SWEET DESIRE, WICKED FATE

Published by Ulu Publishing
Paperback ISBN: 978-0-9914111-9-1
Hardback ISBN: 978-0-9914111-5-3

PRÉCIS

Discovering long lost relatives can be a real nightmare. Do you know who or what you are related to?

Jaden Lisette never imagined she might not live through the month to see her sixteenth birthday, or that befriending reclusive triplets and a withdrawn, introverted man could be her only chance of survival. Once she uncovers her family's deadly secret, to survive she must kill.

What Jaden knew for certain:

1. Buried family secrets can be deadly when uncovered.

2. She wanted Briz.

3. The American poet e.e. cummings was right. *It takes courage to grow up and become who you really are.*

Praise for the award-winning novel
SWEET DESIRE, WICKED FATE

"Sweet Desire, Wicked Fate is presented in a gripping way, and is guaranteed to keep readers on the edge of their seats. The characters in this book are well thought out, and it is a delight to meet some really unique and original characters along the way. I also enjoyed the romantic element of the teenage couple in the book."
Readers' Favorite Book Review

"Successfully blending science fiction, fantasy, horror, romance, and coming-of-age genres, the novel is intended as volume one in a three-part series. The story's original characters, well-constructed plot, moving portrayal of teenaged angst and lust, and effective blending of genres should satisfy young adult readers looking for a fresh new fantasy series."
BlueInk Review

"Sweet Desire, Wicked Fate is a hair-raising dark fantasy thriller interspersed with fantastic moments of humor which will hold great appeal for teenage girls. With well-developed characters, and a unique plot, this book is hard to put down."
Literary Classic Review

Sweet Desire, Wicked Fate

Wray Ardan

*For my partner in life, Steven Lee
Smeltzer, without whom this story would
not exist. It is your artistic brilliance and
ability to sculpt otherworldly beings that
gave birth to this story.*

CHAPTER 1

JADEN

Family. Until now, Jaden had done her best to hold onto the comforting idea that family meant something. That you supported one another and cared about each other.

"Get over it, Jaden. Stop acting all broken-hearted."

Jaden crossed her arms over her chest and glanced at her sister. Ava was pushing buttons on the car radio with one hand and steering with the other. Music blasted as they swerved off the pavement skirting a section of the bayou onto a dirt road. Jaden watched the road stretching in front of them like an open wound, slicing through the remains of a sugar cane field and ending at Guyon Manor, the old plantation house they'd inherited.

Tears welled in Jaden's eyes. She knew she cried too easily. She'd never seen Ava cry. Ever. A glance at her own faint reflection in the car's passenger window reminded her how different they were in both temperament and appearance. Ava had their father's hazel eyes, and his chestnut-colored hair. Jaden's hair and eyes were dark as a new moon, and her features held a hint of their mother's Asian ancestry.

Jaden considered Ava's words. "Broken-hearted." Her sister was seventeen, but still clueless. What Jaden felt wasn't a broken heart. It was the broken bond between siblings. But then, how could a sisterly bond be broken when it never even existed?

Ava started in on her again. "Don't be pissed off at me. Or at Briz. It's not his fault," she smirked. "No guy's ever going to be interested in you. You're a joke. An immature *goodie good.* Or is it all an act?"

Jaden knew Ava wielded sexuality like a sword. It was her weapon of choice to successfully maneuver through life, to gain power over men and the rest of the world. Why would today be any different?

"Oh yeah," Jaden replied, "I'm really just like you, an evil back-stabbing baboon-faced princess!"

Baboon-faced princess. Jaden hadn't called her sister that in years. She was almost sixteen. Couldn't she have come up with something better? Anyway, it set Ava off.

"Get out of the car!" Ava's hollering drowned out the screeching brakes.

"No way," Jaden snapped, but she didn't shout. She knew she'd already sent her sister into Ava mode.

"Don't say *no* to me." Ava punched Jaden's arm.

"Is that what you said to Briz before you had sex with him?"

"He wanted it. He was practically begging me." Ava shoved Jaden toward the door. "Now get out! Walking a few miles in the heat won't kill you." Ava glanced out the window. "Maybe the rain will wash off your pissy attitude."

"Stop pushing me!" Jaden looked at the approaching

storm clouds, then glared at Ava. "I'm not walking anywhere."

"*Get out now!* I don't want to see your ugly face anymore." She gave Jaden another shove. "Why don't you make us all happy and disappear? Or better yet, *drop dead!*"

Jaden climbed out of the car to escape her sister's malice. She slammed the door and jumped back as Ava sped off, tires throwing bits of dirt at her—tiny stones stinging of hurt and rejection. Drawing her hands over her face, Jaden wiped away the summer heat along with her tears and searched her mind for reasons why Ava hated her so much. She answered her own question.

I was born.

A damp stillness hung in the air as she walked toward the manor. Jaden's hair felt heavy and hot against her neck. Pulling it up she twisted it into a thick knot, hoping it would cool her off. It didn't. Why hadn't she grabbed her backpack and bottle of water when she got out of the car?

Jaden plodded forward watching the distant clouds' bulging underbellies grow darker. She imagined a funnel cloud sinking down to the ground and spinning toward her as if she were a target in a video game, whipping her up and tossing her body into the bayou, broken and battered. Or dead.

She walked faster.

A quarter of a mile up the road she came to an overgrown path that disappeared into the cane. An abandoned building lay half hidden under a cluster of trees at the far end of the field. Taking in her dismal surroundings and, in her opinion, her sorrowful life, she thought, *why not? A little detour would be good for Ava. Let her think I've disappeared.*

Vanished, forever.

Jaden glanced down the road in the direction of Guyon Manor—gripping her hands as if squeezing out her misgivings, she stepped into the sugar cane. It rose six feet high, its dried, spindly leaves consumed by thorn-covered weeds that scraped against her bare arms and legs as she walked.

The soles of her tennis shoes left deep imprints on the soft path. She thought of a time when this plantation had been fertile and thriving, when plows drawn by mules eased over this trail until they were replaced by steel-wheeled tractors, then rubber-tired vehicles. And then forgotten.

Steam spiraled up from the ground as she climbed over shrubs and through the cane, dodging webs that wove from one plant to the next. She imagined poisonous spiders finding refuge in her hair.

Raindrops drifted over her, mixing with her perspiration and trickling into her eyes. Stretching up on her toes, she watched as the prowling storm dissolved into a wall of rain. Lightning shot through the air, splitting apart like electrified arthritic fingers reaching for earth.

Jaden counted. Twenty seconds passed before the thunder responded. "Four miles away." Closer than she'd thought.

The rumbling silenced the crickets and birds, amplifying the buzzing of the mosquitoes that fed on her skin. "Worthless draguitoes." Her eyes tightened—saying the name she and Briz had given the dragon-sized insects caused her heart to ache.

A rustling and crackling of twigs behind her made her eyebrows spike up. She hadn't considered what might be roaming through the field. Her imagination toyed with her nerves. Alligators? Pythons?

This is crazy! She thought about ending this senseless adventure and heading back to the road. Instead, she walked further into the cane, intent on healing her fractured self-worth by being brave...within reason. After all, she wasn't in the backwaters of the Congo. This was just an old, dried-up sugar cane field in Louisiana.

Jaden hurriedly pushed another branch aside. She wished she had a machete. Her dad's small knife that she always carried with her was useless right now. Checking the time on her phone, she saw that she'd been on her little excursion for less than half an hour. She would have to be gone longer than that if she wanted her mom to worry—or Ava to be reprimanded.

Ava punished. Ha. It was almost seven years ago, the night before Jaden's ninth birthday, when she realized that "Ava punished" would never happen. Ava had snuck into her bedroom and cut off hunks of Jaden's hair while she was asleep—and their parents had blamed Jaden for making her sister mad in the first place.

"Ava: the illusion of the perfect daughter they always wanted." Jaden stuck her phone back in her pocket. A branch poked her arm. Jaden snapped it in half. "*My* birth wasn't planned. I was a mistake. They didn't want..."

Jaden's throat tightened as something slithered over her foot and coiled around her ankle. She tried to take a breath, but her panic wouldn't let it reach her lungs.

The pressure on her ankle increased. She couldn't move; her legs felt like inflexible rods. Summoning her courage, she attempted a glance down and only succeeded in losing her balance. She fell to the ground and came face to face with her adversary.

"A root...*a root*! I thought it was a friggin' snake." She yanked the vine from her foot. "Ava's right, I am a wuss."

Grateful that no one was around to witness her candy-ass nature, Jaden scrambled to her feet, wiped her muddy hands on her shorts, and moved forward.

The clouds were drawing nearer. Raindrops began tapping her skin, their pressure becoming more insistent, as if warning her to hurry. She looked in the direction of the trees and quickened her pace. She could wait out the storm in the old building.

When the tops of the trees were looming overhead, she took hold of another spider-infested shrub, shoved it aside, then stopped. In front of her stood the remains of a small house. Vines wrapped tightly around its ghost of a railing and covered its decomposing walls and roof. It was like an experimental "green living space" that had gone terribly wrong.

Jaden took a step back, expecting something to burst through the door and pounce on her. The rolling sound of thunder sent a shiver up her spine.

She inched up the stairs to the door, turned the knob, and gave a jittery laugh. It was locked. On the side of the sagging veranda, she found an open window curtained with dense vines. She tugged them out of the way and climbed in.

For a moment, she stood motionless, questioning her motives while her eyes adjusted to the gloom. The walls were coated with a thick layer of mildew that permeated the air. Mushrooms sprouted from the floorboards. She strode across the room, the floor squishing under her feet as if she were walking on slugs.

Jaden unlocked the front door, flung it open, and raised her arms victoriously as if proving to her sister that she wasn't a chicken-hearted wuss.

A crushing wind came racing through the field, blasting her brave moment into oblivion.

The storm had arrived.

The wind caught the door, banging it shut. Jaden stumbled back as her knees buckled, along with her courage. The rain pounding against the building sounded like it was trying to claw through the walls.

An old rocking chair thrashed back and forth in the corner. The window next to it rattled as if someone was beating it with heavy chains, then it burst apart. Jaden shielded her face and covered her eyes as glass flew into the room. The rocking chair slammed against the wall, breaking into large pieces.

A bolt of lightning struck a massive oak tree in the backyard and thunder boomed overhead. Jaden's head tingled as strands of her hair rose, and the nerves in her arms felt ignited by the electric current pulsing in the air. More lightning illuminated the house. She imagined her dad glowing in a tunnel of light, beckoning her.

"I don't want to die!" Jaden yelled.

Her voice was lost in the roar as the tree was ripped out by its roots and came crashing through the kitchen ceiling. The impact lifted the house off the ground. Jaden fell back against the wall, fearing it would collapse on her as the wind razed the structure.

She desperately tried to push the door open, but it was stuck. Tears washed her face as she cried, "Let me out!" Giving up, she turned back toward the room. Mold and dust whirled around her as she stood pressed against the wall, trembling, until the storm moved on.

Jaden inhaled a shaky breath. The tree shifted, groaning as it settled. Jaden steadied herself, trying to keep her balance on the swaying floor.

"I'm so out of here." She pushed on the front door. Again, it didn't budge. A hysterical giggle erupted from her. Between her sister and the storm, her day had just gone from bad to worse. It felt as if she'd lived through a mini rite of passage, its sole purpose to force her to grow a thick skin and learn to be brave.

"Help!" A faint voice came from the kitchen. Then a branch cracked loudly, and the voice was choked off.

Now What?

Jaden pulled back her shoulders—as if that gesture would calm the dread swirling through her—and stepped into the kitchen.

The tree had demolished the room's exterior wall and most of the ceiling. Its trunk, stretching across the width of the room, shifted again. The weak floor rippled under Jaden's feet.

A clump of damp leaves moved, and a rat poked its head out. Seconds later two more appeared. The squealing rodents scampered across the limb onto what remained of the counter, past remnants of melted candles and shattered glass.

"Rats." Jaden released a puff of air. "I thought I was hearing voices. I need to get a grip." Stepping over the debris, she walked through the opening where the back door had been.

The yard resembled a slimy marsh. An old barn, worn by years of storms, had long ago been flattened against the earth.

Nearby, the remains of a group of equally battered dwellings rested.

"Slaves' quarters." Jaden's hushed words burned her throat with guilt. Her ancestors had owned slaves. She had never considered that before.

She descended the rickety porch steps and saw a gaping hole where the tree had stood. A nest of mud-covered ceramic jugs was tangled in the exposed roots. Nudging one with her foot, she thought of cremation urns. The sealed containers were half buried, bigger than she'd thought at first glance.

A loud cawing interrupted her morbid thoughts. She glared up at the remaining hunk of roof; several crows were hopping around excitedly. The noise reminded her of the way Ava was always squawking at her, committed to bringing her down. She could hear her sister's voice saying, *"Briz was just using you to get to me."*

The sting of betrayal latched onto her thoughts. There was no way that she could compete with her sister. Ava stood five-feet six-inches tall and was curvaceous. Jaden was three inches shorter than Ava, and her body was still deciding what it wanted to be.

Short. Tall. Curvy.

No wonder Briz wanted Ava instead of her.

Well, she can have the jerk. I'm not going to cry over some stupid guy. Jaden picked up a handful of stones from the mud and began to hurl them at one of the jugs, pretending it was her sister begging for mercy.

As each stone struck the container, a spider web of cracks spread further across its surface. Despite the still air, leaves swirled around Jaden like a swarm of green moths fluttering up toward the screeching birds on the roof.

"I'm not always good! I can be bad!"

She heaved the last stone as hard as she could, and the jug broke into large pieces. The crows flew away with a loud flapping of their wings. A putrid odor floated up from a murky brown syrup that oozed onto the ground.

The hairs on Jaden's arms rose as she saw the jug's strange contents slowly unfold. Tiny limbs stretched and bony fingers moved the ceramic shards off a distorted face. Citrine-colored eyes sprang open.

Jaden's body went rigid. She sucked in a ragged breath as wiry tendrils lashed out from the head of the malformed thing and plunged their sharp tips into her ankle. A searing pain tore through her, bursting in her head with a blinding light. Her heart beat erratically. She rocked back and forth, then sank down and passed out in the mud.

CHAPTER 2

JADEN

Crumpled on the ground, Jaden awoke to the sound of her cell phone ringing. She rolled onto her back and pulled the phone from her pocket. It slipped from her hand and was swallowed by the muck that immersed her. Her fingers probed deep into the slime but came up empty-handed.

She stood carefully, her head whirling. The setting sun had alerted the draguitoes that it was dinnertime, and they were determinedly finding their way to the parts of Jaden's skin that weren't smeared with mud. She leaned against the mass of tree roots and waited until her slender legs could hold her up on their own.

Fragmented images drifted through her mind. The storm. Breaking the ceramic jug. She looked down. It took a moment for her to register all five containers had been broken open.

Slowly raising her head, Jaden shifted her focus to the battered house. There were voices mixed in with the discordant noise of insects. Had her mom sent someone to find her? Still groggy, Jaden wobbled over to the steps onto the back porch and stood outside the kitchen doorway. The diminishing sunlight filtered through a hole where the roof had been.

Her vision was blurry, her thoughts hazy. Her mother was always telling her she had an overactive imagination. *But...?*

Jaden squinted, trying to comprehend what she was seeing.

Four creatures huddled around the tree's broken branches. Malnourished and scrawny, their small bodies appeared human, except their features were reptilian, or rodent, but without any fur. Horns sprouted from their heads and faces, fangs protruded from their mouths, their tattered clothes were covered in slime.

Had a science lab buried experimental rats and chemicals here in the bayou, where they'd continued to grow until they became these *things*? And she'd released them. Jaden wished her phone hadn't been consumed by the mud so she could take a photo.

One of the things, dressed in a filthy green shirt and baggy pants, stood about sixteen inches tall and resembled an old hag. Long tentacles bounced around its head. Its bony hands reached out as it extended sharp claws, ready to shred whatever they had trapped. Jaden would have screamed if she thought any of this was really happening. But it couldn't be.

The thing spoke, and Jaden shivered.

"Ya useless Bellibone, tell us where the Professor's at or we is gonna rip ya apart," it rasped in a curt Southern twang, nostrils flaring as it reached toward something in the leaves. "Yer time is up. The Professor, he don't care 'bout ya."

"You're right, Datura," a weary female voice replied. "He always preferred the five of you."

"That's right. Us Mal Rous is his favorites."

Jaden stepped back to watch from the shadows. She had never heard of a Mal Rou or a Bellibone. Were they a Southern thing? The creatures only came to her knees. How dangerous could they be?

Her thoughts stopped as claws dragged across her calves and pushed against the backs of her knees, forcing her to stumble into the kitchen.

"Datura, look and see what I got," a hoarse male voice spoke from behind her.

The one called Datura gave a low growl and stretched her neck forward to study Jaden. She kneaded her bony hands together, then ran them over her oily face.

"Ivan, ya dummy." Datura's eyes were beady aqua spheres that followed the sweat dripping down Jaden's brow. "What'd ya bring *her* in here for?" Datura snapped her fingers, as she called to the others. "Anders. Tig. Esere." Snarling, they moved closer to Jaden.

"I ain't no dummy! She were spyin' on ya. She'll tell people 'bout us."

Jaden glanced back at her captor. This Ivan creature stood a few inches taller than the rest, which seemed to make him feel superior. Like the others, he had sharp fangs that jutted out over his thin lips. His clothes were threadbare, his physique human. He appeared to be part horned lizard, with a reptilian hide that resembled dried mud. His eyes were electric green. Horns were scattered over the crown of his head, even on his pointed ears.

"What's ya scared 'a?" Datura lunged at Jaden. "We ain't hurt ya. Tig just injected ya with a little 'a her spurges poison." Datura smiled, patting Tig on the back. "Then she set us free."

Stubby horns hung from Tig's drooping jowls, bouncing up and down when she moved. She wore a dingy yellow jumpsuit that clung to her salmon-colored flesh. The thin strands of wiry hair that she had used to puncture Jaden stuck out on the back of her head. There was a youthful arrogance about her; in spite of her fangs and horns and pointed snout, she reminded Jaden of one of the mean girls at school.

Datura screeched, "What's yer name?"

Jaden replied in a whisper. Stepping back, she tripped and crashed onto the floor next to Ivan. He lifted his arm, ready to smack her across the face.

"Sorry, sorry..." Jaden cowered.

With a snicker, Ivan lowered his hand.

The Mal Rous cackled. Their stench made it hard for Jaden to breathe. Her insides felt as if they were being stuffed through a meat grinder.

No, no, none of this is real. She shook her head.

Datura raised a finger, and the others became silent.

"I...I won't tell anyone about you," Jaden stammered, her gaze shifting back to Ivan. "W-who would believe me, anyway?"

Ivan crouched next to her, his head twitching from side to side as he slobbered, "Ya ain't gonna tell no one 'bout us, cause if ya does, ya'd be better off dead."

His spit cascaded across Jaden's face, arms, and the tops of her legs, sending a burning sensation through her capillaries. Red welts emerged, itching and throbbing as if fire ants were under her skin, biting her, struggling to burst free. Seconds later pus oozed out.

"Relax," Tig said. Her salmon-hued hand roamed tenderly over Ivan's shirt. "It's only poison ivy. He could'a bit ya with snake venom."

"Quiet!" Ivan pulled away from Tig. "What'd ya tell her for? I liked seein' her squirm."

"Jaden, Jaden..." Datura pushed Ivan aside and inhaled a deep breath. "Hmm, somethin' 'bout ya."

Datura's tentacles were crawling around on her head like fat worms trying to escape the sunlight. Several reached toward Jaden, sniffing her.

"Listen up, girlie. Ya is gonna find our Professor. Tell him we is free and bring him to us. If ya don't, like Ivan here says, by the time we be done with ya, ya will be beggin' for us to let ya die." As if drinking in a sweet elixir, Datura inhaled through her tentacles and bulbous nose. "I got yer scent. I can track ya anywhere. *Anywhere.*"

It seemed as though the creatures were gaining strength from Jaden's terror. She scooted back through the wet grunge that covered the floor, sensing that she was nothing more than a toy to them. They would just bat her around for a while, then abandon her when she was no longer alive.

"Ya tells anyone," Ivan said, "and ya is gonna suffer. We'll maim everyone ya know." He jerked his head to the side and stuck out his hand, stopping one of the other creatures strutting toward Jaden. "Esere, leave her be."

From the looks of Esere, Jaden assumed he was another male. He had large bloodshot eyes and a beak-like nose. Despite being smaller than the rest, his frayed red clothes and slate-gray skin made him appear more malevolent. He aimed the stubby horn on his chin at Jaden.

Ivan's slobber had covered her with fiery blisters. Now,

staring at Esere, anticipating his bite, Jaden felt the possibility of death hum through her veins.

"In fact, we'll maim everyone in this here miserable town." Ivan grinned at Esere, then at Jaden. "Ya gets what I'm sayin', ya snivelin' baby?"

"Y-yes, I understand." Jaden stood up. She locked her knees, trying to steady her legs.

"Why don't we just do away with her now?" Tig asked, tugging on her wiry strands of hair. "We could all use a tasty human to dig into."

"I'll look for your professor," Jaden quickly said to Datura. "But I don't know who he is. I...I don't know anyone. I'm not from here. My mom and sister and I just got to town a couple weeks ago. I don't know how or where to find this...this person."

"No excuses!" Datura's lips receded, showing yellow gums and sharp canine teeth. "Find him or ya is gonna pay the price. Slowly. Painfully. We promise."

The rest of the Mal Rous mimicked their leader, waving their filthy claws at Jaden as she continued to back away.

"We want food." Tig pranced over to her. "Cane toads. Peanut butter to dip cockroaches in. Coral snakes. Mmm, the small ones feel good when they squirm down into my belly."

"I, I will." Jaden could feel the remnants of her own breakfast inching up her throat. "I'll get you food. I'll find your professor. Only, I need time." Trembling, she turned toward Datura. "You won't have to hurt anyone."

"Why not?" Tig giggled, her jowls jiggling. "We enjoy teasin' humans, don't we, Honeyboy?" Tig gestured for *Honeyboy* to come closer. "Come on Anders. Check her out."

Anders moved next to Jaden and grinned widely, his

enormous jaws looking lethal. His hide resembled leather. Feelers hung from the sides of his dragon-shaped skull, which seemed too large for his miniature humanoid body. It was obvious that his nickname, Honeyboy, came from his honey-colored irises. Like the others, his clothes were nothing more than dirty rags.

"It's been so long, Datura," Tig whined. "Can't we keep her—just to skewer and flay? Fun treats. The Professor, he won't care. We just has to leave his wife and girl alone." Smiling, Tig pricked Jaden's ankle with her claws, causing her to jump. "The Professor said he were gonna put us someplace safe. That he'd be back."

"Please, it'll take me some—"

"Time." Datura grunted, and her gamey breath hung in the air. "Again, with time." She glanced out at the twilight-blue sky. "Startin' right now, I'll give ya six...no, five days. That should be long enough for ya to find him. And if ya don't, I'll sniff ya out. And yer kinfolk, too."

Jaden winced at the thought of these mutants coming anywhere near her family.

Datura tapped on her engorged nose, sending a group of her tentacles writhing toward Jaden, then tipped her head back, closed her eyes, and took a deep breath.

Ivan leered up at Jaden as if he were imagining breaking her bones. "We is gonna come after ya, and everyone ya love."

A slight movement in the tree caught Jaden's attention, and she glimpsed the Bellibone that Datura had been threatening. One of its legs was caught under a branch. Its complexion was rosy white, with more human, feminine features than the Mal Rous. Unlike the others, it had wings.

Jaden's fuzzy brain cleared with realization—this was what she'd heard calling for help earlier.

"Five more days, five more days," Tig sang in a high pitch, "and we is gonna barbecue ya…" Anders's forked tongue shot out, slapping Tig across her face. The others laughed as Tig rubbed the welt that appeared on her cheek.

Jaden didn't hesitate. She ran out the back door and stumbled down the steps. She could hear them mocking her as she raced through the swampy backyard. It wasn't the first time today that she wondered if she would live to see her sixteenth birthday.

JADEN

Jaden couldn't find her makeshift path hidden in the dusky shadows at the front of the shack, so she pushed her way into the wet foliage and forged a new trail.

Her heart was beating fast. She felt like an animal struggling to get free from a snare. She didn't care about alligators or poisonous insects. She wanted to get far away from this town, from Briz and Ava; most of all from the Mal Rous. She longed to be back home in Colorado.

By the time she found the road, night had settled in. The humidity was smothering her. Her body and mind swayed in opposite directions. She pulled at her filthy, sweaty shirt, ready to peel it off. Her skin itched from Ivan's poison ivy-tainted slobber. Hunching over, she rested her hands on her thighs. Her throat was dry. She needed water.

Scared and confused, she reached for her phone. Then remembered it was long gone. She couldn't call anyone for help, and no cars ever drove on this dead-end road. She had no choice. She'd have to walk back to town to their rental house, or to the so-called mansion.

The mansion was closer.

Jaden willed her feet to move faster with each step. The shrill of cicadas amplified the pounding in her head. She wondered what lies Ava had told their mom about why Jaden hadn't shown up today.

Jaden finally reached the massive stone wall that guarded Guyon Manor from the rest of the world. She opened the iron gate and saw that the house was dark and empty. As she walked along the driveway under the arching oak trees, the glow of the moon enhanced the grounds and softened the two-story manor's flaws. Inhaling the fragrance of magnolia blossoms, she watched as lightning bugs wove in and out of the tall grass.

The house's beauty faded when she stood in front of it. It was dingy white. Its shutters sagged like wet dish towels, pulling remnants of screen away from the windows. The place was as shabby as the nearby town, Belle Fleur.

At the back of the house was the detached garage. It had been the kitchen when it was originally built in the eighteen hundreds.

The sight of the dilapidated building caused the sores on her skin to burn. Were more monsters lurking inside, watching her?

Jaden stepped onto the back porch, scrabbling for the house key her mom had hidden under a paint can. She steadied her trembling hand to fit the key into the lock, turned the knob and inched the kitchen door open; sliding her hand along the wall, she flicked on the light switch.

"Come on, Mom. *Come looking for me.*" Her words were barely audible.

That morning Jaden had woken up so happy, excited to buy a birthday present for Briz. Now she wondered why had she even bothered getting out of bed? Had she unwittingly messed with someone's mojo, and they'd put a big fat Louisiana Voodoo curse on her?

At the kitchen sink Jaden held her mouth to the faucet, drinking as much of the corroded-tasting liquid as she could. Lowering her head under the tap, she let the water flow through her muddy hair, then washed the dirt and pus from her face, arms, and legs.

Enervated, she sat on the floor and leaned against a cupboard. She continued to question why those detestable things had been preserved in slime and buried. Why did she have to be the one to unleash them?

She closed her eyes but couldn't escape from everything that had transpired. The images were too vivid; if she had her sketch pad, she could have drawn the Mal Rous in detail. Getting to her feet, Jaden roamed through the manor's stuffy rooms, turning on every lamp that worked. Even with its elegant crystal chandeliers and gilded mirrors, the place exuded sadness.

And why wouldn't it? It was abandoned, left to die.

Jaden made her way up the grand staircase, opened the door that led into her Aunt Amelia's childhood bedroom and flicked on the light. Sinister patterns crept across the peeling wallpaper. The bed's purple spread was coated with years of dust. The room reeked of mothballs.

She went over to the window and opened it wide. Not that it changed anything. There wouldn't be a breeze unless there was another storm.

Near the closet, her mom had stacked boxes with games, books, and old photographs of her Aunt Amelia with her Grandmother Elvina and Grandfather Dekle. Jaden walked over to the pile. It was as if one day they left and never came back. They didn't even take anything with them.

She inhaled sharply. *They knew about the Mal Rous and ran for their lives.*

They might have known that damn Professor.

Jaden held one of the framed black and white photographs. Her family. They were all strangers to her. She could see how much Ava resembled their Grandmother Elvina, both of them striking. Amelia beamed at the camera with childlike innocence. Jaden's Grandfather Dekle looked very distinguished. Perhaps he'd been a lawyer or a doctor.

Or a professor.

Tig said the Professor wouldn't let them touch his wife or girl. Was my grandfather the Professor? Was he friends with the Mal Rous?

No, that can't be right.

Jaden poked her finger at Amelia's cheerful face. "What'd we ever do to you that you'd leave us this mess?" Jaden tossed the picture back with the others. Amelia was a kid back then and probably didn't even know what was going on. Anyway, Jaden was the moron who busted open the jug.

What have I done? Dry heaves sent her lunging for the open window.

"Please help me," she cried out into the darkness, as if someone was going to hear her and tell her that this was all in her imagination, and she was going to be all right.

She couldn't deal with this alone. She'd tell her mom, and the police everything she knew and then convince her mom that they should leave town.

Jaden stared out the window, hoping that her mom's car would appear in the drive. She resigned herself to wait. Mentally and physically drained, Jaden flopped down on the bed. Decades of dust billowed up, then settled, covering her like a musty blanket as she fell asleep.

Chaotic dreams kept her tossing and turning. She was being chased by the Mal Rous. One caught hold of her arm and shook her as it said, "Ya don't look so good." The sensation was so real, the words so clear, she opened her eyes.

Jaden's breath stuck in the back of her throat. She pulled away from a scruffy man whose fingers were squeezing her shoulders. His slightly pointed ears stuck out from stringy hair that was plastered across the top of his head. What few teeth he had were brown. Bug-eyed, Jaden stared at him, wondering if she was still dreaming.

Equally alarmed by her bedraggled appearance, the man was careful not to touch her engorged blisters as he helped her sit up. "Ya Miss Jaden, right? Miss Jaden Lisette?"

She nodded, watching as he called her mom on his cell, then listened as he went on and on in his Southern drawl, explaining to her mother that he was Officer Duncan and had found her daughter and everything was just fine.

Too tired and apprehensive to argue that point, Jaden kept hearing the Mal Rous' voices threatening her with what they'd do if she told anyone. Besides, from the looks of him, this so-called Officer Duncan could be related to the little cretins.

As she walked to his patrol car, Jaden came to the conclusion that Belle Fleur was a town of misfits. Everyone over the age of sixty had been hexed. At night, the bodies in the graveyard probably crawled out of their coffins and roamed the streets.

When they arrived at the house, Jaden's mother rushed

out to hug her—then quickly recoiled. "What happened to you?"

"Don't ya worry ma'am. She's just fine," the sheriff said.

Jaden's mom turned to him. "Officer Duncan, I'm Brooke Lisette. We spoke on the phone. I can't thank you enough. It never dawned on us...Jaden told her sister she was going to a friend's house. When I called him this evening, he said he hadn't seen her today."

"She says she were out in a cane field. She were just in the wrong place at the wrong time," Officer Duncan replied. "Right in line where that there tornadic storm came a barrelin' through. Lucky for her it kept on movin'. Heard on the news it hunkered down on the next town over." He gestured to Jaden's sores and his head bounced from side to side, reminding Jaden of Ivan. "She got inta some poison ivy."

"Yes, I can see that." Brooke surveyed her disheveled daughter. "Doesn't it normally take a couple of days to get this inflamed?"

"When I was a boy, I got it just the same, ma'am. I reckon the storm uncovered that kinda plant. From what I recollect, it could be lots worse. Ya should get her over to Dr. Schilling. She has an ointment that'll heal it up in no time at all."

Jaden stared at the sheriff. He'd had a run-in with the Mal Rous! She considered the chances that she could end up looking like him.

"Thank you again, Officer Duncan. I'll call Dr. Schilling first thing in the morning."

Unable to find an uninfected area on Jaden, Brooke took hold of the hem of her daughter's grimy T-shirt and dragged her into the house.

Jaden hadn't realized how happy she could be to see the tacky, second-hand furnishings that filled the rental house. When the door shut, the chill of the air conditioner was a welcome contrast to the muggy night air.

Brooke grabbed the remote from Ava and clicked off the television.

"Okay, I'm going to try to stay calm. Where were you all day?" Jaden stared at the blank TV screen, her lips flattening into a straight line as she listened to her mom's tirade. "*We were worried sick about you! What were you thinking? I drove back to the mansion a couple of hours ago and you weren't there.*" Brooke's grand intentions of staying calm had rapidly devolved into a stream of ranting. "Where have you been? Why didn't you call? What's the point of having a cell phone if you don't use it when there's an emergency?"

Jaden held out her empty hands. The gesture causing her mother's voice to go up an octave. "Are you implying that you lost your phone?"

Jaden gave a timid nod.

"Well, you're going to have to pay for a new one!"

The tirade continued, but Jaden was too tired to pay attention. When her mom ran out of steam, Jaden looked at Ava, who was sitting on the sofa, watching complacently. "You almost got your wish," Jaden told her sister. "I could have been killed."

"Jaden Olivia Lisette, that's enough! Your sister's been here all night pacing the floor with me."

"Yeah, Mom." Physically and mentally drained, Jaden walked toward the bathroom. "I'm sure you were *both* upset."

"Don't you walk away from me, young lady. We're not done here."

"Mom, I really need a shower."

"Just know this conversation isn't over." Jaden nodded as her mother walked into the kitchenette. "Make the water as hot as you can stand it. It'll help stop the itch for a while. There's some baking soda in the fridge. I'll mix up a paste for you to put on the blisters."

Jaden stood in the shower letting the hot water penetrate her sores, gradually easing her discomfort, her resentment toward her sister, and her anguish over the events of the day. Crying, she stayed under the water until it turned cold. As she shut it off, she realized that she'd never be able to wash away her fears.

She spent that night quietly weeping.

When she woke the next morning, her skin was an itchy, oozing mess of poison ivy rashes. A screaming reminder that the Mal Rous were real.

She desperately wanted to escape from her body. Her world would never be the same; *she* would never be the same. If her family remained in this town, none of them would be safe.

Was this to be her fate, dying at the hands of ruthless mutant pond scum? She wanted to leap up and start running. It had always been a way for her to clear her mind—the same mind she felt certain she was now losing.

"I'm exhausted," Ava complained, all comfy in her twin bed. She propped her head up and looked down as Jaden rolled off her air mattress onto the carpet. "I didn't get any sleep last night with all the scratching and racket you were making. You're sleeping in the living room tonight." Ava crinkled her nose. "You look so gross. What *did* you do after you jumped out of the car yesterday?"

Jaden stood up and looked at Ava's oh-so-cute dimples

accentuating her annoyingly perfect smile. "*Jumped out?* Yeah, sure, that's what happened."

Jaden stalked from the room, closing the door behind her, then gagged. She hated it when she sounded like her sister. Their similarities bothered her way more than their differences. Preparing for a long lecture with some fuming tossed in, she took a deep breath and went into the kitchenette.

"How are you, sweetie?" Her mom poured cereal into a bowl, averting her eyes from Jaden's blotchy skin. "I called that doctor Officer Duncan recommended. She's going to work us in, so we need to leave soon."

Jaden deliberately blinked in slow motion. "Who are you and what did you do with my irate mom?"

Brooke smiled kindly and shrugged her shoulders.

"Are you sure he was a real officer?" Jaden asked. "He didn't even have a uniform."

"Sweetie, he brought you home to us. That's all that matters. I'm sorry I was so angry last night. I...I was afraid that something terrible had happened to you."

It did.

"So. Are you ready to tell me where you were?" Leaving her breakfast on the kitchen counter, Brooke sat at the table and beckoned Jaden to sit in the chair next to her. "I promise I won't overreact."

Jaden eyed the bowl of cereal still on the counter. Ava was right. She was disgusting. Her mom couldn't even eat in the same room with her. Jaden's hand hovered over a patch of her poison ivy as she fought the urge to scratch her sores. She sat on the edge of the seat. Her thoughts hopped around as she searched for the right thing to say.

"Yesterday I—I found these things on the property that

are really dangerous." She lowered her voice, not wanting to sound like a whiny kid. "We have to get out of here."

"Jaden, poison ivy is not dangerous. It's just a pain in the butt. You will survive."

"No, I'm not talking about this." Jaden gestured at her inflamed skin. "Mom, we need to get out of town. I know why Dad's family left this place."

"I'm listening. Go on, tell me your story." Brooke always used that tone when she expected her daughters to tell her a tall tale. She leaned her elbow on the table and rested her chin in her palm.

"Something horrible is going to happen to us, Mom. You have to believe me." Jaden pressed her lips together and looked out the window, wondering what the repercussions would be for sharing her disturbing secret. After all, the Mal Rous wouldn't necessarily know.

"Jade, just tell me what happened." Brooke tapped her fingers on the table to get her daughter's attention.

"What do you know about Dad's family?" Jaden's gaze shifted to her mother's hand. "I know his father died before Dad was born. Was he some kind of *professor?*"

"I don't know. Your dad said your grandmother was so heartbroken that she never talked about him." Brooke gestured toward a FedEx box on the counter. "If your Aunt Amelia hadn't died, I wouldn't even know about this estate. I was surprised when she left us everything. I didn't think she...or your grandmother, wanted anything to do with us. Especially after your dad..."

Jaden knew her mother had never thought she would marry a career military man. "Love is blind," she'd said every time her husband had shipped out. But he was so much more than his career. He was a great dad. A good person.

It had been five years since he'd been deployed to fight in what Brooke always referred to as another pointless war. And four years since he was declared missing in action. Eleven months later, when his body was recovered, Jaden thought she'd feel a sense of closure. She was still waiting.

"Guyon Manor," Jaden whispered, looking at the FedEx box. "Do you think Dad ever got to see it?"

"He never mentioned it to me."

Jaden expelled an exaggerated sigh. "Maybe he did. Maybe he knew *all* about it and that's why he never said anything."

"Jade, what's going on? What's this about?"

Tears rimmed Jaden's eyes.

"Honey, will you tell me what happened?"

"Will you keep a really open mind?" She held her mother's gaze. "Don't say I have a *remarkable* imagination. This isn't like one of the stories I write for extra credit in English class."

Before Jaden could explain anything, Ava walked into the room and plopped on the sofa with her phone, ready for a busy morning of texting. Jaden crinkled her eyes to stop the tears from reaching her lashes and stared at her sister until she appeared distorted, resembling a wicked witch.

That's it! I must have hit my head during the storm. Instead of seeing Munchkins, I'm seeing Mal Rous.

"Sweetie? Jade...?"

"I'll tell you later, Mom. Don't we have to leave soon?"

Fifteen minutes later, the two of them were alone in the car. Clicking on her seatbelt, Brooke looked over at her daughter. "Okay, I'm listening. Start talking."

CHAPTER 4

BRIZ

The clock in Briz's room clicked to ten A.M. and he called Jaden's number again. He'd left a dozen messages and texts for her. Jaden always returned his calls. Again, he got her voicemail.

"This is Jaden. Precycle. Recycle. Plant a tree." *Beep.*

Still no answer. Now he felt more anxious. They'd only met four weeks ago, but he considered her a good friend. Had he done something to make her mad? Did something happen to her? He sprang from his desk as if he'd just had a shot of crystallized caffeine, grabbed his key and drove to her house.

When he knocked on the door, Ava greeted him. Her damp hair trailed down the front of her skimpy tank top, making the fabric almost transparent.

"Hey, gorgeous." Ava's eyes slowly scanned his nearly six-foot frame. "Too bad you weren't here earlier. You could have showered with me."

Briz blinked in surprise. Though he was originally from Seattle, he couldn't help feeling that Ava saw him as her southern boy toy. He was all too aware of the khaki shorts hanging loosely on his hips, and that his shirt was only buttoned halfway up. He suddenly understood what his sisters said about feeling self-conscious and unempowered when guys undressed them with their eyes.

It took Briz a moment to remember that he hadn't come over to see Ava. "Is Jaden home?"

"No. The idiot got into poison ivy. It's all over her. My mom took her to a doctor." Ava took Briz's hand. "Come on in. I have something for you."

He didn't move.

"Come on. I won't bite."

Briz let his hand fall away from hers as he followed her into the house.

"I picked this up for you." Ava handed him a bag. Standing on her toes, she put her lips next to his ear and added breathlessly, "For your birthday."

Briz couldn't ignore the surge of energy. His skin tingled. He opened the bag and pulled out a book. His eyebrows rose. "*You* got this for me?"

"Yeah. Jade said you'd like it. You don't already have it, do you?"

"No." He tried to speak up, but it was as if someone was flicking his voice on and off with a mute button. "I, I don't."

"Well." Ava leaned against him. "You don't sound very grateful."

"I just didn't expect to get anything from you."

"I know. But giving just the right gift is one of my many wonderful assets."

Ava's *assets* were pressing against him, making him feel as if he was a soft furry bunny and she was the big bad wolf. He was used to being the pursuer, not the pursued. She ran her fingernails along his arm, which was hanging at his side like a piece of cardboard.

"Relax, Briz. I'm sorry about yesterday. I was in a bit of a mood."

"Yeah, no problem."

The fragrance of her shampoo invited him to lower his head next to hers. "Thanks. This is great." Fumbling with the book, he walked to the door. "Uh, yeah...well, I better get going. I'm supposed to help my dad with some stuff. Tell Jaden I hope she feels better soon."

"Sure." Ava gave him a mischievous smile, her eyes fixed on his mouth.

Briz sprinted to his car as Ava's landlady came scurrying up the driveway and called out Ava's name.

CHAPTER 5

DATURA

Datura glanced into the kitchen at Violet. Trapped under the branch, the worthless creature looked frail, her leg broken. Datura flicked her tongue against her canine teeth with disgust. She had always hated Violet. All the Mal Rous had. The characteristics that marked her as a Bellibone, her feminine features, educated speech, and annoyingly kind demeanor were so different from their own. And there was the fact that the Professor had made her first. But he preferred his Mal Rous. Their blend of human, rat, tardigrade, lizard, and poisonous plant DNA meant they would have a better survival rate than the less aggressive species from his earlier experiments, like the inferior Bellibone. Violet was the only one that had lived.

"That kid ain't comin' today." Esere's words brought Datura's attention back to her siblings and the girl who had set Tig free. "She ain't got no idea what we can do to her, or her kin, or this here town."

"Quiet, Esere. If she don't show up, we'll find her," Datura said. "She'll be an easy one to sniff out. It'll be like when the Professor would take us to town at night to tease and feed on the locals."

"Yeah," Tig echoed, "to tease and feed on the locals."

Datura grinned. She and her family were recovering from their dormant state much more quickly than she'd expected.

"To tease and feed," Tig said again.

Datura looked at Tig from the corner of her eye. At times her family seemed a bit mindless. But she knew, like her, they were always cunning. Their caustic bug instincts ruled the pack's actions.

The Professor had never been able to teach her and her siblings to restrain their predatory natures. After a while, he'd just given up. Datura remembered the day they'd captured a hummingbird, delighting in the bird's agony as they plucked the feathers from its tiny frame. When it died, they just tossed it aside like a filthy rag.

Soon after, without the Professor's resistance, they began to direct their brutality at humans. That brought them even more joy. Still, they could be nurturing. Once, when they were young, they'd cared for an orphaned baby opossum until it was old enough to fend for itself. And last night, they'd let Violet sleep. More or less.

And of course, they truly loved and adored the Professor.

Where *was* he? Clever as she was, Datura could not figure out their current situation. Everything she saw and heard made no sense. Saliva dripped off her jutting fangs as she turned and stalked into the kitchen.

She stuck her face close to Violet's, making the Bellibone cough from the odor of the cockroaches Datura had recently fed on.

"Where are we?"

Violet didn't respond.

"I know ya heard me, ya mangy runt!" Datura jabbed Violet in the arm. "Don't know what the Professor made ya for. Now answer me, or we is gonna fill yer days with misery. What is this here place?"

"I told you yesterday, you are in the caretaker's house. Or what is left of it." Violet's contentious tone and well-spoken words rankled Datura, causing the tips of Datura's tentacles to arch and crimp.

"No way! I ain't blind." Datura surveyed the room. "This here place is fallin' apart. 'Sides, if this is the caretaker's house, where's his boy? Where's all his stuff?"

"Don't you remember? After the five of you brutalized the little boy, they moved away."

"What 'bout the Professor's wife? She would'a stuck someone else in here to do her chores."

"She left a long time ago."

"The old slug took off, did she?" Datura sniggered. "Then where's our Professor Dekle?"

"As I said before, I Do Not Know!" Violet exhaled with exasperation.

"And that girl? Why were she here? Her scent was familiar. Is she a Thatcher?" Datura's eyes narrowed. "Or one of Elvina's relations?"

"I've never seen her before."

Datura rubbed her fingers over her thin lips as she studied the Bellibone. Violet was hiding something from her. She raised her hand and scraped a claw over Violet's chin, drawing a thin line of blood. Inflicting pain would get to the truth. It was also the part of Datura's genetic makeup that she most enjoyed.

Violet's brow creased, and her lips pursed. *She's tryin' to stop her tears*, Datura thought.

"Well, I'm askin' ya again. Where is he? He was comin' back for us."

"I presume he is deceased." Violet said as she wiped the blood from her chin.

"Not possible!" Several of Datura's tentacles lashed out at Violet. "He's one 'a us now."

Violet shrank back. Datura noted that the movement sent spasms shooting down the length of Violet's ensnared body. She'd better not die before they could torture her. Datura knew that would infuriate her siblings—ruin all their fun.

"How long was we buried for?" Datura realized her shrill voice exposed her frustration, her need to be reunited with the Professor. "Answer me! How long was we buried for?" She snatched a handful of Violet's hair, yanked her head back and inhaled the Bellibone's emotions—the palpable aroma of physical pain, and an aura of fear Violet could no longer hide.

"A little more than fifty years," Violet said, her tone no longer combative.

Datura's oversized nose pulsed as if it were a beating heart. Her tentacles extended, the wormy strands longing to drain Violet's blood or inject her with venom. Datura gulped in air to calm her tentacles and gave Violet's head a jerk before releasing her hair. Today was not the day for Violet to die.

"That'd mean our Professor probably is dead." Anders spoke from the doorway. The meaning of his own words struck him, and he staggered back as if a spear had been thrown at his chest.

"So, we is all alone?" Tig took hold of Anders's hand as she and Ivan entered the kitchen.

Datura observed her family. None of them had ever been on their own. She knew how dependent they were on the Professor. He'd been their father figure.

"Ya chumps." Ivan stepped forward, his slobber cascading onto the floor. "Y'all trust that Bellibone? She just suckered y'all in."

"He's right. Why we listenin' to her?" Esere pushed past Datura. "We should pluck out her eyeballs while she's alive." He flicked his claws in Violet's face. "'Sides, why weren't she buried, too?"

Violet squeezed her eyes shut.

"Look at me!" Datura demanded, squeezing a clump of her less complacent tentacles and sending thick globs of yellow gel onto the floor. "Why wasn't ya buried? The Professor, he had jugs for all 'a us."

The Bellibone's eyes opened wide, as if she was worried the wrong answer would give the Mal Rous an excuse to attack her.

"After he had you situated..." Violet paused. "The Professor decided I should keep guard and ensure no one would find you. For your safety."

Datura's tentacles contracted, as if smelling a lie.

Violet looked at her. "As you said Datura, he is one of you now. He'll probably live forever." Violet glanced at each of the Mal Rous. "It hasn't been fifty years. I only said that to upset you."

"I ain't buyin' it." Datura glanced at the decaying walls. "This here place weren't rottin' the last time we seen it. And ya ain't so young lookin' no more."

"The house was fine prior to when lightning struck the

tree." Datura cocked her head, taking in Violet's words and scent. "If you release me, I...I might know where to find him."

"Ya is lyin'." Datura slapped Violet, leaving a palm print on the Bellibone's pale cheek.

"Enough 'a this," Ivan said, marching to the front door. "I ain't sittin' around waitin' for that kid. I'm feelin' pretty good. Not so tired no more. Gonna make my way on up to the house and look for the Professor! Ya comin'?"

Datura placed her arm on the tree branch; bearing down with all her weight, she chuckled. "Hurt much?" Then she turned to follow Ivan outside, the others tagging behind.

"Let's get goin'." Ivan spoke loudly from the porch, so Violet would hear. "We can eat on the way. Scrounge up a few rats for ya to suck a drink from, Datura. If that mousey girl's here when we get back, she can be our main course." Snickering, he added, "Right after we hack apart the Bellibone."

CHAPTER 6

JADEN

Jaden caved as they were driving back from the doctor's office. Despite the Mal Rous' warnings, she told her mother about the miniature, walking, talking, humanoid fiends. Her mom's reaction wasn't a surprise. Jaden had expected her to think this was another one of her daughter's elaborate fables. In fact, the entire time Jaden was trying to convince her mom that the Mal Rous were real, Jaden was hoping they weren't.

"If you're making this up because you're mad at your sister, stop it," was Brooke's only response. "Don't blame Ava. You shouldn't have run off to find Briz. It's not her fault that he asked her out instead of you."

Asked her out? More like jumped her bones.

"Mom, I'm telling you the truth—unlike your other daughter, who despises me."

"Jaden, I'm not blind. I know how different you two are. But Ava doesn't despise you."

Did her mom honestly believe that? Ava found ways to make Jaden feel worthless every day.

"Oh baby, I'm not so old that I don't remember what having a crush is like. Especially when it's not reciprocated."

"The only crushing I'm worried about is how the Mal Rous are going to pulverize *us.*"

"Jade—"

"Well, it's the truth!"

"The truth, huh? Well, I don't believe your alien monsters are real. End of story."

Jaden knew *end of story* didn't mean end of lecture.

"And as far as Briz goes, he's too old for you."

"What? He just turned eighteen yesterday, and I'll be sixteen in a couple of weeks. That's only two years difference!" Jaden slumped down in the seat. "It doesn't matter anyway. Ava stole him."

"Jaden, let it go. We're here to fix up that house, not have fun. We need the money we can make selling the estate. I'm a schoolteacher, not a plastic surgeon. Will you just try to get along with your sister? For me? By the end of summer, we'll be back home, and you'll never see Briz again."

In truth, Briz and Ava were the least of her worries.

"You're going to ignore the fact that monsters want to kill us."

"Oh, please!"

"No, Mom, *you* please! You don't get it. They want to skewer us like shish kebabs. They're real!" Jaden felt a painful heat flare from the lesions that covered her body. At the same time, shame needled its way into her heart. She had never raised her voice at her mother before.

"Sorry," she murmured.

What was wrong with her? Was it the anger she felt at the idea of Briz hooking up with Ava? Frustration that her mom wouldn't believe they were in a life-threatening situation? Or had that Tig creature's venom and Ivan's poison ivy somehow caused a glitch in her personality?

"Dr. Schilling said to keep a thick coat of this on and to stay calm," Brooke said, parking in their driveway, handing her the large jar of ointment, and sweeping her fingers through Jaden's hair. "Getting upset will only make it worse."

"Yeah, I know." Opening the car door, Jaden looked at the inflammations on her arms and muttered to herself, "No worries, just stay calm. Why go postal about rank mutations from the bayou mutilating us while we beg them to finish us off?"

When they entered the house, Ava was lounging on the couch wearing her normal aggravated expression.

"What took you so long?" Like a hawk honing in on a mouse, she fixed her gaze on Jaden. "By the way, Briz came by. Yum. Who knew I'd ever think a book nerd was hot? Ends up he's just my type. I told him what a twit you were, falling into the poison ivy. How disgus—"

"Ava, that's enough!" Brooke walked past her to the kitchen and grabbed a bottle of juice from the refrigerator.

"What guy isn't your type?" Jaden squeezed the jar of ointment; nothing would have made her happier than flinging it at her sister.

"Jaden!" Brooke snapped, then aimed her exasperation at Ava. "Ava, go get dressed. We're leaving now."

"*Duh*, I *am* dressed."

"Get *more* dressed." Brooke looked at her older daughter's ensemble. "We're going to work, not to entertain the crew."

"Come on. It's too hot to wear more."

Stone-faced, Brooke held Ava's gaze until her daughter

sauntered off to the bedroom. After she poured a glass of juice, Brooke turned to Jaden. "I want you to stay here today and rest. Now go put that stuff on your sores."

Jaden went in the bathroom and opened the jar. The ointment was bright fuchsia. Her face wrinkled like a prune at the awful smell. "This stuff is nasty."

Once it was on, she balked at her goop-covered reflection in the mirror. Still, it did soothe her festering sores. As she emerged from the bathroom, Brooke did a double take while Ava howled with delight.

"What's in that, fresh cow dung?" Ava laughed as she picked up the car keys.

"Ava." Brooke's tone held a note of understanding—even she couldn't stop her nose from crinkling as Jaden came closer.

"Hey," Ava retorted, "I'd glob it all over myself if it meant I could stay here with the air conditioner, instead of sweating under those ancient fans with a bunch of grungy carpenters."

"I bought floor fans, too!" Brooke protested.

"Like they really help." Ava opened the door, ushering in a blast of heat. "*Oh, lovely!*" she said, walking out to the car.

"Mom." Jaden peered out from behind her mask of pink cream. "What I told you earlier? I wasn't making it up."

"Jade..." Brooke's expression was the voice of her unspoken words: *I don't want to hear another word about monsters.* "The sooner you accept that we're going to be here at *least* another month, the better off we'll all be." Then she stepped outside and closed the door.

"In other words, accept my early demise," Jaden complained to the empty house.

Jaden closed her eyes, wishing that when she opened

them, Louisiana and everything that was happening would turn out to be nothing more than a bad dream. Maybe Belle Fleur didn't even exist in the real world. Leaning her head back, she peeked through slits in her eyes and moaned. Nothing had changed. She was still here.

With resignation, Jaden decided to return to the shack before the demonic mutants came looking for her. If she left now, she'd be there and back without her mom being any the wiser. She looked at the gunk slathered on her skin. She'd have to ride her bike along the side streets to avoid public humiliation.

CHAPTER 7

JADEN

Jaden arrived at the path at mid-day. The heat was sweltering, causing the so-called miracle ointment on her sores to drip from her oozing blisters and merge with her perspiration, reminding her of melted cherry sorbet. Stashing her bicycle, Jaden trudged through the maze of vegetation toward the shack, mimicking one of the hot babes in a *Final Fantasy* video game, trying to psyche herself up and figure out what to do. If only it really were all cyber simulation and not her own personal tale of horror.

Jaden swiped her hand through a large spider web, then stepped out from the protection of the foliage, aware of the exaggerated rise and fall of her chest. She had to quell her urge to dash back into the plants.

Her body jerked up the stairs with robotic motions as the nerves of steel she'd had on the trail turned into a puddle of Gerber baby food. Chicken, to be exact.

"Hello?" Her voice and legs quivered. "I brought some peanut butter."

There was no answer. Only the draguitoes relentlessly

buzzing around her in their quest to find their way through the ointment. Jaden pushed the door open, surprised that it was no longer stuck. She paused to see if it would fall off its hinges. When it didn't, she walked into the decrepit dwelling.

A poorly filmed animal documentary began streaming in her head, flashing gory images of cheetahs pouncing on gazelles and tearing them to shreds. Jaden teetered back on her heels. She was the gazelle.

She scanned the room, peering into the dark corners expecting to see a Mal Rou looking back at her. Not seeing the vengeful creatures, Jaden grew hopeful. Maybe they didn't really exist. She'd whacked her head when she'd fallen and imagined it all. She didn't get poison ivy from an evil monster, but from a rare plant the storm had uncovered, just like Officer Duncan said.

Then Jaden inched into the kitchen and stared at the very real creature that lay pinned under a branch of the huge tree.

Jaden made a choking sound. The thing's eyes fluttered open. Taking off her backpack, Jaden removed a partially eaten jar of peanut butter, then set the jar and her pack down. She picked up a stick and pointed it at the small pixie-like thing. It wrinkled its petite nose as it looked at her.

"Jaden?" it said. "Is that correct?"

Jaden nodded nervously.

"Is that because of Ivan?" The soft feminine voice with the subtle fragrance of violets floated through the room.

"What?" After a moment, Jaden realized the creature was looking at the fuchsia cream dripping off her skin. "Oh. It's supposed to heal the poison ivy rash."

"Yes, I am sure that Ivan has missed infecting unsuspecting humans."

Jaden considered that the ointment might be the one thing that could keep her safe. Nothing would want to bite her through that stuff. Still, she kept her stick aimed at the creature.

"As you can see, my relatives are not here."

"Your re-relatives...? The—the Mal Rous called you a... what was it? A Bellibone? They sounded like they hated you."

"Yes, it is true. We are different. And they are quite hostile toward me."

"Hostile? They wanted you *dead*."

"They are the only family I've ever known," the pixie sighed. "In the past I tried to set our differences aside, though they have always, and *will* always, consider me their enemy."

"It's the same way with me and my sister." Jaden replied.

"My name is Violet."

Of course it is. Jaden breathed in Violet's floral scent and eyed the purple jumpsuit she was wearing.

The Bellibone seemed to be regarding Jaden with kindness. There was a long silence, as if it wanted to tell Jaden everything was going to be all right, only couldn't. Jaden suspected that the Bellibone knew nothing in her life would ever be *all right* again.

"So, Violet." Jaden paused, half-wishing the Bellibone would just go *poof* into thin air. "What are the Mal Rous going to do to me?"

"You must understand that the Mal Rous love to play games, and humans are their favorite conquests. As you have seen, they do not play nice. And they don't fight fair. They enjoy inflicting pain, breathing in the scent of fear. In the past they did not take pleasure in the consumption of human flesh. They have killed once that I know of, though they didn't normally put an end to people's lives. However, that was when the Professor was here to keep them in line."

How many people have you killed? Biting her lip, Jaden didn't ask.

"Do you know where I can find the Professor?"

Violet lightly shook her head.

The stagnant air and incessant buzzing of insects was making it hard for Jaden to think. She was positive the pesky bugs were on a mission to eradicate any sanity she had left.

Jaden knew it wasn't the insects that were really eating at her. She had bigger concerns. Was Violet like the rest of her so-called family? Maybe Violet wasn't as demure as she was acting—this was a trick to befriend her so she could finish Jaden off on her own.

Jaden stood fidgeting, struggling to gather her thoughts. Her chances of surviving the Mal Rous unscathed were slim, and the Bellibone seemed amiable. Besides, what choice did she have but to trust this pixie? Setting her stick down, she studied the branch that held Violet captive. If she set the Bellibone free, would she help Jaden in return?

She reached over to remove the branch; if she was going to be murdered by anyone—anything—Violet seemed to be the better option.

"No, please don't." Violet raised her voice with some effort. "They'll know it was you that helped me. They will harm you sooner than they have already planned."

Jaden feigned courage. "If they're going to waste me anyway, I might as well save *you* from them."

"It is very kind of you, but I fear it is not a good idea. Besides, you are not obliged to me."

Obliged. Jaden had only heard people say that in old movies. She took a step back. "Yeah, well, it's because of me the repulsive things are free."

"True," Violet agreed. "Though it is because of the Professor that we exists."

"How am I supposed to find this professor?" Jaden held her stomach, which was churning as if she'd drunk a carton of curdled milk. She wanted to dash out the door and keep going until she reached Colorado. But she couldn't leave her mom and sister here to deal with this mess she'd unleashed. "Where can I go for help? Everyone's going to think I'm nuts. *I* think I'm nuts."

"My dear girl, you are in your right mind. We are real. I suspect that if you inform others about our existence, the Mal Rous would make certain that all involved would live to regret it."

"Oh, that's comforting. It's a real win-win for me." Jaden spoke more loudly than she'd intended.

"Yes, you have created quite a destiny for yourself."

"Nightmare! Nightmare is the appropriate word! I don't get it. Why don't you want to run away? I would if I could. What's wrong with you?"

Jaden felt her panic growing, giving birth to feelings of defeat. She didn't want to take it out on the Bellibone, especially since Violet was probably her only hope of survival. Shifting from one foot to the other, she glanced down at her backpack. "You must be thirsty. I have a flask of water. Do you want some?"

"I would appreciate that," Violet replied and Jaden placed a cap full of water in her hands.

Jaden stepped back and studied the Bellibone. Everything about her seemed so vulnerable. Pitiful. Reminding Jaden of herself.

Violet drank from the cap, then it slipped from her hands. "I am sorry."

"For what?" Jaden asked, picking up the cap.

"For everything." The Bellibone sounded as if she felt guilty for having been created.

"Will you help me?" Jaden could hear the despair in her own voice.

"I can give you information. It may help you stay alive."

Stay alive. Jaden swallowed hard as the realization lodged in her throat. *I could really die.*

"What kind of information?"

"As to how the Professor created us," Violet replied.

"Created you?" Jaden's eyes widened. "*On purpose?*"

"Yes, that is correct. May I ask why you and your mother and sister are renovating the large house? Have you purchased the plantation?"

"How do you know about my mom and sister?" Jaden asked sharply.

"I saw the three of you at the house. And you mentioned your family to Datura. Jaden, you need not worry, I would not hurt you or your mother and sister. I have never harmed anyone. The manor is my home. When you arrived, I came out here. I had nowhere else to go."

Violet flinched, her discomfort more apparent. "Of course, I had no idea of the danger I was placing myself in. But who can predict when or where lightning will strike? My life is in the hands of the fates. Why else would I end up trapped beneath the same tree the Professor wanted to bury me under so long ago? Again, why are you here?"

"We inherited this place from my dad's sister, Amelia." Attempting to exude the persona of a fearless badass, Jaden put her hands on her hips, taking stock of the dump.

"Elvina had a son...?" The creases framing Violet's eyes deepened as she stared into the distance, before continuing, "Professor Thatcher didn't harm her! Elvina was pregnant. That must be why she moved away when he threatened her. Did Dekle know...or did he go with her?"

"*Thatcher*," Jaden squealed, ignoring Violet's other ramblings. "Thatcher was the professor's name? Not Lisette?"

"Yes, child. Professor Dekle Thatcher."

"How did my grandparents know him?"

"Jaden," Violet spoke slowly, "Professor Thatcher was Elvina's husband, which would make him your grandfather."

"No, no, no." Jaden's head bounced forward with each *no*. She found herself almost yelling. "My grandmother's last name was Lisette. Even the deed to this land says Lisette. My dad's last name, *my* last name is Lisette."

"Jaden, Elvina's maiden name was Lisette. This is her family's estate. I gather that when she left Louisiana, she chose to no longer use the last name of Thatcher."

Jaden looked frantically around the disheveled room. "You're wrong. You have to be!" In Jaden's mind, the photograph of her grandfather burned brightly. A part of her knew it was true. "There's no way that I'm related to that Professor Thatcher."

Compassion filled the Bellibone's eyes, making Jaden feel worse. Her skin crawled, and not because of the sores Ivan had inflicted on her. Was she really related to a mad scientist who created demented demons?

And now they were *her* demented demons.

"What am I going to do? No one's going to believe me. No one's going to help me."

"Perhaps someone will. Elvina found herself in a terrible situation many years ago and seemed very alone. I've come to believe her friend Dr. Whiting assisted her."

The weight of Jaden's fears was compressing her chest. She sat on the floor, tugging at the front of her shirt as if it could relieve the discomfort.

"Jaden...are you all right?"

"Oh yeah, sure. Maybe I can get beamed up to the mother ship with all the other wackos." Sarcasm had always helped keep Jaden sane while living with Ava. Right now, it only made her feel worse. Her questions rattled in her mouth before rushing out. "What are you, anyway? And the Mal Rous? You said the Professor *made* you. From what?"

Violet held a hand over her heart as if she were shielding herself from Jaden's outburst, then said, "It is my assumption that your grandmother never spoke of your grandfather Dekle. Is this correct?"

"I never even met my grandmother." There was sadness in Jaden's voice, not for the family she'd never known, but for the mess they'd left behind. "I don't know anything about her or my aunt. I only saw Amelia on the day of my dad's funeral."

"Oh. I am so sorry for the loss of your father."

Jaden felt her throat constrict. She swallowed hard, pushing her grief back down into the small hollowed-out place in her heart where it normally resided.

"Yes, well...the loss of a loved one is never easy." A moment later Violet continued, "As for the Professor, he was a very brilliant man. He created us from unique blends of DNA. At the time, he was the only one in his field to accomplish such a feat."

Jaden considered the fine line that lay between brilliance and insanity. "So you're genetic experiments gone bad?"

"I understand why you might think that. I was the Professor's first successful attempt at cloning, though he had conducted other experiments in England, before he moved to Louisiana."

"My grandfather was British?" That made sense. Jaden could see the influence in Violet's demeanor and the proper way in which she spoke.

Violet gave a nod, then averted her eyes. "There were other Mal Rous before these five. The Professor took them away."

"Took them away?"

"Yes. They were a bit...cannibalistic."

And you? Are you a cannibal? Hateful and bloodthirsty like the others?

"So, why aren't you vicious?" Jaden asked, hopeful that Violet was a vegan.

"I was created with DNA from your grandmother Elvina. 'Bellibone' is a long-forgotten word meaning 'a female excelling in beauty as well as goodness.' To the Professor I was akin to Elvina, which was wonderful in the beginning. Until he changed. As he grew to detest her, he felt the same toward me." Violet shifted, flicking her elegant wings. I also have damselfly DNA. And pampas grass. And violets, Elvina's favorite flower. Each of us is named after the plant DNA from which we were created: Anders for oleander, Ivan, for...well..." Violet gestured at the poison ivy sores under Jaden's ointment.

With a long, drawn-out sigh, Violet added, "I will never forget when Elvina discovered us. She was terrified."

Jaden could hear sadness in Violet's voice, but couldn't comfort her. She was trying to cope with her own perverse reality. "What can you tell me about the others?" she blurted. "Please, I need to know."

"For them, your grandfather mixed his own DNA, which gives them their human characteristics. They also possess the DNA of newt, tardigrades, myomorpha, poisonous plants, insects, venomous snakes—whatever he found to be tenacious survivors in the elements. Their unusual molecular makeup is apparent in their faces and the unusual shapes of their heads."

"Tardigrades? Myomorpha?"

"Yes, tardigrades, also known as water bears." Jaden gave Violet a blank expression. "They are considered to be one of the most resilient known micro-animals. And myomorpha are rodents."

"So why did he call them Mal Rous?"

Violet's long pause made Jaden even more uncomfortable.

"In Latin, *mal* means bad, evil. Cajun folklore tells of a beast that is said to prowl the swamps, a *rougarou*, part human, part animal. The first batch of Mal Rous' genetic dispositions inspired the Professor to give them this nickname. He rather enjoyed the sound of it." Violet shifted her gaze away from Jaden. "Their scientific name is *Cerophagous Cautelosus*."

"Do I even want to know what that means?"

"No. Nonetheless, you should, so you will better comprehend what the Mal Rous are capable of—if they become as inhumane as their predecessors." Violet spoke calmly. "*Cerophagous* is Latin for flesh-eating. *Cautelosus*, for treacherous and cunning."

Jaden slumped forward. There was a loud pounding in her ears.

In the distance she heard Violet repeatedly saying her name, but Jaden couldn't respond. She could barely breathe.

CHAPTER 8

DATURA

The raw elements thriving in the tangled mass of undergrowth invigorated Datura and her family of Mal Rous. The damp earth enveloped their bodies like a moist mantle of belonging, enlivening their self-righteousness. They knew their innate cruelty came from the poisonous sources of DNA they were derived from. The poisons were not only harmful to their victims, but to their own souls as well. This awareness empowered them. They equated kindness and soulfulness with weakness. The Mal Rous believed the part of their DNA that was human gave them a bit of compassion—at least, toward the Professor.

Datura's saliva overflowed from the excitement of knowing they were closer to finding their creator. Spittle rolled down her chin, splashing onto the ground. She knew the others missed the Professor as much as she did and would do anything necessary to get him back—destroy whatever or whoever got in their way.

"Is ya sure we goin' the right way?" Ivan interrupted Datura's thoughts.

Datura didn't answer. She looked back at Ivan. His ears were twitching as his eyeballs swiveled like marbles and settled on Tig.

Datura and Ivan watched as Tig snuffled the air. A snake spiraled up behind her. When it rose to the full height of her fifteen-inch body, Tig's tendrils sprang from her head and hit the snake dead on, piercing its scales, sending it squirming and hissing to the ground.

The Mal Rous feasted on their unexpected treat while it was still alive. It was only a mud snake, not poisonous, but still a delectable snack.

With their stomachs full and their minds dulled, they continued their journey. The trek through the mud and dense growth was harder than Datura had expected. Judging from her siblings' appearance, they were as tired as she was by the time they got to the open space at the back of the old estate.

At least an acre of land stretched between them and the house. Ivan's ears curved forward, taking in the sounds of the hammering and chattering.

Datura sucked in a breath, hopeful to smell their dear Professor Dekle. Her tentacles hung limp on her head. "This ain't good. My feelers should 'a picked up the Professor's scent from here. Somethin' ain't right. We should wait. Let that girl bring him to us."

Esere got in her face. "We come all this way, we gonna see what's up. He might be sick. Or maybe he's in the cellar. We got to look in there. Maybe he needs our help."

Ivan stood at least three inches taller than Datura. Straightening up, he looked down his nose at her. "I agree with Esere. We is this close, we're goin' in. 'Sides, if the Professor ain't here, we'll get to see who is."

"Fine. Ya thinks yer so smart." Datura's remark implied, *if yer wrong I'm gonna punish ya.* "But we has to split into two groups, so we don't get caught."

"Ya gone soft." Esere flicked one of Datura's limp tentacles. "When has anyone ever tried to capture us?"

"I ain't soft! The Professor never released us in daylight. Them times we snuck out, he was mad as all get-out. He had his reasons. So we is gonna be careful, not stupid."

"She's right." Ivan grabbed Esere's arm and yanked him away from Datura. "Us bein' seen in the day would upset our Dekle. Datura and me will check the cellar."

Datura didn't argue. She knew the blood coursing through a tasty human could trigger her mosquito instincts and Ivan had the strength to overpower her. The rats she'd fed on earlier would help buffer her appetite, but the sweet smell of human blood would make her want to go after any unsuspecting prey.

"Tig, Anders, Esere, y'all shimmy up that lattice beside the house," Datura ordered. "Find the Professor's bedroom. If his belongings is there, it means he's alive. And sniff around for Elvina. With her perfume she'll be easy to find. Just 'cause that stinky Bellibone says she's gone don't mean it's true."

Esere nodded, pretending to agree. But he had no interest in snooping around the house. The cellar was *his* idea. *He'd* be the one going there. Before the others could stop him, Esere charged out from the cane field and ran the distance to the garage; hiding in the shrubs next to the building's thin walls, he rooted among the plants, searching for the window they used to climb through after their nighttime jaunts to town.

He stopped himself from letting out an excited squeal when he found it. He was certain his creator would be inside. Dekle practically lived down there with the Mal Rous. Squeezing between the iron bars, Esere pushed on the filthy glass. The small painted window opened, welcoming him in.

Elated, Esere climbed down the brick wall into the Professor's laboratory. His beak-shaped nose rose up, seeking the comforting odors of sulfur and chloroform.

Instead, the air smelled musty and organic. Esere's eyes adjusted to the muted light. His head moved like a mechanical toy, turning to look for the Professor's lab table and its simmering test tubes, cages of toads, and jars of cockroaches.

There was nothing.

He hurried over to the corner. The pens they used to sleep in were missing. The room was devoid of everything that once was home. Only the large wooden crate where the Professor had kept snakes sat in its original place. But it was empty.

Heat rushed through Esere's body as he recalled the last time he had seen the Professor. It had been mid-day when Dekle came into the cellar inhaling a slow, deep breath. His face had contorted, and his tongue slid out, lapping up the air, tasting Elvina's perfume that lingered in the room.

The Professor shook with anger as he read aloud the words he'd so meticulously printed on the cover of his journal, "Book Four, 1959: DNA/Genetic Testing, by Professor Dekle Thatcher." Then he left, cradling the journal in his arms.

By the time Dekle returned, the sun had set. The Mal Rous watched as the Professor hauled large stoneware containers into the cellar. He worked late into the night, accompanied by Tig singing along to Rosemary Clooney's voice as it crackled through the speaker of a small phonograph.

"You'll be safe," Dekle told them. "You can live for years in the solution I germinated you in. I'll hide you where no one will find you. Trust me, you'll be fine."

At first Esere didn't understand. Then he thought the Professor must have gone mad as he stuck each of them into a vessel. Esere couldn't stop coughing as the dense liquid slowly flowed into his nose, his lungs, his ears, gradually muffling the Professor's loud, confident words, "I promise, I will come back for you."

Esere was certain he was going to drown in the horrible stuff, but a few minutes later he fell into a deep state of hibernation—until Tig freed him yesterday.

Now, looking around the cellar, he missed the Professor more than ever. The empty room made him feel hollow inside. Esere leaned against the wall, slid down to the cold damp floor and wept—crying had never been acceptable to his siblings—this was his only chance to grieve.

His ears spiked up as the door at the top of the stairs opened. Through his tears, he saw the faint image of a man. With a surge of excitement, Esere stood to greet his beloved creator.

The light clicked on and a bulb overhead flickered, then popped. The man cursed as he came down the stairs.

Esere's feral instincts erupted. The voice and scent, everything was wrong: Professor Thatcher was tall and slender. This man was stocky and looked as though he'd stuffed a large rubber ball under his stained shirt. He wore shorts that accentuated his thick calves. Stomping down the steps, he skimmed the railing with one hand, while the other held a bucket filled with tools. He reminded Esere of those halfwits they used to terrorize in town.

The man stopped, looking at him in the dim light. "What the—?"

Esere leaped up, embedded his claws in the intruder's leg, and rammed his chin horn into his calf. The stunned man screamed. His tools crashed to the ground. Esere leaned back, ready to stab again, when someone called from the top of the stairs.

"Carl, what's goin' on? You all right down there?"

The poison pumping into the man slowed his pulse. He wobbled as he gulped for air. "Rick, help me," he muttered. His body lurched like a boat in a storm.

Esere sprang off him, feeling a confused mixture of excitement at assaulting a human, anger at being caught off guard, and sadness that his home no longer existed.

The man tumbled down the remaining stairs, unconscious.

Esere scrambled across the dank room and out the window. When he reached the safety of the cane field, he sank to the moist ground. He was certain that any punishment Datura inflicted on him for leaving the pack and letting himself be seen would not be as agonizing as the pain he felt at knowing Dekle was gone.

CHAPTER 9

JADEN

"Jaden...Jaden. Say something. Jaden—" Violet continued calling out to her.

Jaden wanted Violet to leave her alone. The more she learned, the worse she felt. *Cerophagous Cautelosus.* She could barely pronounce the words, but their meanings, *flesh-eating, treacherous, cunning,* simmered in her head and threatened to boil over. It was bad enough that this professor was related to her. But was she really any better? After all, she had released his sleazy creations.

The Bellibone stretched out her neck and inhaled Jaden's guilt as if it were a cloud of spores floating through the air. Jaden doubted whether guilt had ever entered her grandfather's conscience. At the same time, she knew that she had to get all the information she could while the Mal Rous weren't around. She steadied her breathing and found her voice again.

"So, what's *your* scientific name?" She waited to hear some word she'd never be able to spell, a word that would mean she'd better run and hide before Violet revealed a set of fangs.

"He just referred to me as a Bellibone." Violet smiled at her, obviously relieved that Jaden had survived her mini meltdown. "Jaden, Professor Thatcher wasn't always a misguided man."

"*Misguided*! He was certifiable."

"Yes, yes, I know how this must sound to you, but when he first began developing us, he was brilliant and kind. I understood why Elvina fell in love with him. Over time, his experiments had a negative effect on his health. It was Datura's bite that caused him to change so drastically, physically, mentally...emotionally."

"Why would Datura bite him?" Jaden asked.

"The Professor was always experimenting on the Mal Rous. I like to believe that he was trying to discover a way to humanize them—"

"Humanize? What's the point? Have you read the news lately?" Seeing Violet's bewildered expression, Jaden said, "Go on."

"One day the Professor came into the cellar with a special mushroom brew he had asked one of the triplets to mix for him."

Triplets? More bizarre DNA experiments gone bad? Jaden felt as if she were sinking further into a bottomless pit.

"Prior to that, he had given the mixture to the Mal Rous in small doses. This time, before he could open the container, Datura went after him. She got hold of the bottle and broke it with her teeth. Her gums were bleeding, but she didn't care. When the Professor tried to take it from her, she slashed her claws into his arm and sank her teeth into the open wound, sending her blood into his system, mixing with his blood. While Datura was latched onto the Professor, a sixth Mal Rou, by the name of Talis, consumed all of the elixir.

"The Professor fell to the floor, convulsing, and became unconscious." Violet's voice quivered. "There was nothing I could do. The next day, when the Professor woke up, Talis was dead. While a mere teaspoon of the elixir invigorated them, apparently too much would cause their demise. The Professor had created the Mal Rous with a substantial amount of tardigrade and newt DNA and thought them to be indestructible. It is my understanding that newts can regenerate their limbs, spinal cord, eyes, intestines. And it is said tardigrades can survive in environments that would kill other animals."

Indestructible. The word sat on Jaden's tongue like a fat maggot.

"From that day on, the Professor enjoyed seeing how much suffering the Mal Rous could create. It was as if he had been taken over by a sinister force. By Datura."

Jaden's eyes widened. Had Datura's blood mixing with the Professor's allowed her to manipulate him? Tweak just the right mind strings to make him do what she wanted? Had she intentionally changed him into a Mal Rous?

"Are you telling me he became an indestructible super-human?" Jaden's body tensed, picturing him turning into Wolverine.

"No, no, by no means. We are not magical super-beings. But the Professor acquired certain traits of Datura's. He enjoyed coming into his lab in the cellar to eat raw meat with his 'little darlings.' I believe it was because he was unable to extract blood from animals or people, the way Datura can."

"She drains blood from people and drinks it?" Jaden

gagged as if she'd swallowed the imaginary maggot. "Datura's a miniature vampire? I'm so screwed."

"Oh no, she is not large enough to drink that much all at once. She pumps small amounts from her catch with her tentacles. Do you remember the way some of them reached for you? She is part mosquito. It is one of the reasons she dislikes me; damselflies are mosquitoes' natural predators. She uses some of her tentacles for tracking her game. A few carry the toxic sap of her namesake, the datura plant, also known as thornapple. Are you familiar with it?"

Jaden shook her head, numb with the consequences of what her simple stone toss had unleashed.

"Do you think the Mal Rous know I'm related to the Professor?" she asked.

The tilt of Violet's head and her sad expression made it clear. The Mal Rous would figure it out soon enough.

Jaden raised her finger to her lips as she looked at the front door. "Did you hear that?" she whispered.

Not waiting for Violet to reply, Jaden tiptoed into the other room and peeked out the window.

If the Mal Rous were back, they were hiding. Jaden stepped into the shadows and waited for the Mal Rous to storm the house and pummel her.

After a few minutes her jumpy nerves settled. She went back into the kitchen.

"It was not the Mal Rous, Jaden. I will smell them long before their arrival." Violet exhaled, sending her floral essence wafting through the room. "We all have an excellent sense of smell, sight, and hearing."

Jaden inhaled Violet's fragrance and found herself feeling emboldened. She rolled her shoulders and stretched her neck as if she were preparing for a boxing match.

"Then what about Ivan?" Gesturing at her skin, Jaden continued, "I know he can spread poison ivy. Plus, Tig said he has snake venom."

"Yes. You were paying attention yesterday. Ivan also has the DNA of horned lizard, and coral snake. A bite from him can be lethal. The Professor taught him to inject only small amounts of snake venom, not quite enough to paralyze a person's breathing muscles."

"What can Tig do?" Jaden asked.

"The spurges poison she injected into you with her tendrils can cause inflammation, paralysis...even death. She also has black widow DNA. You were lucky that she did not bite you as well. That could have sent your body into shock."

"I'm never going to remember all this." Jaden pressed her hands against her head, as if would simulate her brain. "Umm...Datura: part mosquito, uses her tentacles to drink people's blood. Ivan: poison ivy toxins and coral snake. Has the ability to paralyze me."

Jaden looked over at Violet, who was nodding. "Tig: black widow poison plus spurges plant, which obviously causes psychotic episodes," Jaden said with sarcasm, gesturing to herself. "So that leaves Esere and Anders. What about them?"

"Esere has scorpion DNA. The toxins are in his chin horn and can cause increased heart rate. He also has Calabar bean DNA, which can be fatal if he gets too carried away." Tapping her own nose, Violet added, "Do you recall the shape of his nose? That comes from vulture DNA."

"What the blazes was wrong with my grandfather?"

"Funny, 'blazes' is a word your grandfather often used."

Jaden gaped at Violet, remembering how often her father had said the word, and wondered if slang words were genetically passed from generation to generation, like hair and eye color.

Violet reached her hand toward Jaden as if wanting to comfort her. When Jaden didn't return the gesture, Violet pulled back.

"With Anders, the Professor's results exceeded his own expectations. He used the oleander plant—the poisons are in his fangs. Also centipede—the venom is released from the tendrils on the sides of his skull. And DNA from a Komodo dragon. Did you notice the shape of his head, the way that it sways when he walks, and the size of his jaw? For being only seventeen inches tall he can cause quite a bit of damage."

"A Komodo dragon?"

"I don't believe it was difficult for Professor Thatcher to find a source of DNA for one. The scientific community was quite close. He had connections all over the world."

"So, if the Professor was so brilliant, and they have his DNA, why are they so...*backwards*? You seem intelligent."

"Well," Violet beamed, "though I never knew Elvina, I have always assumed she had an inquisitive mind. I too have a passion for knowledge. You saw all the books she left in the house. I have had many years to read."

A frown passed over Violet's face. "However barbaric the Mal Rous are, the Professor did his best to teach them. Still, he could never rein in their eagerness to cause havoc, nor their joy for tormenting humans. But don't be fooled by Datura. She is extremely bright. She pretends to be a simpleton for the others. And though they are not intellectual, they are quite conniving, very quick to find a way to gain control of a situation."

"Anything else I should know?" Jaden spoke more

urgently. Aware of how long they'd been talking, she worried that the Mal Rous might return.

"Yes," Violet answered quickly. "Datura's thornapple sap produces delirium. Even hallucinations. An adequate dose will last for several days. The toxins can cause her quarry to forget how they came to be injured."

"So that means no one would know what made them sick. No one would have any memory of being attacked." Jaden lowered her gaze to avoid making eye contact with the grim reaper that she imagined standing before her.

"There may be one person who remembers. A little boy who lived in this house many years ago. Regrettably, he saw the Mal Rous and experienced all their effects. Datura boasted that she chose not to give him any thornapple. If he is alive, he probably remembers them, and he may be willing to help."

"Were any other townspeople changed?" Jaden asked, thinking of Officer Duncan.

"Besides the Professor, I don't know of the Mal Rous ever mixing their blood with anyone else's—only their poisons, which made people ill or delirious. The effects normally passed in a few days, though there may have been lasting maladies such as skin disorders and learning disabilities. I recall the Professor saying one person had gone insane. It was very upsetting to him. However, that was before Datura bit him."

"I don't understand. Why did he want them to hurt people?"

"I believe at first, he found their actions unsettling. Over time, he grew accepting of it. His *need* to observe the Mal Rous attacking people developed after Datura's blood merged with his, and her desires became his."

An acidic taste filled Jaden's mouth. "I'm doomed."

"I am very sorry that I cannot be of more help."

"Well, like it or not, I'm helping you." Finding a broken tree limb, Jaden ignored Violet's plea to let her be. Prying apart the two branches that trapped the Bellibone, Jaden wedged a hunk of wood no bigger than a large pack of chewing gum between them, leaving enough space for Violet to maneuver her leg free, if she chose.

Violet eased into a more comfortable position.

"The Mal Rous shouldn't even notice." Jaden arranged the leaves, so they hung down, concealing the gap. "Besides, they're going to come after me whether I help you or not." Sitting back down, Jaden considered all the stories she'd read, movies she'd seen that taught good wins over bad, right is might.

All lies. In this scenario, she would never be the victor.

"The Professor did keep records of his research. They might be in his main laboratory." Violet gave a strained smile of encouragement. "It is also possible Dr. Whiting has them. He may have found them on one of his visits to the manor. He kept an eye on it when your grandmother left. I think it was a way to feel close to her. He missed her terribly."

"Records could be helpful," Jaden mused. "When I'm at the house, I'll look around. Maybe they're hidden somewhere."

Jaden leaned back, and her palms landed in thick globs of sap that stuck to her like glue. "Oh yuck, this isn't Ivan's slobber, is it?" She rubbed her hands together, trying to ball it up, but that only made it worse, blending with the pink goop from around her wrists and making a sticky mess that seeped into her skin.

"May I see your hands?" Violet asked, trying to look at

Jaden's palms. "You shouldn't go to the manor now. The Mal Rous will be there."

"What?" Jaden jumped up. "My mom and sister are there! I've got to go."

"Jaden, please, let me see your palms. If it's Datura's—"

"I have to hurry!" Tossing her flask of water into her pack, Jaden ignored Violet's plea.

Chapter 10

Jaden

The neurons in Jaden's brain were tingling. Her thoughts were whirling faster than her bicycle pedals as she rode to the mansion. She didn't care what Violet had been saying about her hands when she'd rushed out of the shack. Her only concern was getting to the Mal Rous before they could hurt anyone.

Jaden skidded onto the estate's driveway, then paused. Everything appeared charged with energy. The colors were glowing and vibrant. The magnolia blossoms were singing. She let out a belly laugh at such a crazy idea.

Her palms were stuck to her handlebars. She shook them free, dropped her bike to the ground and barreled into the kitchen.

Carl was sitting on a chair surrounded by his four crewmen, her mother, and Ava. Brooke looked up. The set of her jaw made it clear that she was not pleased to see Jaden.

Jaden didn't say anything. She turned away, trying to hide her toothy grin.

They were all listening to Carl, who was covered in

perspiration and gesturing at his leg. His speech slurred as he complained of chest pains and insisted that a critter resembling a two-legged, human-looking rat wearing clothes had attacked him.

Everyone's faces held lines of tension, along with disbelief. Rick said he hadn't seen any rodents in the cellar. They thought Carl must have had a stroke and fallen on a sharp object that gouged him in the calf.

He lost them when he said the rat was wearing clothes. Jaden glanced around looking for signs of the Mal Rou that had attacked him.

"My vision is messed up," Carl said, blotting the moisture from his face with his handkerchief. "Maybe that there critter didn't have on clothes." He looked at Jaden and rubbed his eyes.

"Your eyes are just fine, Carl. I really am covered in pink slime." Jaden giggled. "I probably look like I've stepped out of a Salvador Dali painting."

She was still laughing as Ava spun her around.

"Are you drunk?" Ava scrutinized Jaden's dilated pupils. "Drugs! You're on drugs."

Brooke stepped closer. Jaden could tell her mom was ready to lose it. Stress was scribbled over her face like a splotchy red tattoo. She was obviously concerned about Carl's health. Worried he might sue her.

Jaden wondered if her mom could hear the fans clinking and clanking in every room of the house, nattering on about Jaden riding her bike all the way here, Jaden possibly drunk —or worse, Jaden being on drugs.

Ava pushed Jaden aside. She was in drill sergeant mode. "Carl, you have to go to the hospital."

"Y-yeah, yeah," Carl said meekly.

"Rick, you take him." Ava snapped her fingers inches from Rick's face. Then she barked at the rest of the crew, "Get back to work."

Jaden watched as Ava seized their mother's arm and hauled her toward the back door. "Jaden, put your bike in the back of the car," she commanded over her shoulder.

"Yes, ma'am." Jaden was doing her best to walk like a sober person while giving a limp salute as Ava turned away.

Moments later, Ava was driving the three of them to their small rental house. Pressing her fingers against her eyes to stop the rush of colors whizzing by Jaden smelled Datura's sap on her palms. She smeared the noxious secretions onto her shorts. Violet's words of concern sank in.

Jaden tried to remember the Mal Rous' various vile abilities. She couldn't think straight. *Which poison is this? Oleander? Spurges? No...Thornapple!*

Ava turned up the volume on the radio, sending Jaden's loopy brain reeling. She knew Ava hated the quiet. It was as if the noise filled up the holes in her sister's heart and stopped unwanted memories from taking hold. *Or maybe she's not as smart as she thinks she is, and the noise just rattles around in her head.*

The car pulled into the driveway, and Jaden watched her sister jump out and dash to the front door. Ava snatched a note from the doorjamb and smiled as though she'd won the lottery.

"Mom," Jaden scooted forward. "I know you're not in a good mood, but now do you believe me about the Mal Rous?"

"You're right," her mom said, turning toward the backseat. "I'm not in the mood. One more word about Mule Rules—"

"Mal Rous, Mom. Mal, as in bad and evil!"

"I mean it, Jaden, stop it." The sealed car was turning into a steam room on wheels. "You're not going to read any more horror books. They're spinning your imagination out of control."

"Hah! I couldn't make this up if I wanted to."

"What's wrong with you lately?" Brooke demanded, practically jumping over the seat. "Is Ava right? Have you been drinking? Taking drugs? Is this all because of that boy?"

*Speaking of drugs...*Jaden realized her sap-induced giddy mood had dissolved. Violet had said thornapple poisoning could last several days, cause hallucinations and dull a person's memory. Obviously, the sap didn't have as long-lasting an effect on the skin as when it was ingested.

"Oh yeah, as usual, Ava's right. I'm a closet alcoholic. I rolled around in poison ivy so I could stay at this deluxe rental house drinking beer all day." Jaden flopped back against the seat. "We don't even have alcohol in the house! You think I go out and steal it? Oh, and just so you know, I sneak into the landlady's house and take her painkillers, too."

Her mother's mouth shut, teeth striking together loud enough for Jaden to hear. Without another word, Brooke exited the car and slammed the door shut.

I'm such a jerk.

Jaden hurried after her mother. She knew it was no use telling her the truth. "I'm sorry, Mom. I must be allergic to this ointment. It makes my mind all sketchy. I just wanted to help 'cause I know how badly you need to get the place ready to sell."

"Aww, isn't that sweet." Ava was still standing by the front door. Jaden looked over to see her clutching the limp piece of paper to her chest.

"It's from Brisbane," Ava gloated. "He said I forgot to give him my cell number and that he was hoping to see me." Delighted with herself, she opened the door and sashayed inside.

"Ava, stop it." Brooke's tone was weary as she followed her oldest daughter.

"I forgot to tell you, this morning when you were at the doctors the landlady stopped by. She's going to New Orleans for a few days and taking her dog with. She wants us to watch—" Ava's words faded as the front door closed.

Jaden put her bike in the shed, then stormed into the house, glaring at Ava. Even if they had sex, Ava didn't have the right to call Briz by his full name. In another month he'd be leaving for Europe. Why couldn't it be now?

Jaden went into the bathroom and scrubbed her sap-covered hands until they were raw. Wearing a fresh coat of Dr. Schilling's cream, she snatched the FedEx box from Amelia's lawyer off the kitchen counter on her way out. The decaying picnic table in the backyard was one place where she knew she could have some privacy. No sane person would willingly sit in that bug-infested sauna.

She was at an ultimate low point—swimming in a septic tank would be an improvement. Jaden gazed at the white clouds that adorned the horizon like a string of misshapen pearls against the azure sky, wondering how such a beautiful place could be the spawning ground for miniature devils.

Jaden opened the box that held the legacy her father never knew he had, and sifted through the paperwork, looking for what? A clue, or hidden note that said, "Beware! Mal Rous!"

The legal mumbo-jumbo made for a boring read, but it reminded Jaden that her family had also inherited Aunt

Amelia's home in North Carolina—only they couldn't take possession of it until Amelia's man-friend died or moved out.

Another house! What all have you got hiding there, Auntie?

At the bottom of the box was a black velvet pouch holding a small key, and a heart-shaped locket with tiny pictures of her grandparents.

Brooke came around the side of the house fanning herself with a piece of paper. "We're going back to the estate. You get some rest. Don't stay out here too long. You could pass out. I can't handle another person doing that today. We'll see you this evening. *Don't go anywhere.*"

Jaden wasn't sure if her mom was swatting bugs away or if she actually thought flapping that piece of paper was going to cool her off. "Yeah, okay. Mom, are you all right?"

"I'll decide how I'm doing when I hear how Carl is." Brooke flapped her makeshift fan faster. "I left my phone on the kitchen counter. If you need to reach us, call Ava's number. And try to remember what you did with your phone."

Jaden nodded, knowing her mom wouldn't believe her if she told her.

"Hey Mom, did you know Amelia left us some kind of key?"

"I saw that. I think it's for a safety-deposit box. Don't lose it."

A few minutes later, Jaden listened to the car driving away, hearing words in the rhythmic repetition of the tires as they whirred into the distance. *Your life sucks, you're helpless and alone. Your life sucks, you're helpless and alone.*

Jaden gathered up the contents of the box and went back into the house. Setting the box onto the kitchen counter, she scowled at the goop covering her body—the body Briz wasn't interested in, and that the Mal Rous wanted to torture. Was feeling like a reject part of being a teen, or was Ava right? Jaden was just a born loser.

Her attention shifted to a stack of photo albums her mom had brought from the estate. Brooke said the girls would appreciate them one day as part of their father's history. Thumbing through the pages, she saw an older sepia photo of Elvina as a young girl, hand-painted to give it a hint of color. She was standing next to a good-looking boy who had his arm around her. Both of them were smiling.

In another album, Jaden noted the contrast between her grandparents' happy faces in their wedding pictures, to their dour expressions in later photos. Jaden knew she'd been wearing similar expressions ever since she first encountered the Mal Rous.

"Okay," she glared at her grandfather's photo. "I have a key—whatever good that is—and Violet...sort of. If I can keep her alive, she might help me."

Her glance fell back to the goo on her arms. "Whoever's making the ointment might know something about Ivan." Locating the doctor's business card on the counter, Jaden grabbed her mom's phone and called Dr. Schilling's number.

She listened as the receptionist repeated what the doctor had told them earlier. Then the woman added in her thick southern drawl, "I think it was Dr. Shilling's father-in-law... well, ex-father-in-law that first created the formula, Dr. Whiting."

Jaden's ears perked up. Could it be Elvina's Dr. Whiting? Could he still be alive?

"Is he...does he still make it? Does he live here in Belle Fleur?"

"Just outside of town, at the Meadow Seniors' Facility. I have to go now, Miss Jaden. I'm gettin' another call."

"Oh, okay, but real quick, who do you buy the ointment from?"

"We get it from a man named Hubs." The receptionist hung up before Jaden could say anything else.

If this was Elvina's Dr. Whiting, Jaden had to talk to him. And track down this Hubs person.

She looked at the clock and groaned. If she left the house again today and her mom caught her, Brooke would set her up with a GPS child-tracking device. Turning on her iPad, Jaden found the address to the Meadow Seniors' Facility. Then she began researching things Violet had mentioned.

She started with centipedes; clicking on a site, she learned that centipede venom could cause chills, fever, and anaphylactic shock. She imagined Anders's thick tendrils burrowing into his victims and shuddered. Moving on to oleanders, her stomach turned. The plant poisons secreted from Anders's fangs could cause tremors, seizures—even a coma.

My grandfather was a real sicko.

She knew enough about Datura's bloodsucking mosquito abilities. What about thornapple? A picture of the thornapple bloom, a.k.a. *Datura stramonium* appeared on the screen. It was hard to comprehend how Datura could be named after such a beautiful flower. Like the Mal Rou, the entire plant seemed to be pure evil. Its poison was capable of causing amnesia, delirium, and death.

On to scorpion venom. Judging from Carl's symptoms, Jaden was positive Esere had been the one that skewered him. Her next click revealed another disturbing fact: Esere's Calabar toxins could affect people like nerve gas. Jaden hadn't thought it was possible to feel more hopeless and overwhelmed, but facing the combined scope of the Mal Rous' powers did just that.

She doubted her grandfather was still alive and couldn't stop herself from hoping that he had died a painful death. With a feeling of unease, Jaden worried this meant she was no better than him?

Through the window, she saw their landlady loading up her car. Like both of her houses, the woman was old and could use a makeover. She was also leaving town just in time. Jaden would have traded lives with her in a second.

"Forget it. I'm calling the police."

Dialing 911, Jaden blubbered about mutant creatures. Before she could finish, the operator hung up on her.

CHAPTER 11

JADEN

With her hair flowing down her back and her sheer dress billowing in the breeze, Jaden stood on the exquisite white beach, her toes curling into the warm sand. She stepped into the cool turquoise water and felt it lapping over her ankles. She knew she was dreaming. The real giveaway wasn't the breeze or the water, but the dress. She didn't own one like that. Only alluring femme fatales wore them. Well, the dress, and that Briz was there reaching out to her. *To her, not Ava.* She leaned toward him as he gently touched her cheek. A glass of water appeared in his hand, and he guided it to Jaden's lips, tipping it slightly. She swallowed the liquid, expecting it to be followed by a passionate kiss.

This was *her* dream. She might as well make it unfold in her favor. At least she could have Briz when she was asleep. She placed her hands on his hips, pulling him toward her. Laughing, he intentionally spilled the cold water onto the thin fabric of her dress.

His laughter changed into Ava's piercing cackle and Jaden woke up.

Water was dripping down Jaden's chin onto her pillow. Scrunching up her face, she opened an eye and focused on a soggy washcloth hanging above her head. Ava was holding it, smirking.

Of course. Snatching the wet cloth, Jaden tossed it onto her sister's bed.

"Hey, you snot, you got my spread all wet." Ava pelted it back at her.

"*Right.* I'm the snot."

"Well, Mom told me to wake you up. She wants to talk to you before we leave."

With the dripping cloth still in her hand, Jaden walked to the bathroom—standing in front of the mirror she saw that last night's layer of goop had soaked in, leaving a sheer pink film behind. She washed her face and studied it. Dr. Schilling said that the cream would work fast, and she was right. Her skin was almost healed. Jaden piled on more ointment to hide that fact. She'd barely opened the door when Ava marched up to her.

"I didn't see any festering sores when we were in the bedroom." Ava eyeballed the slime as if she could see right through it. "Mom, she's just trying to get out of cleaning up that dump. She's fine."

"Give it a rest, Ava," Brooke said, putting their lunch into a canvas bag. "By the way, that *dump* will end up buying us a new car, and with any luck, pay for your college education."

"It's not fair." Ava flopped onto the couch. "I always have to do everything."

"I don't mind helping." Jaden knew it would give her a chance to look for clues about the Professor. She'd have to remember to bring the key Amelia had left them in case it unlocked a hidden box with his records. "It's kind of boring hanging out here."

"Well, if you're up for it, baby. But let's wait till this evening. It'll be cooler. Nothing too strenuous. Box up some clothes for the homeless shelter. Wipe down some cupboards."

Even better. It would give her time to go see Elvina's Dr. Whiting this morning.

"Oh, yeah," Ava whined, slipping on her sandals. "It'll be nice and cool, *'baby.'* Like working in a vat of warm Jell-O."

"Go start the car, Ava." Brooke slid a stainless-steel jug of water in Ava's direction. "Carry this."

"*Go start the car, Ava.*" Ava sounded like an angry parrot.

"Your sister will be here at six." Removing some cash from her wallet, Brooke handed the money to Jaden. "Order us a pizza for dinner, whatever toppings you want."

"Wow, Mom. You're giving us junk food? What a great reward for slave labor." Ava grabbed the water and opened the door, mumbling about the heat.

"It's a treat, so appreciate it." Brooke spat back, following Ava to the car.

As soon as the two of them drove off, Jaden removed her coating of smelly ointment and applied some of Ava's makeup over her fading sores.

The Meadow Seniors' Facility was forty minutes out of town by car. She didn't have the time or patience to clean the thornapple sap off her bicycle handlebars, so she covered them with masking tape she'd found in the shed. With a photograph of Elvina in her backpack, she set off to visit Dr. Whiting.

Jaden pedaled her bike like a wild woman on a mission,

despite the awful heat. The desire to stay alive was proving to be a great source of motivation.

She rode through the old part of town, where Belle Fleur wore its history like a great-grandmother's faded housedress. The gas station was built back when attendants had uniforms, filled gas tanks, and washed customers' car windows. Its sign proudly stated, "Established 1927." The barbershop had opened a decade before the depression. It seemed to Jaden, every patron left the building with the same buzz cut.

Three blocks north was the newer section of town. New for Belle Fleur, anyway. At least the stores had air conditioning. But they were in ragged shape from the multitude of storms and hurricanes caused by global warming.

Strands of hair escaped from Jaden's ponytail and stuck to her face. Her sunglasses steamed up, blurring her vision, so she barely glimpsed the car that swerved in front of her. Screeching to a halt, she planted her feet on the ground, stopping herself from flying headfirst over the handlebars and bonding with an oak tree.

She snapped her head up, expecting Ava to jump from the car and start verbally blasting her for leaving the house.

Instead, Briz's ultra-quiet Prius blocked her way. No wonder she hadn't heard him driving up next to her. He was the only guy in this town who didn't own a noisy pickup truck. She thought about maneuvering her bike past him.

She was caught between her battered ego telling her to hurry up and her heart saying *slow down, let him catch you.* Her heart won.

Briz jumped from the car and rushed over to her. "Jaden, I'm so sorry." As he grabbed her bike's handlebars, she couldn't help thinking it was too bad she'd covered up Datura's sap with the tape. "Are you okay?"

No! She thought, gritting her teeth. He dumped her for Ava. It would serve him right if she rode away and left him standing there with a dazed look on his face. She meant to—until he placed his hand on her shoulder and electricity shot through her.

Could he feel it, too?

Jaden's body betrayed her, surrendering to his touch. When he removed his sunglasses, she fell into his blue eyes. Back home she had plenty of guy friends, some she'd even had minor crushes on, but not one of them had this effect on her. She longed for Briz to touch her, and not just her shoulder. Only he didn't want her. Not even close.

Briz's fingers skated over the top of her arm, causing her skin to tingle. "How are you? Why haven't you called me back? I've left messages on your phone, sent you texts. Did I do something wrong?" With a guilty smile he added, "I mean, besides almost making you crash into a tree."

She'd missed hearing his voice. Now it was caressing her like the gentle waves in her dream. But thoughts of him with Ava flooded her mind, and the waves turned into a tsunami.

"What are you talking about?" Her words rushed out. "Why should I call you?"

"Uhh...because that's what friends do?"

A friend. He might as well strangle her with her bicycle chain.

Briz brushed a strand of hair from her face and her knees went weak. Jaden turned away, wishing she could feel distant and bitter. She gripped her bicycle's handlebars, wanting him to come closer, to kiss her and end the spell that her shallow sister had cast on him.

"I lost my phone, so I didn't get any of your messages," she said, slouching forward.

"Oh, I thought you were mad at me about something."

Something besides doing it with my sister?

Jaden watched Briz pluck his sweaty T-shirt away from his chest. She wasn't surprised that he didn't notice her clinging top. Why should he bother? He wanted Ava's flawless body.

"I'm not mad at you, Briz." Jaden didn't bother to hide her insincerity. "I have to get going. I need to get to the seniors' home and back before my mom...I'm supposed to be recuperating."

"Yeah." Briz stepped back. "Your sister said you had poison ivy, but it doesn't look bad. You using Dr. Schilling's cream?" Jaden gave him a funny look. "It's like a miracle ointment. Everyone in town uses it."

"Yep. Okay, well, I'll see you around."

Briz nodded and leaned against his car. A sense of humility with just the right amount of confidence emanated from him, as if he'd started meditating when he was in the womb. Why couldn't he be egotistical, cocky, and rude? It would be so much easier to hate him. Glancing over her shoulder as she rode away, Jaden wanted to go back and tell him, "Friends is better than nothing. I'll take it."

She pedaled faster.

A block away, Jaden's thoughts remained wrapped around Briz so tightly that nothing else could get in or out. She hadn't realized a car had purred up next to her until it dawned on her that Briz was actually there, talking to her.

"Hey Jaden...Jaden? Can I give you a ride?"

A goofy grin spread across her face as she nodded and veered to the side of the road, suspecting he might be using mind control on her. She willingly surrendered to the possibility.

The forty-minute drive seemed like ten. For a while, it was as if the events of the past few days had never happened. No Mal Rous. No older sister aggravating her.

When they arrived at the Meadow Seniors' Facility, Jaden saw what a well-groomed southern estate should look like—instead of the mess that her family had inherited. The entrance to this place resembled a hotel lobby, not a convalescent home.

Jaden hadn't thought of calling first. Suddenly she worried that they might not let her see Dr. Whiting. Combing her fingers through her hair, she approached the front desk. To her relief, the receptionist seemed delighted that the doctor had a visitor. Briz waited in the lobby, as Jaden followed directions down the corridor to Dr. Whiting's room. She knocked on his door, agonizing over how much she was counting on this stranger to help her.

A man's voice said, "Come in."

It was a private room, similar to any other in this kind of facility, sterile and medicinal. Though he'd tried to make it a cozy space, the only signs of it being Dr. Whiting's so-called home for this stage of his life were two matching reclining chairs, a full bookcase, and an oak dresser covered with framed photographs. Considering that he was at least ninety years old, he wore his age with dignity. His hair was silver, and he was dressed in jeans and a long-sleeved blue button-up shirt.

Jaden had expected to find him bedridden, not sitting in a leather chair, reading.

She meant to say hello. But she found herself walking right past him to his nightstand, where an ornately framed photograph practically jumped into her hands. Like the sepia-colored photo she'd looked at earlier, it showed Elvina in her youth and a young man with his arm around her. The boy in the picture was a much younger version of the man sitting in the recliner.

Jaden's curiosity was now fully awakened. Dr. Whiting's past was obviously more entwined with her grandmother's than Jaden had realized. And now it was linked with her own future. Returning the picture to its prominent position, she turned and found the doctor watching her, clearly wondering who she was.

"Hello, Dr. Whiting." She smiled sweetly. "Forgive me, I didn't mean to be impolite. My name is Jaden. I'm Elvina Lisette…Thatcher's granddaughter."

He stared at Jaden as if she were an apparition. It looked as if he'd stopped breathing. She was ready to call for help. Then slowly exhaling, he set his book down and gestured for her to sit in the chair across from him.

Jaden's body relaxed as the color returned to his face. She opened her backpack, removed the photograph of Elvina she'd brought with her, and handed it to him.

"I can see a bit of Elvina in you," he said, looking at the photo. "You have her smile. How lovely."

Jaden knew that with her dark eyes and raven hair, she resembled her maternal grandmother Jin, not Elvina. Her smile was the only part of her that resembled her dad's side of the family.

"It's a pleasure to make your acquaintance." As he spoke, his Southern accent draped over Jaden like a fine lace antique shawl. "My dear Elvina…" He handed the photograph back to Jaden, took a handkerchief from his pocket and dabbed at his eyes. "I heard of her passing a while back." The doctor's words held more grief than Jaden had expected. "And Amelia, how is she?"

The doctor might have been old, but he didn't appear senile. Jaden's silence said it all.

"Oh no. She was near my son's age, so young. My deepest condolences for your loss."

To the doctor, it must have appeared that Jaden was withholding her grief. But she had never even known the two women. She nodded, aware that the only remorse she felt was for having freed the Mal Rous.

His eyes searched her face. "What may I do for you?"

Grateful that he didn't ask her more about her grandmother and aunt, Jaden realized that she hadn't thought any of this through. She couldn't just blurt out that she needed to know how to get rid of the Mal Rous. If he knew about them, just hearing the name might give him a heart attack. After all, he was living in a convalescent home. Perhaps he wasn't as healthy as he looked.

"Well..." Sliding the photo into her pack, she considered what to say. "We inherited Elvina's estate, and we're fixing it up to sell. I was hoping you could tell me about the place and my grandparents. I don't know anything about my father's side of the family."

"Your father..." With a sad smile, the doctor said, "Of course, Elvina would have had another child. She loved being a mother. I hope she was happy."

Jaden nervously coiled the nylon straps of her pack around her fingers as Dr. Whiting looked at her as if she were a long-forgotten friend.

CHAPTER 12

JADEN

Jaden quietly waited. And waited. She folded her hands together to stop from fidgeting. Dr. Whiting settled back into his leather chair as he conjured up old memories.

Finally, he spoke.

"Ah yes...Elvina." His shoulders rose and lowered again as he sighed. "So, you're going to sell the plantation?" He ran his hands over the chair's armrests. "You know, it's been in your family for...I'd say seven or eight generations now, counting you." Resting his palms on top of his thighs, he said, "If walls could talk, I'm sure that house would have many stories to tell."

Jaden thought, *If walls could talk, I wouldn't be here.* Then she asked, "How well did you know Elvina?"

"Both of our families have lived in this area for a long, long time." He chuckled, before adding, "When we were children, I'd push her on a swing that hung from the oak tree in her yard. She was always a sight to behold. She never did go through an awkward stage." Dr. Whiting looked as if he longed to reach out and touch Elvina's wavy chestnut-colored hair. "Your grand-mere went from being a pretty child to a lovely young woman. Like every other boy in this town, as well as the next parish over, I imagined that one day I would proudly call her my wife."

Jaden found herself falling into the lyrical rhythm of his voice.

"Of all her suitors, I was the lucky one. She was most fond of me. Probably because we'd been childhood playmates. Though I prefer to believe that she was also smitten by the man I became. After high school, she all but agreed to marry me. It was in the summer of 1938. She promised to give me an answer when she returned from Switzerland. It seems her parents had decided she should be even more of a Southern lady than she already was. They sent her off to a finishing school, the Institut Alpin Videmanette."

With his elbows pressing into the armrest, the doctor propped himself up as if what he had to say next was very important. Jaden found herself mirroring his actions.

"The following summer, instead of returning to Louisiana, she went with a girlfriend to England. There she was introduced to Dekle Thatcher. I was told he swept her off her feet. Within a year they were married, happily living in Cambridge—and, as they say, I was history." Another wave of sadness flitted over the doctor's face.

"What did you do then?" Jaden asked.

"At the time, I was going to medical school in Mississippi. When I finished, I moved up to West Virginia and worked at the VA Hospital in Martinsburg. That's when I met Sara."

He pointed toward a photograph of a woman on his dresser. Jaden found it odd that the picture sitting next to his bedside wasn't of his wife.

"Sara was from a very wealthy family. Though…" the doctor clarified, "that is not why I married her. She had such warmth and vitality. I suppose I had hoped she would help me to forget Elvina. Sara was five years older than I was and had been married before. When she was in her early twenties, she'd given birth to triplets."

Triplets? Scooting back in her chair, Jaden listened even more intently, recalling Violet's comment that triplets had made a brew for the professor.

"Because they were albino…" Dr. Whiting paused, looking at Jaden as if expecting to see an adverse reaction. Jaden's expression remained curious, not judgmental, and he continued. "Sara's husband abandoned her. He cruelly declared Sara to be damaged, not worthy of him. It was a very difficult time for her. I am sure she felt for him the way I always have for your grand-mere.

"Sara's daughters were seven years old when we married. Two years later we had our son, Cape. That's when I legally adopted the triplets. The girls were so scorned in our town that at the end of the war we decided to move to Belle Fleur. I had relatives here, and friends. It never dawned on me that they wouldn't be accepting of my daughters." He slowly shook his head from side to side. "I was so wrong."

"When did my grandparents move back?" Jaden asked.

"Well, Elvina's only brother had been killed in the war. It devastated her father. Soon after, he unexpectedly passed away. Elvina's mother didn't want to live at the estate any longer."

The doctor looked up toward the ceiling as if he were studying an invisible calendar.

"It was 1946. That's when she went to North Carolina and gave Guyon Manor to Elvina. A year later Elvina moved back. It seems the timing was perfect. I never did learn exactly what had happened with Dekle's research position at Cambridge. He had become a professor by then. All I know is that for some reason his relationship with his colleagues fell apart and they asked him to leave."

Sadness creased his eyes as he said, "World War ll had taken its toll on everyone in England...well, everywhere."

Jaden couldn't help but think of her dad and all the stupid people in power who instigate wars.

"Elvina was delighted to come back home with her 'wonderful' husband and sweet daughter. Amelia must have been three or four years old at the time."

The disdainful tone he used when he referred to her grandfather made it obvious to Jaden that Dr. Whiting had known him all too well.

"Oh my, the sight of Elvina when she returned. I tried to hide my feelings from everyone. Especially Dekle and my lovely wife." He held Jaden's gaze. "How do you conceal the exuberance of pure joy when you are in the presence of certain people?"

The doctor's expression filled with delight as he savored his memories. It was obvious that there was much more to him than the weathered man he was now. His age hadn't erased his youthful desires. Jaden was struck by the connection she was feeling with him. They were kindred spirits, both broken-hearted after losing their unrequited first loves. Obviously, Dekle and Ava were related—the backstabbing louses.

"To be honest, I only befriended Dekle so I could be near Elvina."

"Excuse me, Dr. Whiting...Miss..."

Startled, both Jaden and the doctor looked up and saw a nurse standing in the doorway.

"Excuse me, Dr. Whiting," the nurse repeated. "Sir, it's time for yer physical therapy. And it's time for ya to leave, Miss."

An unnerving sensation of panic rushed through Jaden. She couldn't leave yet! She still needed to learn more about the triplets! Jaden looked imploringly at the old gentleman. "I—I can wait in the lobby—and you could tell me more when you get back," she practically begged.

"Miss, Dr. Whiting will be takin' a nap when he's done."

"I'll tell you what, Jaden," Dr. Whiting said. "You come back tomorrow, and I'll continue the story."

The nurse moved between Dr. Whiting and Jaden. She spoke in a sharp, abrupt tone. "So, Miss, we'll see ya tomorrow."

Jaden's face pinched. She didn't have the luxury of time. This man had answers that could affect her entire life. The nurse mimicked Jaden's expression, and Jaden found herself agreeing to return the next day.

At the door, she paused and turned back. This was the grandfather she should have had. Kind and gracious. Not what she imagined Dekle Thatcher was—a bottom feeder whom she was happy to have never met.

Dr. Whiting was rubbing his thin fingers against his forehead as if his mind was filled with too many memories, all of them sheathed in a layer of longing for what should have been. Jaden wondered how many people actually lived the life they dreamed of.

Without question, there had been some major glitches in Dr. Whiting's plans. His life had not been the glorious adventure he'd envisioned as a young man with Elvina by his side. Still, he seemed to have loved his wife, his kids. So, he had a good life, an acceptable journey...right? Maybe more than fine only happens to one in a million people.

CHAPTER 13

JADEN

With one look at Briz, Jaden didn't care that her time with Dr. Whiting had been cut short. He had the ability to create a chemical reaction in her that made her thoughts travel at warp speed into the La-La-Land of Briz. Part of her savored the feeling. Another part didn't want to act like a lovesick puppy. Especially for someone who didn't feel the same about her.

"That was fast. Did you have a good visit?" The rich tone of Briz's voice took her further into La-La-Land.

"Sort of. I have to come back tomorrow."

"I can give you a ride...if you want," Briz offered, opening the lobby door. "It's sort of far to ride your bike. You could get sunstroke."

"Are you sure you have time?" Jaden walked as close to Briz as possible without bumping into him; smiling as he opened the car door for her.

Proof that he liked her?

Her smile vanished as he said, "Hey, that's what friends are for."

Friends. She could really learn to hate that word.

Briz started the car, as he cheerfully asked, "Where to now?"

"I'd better get home. My mom would be furious if she knew I was gone. And Ava would probably claw my eyes out."

"Yeah, you and your sister have an interesting relationship."

"Yep, one of those love-hate things—without the love on her part."

"Jaden, I know it's only been a few days, but I've missed hanging with you."

Briz leaned toward her. Ever hopeful, Jaden sat perfectly still, anticipating his taking her hand in his. When he popped open the glove box, pulled out his phone charger, and plugged it into the USB port, she wilted in her seat.

"You want to listen to some music?"

Jaden gave a nod. She was such a dork. He wanted to charge his phone, not hold her hand. Was this how Dr. Whiting had felt around Elvina?

Would anyone ever be attracted to her the way they were to her sister?

Friends. In rhythm to the music, Jaden kept repeating the word in her head as the car hummed down the highway. At her house, Briz unloaded her bike while she made a beeline to the front door. Briz had done his good deed for the day by helping the new kid in town. Now he was free to find some awesome babe to make out with.

Jaden was fumbling with her key when he came over to her, standing only millimeters away. Shaking visibly, she made a feeble attempt to dampen her excitement as he placed his hand on hers to steady the key. When she glanced up, she saw his lips pressed together, hiding his amusement as he helped her guide it into the lock.

She stared at the doorknob. *Cooyon. Betasse.* Her giddiness subsided as she remembered the Cajun words her landlady had told her meant stupid and foolish. *That's me.* Opening the door, Jaden swiveled around. "Do you want to come in?" Nervously snorting in air through her nose, she made a sound like a hippo.

With a chuckle, Briz gently took hold of her hand and folded her fingers around the key. Jaden could feel her lips swelling, craving his. She swallowed to stop the moisture that was seeping toward the corners of her mouth.

Cooyon might as well be my nickname. He's not flirting. He just thinks of me as Ava's little sister. Jaden backed into the house, silently yelling at herself, deep in the small space where her brain had once resided. She tried to think of the Mal Rous. They were amped up, ready to stick their canine teeth into her. She could die! Her whole family could die! Here she was, obsessing over some guy. Because Briz was standing next to her, touching her, the genetic barbarians faded from her mind.

"Jaden—" Propped against the doorjamb, Briz tilted his head, watching her.

"Yeah?" Avoiding his eyes, she pinched the bridge of her nose, trying to stimulate her brain to work.

"You okay?"

"I'm fine." Jaden lowered her hand, thinking that feeling *fine* would be an improvement.

He smiled. He might as well have injected her with a drug.

She craved more from Briz—more of anything, as long as it wasn't rejection. Jaden couldn't stop her lips from quivering into a pucker. Her mouth fought against her as she tried to force it into a straight line. Briz lowered his eyes. He was probably trying not to laugh at her.

Could she be more pathetic?

She wanted him to hurry up and leave, and at the same time, to stay. Her emotions were bouncing around as if they were stuck in a pinball game. Couldn't they be friends with benefits?

"What time should I pick you up tomorrow?" Briz asked.

"I'll have to wait for my mom and sister to leave. Would nine be okay?"

"Whatever works for you."

"Um, if you see my mom's car, don't stop. She doesn't know I'm...researching my family."

"I won't say anything." He raised his hand to give her a fist bump. "Friends should help each other out."

There was that F word again. Jaden reluctantly returned the gesture.

"So, I'll be back tomorrow." Briz turned and headed for his car.

Jaden left the front door open a crack; peeking out, she followed his every move. Then something caught her attention.

It was Ava, bouncing up the driveway. Jaden shut the door and inched aside the edge of the living room curtain to spy on them.

All of her poison ivy sores throbbed as Briz turned to face her stunning rival. Ava reached up and ran her perfectly manicured nails through his hair. What was it with her sister? She'd never liked a vegetarian, or someone that owned a hybrid car, especially a used one.

Though he had his back toward her, Jaden saw the way

Briz lightly touched her sister's arm, maneuvering her just enough so he could open his car door. With an impish grin, Ava stepped closer—if that was possible—and they kissed.

And I got a fist bump. Jaden hunched forward, pressing her clenched hand against her chest to stop the sharp pains of self-pity and wistfulness from consuming her. "He was supposed to choose *me*...to kiss *me*."

She knew exactly what Ava's snide response would have been if she'd heard her: "*Kiss you? You're not just immature, Jade. You're delusional. I bet you think he wants to cop a feel, too? Oh no, you'd actually need breasts for him to do that.*"

Jaden yanked the curtain closed. "I have breasts!" She stuck out her chest. "They just aren't the size of soccer balls."

She turned away and went to hide in the bathroom. Jaden looked in the mirror, checking her messy hair, baggy green T-shirt, and capris. Her sister was right. There was no reason for Briz to be interested in her. He'd just been using her to get to Ava. Jaden had never thought of herself as a jealous person. But she'd never had a reason to be jealous before.

Jaden was piling on ointment, wishing she could escape through the small bathroom window, when Ava made her triumphant entrance into the house. Jaden turned on the water, determined to drown out any words of glory her sister was going to shove down her throat.

"I'm home." Ava chuckled. "But you knew that, didn't you, you peeping perv."

Jaden heard her loud and clear. Ava always made sure that she heard her biting comments.

"I talked Mom into quitting early. She's going to go see how Carl's doing, then she's stopping at the market. So lucky you, you don't have to work tonight, even though I told her you're fine." Ava happily added, "Tomorrow night, you're going to be sweating like a pig, Jaden *baby*."

Jaden turned off the faucet and stood glowering at the turquoise poodles on the plastic shower curtain and the matching crocheted toilet paper cover.

"Hey, hurry up. I want to take a shower."

Covered in her fuchsia coating, Jaden came out of the bathroom and almost walked into Ava.

"Still faking it, huh?"

Jaden didn't make eye contact with her black-hearted sister, who thrived on ruining her life.

"That Briz sure is delicious."

Jaden wanted to punch her in the face. She thought of her mom's advice: "When it comes to your sister, pretend you're walking on eggshells. Let her have her way; it's easier on everyone."

More like rotten eggs, if you ask me.

Then again, no one ever asked Jaden. It seemed better for everyone if they didn't know what she thought. She'd grown up trying to avoid the wrath of Ava on a daily basis. Though here in Belle Fleur, with the three of them in this small house, plus working together cleaning up the old estate, there was no way to keep clear of her.

Maybe it didn't really matter. The way things were going, this could be Jaden's last night alive.

CHAPTER 14

JADEN

The next day, the last person Jaden wanted to see was Briz. It was bad enough having to interact with Ava after watching them kiss. Jaden texted Briz to let him know she'd changed her mind and was going to ride her bike to Dr. Whiting's. Briz wouldn't have it, insisting it was already too hot. Fine. But that didn't mean she would talk to him.

Briz greeted her with a smile. "You look nice today."

"I did it for Dr. Whiting, not you," Jaden muttered as she walked to his car.

The drive took forever. Briz kept talking about the new book he was reading and how much he thought she'd enjoy it. Unlike her, Briz had even read a lot of Shakespeare, though he probably hadn't had a choice since his mom was an English professor. When Jaden didn't reply, he eventually stopped talking.

At the Meadow Seniors' Facility, the staff was busy getting the residents ready for the day. Jaden left Briz in the lobby and walked down the seemingly endless corridor filled with life-support equipment. She imagined herself in an old movie—the tormented heroine walking down a shadow-filled hallway. At the end, an ornate mirror hung on the wall. When the anxiety-riddled character gazed into it, she would see visions of demons mutilating innocent people. Realizing that the destruction and devastation of the entire town was because of her, the actress would collapse onto the cold floor, sobbing.

The scenario filled Jaden with a sense of shame.

As she entered Dr. Whiting's room, his exuberant southern hospitality felt contagious. She half expected him to offer her a mint julep. Instead, he welcomed her with a pitcher of lemon water, saying he was happy she'd come back.

Like her, he was wearing a crisp white shirt and jeans, though his shirt was long-sleeved and buttoned up all the way, and her jeans were capris. Also like her, his eyes shimmered with hope.

Jaden sat in the chair across from him—prim and proper, a clip holding her hair in a neat ponytail—questioning her own motives. What did she expect him to tell her? How to pickle the Mal Rous?

"Are you ready to hear more of my story?" He sounded as if he couldn't quite believe that he had a willing audience. "Or are you just being kind to an old man?"

"I'm really interested in hearing what you have to say." For whatever reason, Jaden found her newly discovered relatives intriguing. This was her own personal Transylvania soap opera, pint-sized vampires and all.

"All right, Miss Jaden, do you recall where I leave off?"

"The triplets. You were just starting to tell me about them."

"Mm, yes, my lovely, brilliant daughters. They adored

your grand-mere. She was so good to them. Elvina was always the perfect lady, as well as intelligent, the kindest person I've ever known." Jaden tried not to frown when Dr. Whiting's recollections shifted to her grandmother. "Amelia and my son Cape were close to the same age, and became friends. It reminded me of Elvina and myself when we were children."

"You said the triplets were scorned in Belle Fleur, too, after you moved. Do they still live here?"

"Back then," the doctor paused, the lines in his face deepening, "living in the South, it was more difficult being an albino than being a person of color. *Everyone* discriminated against you, blacks and whites alike. They were all terribly unfair to my girls. I like to think things have changed. I'm not proud of the way some of us Southerners have treated people."

"What happened to them? Do they still live here?" Jaden asked again.

"Well, when people in town began getting ill, a lot of uneducated, superstitious people believed it was because of our girls. Some even threatened their lives. The kinder ones questioned why God was punishing Sara, having her give birth to such repulsive children."

Misty-eyed, the doctor continued, "The girls wanted to run away. But they were convinced it didn't matter where they went in the world. They were certain to be treated badly, as if unworthy of living on this earth. They never socialized. We home-schooled them. Even Cape's little friends accused them of practicing black magic. So many cruel lies were spread around town!

"When our Olympe was seventeen, she fell in love with

a sharecrop worker's son. His name was Billy. It didn't bother Sara and me. In our eyes, there was no difference between Olympe's sheer white skin and Billy's ebony. We had lived with so much color discrimination, we weren't about to be that way, too. They were both good kids, shamefully mistreated."

Dr. Whiting cleared his throat as he glanced at the door. "I must admit, Sara and I weren't all that surprised when Olympe became pregnant. All of our so-called friends would have sent their daughters away to get rid of the baby. Of course, everyone in town rejected her even more. Billy's parents were beside themselves when they learned he was in love with an albino. They packed up and left and took Billy with them.

"It's hard to know how to be a good parent. Children don't come with a book. It sure would be helpful. Billy was gone. We were there for her, though my sweet Olympe felt that she and her beautiful baby were all alone. She went into a deep depression. So did her sisters, Tamara and Isadora. I don't know if you've ever been around triplets. They have a remarkable connection. When one of the triplets feels pain, they all do. I suppose it's that way with all siblings."

Jaden was living proof that not all siblings were like that. She knew for a fact that when she was sick or unhappy, Ava rejoiced.

"Well, the three of them decided they'd prefer to live outside of town, on the bayou, where no one would bother them. Sara purchased the land. We thought it was a temporary decision. We believed that someday our girls would find a way to live comfortably in society. Still, what mattered most to us was that they were happy."

Jaden nodded, though she really wanted to jump up and shout, *Do the triplets still live on the bayou? Can I go see them?*

"We got a skiff to haul supplies out to the land. We didn't dare hire people to build a house for them. It was to be the one place where they could feel safe. Though we weren't carpenters, somehow, between the five of us, we built an acceptable structure. They had a generator for electricity.

"A year later, Billy returned and constructed a real home for them. Your grand-pere Dekle even taught Billy how to set up a decent solar power system; back then, no one around here had ever considered it."

Jaden gave him a surprised look.

He responded with a smile, "Why Miss Jaden, you thought solar power was a new concept? It's been around in one form or another since the sun's been shining. In fact, your grand-pere had exchanged letters with one of the men who developed the first solar batteries."

Dr. Whiting chuckled, then glanced at the photo of his wife. "You know, I haven't spoken about this for years." Then he turned toward her grandmother's picture on his nightstand. "I've never had anyone I could talk to about Elvina."

Though Jaden's reason for tracking Dr. Whiting down had been sheer desperation, she found herself fascinated by his story and who he was as a person.

"Over the years, Elvina and Sara became close friends. Your grandparents were the only ones in town who knew where the triplets were. Most people didn't want to know. They were just glad they were gone. Elvina gave Billy a job as caretaker on their property. Billy was always a good papa and husband. When their son, Hubbard, was old enough for school, he'd stay with Billy during the week. Then they'd go to the triplets on the weekends. Olympe agreed that it was best for the boy.

"Then one day, when Hubbard—Hubs—was six years old, he was attacked."

Jaden knew that name! Hubs was the name of the man who sold the poison ivy cream to Dr. Schilling!

The doctor sunk back in his chair. Jaden felt a cold chill as a realization took hold. That meant Hubs was also the little boy Violet remembered the Mal Rous had attacked.

"Billy had left him alone at the cottage, just for a short while. When he returned, he found Hubs in a coma. Sara and I were visiting her kin in West Virginia, so Billy rushed Hubs to the hospital. In spite of Billy's begging for help, the staff left my dear grandson unattended for hours. You see, people of color weren't welcome there. Billy had no other choice but to take his son home.

"Olympe tried to heal Hubs with herbs. Billy contacted us, and we returned right away. I did everything I could. Nothing helped. So I enlisted the aid of your grand-pere Dekle. He seemed to have an innate knowledge of what was wrong with Hubs."

Innate knowledge. Yeah, right. Of course, her brilliant grandfather had known what was wrong with him.

"In the end, I don't know. I guess I waited too long to ask for his help. Hubs...he's not mentally disturbed the way the townspeople claim. It's just that his speech is a bit slow. He's a good person. A proud man. Won't ever take a handout.

"From then on, Dekle formulated cures for the different diseases that had been infecting the townspeople. Eventually the triplets started making them for him."

"Did you learn why everyone in town was getting sick?"

Dr. Whiting sat up straight in his seat, as if he were on trial.

"Apparently Dekle was a bit of an outdoors person and enjoyed exploring the bayou. He said that shortly after they first arrived in Belle Fleur, he was hiking one day and came across an abandoned salt cave that had been used by the government as a chemical dump site."

The wrinkles around the doctor's eyes tightened.

"He claimed he'd never thought it necessary to test the toxic waste prior to my asking for his help. Then he insisted that poisons were leeching into the bayou, penetrating the town's water system, and causing the illnesses. I had no reason to question his opinion."

"Dr. Whiting..."

He held her gaze. She felt queasy as she asked, "Do you know what attacked Hubs?"

The doctor nodded very slowly. "One night a few years later, Elvina came to our house and begged me to help her. She said she'd seen horrible creatures in their cellar. She told me about the dreadful things Dekle had done to her. I accepted what she told me as the truth. It was obvious to everyone that Dekle had been changing. He'd become a different man. I was not going to let him hurt my precious Elvina again. She was afraid for her life—and Amelia's. So I went with her."

His eyes briefly swept over Jaden's face.

"I called the police and had your grand-pere taken away and committed to a mental institute." He bowed his head. "I'd believed Dekle was sincerely working to help the people who lived here, creating elixirs and preparations to heal them. *I had no idea.*"

Jaden wanted to interrupt the doctor, tell him that the

Mal Rous were back, and beg him to help her. But he continued emptying the cracked and tired old trunk of painful memories he'd locked away in the depths of his soul.

"When others in town learned the news about Dekle being taken away, they turned Elvina into an object of contempt. So much gossip in a small town. After Dekle was committed, Elvina and Amelia spent a lot of time with Sara and me. Elvina hated being alone in that big house."

He examined his hands in his lap. "I'm certain that over the years, Sara couldn't help but see how besotted I was with Elvina. I know she had faith in me and that I would never act on my affections. She also trusted that Elvina would never intentionally hurt her."

The doctor pressed his hands against the chair's leather armrests to stop them from trembling. It didn't help.

"One day, Elvina came to my office and told me that she and Amelia were leaving. When we embraced, Elvina began to weep. She told me all the things I'd always longed to hear." Guiltily, Dr. Whiting lowered his eyes. "We kissed, and...well, that moment of passion..." his voice wavered. He spoke more slowly. "That moment of passion would have to be enough. It would have to last the rest of our lives."

The air conditioner droned in the background. Jaden questioned if the noise was resonating from the doctor's broken heart.

"I wanted to go with her," he confided, meeting Jaden's eyes. "I believe she wanted me to. We both thought she would only be leaving for a few months. That when she returned, we would work things out. But it wasn't meant to be." He paused. "Once she left, Elvina determined that we could never truly be happy if it meant hurting Sara. She was right."

His fingers curled around a glass of water that sat on the table next to him, but his hand shook too much to raise it. Releasing his hold, he continued, "Elvina and Amelia decided not to return. I never saw either of them again. Elvina and I wrote for a while. Then she stopped answering my letters."

Dr. Whiting's gaze fixed on Jaden and he smiled gently. "I never imagined Elvina being a grand-mere. I have always pictured her as she was the last time that I saw her."

Jaden looked over at the photo of her grandmother on the doctor's nightstand. Truth was, the local grocer's wife back home was more like a grandmother to her than Elvina had ever been.

"My oh my, I've gone and talked a blue streak, haven't I." The doctor's smile faded.

It was time to come clean about why she was there. Sitting up straight, Jaden tentatively asked, "Do you know if my grandfather is still alive?"

The doctor shrugged his shoulders, clearly worn out from all the memories.

"Did you ever see any reports of his experiments, or notes with his formulas?" Jaden pressed back against her leather chair, wishing it would swallow her up for being related to such a depraved man.

Dr. Whiting stared as if looking right through her. Finally, he responded. "The triplets might have copies of the cures Dekle created. Though once he was locked up, people were no longer plagued by the unusual illnesses. We never did find the strange creatures that Elvina had seen."

Jaden's spirits lifted. The triplets were still alive! If they had that mushroom brew Violet had mentioned, Jaden's troubles would be over. "Would it be possible for me to meet the triplets and Hubs? I really need to talk to them."

"I suppose so." His head teetered back and forth. "I could call Hubs. He could take you there." He paused, and the corners of his mouth sagged. "Why would you want to see them?"

Jaden could almost hear his unspoken fears that she, like everyone else, would be unkind to his daughters.

"I need their help, Dr. Whiting." She couldn't look at him. Focusing on the collar of his shirt, Jaden let the words tumble out. "It's about—it's about the Mal Rous."

The doctor slumped forward. "That's what Hubs called them." His narrow chest slowly expanded, then caved in as he exhaled his sadness. "We didn't know what he was talking about. He was a child. We thought he didn't understand that he'd been attacked by some kind of animal. Then Elvina found those, those *things*. Her description of them matched Hubs's."

Dr. Whiting's eyes glazed over, and his head dropped against the back of his chair. Jaden feared that his heart had stopped. Meanwhile, hers was banging a chaotic, abstract beat.

She rushed over and pressed a button next to his bed. Seconds later, a nurse flew into the room. The woman took Dr. Whiting's blood pressure, inserted a pill into his mouth, and held a glass of water to his lips.

"Ya'd best leave now," the nurse ordered.

"Is he going to be okay?" Jaden words felt heavy with guilt. "Can I come back tomorrow?"

"Ya can call to see how he is. Don't you just go stoppin' by." The nurse firmly guided Jaden to the door.

Even though the nurse said Dr. Whiting should be all

right, Jaden was ashamed of the pain she'd inflicted on him. She had reminded him of the Mal Rous and all the sorrow they had caused in his life—hurting his grandson, causing Elvina to leave him.

The door closed in her face. She stood there, worried that she had just given Dr. Whiting permission to die.

CHAPTER 15

JADEN

Jaden's vision settled on Briz as she returned to the lobby. He was leaning back on the sofa, his legs stretched out in front of him, his hands clasped behind his head. She exhaled a long, slow breath. The image of Dr. Whiting slumped down in his chair remained fixed in Jaden's mind. Briz gave her a smile. Then, seeing her tear-filled eyes, his smile faded, and he hurried over to her.

"What's wrong?"

Jaden didn't respond as her body sank against his. Briz placed an arm around her slender waist and guided her to the car. Lost in thought, she sat gazing out the passenger window.

"Jaden, what happened? Are you all right?"

"I'm okay." Her words were garbled. "I am, really. I need to get home. I have to go feed the little cretins—"

Briz leaned nearer. "I can hardly hear you. You have to feed what?"

Mal Rous, she thought, clearing her throat and speaking

louder, "I have stuff to do before Ava picks me up. I'm helping at the estate tonight. Unless you know somebody called Hubs."

"Yeah, I know him."

"You do?"

"Yeah, he's...a little different, but he's a good guy. I heard when he was a kid he was bitten by some kind of wild animal."

Wild animal. Close enough. Jaden sat up straight. "Can you take me to him?"

"Sure, no problem."

As the car turned off the highway onto the narrow road leading to Belle Fleur, Jaden asked Briz about Hubs. He couldn't tell her much, besides that the local kids enjoyed picking on him, and that he lived in a trailer behind a coffee shop in the old part of town. He cleaned the place and did odd jobs for the shop's owner.

Briz was parking the car in front of a vintage Airstream trailer when a slender man came out the back door of the café.

Hubs.

Jaden assumed it was him; limping toward his metal home, his head swayed slightly. Because of childhood injuries from the Mal Rous' attack? If he stood erect, he'd be as tall as Briz.

Briz jumped from the car and greeted him as if they were old pals. "Hi, Hubs. This is my friend Jaden." He gestured toward her as she exited the car.

That "friend" word again. It wailed loud as a siren in Jaden's head, fueling her melancholy. Hubs looked up and nodded hello. He had a kind face.

"Her family just inherited the old Guyon Manor," Briz added.

With an alarmed expression, Hubs scurried into the trailer and locked the door.

"Good move, Briz." Jaden grimaced, knowing she sounded like her sister.

"What'd I do?" Briz stared at her as they walked over and he knocked on the door.

When there was no answer, Jaden reached past Briz and knocked harder. "Hubs, I just saw your—" She glanced at Briz and decided not to say *grandfather*. Maybe that was another family secret. "I just saw Dr. Whiting. He was going to call you. He said you could help me."

She knocked again, with the image of Dr. Whiting unresponsive in his chair vivid in her mind. "Dr. Whiting said you would take me to the triplets. Hubs, I need your help!"

Nothing. No response, not even a "go away" or "leave me alone." The only sounds Jaden heard were cars driving through the parking lot, the rumbling of an air conditioner, and mosquitoes buzzing. After knocking on the door for five minutes, and her pleas becoming more and more desperate, she stopped.

"Jaden..." Briz had been waiting in the shade of the trailer. Now he walked toward her.

She hit her fist against the metal door once more.

"He's not going to answer." Briz slid between Jaden and the door. "Come on, I'll take you home. Dr. Whiting probably hasn't called him yet."

"Sure, that must be it."

Jaden dragged her feet across the asphalt, following Briz

to his car, worrying about the doctor, and the possibility that the Mal Rous were going to show up on her doorstep. As they drove out of the parking lot, she was looking back at the trailer, still hoping Hubs would emerge, when she felt a static shock on her wrist.

She turned to Briz. His touch fully captured her attention.

"Jaden, I'm sorry I messed things up with Hubs," Briz glanced in her direction, "but I'm glad we've been able to spend some time together today. I wanted to talk with you..." He pulled his hand away. "...About your sister."

The one and only traffic light turned red, and they slowed to a stop. Jaden considered jumping out of the car. She wasn't interested in hearing Briz tell her that he wanted to be with her sister. Right now, her frustration level was maxed out.

"I don't know what Ava might have said to you, but I'm not interested in her."

"What?" Jaden's heartbeat quickened.

"I said, I'm not interested in your sister."

"She told me the two of you had sex."

"No way!"

"I saw you kiss her, Briz."

"No. No, she's the one that kissed me. I just sort of fell into it. She's really aggressive when she wants...something."

Jaden gave Briz a sideways glance. Was he just feeding her a line? Her skepticism must have shown.

"I did not have sex with her! Not even close." Briz blew out a frustrated breath. "She kissed me," he repeated, gripping the steering wheel tighter. "Hey, I'm a guy. Pretty lame excuse, but I am. I got in my car and drove home when I realized what a dope I was being. I don't like her, Jaden!"

Jaden stared straight ahead. She could see Briz looking at her, hoping for a sign of forgiveness. Or understanding. Or acknowledgement that guys could be something more than testosterone-driven hounds. Instead, she rolled her eyes.

Though, Jaden had to admit that if Briz was telling the truth, that he hadn't gone for it with Ava said a lot about him. Ava's sexuality permeated the air around her. What guy wouldn't respond to her advances?

"Since you never returned my calls, I went over to your house a couple of times to see you. I even stuck a note on your door."

"That note was for me?"

"Of course it was."

"I never got to read it. Ava—"

"She's a real case," Briz said, shaking his head. The light turned green, and he pushed down on the accelerator.

Jaden's emotions were ricocheting from her heart to her head. If Briz didn't like her sister, why was Jaden mad at him? Why was she acting like a jealous girlfriend when they were only friends?

"She gave me a birthday gift, too."

"*Ava* gave you a present?"

"Yeah." Briz grinned as if he'd just scored a point. "That artist's book you told me about."

"That harpy!"

Briz cracked up, repeating the word *harpy*.

"I bought you that book!" Jaden's body tensed, her words bitting with annoyance. "Things just got all crazy, with the poison ivy...and other stuff...I forgot all about it." With each word, dread crept back into her thoughts as she was reminded that her world now revolved around the Mal Rous.

"Since it's from you, I'll actually read it. Thank you for

the thoughtful gift." Briz reached for her hand and gave it a squeeze. "Your friendship means a lot to me." He released Jaden's hand, his voice fading as he said, "Yeah, you're a really good person."

Oh, perfect. He thinks I'm like Mother Teresa.

Jaden shrank down in her seat. Friendship. What had she expected? He'd never actually said he wanted to be with her, only that he didn't want to be with Ava. The speck of happiness he'd bestowed upon her moments ago was now crushed, run over by the boy driving a Prius.

When they arrived at her house, Jaden gripped her key, determined to keep her hand steady even though Briz was right next to her and her arms and legs were turning into ropey strands of putty. She opened the door and quickly stepped inside, stopping herself from spinning around and blurting out something completely embarrassing, like her loins ached for him.

Then she felt Briz behind her, so close that the heat from his body enveloped her. His fingers slid under the straps of her backpack, and he lowered it to the floor. Her arms dangled at her sides and her knees wobbled. He pressed his palms against her hips, then gradually moved them upward, pausing at her shoulders. Her face flushed. She willingly surrendered as he turned her around to face him. Then leaning down he kissed the crown of her head.

"Jade, it's you I want to be with."

That did it. She was a pile of quivering gel. A part of her worried that it was a joke and that he was going to start laughing at her.

Briz freed her hair from its clip and ran his hands through the thick strands as it tumbled over her shoulders. Then, cupping her face in his hands, he tilted her head up.

Jaden shivered in spite of the sultry air flowing in through the open door. Her pulse quickened. She was certain that at any minute she would awaken from this dream.

This is real, she silently chanted, *this is real*.

She swallowed hard as his lips glided across her cheek, then hovered over her mouth, the warmth of his breath merging with hers. She could hear her breathing keeping time with his, faster than normal, building like an orchestra reaching its crescendo. And he hadn't even kissed her yet.

Then his lips pressed against hers. Her palms were damp. The backs of her knees were perspiring. She'd never really kissed anyone before. Not like this.

Repeatedly and lightly, he kissed her mouth. She reached her arms up around his neck enthusiastically as his lips melded with hers, separating slightly, inviting her to do the same. And she did. At the same time, she was making an effort to imprint this moment in her mind so she would remember it her entire life—or at least, what was left of it.

Muffled music played in the background. Somewhere in her euphoria it dawned on her that the melody was her mother's cell phone ringing. But the slow, tender kiss had her entire body vibrating. She couldn't have answered the phone if she'd wanted to. She was lost in the sensations surging through her—the heat from Briz's body as he leaned into her, the pleasure of hearing his barely audible moan.

Long after the phone had stopped ringing, Briz slowly brought the kiss to an end. His hands roamed through Jaden's hair, gravitating down to her waist, encouraging her to draw closer.

With his mouth next to her ear, he whispered, "Wow."

"You really aren't into Ava!" Jaden stated breathlessly.

"Jade," Briz's voice was low, seductive, "you're the one I'm interested in."

Jaden tensed. Her sister had spent years convincing her that at best she was a homely misfit.

"I'd better get going." Briz smiled as Jaden's swollen lips mouthed *no*. He brought his mouth back to hers. Where their first kiss had been soft and enticing, making her feel as though she was hovering above the ground, this one was deep, passionate, intense.

Briz stopped abruptly. Raising his head above hers, Jaden felt his chest expand, then he exhaled slowly. "I have to go before this gets out of hand."

All she could do was nod as he left.

Wow is right! What a kiss. For the first time, Jaden didn't feel like one of the guys. She wanted someone, and he wanted her. Jaden was going to enjoy every bliss-filled second of being with him. She couldn't even muster any anger toward her conniving sister. He really was delicious.

Jaden grabbed her mom's phone from her pack. With the punch of a button, Briz vaporized from her thoughts as she listened to the message.

"JADEN! Where are you? You're supposed to be home resting. Call me when you get this. You'd better have a good excuse for not answering! Ava will be there at six o'clock. Be ready to work tonight. In fact, since you're feeling so good, clean up the house and do the laundry. That should keep you busy for a while. And don't forget, call in the order for pizza before Ava arrives."

Jaden called her mom back and groveled. "I'm here, Mom. I was out by the shed cleaning up my bike and didn't have the phone with me."

Her mom was going to be way more satisfied with that

answer than knowing Jaden had been running around town —and hooking up with a guy. The truth would make her mom as happy as thinking she was on drugs. Hanging up, Jaden promised herself that if she lived through this ordeal, she'd never lie to her mom again.

Normally, she didn't have any reason to lie. Only, there wasn't anything normal about her life right now. It was filled with fantasies of Briz—and abhorrent hellhounds. Closing her eyes, Jaden saw the Mal Rous' faces, recalled the smell of their disgusting breath. The mere thought of interacting with the demons made her feel sick.

What kind of grandparent leaves defective DNA experiments for his grandchildren to find?

Jaden shuddered. What would the Mal Rous do to her for not showing up today? Or yesterday? They wouldn't threaten some heinous act on her life, right? Not after she'd spent the last few days piecing together clues about their slimy Professor.

I mean, come on, death by Mal Rous...

It seemed ridiculous to be troubled by something so completely surreal.

Jaden could either pacify her mom or go to the shack to see the Mal Rous. Conscious of how emotionally detached she was becoming over her own possible demise, Jaden conceded to her mother's demands and took the cleaning supplies from the cupboard. What would one more day matter?

A little before six the pizza was delivered, and five minutes later Ava roared into the driveway honking the horn. By then Jaden was mentally back in the La-La-Land of Briz and wanted to stay there for as long as possible.

Covered in pink goo, she couldn't stop smiling as she climbed into the car.

"Cut the crap, Jaden." Ava's eyes shrank to the size of peas. "I know you don't need to wear that crud anymore."

Jaden grinned, determined to keep her thoughts on Briz. She wasn't going to let them stray into the world of Mal Rous or older sisters unless she absolutely had to.

CHAPTER 16

JADEN

Jaden never expected to see Briz at Guyon Manor. But there he stood in the drive, wearing a wide smile, thumbs hooked in his belt loops, a sparkle in his eyes.

"What's *he* doing here?" Ava asked, agitated.

"Maybe he's going to ask you out on a date." Jaden laughed, unable to hold it in. Ava's head spun toward her so fast that Jaden wondered if her sister had figured out the charade was up.

The car barreled up next to Briz and came to an abrupt stop. Ava opened her door and stomped over to him like a steamroller intent on flattening him. Before she could speak, Briz acknowledged her with a lighthearted hello, throwing her off guard. Ava's face quickly changed from annoyed to confused to her favorite, the seductress. She looped her arm through Briz's, claiming him as her own.

Jaden walked toward them carrying their dinner.

"You're beautiful in pink," Briz said, checking her out from head to toe.

"Oh yeah," Jaden replied with a ripple of laughter and a

huge grin. She was enjoying seeing Ava so befuddled. She knew how ghoulish she must look with her goopy skin accented by the colors of the sunset. "What are you doing here?"

"I came to help."

Briz's voice was deep and soft. Jaden wanted to jump into his arms. He stepped away from Ava, letting her arm fall to her side.

"Jade," Briz clarified, looking at Ava. "I came to help Jade."

Ava's eyes seared into the two of them. Jaden felt even more triumphant. Ava snatched the pizza box from her and strutted into the house.

Briz turned to Jaden. "I have to go talk to your sister and set her straight."

"I think you just did."

Briz moved closer. Unfazed by her pink mask, his gaze paused on her mouth. He slowly traced his finger across her lower lip as if she was the most alluring female he'd ever seen. When he took his hand away, she had to stop her head from bobbing forward. She drew in a breath and let it fly back out, trying to clear her head.

She followed Briz into the house, where he disappeared into the kitchen. Jaden stopped in the front hall and loudly said, "Mom, it's time to eat."

Jaden listened for the sounds of her mom working. All she could hear were the fans clanking and Ava's lies rising above Briz's voice, pushing against the kitchen door, drifting out of the room.

"Mom, pizza's here. Mom!" Jaden moved to the bottom of the stairs and shouted again.

There was no answer.

An icy chill moved through her. Then, like the thrust of a jagged knife, Violet's warnings about the Mal Rous cut into the core of her being—how vengeful they were, how they enjoyed brutalizing humans.

Jaden raced from room to room calling her mother.

When she reached the door of Elvina's bedroom, Jaden saw Brooke's lifeless body on the floor, her mouth frozen in a silent scream. Blood, like an elaborate fan of glistening rubies, had soaked through strands of her hair. More of it leaked from two large punctures in her leg.

Jaden's gaze followed a line of blood up the wall to the broken windowpane. In her mind, she could see her mom innocently looking out the window when she was attacked from behind.

"NOOO!" Jaden screamed. Stumbling forward, she fell to her knees next to her mother. "Mom." She touched her mother's shoulder. "Why didn't I do my part?" she wailed. "The Mal Rous wanted me to play their sick game of cat and mouse, and I didn't do it."

Jaden heard Briz and Ava sprinting down the hall. She saw them enter the room. She watched blankly as her sister cringed at the metallic smell of their mother's blood.

Briz hurried over to Jaden. Kneeling, he squeezed her shoulder, consoling her.

She looked into his eyes. "What's wrong with me? I could have stopped them."

He pulled her into his arms. "Jade, this isn't your fault."

But Jaden knew the truth.

She struggled to gather up the frayed threads of her consciousness.

Ava squatted down and felt her mom's wrist for a pulse.

In a meek voice, Jaden implored, "Help me get Mom up."

"No." Ava clutched Jaden's arm. "No, we shouldn't move her. I'll call 911."

"Jade's right. It'll take too long for an ambulance to get all the way out here." Briz picked up a paint rag lying next to Brooke's body and held it against the gash on the back of her head. "We have to drive her to the hospital."

The three of them carried Brooke down the stairs, out to her car. Ava, who never cried, couldn't stop sobbing. Jaden remained dry-eyed as she slid into the back seat and laid her mother's bloody head in her lap.

Why didn't I go to the shack today? Or yesterday? Why didn't they come after me instead?

With brittle movements, Ava put the key into the ignition.

"I'll drive," Briz said, standing next to the driver's door. Ava climbed into the passenger seat without arguing.

While the car sped down the road, Jaden agonized over the last time she'd spoken to her mother. She leaned down, whispering, "I'm sorry, Mom. For releasing the Mal Rous. For making you mad at me. For everything. I love you, Mama. Don't leave me."

Jaden cradled her mother's body in her arms, doing her best to stop it from rocking as the car bounced over the pitted road. At the far end of the field, the cluster of trees stood above the cane like prophets of doom, proclaiming this was all Jaden's fault. Up to now, Jaden had unwittingly accepted Ava's words—that she didn't have a backbone, that she'd never amount to anything. She had already lost her dad, and now her mother was slipping away.

Jaden saw the head of the trail and felt her urgency rise.

She had to find out what poisons were in her mom, or worse, if a Mal Rou's blood was coursing through her veins, altering her cells.

"Stop the car." She raised her voice. "Stop the car now!"

Briz looked at her in the rear-view mirror. Ava unhooked her seatbelt and turned around, her expression lined with panic. The car slowed to a stop.

In.one continuous motion, Jaden lowered her mother's head onto the seat, opened the rear door, and jumped out. The interior car light lit up Jaden's body, exposing fine wisps of heat radiating from her like smoldering anger.

"Take Mom to the hospital. Tell them that something bit her. That she hit her head on a window."

"What? What are you doing?" Ava asked, wiping away her tears.

"Ava, listen to me." Jaden focused on her sister. "Tell the doctors you don't know what bit Mom, but make certain they check for plant and insect poisons. Do you understand? Plant and insect poisons. Don't forget. Go! Hurry!"

Jaden shut the door.

"Jade." Briz leaned out the window. "Get back in the car. We have to hurry."

"I have to go see someone." Her eyes were riveted on the path.

"See someone? No one even lives out here. Get back—" Trapped by his seatbelt, Briz made a futile attempt to grab her.

"Just go!"

Before they could respond, Jaden ran across the road. She glanced back and saw Briz and Ava's expressions of disbelief as she vanished into the thick foliage.

CHAPTER 17

JADEN

Damp leaves pawed at Jaden like slimy hands trying to stop her from moving along the path. She shoved her way through the growth, refusing to let it drag her to the ground. She was determined to right her wrong. With each step, she felt the plants edge around her like wolves intimidating their prey.

A thorn-covered vine scraped over her foot; she kicked it away. Her self-loathing and determination spurred her on.

Head down, following the track underfoot, she didn't notice that the evening stars were blanketed by menacing clouds—not until the downpour soaked her clothes and washed the ointment off her skin. Looking up, she saw a flickering light shining through the leaves in the distance, like a shimmering swarm of fireflies beckoning her forward.

She paused, thinking she heard Briz calling her name. But rain, trilling insects, and croaking frogs drowned any trace of his voice.

When the shack came into view, the rotting walls were stippled with light. As the rain subsided, Jaden heard a discordant tribal beat drumming through the air.

Mal Rous! The words tasted rancid, simmering in her mouth. She tried to lighten her step as the stairs groaned under her weight. Her hand hovered over the doorknob, then dropped away. Lowering onto her knees, she crawled across the veranda to look in the open window.

Remnants of burning candles lit up the Mal Rous, stretching their grotesque shadows across the mold-covered walls.

Esere and Ivan were grinning as they pounded on makeshift drums. Tig was gyrating and kicking at the walls. Datura was frantically twirling the elongated tentacles on her head; they made a haunting whistling sound as they whirled through the air.

They were so completely absorbed that none of them smelled Jaden's presence. All of them looked in better shape than on the day she'd freed them.

"Datura, it's too bad ya wasn't there," Anders shouted over the racket. "That woman never seen me till it were too late. I did just what ya told me. Bit into her leg real good, then rubbed some 'a yer thornapple sap on her gums when I was done; she won't remember nothin'."

Anders had centipede poison...oleander toxins—her mom could be in a coma.

"That there snivelin' girl will take us serious now." Anders jumped around, laughing. "I did more damage than ya wanted."

His words sent a white-hot flame of courage through Jaden's veins.

Too much thornapple sap could kill my mom. What else had he injected? His blood? Jaden wanted answers. Even more, she wanted to strike back. Her rage destroyed all sense of self-preservation. Marching to the rotting front door, she flung it open with such force that it broke free from its rusty hinges, crashed to the floor, and crumbled apart.

The Mal Rous froze, staring at her like statues that Edgar Allan Poe would have sculpted.

"You psycho demons went after my mom. And now you're celebrating!" Jaden yelled. "If you were pissed at me—if you wanted to bite someone—come after me, not my family."

She stormed over to Anders, towering over him. He stood with his mouth hanging open.

"You! I found my mom unconscious, with a gash in her head. Two holes in her leg." Jaden swung her leg back, thrusting it forward with more strength and hate than she knew she was capable of. She struck him in his face; his head snapped back as he dropped to the floor.

"And you!" Jaden rushed to Datura, stopping inches away. "You scuzzbag!" Jaden leaned over her. "You told him to do it."

"Enough!" Datura's tentacles coiled, then sprang toward Jaden, warning her back. "Ya wasn't here yesterday. Or today. What was ya plannin' behind our backs, ya spiteful little girl?"

"You didn't tell me I had to report to you every day. My job was to find your deranged Professor. My time wasn't up. I've been trying to track that lunatic down. This is how you repay me—by siccing one of your puppets on my mom?"

"Don't ya ever talk badly 'bout my Professor."

Moisture covered Jaden's face. She wasn't sure if it was rain, tears of anger and fear, or sweat from the stifling heat that was threatening to suffocate her.

"Ya disgustin' human. Ya don't control me." Datura's

tentacles twitched. "I do what I want, and the others follow my orders."

Before Jaden could respond, Ivan stepped between them, snarling—not at Jaden, but at Datura.

Jaden was stunned. Was Ivan going to defend her?

"Datura, ya ain't in charge 'a *us*," Ivan growled. "We do things 'cause we want to."

Jaden's confidence grew as Ivan confronted his leader.

Datura's tentacles were crimping and twisting uncontrollably as she tried to stop them from lashing against Ivan's thorny head.

"Ivan, get outta my face. Now! This ain't 'bout ya." Datura pointed her crooked finger at Jaden. "She didn't bring us no food. She helped Violet get away. She has no right to interfere with how we treat each other. She had to be showed who's in charge."

Jaden hid her relief at hearing that Violet had escaped. She pointed a rigid finger right back at Datura. "I did come by with food. I left you creeps a jar of peanut butter. You weren't here. You were busy over at the mansion attacking one of our workers."

"Peanut butter, pah!" Datura elbowed Ivan out of the way. "Ya dumb girl. I bet ya never even bothered goin' to the cave to see if our Professor was there."

"What cave, you rank troll? You never told me about a goddamned cave."

Ivan cocked his head, swiveling it one-eighty degrees. He scowled at Jaden, and she knew she'd lost his support. Never really had it.

"Datura's right. Ya is a very dumb girl," Ivan slobbered, sending poison ivy juice across Jaden's bare legs.

The new welts burned and throbbed, but the surge of pain only impelled Jaden to hold her ground.

"What 'bout the Bellibone?" Datura sneered, exposing her fangs.

"I haven't been here for two days." Jaden's voice rose louder than Datura's. "You just said so yourself. So exactly when did I set her free?"

Ivan swept his hand toward Jaden, indicating to Datura that the silly kid was all hers. That simple gesture was all it took.

Jaden knew the consequences could be deadly. But what other choice did she have? Before Datura could spring into action, Jaden snatched up a leg from the busted rocking chair and swung it relentlessly, sending Datura flying across the room and slamming into the wall. Blood spurted from Datura's mouth like soda from a shaken can.

Datura charged at Jaden, digging her claws deep into her leg, flaying it open. She bit in.

The warmth of Datura's blood and poisons penetrated, mixing with Jaden's own blood, pumping through her arteries like hot embers. Jaden began shaking. Droplets of perspiration covered her skin. Foam dribbled from the sides of her mouth. She fought to stay conscious.

Datura abruptly extracted her fangs and jumped back.

Jaden sucked in a breath of air. Her body felt as if it was being wrenched in a vise. Turning her head, she found Briz standing behind her. She realized he was holding her tightly in his arms. Jaden could hear Briz gasp as the sight of the monsters registered.

The Mal Rous' laughter shrilled through the room. Jaden tried to scream at Briz to run before he was attacked, but all her words were garbled together.

"Ain't that sweet." Blood splattered from Datura's mouth as she scoffed. "He's gonna protect her."

"Let me get him." Tig spun around, circling Jaden and Briz. "Let me get him for what *she* done to Anders and ya."

With a bloody grin, Datura nodded.

Jaden tried to kick out at Tig, but her legs wouldn't move. Her body was as useless as a mangled rag doll. She fell limp in Briz's arms.

He was dragging her toward the doorway when Tig clamped onto his leg, tendrils boring into his calf. Holding Jaden, Briz swung his leg wildly, pounding Tig against the doorjamb. The rodent dug her claws in deeper. Struggling to keep his balance, Briz heaved Tig against the frame of the door again, and her tendrils released. Another blow and her hands dropped away. She staggered in a circle.

Briz lifted Jaden into his arms as Anders rose to his feet and approached them.

"Let 'em go." Datura smiled, smearing Jaden's blood over her face, breathing it in.

Jaden could feel the adrenalin pumping through Briz as he carried her to the porch and down the stairs. She saw Ivan standing in the doorway, heard his frustration.

"I don't trust 'em. The Professor said no one can ever know 'bout us. They is gonna tell others."

Datura stood next to Ivan, laughing, her beady eyes on Briz, watching his muscles spasm as Tig's poisons worked their way into his system.

Briz let Jaden slide from his arms as he sank to his knees. Then he pulled himself upright and drew her back to her feet. As they plunged into the growth, Jaden felt her legs being dragged over the ground like useless baggage. The sensation of branches scraping her fresh poison ivy welts was a painfully pleasant reminder that she was still alive.

She became aware of the aroma of blood on Briz's calf. It smelled sweet. Her own blood stank like a dead animal. With her eyes closed, she saw flickering images of the Mal Rous. She knew if the beasts were following them, there wasn't anything she could do to stop them.

Briz scooped her up into his arms, Jaden's head flopped back. Opening her eyes, she saw that the sky had cleared. The stars above were plummeting toward her like shards of colored glass.

The feeling of burning embers moving through her veins subsided. But her mind continued spinning in and out of consciousness as if she were sinking into a hot whirlpool.

When they finally broke free from the tangled plants, she could smell Briz's sweat more intensely than the fragrance of his blood. She inhaled it as if it were a drug that aroused her animal instincts. She knew that the fear and confusion pumping through him was propelling him forward.

He didn't slow down until they reached the estate.

Jaden raised her head and tried to focus. Briz's parked car was a fuzzy blob in front of the house. Had it only been a couple of hours since he'd come to help work on the place?

Briz carried her into the sitting room and laid her on Elvina's tattered Queen Anne sofa. Jaden watched his blurry form turn on a lamp and walk into the kitchen.

The stillness closed in around her. It seemed as if he was gone for hours. When he reappeared, he was carrying a pan of water, a towel, and the first aid kit her mother had been adamant about buying after Carl was bitten.

Jaden could hear Briz talking to her, though he sounded

far away. It was as if she was immersed in a clear liquid resin that blocked not only his words, but also her ability to think sensibly. When he knelt down to clean the deep slash in her leg, she leaned forward and took a deep breath.

His sweat, mixed with the smell of his blood, was intoxicating. Jaden slipped off the couch and pressed herself against him. He gently pushed her away, but she didn't care. Coaxing his head to hers, she bit lightly down on his earlobe.

He shifted back, looking at her warily.

The innocent girl she'd been earlier today, trembling at her first kiss, was nowhere to be found. Now she wasn't feeling the least bit pure or virtuous. Taking hold of his shoulders, Jaden drew Briz closer, letting her lips fondle his.

This time he didn't stop her. He let out a sigh—not of protest, but longing. His mouth willingly melted into hers. Sliding down, lying on the floor, the sensation of losing control began to overtake them both.

CHAPTER 18

BRIZ

Briz rolled onto his back and pulled Jaden on top of him. Her deep kisses electrified his body. His mind, yanked out of a state of shock, was now racing toward a libido-driven joy ride.

Jaden sat up, lifted Briz's shirt and ran her fingers firmly over his chest. Then he watched her pull up her own shirt high enough to reveal her lacy lilac bra. He felt a grin tugging at the corners of his lips. He had never imagined her wearing a lacy bra. Well, maybe he had. But he hadn't imagined her being so aggressive.

She lowered her body on top of his. The feel of her skin touching his, her lips pressing against his—Briz questioned why he'd ever wanted to take things slow with her.

Then her body convulsed. Her mouth slid from his and she went limp in his arms. Briz shifted her onto the faded rug and pressed his fingers against her neck. He felt her pulse surge, then it seemed to stop. He pulled Jaden's shirt back down, put his head to her chest and listened. A beat, fading into the distance, barely reached his ear.

He felt her cheek. Her skin was no longer feverish but ice cold.

What had he been thinking? Jaden was hurt. She could be dying. Not to mention, no birth control.

A noise brought him to his feet. He stood protectively next to Jaden's unconsious body, listening to the sound of wings flapping. Whether it was because of the gouges in his leg, lust, or fright, his heart was pounding. Lightheaded, he wiped moisture from his brow. His skin was hot.

He tried to spot where the noise was coming from, then saw something hovering up near the ceiling.

Briz gasped.

No. Fairies aren't real. His chest felt compressed. He couldn't breathe. His head fell forward, and he sank to the floor.

When Briz opened his eyes, the flying thing was chewing on Jaden's leg. Raising himself onto his elbows, he managed to force out the words, "Leave her alone. Please, please, leave her alone." He tried to swallow, but his throat was too dry.

The thing lifted its head and spit blood onto the carpet.

Briz tried to stand, but his legs wouldn't respond. All he could do was watch the creature as it fixed its mouth on Jaden's leg again. He could hear a slurping as it sucked out more of her blood. His face contorted. It was a bizarre pixie vampire, and he'd be next. No, no, vampires didn't exist—or maybe they did. After what he'd seen tonight, how could he say what was real and what wasn't anymore?

Again, the thing raised its small head from Jaden's leg, spat, and wiped its mouth. Removing disinfectant and gauze from the first aid kit, it cleaned and dressed Jaden's wound, spreading salve over the poison ivy lesions that covered her legs.

When it was done, its attention turned to Briz.

He sat up, squeezed his eyes shut, then quickly opened them to make this nightmare disappear. His mind was playing tricks on him. He was hallucinating. Wasn't he?

The fairy-like bloodsucker stood up. With its left leg hanging limply from its hip, it raised its hands as if to show him it wouldn't harm him.

"You may call me Violet," it spoke in a soft voice.

"What are you?" Briz asked, still doubting it was real. He'd had LSD once, when his so-called friend Marcus had snuck a tab in his lunch. Was he having some kind of flashback?

"I am a friend of Jaden's. I was not hurting her."

It was talking to him, but Briz was positive he was imagining it. "Friend, yeah, right."

"I was trying to remove any possible traces of poison from her leg."

Briz's eyes widened.

"I assume you were at the shack?" Violet gestured toward his wounds. "The Mal Rous did this to you?"

Briz's shoulders rose as he dragged in a breath of stale air. "Mal Rous...? That's what those *things* were? They seemed almost...almost human."

"Yes, Mal Rous, and only partly human," Violet responded. She pointed at Briz's leg. "May I examine—"

"What's going on?" Briz cut her off, shrinking back as she hobbled closer. "Where did you—they—come from? Are you even real?"

"Yes, we are real." She stepped closer.

"Are *you* a Mal Rou?"

"No, I am not; I am a Bellibone. We were...are...genetic experiments." Violet knelt down next to him.

"The dark side of cloning," Briz whispered. Then he became still as a hunted deer.

"Many years ago, Jaden's grandfather, Professor Dekle Thatcher, created us." Hesitantly touching his leg, Violet cleaned off the blood. "May I ask your name?"

There was a lump in Briz's throat the size of a rotten apple. Pulling on his collar, he mumbled his name.

"The one that did this, what did it look like?"

Briz rubbed his throat. "It jumped up in the air, circling around, then stabbed me with..."

"That would be Tig."

None of what happened in the shack—or was happening now—made any sense. Briz steadied his breathing as Violet's small hands kneaded around the punctures in his calf, releasing a pocket of pus. She pressed her lips to the openings and carefully sucked out any remaining poisons, then applied a disinfectant.

"It seems that Tig's tendrils did not penetrate completely." Violet took note of Briz's sallow skin and enlarged pupils. "However, she injected enough spurges poison to cause dizziness and shock. I am surprised the two of you were able to walk all the way to this house."

"She didn't." Briz looked over at Jaden. "I carried her."

"Do you know which one attacked her?"

"It had worms all over its head. Jade must have hit it with something. Its mouth was bleeding. When I got into the shack, it was biting into a gash in Jade's leg."

"Datura," Violet said the name with disdain. "Are you certain its mouth was bleeding?"

Briz nodded.

"Oh no..." Violet's hand hovered over her mouth. "The Mal Rous will trust her now."

"What are you talking about?"

Violet didn't respond. Her silence weighed on Briz's body like a cement casket. Refusing to submit to the mania that threatened to take hold of him, his mind pushed against the weight. "I have to get Jade to the hospital."

"The hospital will not be able to help her," Violet said matter-of-factly.

"Well, that's where her sister took their mom. I'm guessing one of those things got her, too."

Or was it you?

"Jaden's mother was attacked?" Wisps of Violet's hair stood straight up.

"Yeah, earlier, upstairs. I figure Jade knew about them, that's why she went after them."

Violet's shoulders drooped. "Fair is foul, and foul is fair—"

"Hover through the fog and filthy air." Briz finished the quote. *This is crazy; she's read Macbeth?*

"This is my fault." Violet surveyed Jaden's inert form. "The Mal Rous were digging their claws into me, threatening to dismember me."

Dismember? Briz pulled on his ear as if something was wrong with his hearing.

"I...I panicked." Violet looked back at Briz. "I told them Jaden might be the Professor's granddaughter, hoping it would make them stop. A short while later, they went hunting, and I fled. If I hadn't left, they wouldn't have hurt her mother. Jaden wouldn't have been attacked."

"Hey, I don't really get what you're talking about...or if any of this is even real..."

"We are quite real."

"Sure, you are." All Briz knew was he wanted to get Jaden out of there. "I have to get her to a doctor." He motioned toward the two gouges in his leg. "We both need medical attention. I should call the cops, too."

"The hospital, the police...they will be of no help."

Briz wasn't interested in arguing with an imaginary creature about what he should or shouldn't do.

"To save her," Violet continued, "it would be best if you could find the triplets."

"Triplets. What the hell are they? Shakespearean fairies that'll make everything all right? We don't need any more bayou fairies."

Violet cocked her head. Her hair bristled. "Fairies don't actually exist, Briz."

"Well, you look like one."

"Trust me, I am not a fairy." Her tone was crisp, but her touch remained gentle as she secured a piece of gauze to his leg. "I have always thought the triplets could have stopped the Professor from becoming one of them."

Briz narrowed his eyes, taking in the Bellibone's words. "One of what? What happened to the Professor?" As he waited for an answer, he thought he could hear the rapid beating of the Bellibone's heart. "One of what?" he asked again.

"A Mal Rou." Violet's wings contracted.

"That's impossible." He rubbed his eyes, then looked at the gauze on his leg. "Shit, I'm messed up. None of this is really happening."

Violet pressed her small fingers against his leg.

"Briz, look at me. I am real. The Mal Rous are real. At

one time the triplets prepared the Professor's formulas for him. They may be able to help Jaden."

Briz brushed Violet's hand away. Both hemispheres of his brain were working overtime. Then a memory prickled under his skin. When he found his words, his voice was tight. "Jade...Jade asked Hubs to take her to the triplets."

Violet murmured Hubs's name.

"Did they change Hubs, too?" Briz asked. "Is that what's wrong with him?"

"Hubs, Hubs..." Violet kept repeating his name. "Of course." She spoke slowly. "Hubbard was the name of the little boy that lived at the shack. No, the Mal Rous only tortured him."

Tortured him.

"That's why he locked himself in his trailer when I mentioned Guyon Manor. Jade's not going to end up like *him*...is she?...Am I?!"

"You must find Hubs."

"There's no way Hubs can help her..." Briz's energy was dwindling. He had to do something *now*. He had actually started to believe that this was all real. "I'm taking her to the hospital. It'll be faster, safer. *Saner*."

"Briz. Please, go to Hubs. Tell him what happened. Tell him that Jaden may take on their traits. Have him take her to the triplets."

"The Mal Rous' traits?" The words felt as if they were choking him.

Violet and Briz looked at Jaden. Moments ago, she had seemed fevered. Now she appeared pallid and cold. Dark red spots were already showing through the gauze Violet had fastened to her leg. "If you get her to the triplets right away... they *might* be able to stop her from becoming one of *them*."

"*Might* be able to—? No, I'm taking her to the hospital."

"The hospital staff, those medical doctors, *won't* be able to help. They won't understand what is happening to her. *You* have no idea of what is happening. How are you going to explain it to them? Do you honestly think they would believe you?"

Briz pushed himself up. Surrendering to the possibility that he wasn't hallucinating, he tried to steady his legs as well as his mind. He ignored the pain and weakness of his own body and lifted Jaden in his arms. Blood oozed from his bandage, trickling down his leg as he carried her to his car.

"The triplets, Briz," Violet called from the front porch. "And please, don't tell anyone about me."

"They'd just laugh me off." Under his breath, he mumbled, "Or lock me up." He looked past Violet at the house. During the day, it exuded the aura of a southern mansion being resurrected. Now it was ominous, foreboding.

As he placed Jaden on the front seat, he heard Violet recite more lines from *Macbeth*.

"When shall we three meet again? In thunder, lightning, or in rain. When the hurly-burly's done, when the battle's lost and won."

Driving away, Briz gripped the steering wheel and yelled, "WHAT THE HELL IS HAPPENING?

CHAPTER 19

AVA

Ava pulled up to the hospital and wiped her face, smearing tears and mascara across her cheeks. She glanced at her mother's lifeless body on the back seat of the car, then at the building. Ava hated hospitals. She could never fathom why anyone would choose to work in one. They were always full of sick people. Finding no one around to help her, she struggled alone to get her mom into the lobby.

Now, at the sight of Brooke slumped over in a plastic chair, the taste of hysteria filled Ava's mouth as if she'd gargled with ammonia. Her head was pounding. Her nerves were shredded. Her mother's blood covered her hands. It was smeared across her arms and blouse.

"Is anyone here? Come on, someone help me! My mom's dying here!" Ava was shouting at the stark white walls when a middle-aged woman came through a set of swinging doors. "This dump *is* the hospital, right? It looks like a cheap motel. I drove past it three times."

An ex-boyfriend had once told Ava that her overbearing and bossy nature was like a tear gas grenade. She accepted that as true. The grenade was detonating now, and as usual, she had a deep-seated unwillingness to control it.

As the woman sat down at her desk, Ava kept talking.

"I don't get you people. Are you blind, or are your brains clogged up from eating too many fried foods? Why are you just sitting there?" Ava flattened her hands on the desktop and leaned into the woman's face. "My mom's hurt. She's dripping blood all over your cheap vinyl flooring." Reading the woman's nametag, Ava straightened up. With perfect posture, she looked down her nose and snarled, "So, *Jezebel*, my mom is in some kind of a coma. She's unconscious."

Jezebel frowned while repeatedly pressing a button on the wall.

"Look, lady, my worthless sister and her fathead *boyfriend* jumped from the car and ran into a cane field. The asses left me alone to take care of my mom. I had to drive all the way to town. I had to do everything *alone*."

Ava shoved her hands toward Jezebel. "Did you see this?" Flailing her arms in the air, her voice rose to a high pitch. "My mother's blood is under my fingernails; now they're ruined." Ava understood the absurdity of her words, but continued, "I need to get home to clean them up and apply a new coat of polish."

"Calm down, child." Jezebel slid her chair back from her desk, farther away from Ava.

Ava mimicked her Southern twang. "Calm down, child? Calm down, child! Something bit my mom. She cut her head on a window. Look, are you going to help me, or—"

She stopped mid-sentence as the swinging doors burst open. A nurse hurried into the lobby, quickly maneuvered Brooke into a wheelchair, and rolled the chair back through the doors. Ava followed close behind as if she were attached to her mother by an umbilical cord.

After Jezebel helped the nurse lift Brooke onto a bed, she guided Ava to a neighboring bed and rolled the screen aside, letting Ava see her mother.

"Where's the doctor?" Ava demanded, sitting on the corner of the mattress, pointing and shaking her finger. "She's just a nurse. My mom needs a doctor."

"It's all right, darlin'." Jezebel patted the pillow, encouraging Ava to scoot back and lie down. "Don't ya fret. The doctor will be here any minute now."

Ava didn't budge. She could tell from Jezebel's demeanor, the woman thought she was a spoiled brat, and she didn't want to excite Ava any further. This realization thrilled Ava. It meant she'd get her way.

"Your mama is bein' taken care of." Jezebel stuffed her hands into the pockets of her uniform. "Now, if it's okay with ya, I'm gonna have the nurse give ya a sedative to calm yer nerves."

"Good idea—*you think!*"

Ava doubted they could legally give her any medication. Even in the South, it had to be against the law to give a drug to a minor without parental consent.

Her eyes cut into the two women as they whispered back and forth. Then Jezebel walked over to another cart.

The nurse caring for Brooke never looked at Ava. The woman's attention stayed on her mother. When Jezebel returned, she handed Ava a white pill and a glass of water.

Ava popped the pill into her mouth; a bitter taste coated her tongue. "Did you just give me an aspirin to help me relax?"

"Just swallow it, child." Jezebel turned her head and mumbled, "*Betasse.*"

"Hey, I understood that. My landlady speaks Cajun. Don't call me stupid."

"Ya hear that one a lot, do ya?"

"Real nice. Very professional," Ava said, tossing another grenade of attitude.

"I'll be back with paperwork for ya to fill out." Jezebel gestured toward a closed door. "Ya can wash up in there."

Ava looked at her mother's blood on her arms. She wiped her eyes, but they were dry. She had run out of tears. She disappeared into the cold, antiseptic washroom.

Cleaner, though not any calmer, Ava went from room to room, checking out the institution she was relying on to save her mom. At least the inner workings of the hospital appeared legitimate. Smaller than a general hospital, it looked sufficiently set up to help people—despite what she considered to be an unqualified staff.

Down the hall were two rooms, each with four beds, all empty. Ava opened another door. The sterile room was set up for performing rudimentary surgeries. Everything seemed foreign to her. Yet right now she had to accept that this wasn't about her. This place was her mother's lifeline to recovery.

When she returned, Jezebel was waiting for her, hugging a clipboard. From Jezebel's expression Ava thought she was ready to lock her in a padded cell.

"Don't *fret.*" The bed's springs objected as Ava plopped down. "I didn't go off to find a *real* sedative."

Jezebel grunted while repeatedly clicking her pen. "Just explain to me what happened to yer mama."

"Something attacked her. Look at her leg," Ava half-hollered. The twitching of Brooke's closed eyelids was the only sign that she was alive. "And she hit her head on the window. What's so hard to understand?"

Jezebel had already had her fill. Squaring her shoulders, she stood like a pit bull prepared to defend itself. "Well maybe it'd be easier if ya'd stop barkin' at me."

"I told you." Ava shifted to the edge of the bed, closer to the woman. "A bug or some kind of animal bit her. What don't you get? I have no idea what it was. I wasn't there. My sister said to check her for plant poisons, too."

"Oh..." Jezebel clicked her pen closed and slapped it against the clipboard. "So ya tellin' me a poisonous plant came into the house and gouged a hole in yer mama's leg?"

"Listen, if my sister said to do it, I'm sure she had a good reason."

"If ya were my kid, I'd go into a coma, too," Jezebel said, walking away.

"I didn't come here to win a popularity contest. Just help my mom."

Chapter 20

Datura

Datura was feeling good. *Really* good. Biting into Jaden had made her hungry. Datura's slender tongue skimmed over her lips, tasting the lingering smears of the girl's blood. It was different from Dekle's but had the same bitter flavor of raw chocolate. Jaden's scent had been familiar. Was the Bellibone telling the truth? Was Jaden related to the Professor? Either way, Jaden would soon be faithful, even devoted to them. Another reason to celebrate.

Now for a more savory treat.

"Let's go to town." Datura's happiness filled the room. "I need a good *feedin'*."

"Yeah, it's 'bout time," Ivan said. "I don't just wanna fill my belly. I wanna gorge on some tasty human *emotions*."

Datura understood what Ivan meant. They all did. His unspoken words, *pain, agony, abuse*, were the flavors they all longed for.

The Professor had often shared with Datura that the Mal Rous satisfied his need to avenge himself against all those who had dismissed his talents back at Cambridge.

Even now, Datura could hear him as if he were standing right next to her. "Remember, my little darlings, having control over people is empowering. It's how a dictator feels, filling his subordinates with intimidation and dread." The Professor had always encouraged those behaviors in them.

Datura knew he would be upset with her for letting her blood mix with Jaden's tonight. None of them were ever supposed to do what she'd done. She'd lost control.

Even so, it had felt so good.

She promised herself that she would never inject another human with her blood again. Or at least *try* not to.

The sounds of life around her were inviting Datura to terrorize the town. She had a hankering for one thing—the gratification of releasing her venom; knowing it was flowing through her chosen victims, making their bodies sick, altering their minds.

"Mm, fear." Datura's tongue sliced through the air. "Like the Professor would say, it has such a distinctive, succulent bouquet."

The Mal Rous had been locked up too long. The others inhaled Datura's cravings until her cravings became their own. Enhanced by the delectable fumes of Jaden and Briz's blood, the smell of their terror that lingered in the shack, the Mal Rous were anxious to attach their fangs to human flesh.

They'd been planning a feeding binge since the day they were set free. It was time to appease their insatiable appetites for gorging on the secretions of fright. Salivating with excitement, they charged into the field. Nighttime had always been when they'd thrived. The best time for the Mal Rous to stalk.

When they approached town, Datura observed her siblings, sniffing for familiar odors. Things weren't as they'd remembered. Some places were run down, while others were glaringly new. Cane fields used to butt up to the dodgy bar that thrived on the outskirts of town. Now a brightly lit shopping mall scarred the ground.

"This could be good." Datura grinned. "More humans to play with. And they is gonna remember us! They ain't gettin' any of my thornapple sap to make 'em forget what happened." Somewhere deep inside, she could feel the Professor's disappointment in her, but her need to indulge her predatory nature was stronger.

Datura looked at Esere. The sight of a few drunks and druggies behind the mall caused the blood vessels in his eyes to bulge, sending him into a frenzy.

Esere's body quivered as he squealed, "Starter food! No one's gonna care 'bout 'em."

"What's the fun in that?" Ivan patted the back of Esere's head. "Let's find us somethin' worthwhile."

Esere snarled, swatting Ivan's hand away. Crouching down on all fours, Esere let out a howl. He charged for the nearest human, pulled up the man's shirt, then stabbed his chin horn into the man's soft belly.

Anders watched Esere—breathing in his brother's excitement, he drooled at the sight of a teenage boy emerging from a metal door at the far end of the loading dock. The kid leaned against the brick wall and lit a cigarette. The flame from his lighter illuminated his arrogant youthful countenance.

Datura signaled to the others to stay back as Anders took off, scampering in and out of the lights and darkness. Sneaking up to the teenager, Anders cocked his large head and clamped his massive jaws down on the boy's tender leg. The cigarette fell from the kid's mouth as he yelled in pain.

None of the derelicts in the alley seemed to care, and the building's thick walls prevented anyone inside from hearing.

Datura could sense Anders's elation as his catch trembled under his touch. She felt the ecstasy as his teeth sank in, releasing his venom into the mouthwatering flesh.

Paralyzed, the boy collapsed onto the ground. He would wake up sick and weak.

Datura slapped Tig and Ivan on their backs. "Let's check out the rest of the town. These two are happy grazin' here."

The smell of deep-fried fat dangled in the air as they neared a grungy cafe, making Datura long for bygone days. She missed the Professor, especially the way he'd changed after she'd bit him. From then on, instead of dropping them off in town and leaving them to hunt on their own, he'd stay and watch. A voyeur in the shadows, he let his desires surge. He lived vicariously through his creations, envying them as they assailed their human targets. Datura loved how their needs had become his.

Ivan elbowed Datura, bringing her out of her reverie. He gestured at Tig.

Mesmerized by an ice cream shop's flickering neon sign, Tig was squeezing drops of poison from the tips of her tendrils. "After they close, let's sneak in. Add a little *zest* to the ice cream. Ya know, put Ivan's poison ivy juice and my spurges poison in one of 'em special toppin's."

"Don't think so," Ivan responded. "I like watchin' my victims suffer."

Tig released a long sigh. "I miss huntin' with Talis."

Ivan gave a nod. Before her passing, Tig and Talis had been inseparable.

Datura walked past the two of them, intent on finding a human sacrifice to satisfy her cravings. Trusting her instincts,

Tig and Ivan followed, scuttling behind trash bins, hiding in the darkness.

The warmth of the night settling on their skin comforted them, but it did not diminish their hunger. Passing a hole-in-the-wall bar, Tig spotted a man in an alley.

"Come on, Ivs, Dat." Tig twisted and squirmed from side to side. "I can't wait no longer. I should'a stayed with Esere and Anders. They is havin' fun while we is waitin' for the perfect treat."

"Fine." Datura's tendrils cuddled against Tig's head, soothing her. "Go on."

Tig eagerly ran and pounced on the drunken man. She wiggled her tongue over his arm, licking it clean before biting down and injecting her poisons—pressing her fangs in deeper, the man's head thrashed back and forth. She released him with a sigh of pleasure as Ivan, and Datura approached.

"Let's go." Ivan leaned over. He spit on the man's face and walked away, not waiting to see the poison ivy bloom and cover the stubble on the man's chin. "I'm gonna find me a more tasty, healthy morsel."

The Professor always said it was about the joy of the chase, the act of violence. The scent of their catch's fear when their fangs dug in. These were the emotions, the pleasures that motivated the Mal Rous to hunt. These were the sensations that Datura and Ivan hungered to experience now. Leaving Tig behind, they headed for the residential part of town.

They made their way through tree-lined streets of older wooden houses. They were entering a subdivision of identical stucco homes when they caught a whiff of a girl jogging a short distance ahead of them. Her firm legs called out to them.

"That's the one," Ivan said, peeking out from behind a parked car.

Datura was interested in this quarry, too. But hearing the delight in Ivan's voice, she backed down. For now, she was content tasting the traces of Jaden's blood in her mouth. Ivan was in for a good chase. She knew he'd win; he always did.

Datura grinned, remembering more of the Professor's wisdom: *There is such fulfillment in the act of pointlessly torturing and tormenting someone. There's no mental challenge between right and wrong, only the need for victory. You must achieve it in whatever way you can.*

She'd always loved the Professor's feral nature.

Datura followed Ivan as he bounded after the girl. He wasn't as fast as he used to be—none of them were—and the girl was moving at a good pace. It would take a few more outings before he would be back up to par. Still, he was in his element.

The girl continued down the block, unaware that she was being pursued. She jogged up to a small house. Ivan waited for her to reach the front door. Then he made a mad dash toward her.

Datura loved the way the porch light lit up the horror that etched the girl's face. Kicking at Ivan, the girl cried for help, which excited Datura and appeared to fill Ivan with greater strength and determination.

Like Datura, he'd always loved a worthy opponent. Even at this distance, Datura could smell the fear exuding from the girl's pores.

The girl tried to put her key in the lock as Ivan spit gobs of saliva onto his filthy claw, jabbed it deep into her leg, removing it when the key dropped from her hand. She reached down, but it was too late; her fingers were curling under, cramping and burning. Ivan's poison ivy was already penetrating her system.

Datura grinned, her fangs throbbing as she watched.

Ivan cheerfully looked up at the girl, extended another saliva-covered claw and stabbed it into her ripe, succulent thigh. The girl fell to the ground, crawled over to the side of the porch, and huddled in the corner as if trying to hide.

Datura could tell Ivan wanted to taunt her more, make this playful little game last, but it had been too many years. He was too excited. *Next time*, Datura thought. On the next outing, Ivan would tease his catch into exhaustion.

With a rhapsodic hissing, his forked tongue lashed out and swept over the girl's neck. Pressing his lips to her skin, Ivan bit in, savoring her flavor, then leisurely released his snake venom. When the girl became still, he withdrew his fangs and stepped aside. Datura joined him then, her tentacles aching with the need to consume fresh human blood, and took her turn.

The girl would never be the same.

Datura and Ivan went to find the others.

When the Mal Rous gathered back together, Datura took charge, giving orders: "Infect vendin' machines and door handles. Just for a lark. We is overdue for a good laugh," she cackled.

Phlegm dripped from Anders's fangs as he panted. "Datura, let's go find that horrible kid. It's time for some payback. I want to chomp down on her skinny legs for when she kicked me."

Datura considered Anders's need for revenge.

Dekle always said they hadn't gotten any of his compassion. It seemed to her that after she'd bitten him, her blood had burned all feelings of tenderness out of the

Professor, too. She'd found this comforting, even though she knew that being sentimental was an oddly human trait.

Again, his words chimed in her head.

"Cruelty. How dark it is. Revenge. How sweet it can taste."

CHAPTER 21

BRIZ

Belle Fleur had never felt like home to Briz. Now it was less so. With Jaden still unconscious in the front seat of his car, he sped into town. Every pothole in the road grabbed at his tires. Most of the streetlights had been shot up by bored kids with hunting rifles. The few that remained gave off a faint glow and a crackling hum. Were they prophesying what the night would bring? Briz was watchful, his attention skittering from one side of the road to the other. He was anticipating the creature from the black lagoon—or in this case, the mucky green bayou—to come charging at him.

He swerved into the parking lot by Hubs's trailer. The light escaping from under the edge of the curtains should have filled Briz with hope. Instead, doubt took hold.

He meant to knock calmly on the hobbit-sized metal door, but his fist struck with force. There was no answer. He inhaled a sharp breath. Violet had said Hubs was the only chance for Jaden's survival. Briz called out Hubs's name.

The door opened.

With great effort, Briz stretched his lips into a crooked smile. *Now what? What do I say to get him to help us?*

"Hey, Hubs." Gesturing toward his car, Briz kept his voice as calm as he could. "I...I need your help."

Normally when any kid Briz's age approached Hubs, it was to play a joke on him. Briz's saving grace was that he'd never been involved with their mean tricks. In fact, more than once, he'd called off some of his so-called school buddies and made them leave Hubs alone.

He hoped Hubs remembered his good deeds.

Hubs hesitantly followed him over to the car. The streetlight shone through the windows on Jaden. Her head hung limply, and foam dribbled from the sides of her mouth.

A stammer and slow drawl were both evident as Hubs insisted, "I-I d-didn't d-do any-anything."

"I know. But you're the only one who can help her." Briz scanned the parking lot nervously, expecting a Mal Rou ambush at any minute.

"This isn't a prank, Hubs. Her name is Jaden. I introduced you to her the other day." Briz was doing his best to speak clearly and slowly. To relay the urgency of the situation without prompting Hubs to lock himself back in the trailer. "We need to get her to the triplets. Dr. Whiting told her you'd take her to them. She needs to go there *now*."

Hubs looked from Jaden's inert form to the gauze bandaging Briz's leg. He fidgeted, buttoning his shirt all the way up, hiding the scars on his throat.

"W-what happened to her?"

Hubs's anxiety was obvious.

"She was at the shack, at the back of Guyon Manor. She got bit." From what Violet had told Briz, he trusted that

Hubs would understand. To be clear, he added, "Like you, when you were little."

Agitated, shifting from one foot to the other, Hubs ran his hand over his mouth as if sealing in the pain of Briz's words.

"The bite isn't going to kill her. But it could make her..." Briz couldn't bring himself to say *one of them*; he wouldn't allow himself to believe it. Maybe Violet was wrong. Maybe Violet didn't even exist. "Please, Hubs. For her sake.

"For the whole town's sake."

Hubs's eyes were fixed on Jaden. He could see that her body was succumbing to the venom that was overwhelming her nervous system, her organs, her mind. "Mal Rous," Hubs mumbled as he leaned against the car for support.

"Help us." A tear escaped from Briz's eye. He wiped it away before it reached his cheek. "Please. Take us to the triplets. She's a good person. She doesn't deserve this. *Neither did you.*"

They both watched Jaden's body convulse.

"If you won't take us, tell me where to go," Briz pleaded. "Where can I find the triplets?"

Hubs didn't respond. He returned to his trailer and shut the door.

Briz slouched against his car. He could hear Violet's voice telling him it would be useless to take Jaden to the hospital. Now he had no other choice.

Then Hubs came back. Carrying a set of keys, he walked over to an old Chevy Impala. "Fo-follow m-me."

Without saying a word, Briz got back in his car.

They drove for thirty-five minutes, on the highway, then on a dirt road skirting the new part of town. Briz wondered if

Hubs was just going to abandon the two of them out in the boonies.

*What the...*Briz slowed as they turned onto the grassy mead. Thirty yards in front of them, an old boat shed sat on the rim of the marsh. *The triplets live on the bayou?*

Moonlight played across the water. Nothing about the tranquil scene reflected the nightmarish event it truly was. Hubs jumped from his car, pulled a small flashlight from his pocket and started up the path, leaving Briz to lift Jaden into his own arms. Hordes of croaking toads hid in the grass, vying to see who could bellow the loudest.

When Briz reached the shed, Hubs was standing next to a flat-bottom skiff, lighting a cobweb-filled camping lantern.

Briz lowered Jaden onto the front bench of the skiff as Hubs hooked the lantern to the bow near a broken lamp.

"Ya kn-know, ga-gators have g-great night vi-vision," Hubs said, as they maneuvered the boat into the water and climbed in.

The motor growled and sputtered as the boat moved forward. Briz remembered going on the jungle ride at Disneyland when he was seven years old. It had seemed so real to him. He'd sat holding his dad's hand to feel safe. Only this wasn't Disneyland. This was real—and nothing was going to make him feel safe.

The smell of the bayou reminded Briz of his mom's fermented tofu. Mosquitoes swarmed Jaden and Briz, loudly informing him that this was *their* element. He couldn't swat them fast enough. He gave up keeping them away from himself and tried to keep them off Jaden. Sliding his palm over her leg, he transformed her skin into a canvas of modern art smeared with the draguitoes' black bodies and her red blood.

Briz glanced back at Hubs. The bloodsucking pests weren't bothering him.

The somber man tossed him an herbal-scented clump of soft wax. Briz rubbed it over Jaden's fevered skin, then on his own bare arms and legs.

Once the onslaught of mosquitoes dissipated, he took in their surroundings. A cloud wandered in front of the moon, washing away all color, bathing the bayou in a dismal gloom. The bald cypress trees rose from the water like sentinels guarding their domain. Spanish moss hung from branches like tangled hair. Steam blanketed the surface. It was as if they were on their way to perform a macabre ritual with Jaden's sickly body.

The golden flame from the lantern shimmered on the water, highlighting the bumpy backs of alligators as they glided by. From the way that Hubs navigated the boat through the channels, Briz figured the man could do it in his sleep.

Almost an hour passed before they came to a sharply angled outcrop nestled in a mound of bog. Briz could see lights glowing from a house. A shroud of mist gave it the appearance of floating in space. Hubs turned off the motor and guided the skiff with a long pole to a small dock and boathouse at the water's edge.

With a boisterous voice, Hubs called out, "Ooo-ee."

Three women emerged from the house.

"It's me, Hubs."

Briz blinked the sweat from his eyes and stared. The women had long silver hair that billowed around them as they crossed a raised walkway to the boat, a lantern guiding their way. In the distance, they seemed almost translucent.

"Hubs, what are ya doing here now?" The woman's

voice held a rich tone that embodied the bayou. "Ya never come here in the night."

Hubs tied up the boat as the women approached. The moon rushed out from behind the clouds, casting its light like a fluorescent net that captured the dock and lit up the triplets.

Briz's mouth was hanging open. He snapped it shut. *No wonder they look translucent. They're albinos.*

The matching women wore matching bathrobes. Petite in stature, everything about the women was unique, from their pale skin to their pale blue eyes. The lines on their faces were like embroidered patterns of knowledge.

If fairies were real, the triplets looked as though they would be the ruling fairy queens of the bayou. Briz leaned to one side to see if they had wings. Maybe they were related to the Bellibone, Violet.

"Th-they needs y-yer help, Mama." Hubs raised the boat's lantern to illuminate Jaden and Briz.

Hubs is related to the triplets? His mom is an albino? Things just keep getting weirder.

"She's b-been bit—" Hubs's voice quavered, as if he was afraid to say the words, "—b-by a Mal Rou."

The women gasped.

"Th-they was at th-the shack." Hubs gestured toward Briz. "He s-says Grand-pere wanted me to b-bring them here."

Grand-pere. Briz stood next to Jaden, rubbing his forehead. *Who's Hubs's grandpa?*

"Hubs, ya carry the girl. That boy is weak with fever."

"Yes, Mama." Hubs stepped back onto the boat, set the lantern down and lifted Jaden into his arms. He held her body away from his as if she had a contagious virus.

Briz's plan for the night had been so simple: put Ava in her place, help Jaden and her mom paint some walls. Now, for some bizarre reason, he'd stumbled into the world of Shakespeare's weird sisters and the lore of the three fates. *Why'd my parents make me read all those stories? They've messed me up.*

Briz carried the lantern from the boat as they walked toward the house. Straggling behind the others, his stomach tightened, and his mouth felt dry. He wasn't sure what to expect out here in the middle of the night. In the middle of the bayou. Voodoo high priestesses living in a shack?

The place was larger than he'd thought. Situated on a parcel of land that rose well above the waterline, the structure was a good six feet off the ground. It was a unique blend of a rustic cabin and a suburban home. A large, screened porch surrounded the building like a moat and obviously kept out rats, snakes, and mosquitoes while giving three tabby cats a refuge from bayou predators. A group of wicker chairs sat at the far end next to a swinging bench.

Moths fluttered around a light above the door. The moths' movements slowed, as if they were watching Briz, wondering who this intruder was. Two hound dogs lay entwined under a hammock, napping. They didn't bother to raise their heads when Briz walked past them into the house.

Hubs and the triplets hurried into a dark room with Jaden. Briz stayed right behind them, uncertain what their intentions might be. He knew that under the dirt and grime, Jaden was burning with fever. Hubs's mother motioned for Briz to set his lantern on top of a chest-of-drawers.

She set hers on a nightstand next to a lamp.

"This here lamp don't work," was all she said, as she

pulled aside the mosquito net and folded back a patchwork quilt. Hubs set Jaden down as if she were a priceless vase.

Briz watched as the women started undressing her. Hubs guided him to the door. Noting there weren't any headless chickens hanging from the ceiling or Voodoo dolls on an altar, Briz felt that it was okay to leave Jaden with the triplets. Besides, he was in no condition to fight them off. Listless, he felt his strength diminishing quickly. He needed to sit down.

I've got to be dreaming. Monsters. Fairies. Albino triplets living on the bayou. I must be delusional from the fever. Maybe too many mosquito bites. I bet I've got the West Nile virus.

The bedroom door closed behind him, and he staggered to the sofa and sat down. For the second time that night, Briz passed out.

When he came to, all he could see was a bright light.

Oh no...Don't follow the light...Don't follow the light. I'll live if I just don't follow the light.

"His pupils are dilated," he heard a female voice declare.

The light clicked off. Briz shrank back as a snow-white face came into focus just inches from his, the delicate features frail under sheer, wrinkled skin. He tried to sit up, but a strong hand clamped down on his shoulder, holding him still. Looking up, he saw Hubs.

Good, okay, I know him.

This time the woman spoke directly to Briz. "I didn't mean to frighten you, son. I'm gonna unwrap your leg now, to see what all you got going on here."

Briz stared into her pale irises. They were crystal clear, fringed with long white lashes. Gradually, Jaden, Violet and the triplets emerged from the quagmire of his mind as the alabaster woman carefully peeled the moist gauze from his calf.

He worked to steady his breathing as he surveyed the large room. An ornate desk was tucked into the corner, surrounded by a wall of books. Three wingback armchairs with handcrafted footstools sat facing a window overlooking the dark bayou. An oversized chair stood across from the sofa. A cloud of incense hung in the air. It smelled like the waxy bug repellent Hubs had on the boat.

Briz's attention went back to the woman as she got up and walked down the hall. Hubs reached down and raised Briz to his feet. With Briz leaning against him, Hubs guided Briz into the kitchen and eased him into an old wooden recliner near a window.

Herbs dangled from the ceiling, making the air spicy and pungent. The woman stood in front of a stove at the center of an island counter that stretched across the room. Pots and pans hung overhead. Under a window was a large sink. Jars containing fermenting concoctions sat in a row along the length of the counter.

Insects attracted to the lights were clinging to the screens, wailing in frustration at their thwarted desire to get into the house. A ceiling fan gyrated, not quite drowning out the humming refrigerator. The room, twice the size of a normal kitchen, included all the conveniences you'd expect in any middle-class home.

Where do they get their electricity? I don't hear a generator. They must have solar energy and backup batteries. They're too far from town to be hooked up to a power grid. They have running water; there's a catchment nearby.

Briz was grateful for every analytical thought that he

could capture in his brain. It made him feel normal, or as normal as he could be right now.

"Hubs, bring that there cup of tea for the boy."

The woman carried a pan of steaming liquid and herb poultice to a small table—sliding a chair over, she sat next to Briz.

"I'm not gonna hurt you, son. I'm Isadora. What's your name?" She spoke with a light Southern accent that faded in and out.

Hubs reached past Isadora, setting the tea down.

She nodded toward the cup. "Drink up. It'll help break your fever." With a reassuring smile, she added, "I'm sure you're a bit nervous about Hubs dragging you all the way out here. So are we. He's never brought anyone to our house."

Briz felt as though he was in a foreign country, uncertain they would understand him. Yet, his voice came out strong. "My name is Briz. Brisbane Nolan." His eyes darted to Hubs, who was leaning against the doorway with his arms crossed over his chest, then back to Isadora. "I suppose Hubs never had a reason to bring anyone here before."

Her gaze met his, and she nodded in agreement. Washing the blood off his leg, she studied the inflamed holes. "This here has been cleaned very well. Did you do it yourself, son?"

"No." Briz wasn't sure whether he should tell her who or *what* had. "A friend who told me to come here did it."

"Hmm, just who might this friend be?"

"Actually, I'm pretty sure you don't know her." Briz glanced around the room while sipping the warm tea. *Or maybe you do.* "A man named Dr. Whiting mentioned you to Jade...Jaden, she's the girl in the other room." Curiosity deepened the lines on Isadora's face as Briz continued. "She went to visit him, to learn about her family history. I guess he knew them."

"Doctor Whiting is our stepfather." A weighty undertone colored Isadora's voice.

Briz wondered what she was thinking. Something prophetic about fate, destiny, timing? Perhaps she wanted to say, *We have all been waiting for this moment. Now you're part of this most regrettable situation*—hopefully including some words of wisdom. She secured the poultice against Briz's leg with a thin towel and strip of gauze. He heard her mutter the word "fate" under her breath as she gestured for him to finish his tea.

Had she just read his mind?

While he was inwardly piecing together this unusual family, one of the other albino women entered the kitchen. From the way Hubs reacted, Briz assumed she was his mother.

"Hubs, help the boy into the other room. I put clean sheets on the sofa for him. He needs to be getting some sleep now." She gently placed her hand on Hubs's arm. "Since yer bed and the sofa is taken, ya is gonna have to sleep in the hammock tonight, son."

Hubs nodded but didn't move away from the door. His golden eyes continued to take in the scene.

"Thank you," Briz said. "Thank you for helping us." Everyone turned to look at him. "Is Jaden going to be all right? That *thing* was bleeding when it bit her. She might have rabies...or *something worse.*" The two sisters blinked rapidly as if speaking to one another in Morse code. They seemed to know what he meant. His voice faltered as he asked, "You're going to be able to help her, right?"

The women seemed reluctant to reply. Finally, Hubs's

mother spoke. "We're not sure. We are counting on the fever burning any poisons outta her system. I need to research what kinda healing tonic to be making for her."

Isadora continued where her sister left off. "You know, when Hubs was a boy, he was attacked?"

Briz gave a grimace of understanding.

"Back then our stepfather did all that was medically possible. But we have other formulas now. One of them may help."

A chill swept through Briz. *What was going to happen to Jade?*

Hubs approached him. Again, taking the brunt of Briz's weight as he hobbled back to the other room.

After that, Briz had fitful dreams about alien-looking rodents, people making him drink a sour-tasting herbal mixture—and Jaden.

He woke with a jolt.

CHAPTER 22

JADEN

A loud screech roared through Jaden's head, and she bolted upright, eyes springing open. A hint of moonlight shone through a small window, offering barely enough light to give shape to the room. In unison, a sea of croaking frogs rattled her brain. She sank back down on the unfamiliar bed, trying to figure out where she was and what had happened. Her leg ached. When she reached under the flimsy cover, she felt a bandage wrapped tightly around her calf.

The frogs were silenced by another loud screech that caused her head to feel as though it was going to burst.

Shadowy patterns covered the walls, reminding Jaden of the Mal Rous. Abhorrent memories of the night came to the surface of her groggy mind. Sitting up more gingerly, Jaden took the covers off and realized she was naked. She traced her fingers along the length of mosquito netting, found the opening and lowered her feet onto the wood floor. Curiosity began to override her fear.

Was she in the mansion? No, the mansion had wood floors, but it smelled like mothballs and disinfectant, not herbs and spicy potpourri, and the beds weren't shrouded in netting.

Jaden stood up, moving as if she were blindfolded she bumped into a nightstand—fumbling she found a lamp; its switch didn't work. She searched for her clothes in the dimness but couldn't find them. Jaden removed the thin sheet from the bed, draped it around her and made her way to the door.

She turned the knob slowly. Then paused. When nothing came after her, she stepped into the next room.

Its larger windows let more moonlight flood in. She could make out a couch with someone sleeping on it. Briz. Jaden smiled as she walked over to him. She looked down at him, feeling as if she couldn't breathe. Except that wasn't the problem. She was breathing.

Heavily.

Jaden traced her fingers along the curve of his chin, down the front of his throat, and lightly across his bare chest. Surprising herself, she lay on top of him. When the weight of her body didn't wake him, she stretched upward, placing her lips against his, kissing him repeatedly until he responded by drawing her closer, his body welcoming hers.

Suddenly he stopped and his eyes flew open. He placed a hand on her shoulder and pushed lightly.

"Shit, Jade! I thought I was dreaming." Before she could respond, his voice changed. He pulled her close. "Are you okay? I've been so worried about you."

She slipped her hand under the sheet that covered him, intent on undoing the top button of his shorts.

"What are you doing?" Clamping down on her wrist, he pulled her hand away. "You were half dead a couple hours ago, and now you want—"

Jaden pressed her lips against his, cutting off his words.

He turned his head away.

"Jaden, NO!" He lowered his voice. "This isn't cool." She could feel his heart thumping against her chest as he tried to slow his breathing. "Get up. Get off me. We aren't doing this. Not here. Not now!"

"Why? Don't you want me?" Jaden stood up abruptly. Her sheet fell to the floor.

"Yes. No." Propping himself up, Briz stared at the silhouette of her body outlined by the moonlight. "Christ, you're naked!" He averted his eyes grumbling, "Go back to bed."

She picked up her sheet, draped it around her, then held a hand out to him.

"By yourself." Briz flopped back down on his pillow.

"You sure wake up grumpy," she said, grinning.

"I'm grumpy for a reason."

Jaden glanced around. "What is this place? Where are we?"

"We're at the triplets. Hubs brought us here."

"The triplets?" Jaden had a vague feeling she was supposed to know who they were.

"Come on, I'll take you to your room." Briz grabbed her hand and guided her toward the bedroom. "I know this isn't you, Jade. This is because of that thing that bit you."

Happily entwining her fingers with his, she walked beside him, expecting a tingling sensation. Instead, she wanted to leap on top of him. She said his name as she climbed into her own small bed and scooted over. "Just lie down with me for a while. You don't have to get under the sheet."

Briz rubbed his face and looked away as if he was willing his brain to make him do the right thing.

"*Come on, Briz.*" For a second she thought he would surrender.

"No." He stepped back.

"Will you at least stay with me till I fall asleep?" Jaden lowered her head onto the pillow.

Briz sat on the floor resting his back against her bed. "Go to sleep. You're safe here."

She slid over and ran her fingers through his hair.

"Stop it, Jade." Lightly tapping her hand, Briz leaned forward. "Or I'm leaving."

Later she woke to the sensation of Briz moving away from her. She wondered if he'd ever really been there.

The room was filled with incandescent light. An angelic being hovered over her. Another angel set a large container of liquid on the nightstand next to the bed, a third appeared carrying a pan and several towels. The three of them were pure white, with translucent blue eyes that studied her. She caught a glimpse of Briz standing in the doorway before he dissolved into the darkness.

Chapter 23

Briz

The sun was rising as Briz watched the triplets come and go from Jaden's room. His eyes twitched as if he'd been gaming for too many hours. Last night he'd tried to keep track of all the different turns Hubs's boat had made as it motored through the bayou. Even during the day, the twists and turns would have bewildered him. He wished he could shove more RAM into his brain to compute everything that had happened.

Cold-blooded mongrels wanted to pulverize us. That pretty much sums it up. Not to mention their transformation of Jade into some sort of lascivious babe. Which was really ratcheting up his dreams. The thing was, he kind of liked the changes to this bad girl version of Jade.

One of the triplets paused and looked at him on her way to Jaden's room. "Son, Jaden is doing better. Her fever is breaking." There was a soft rise and fall to her words. He knew it was Isadora. "Though we aren't sure whether she'll be exactly how she was before. You may see *changes* in her personality."

Changes? Yep, just as he'd thought. Briz added psychic to his list of the triplets' otherworldly abilities. His brain rallied to defend himself. *Lady, I'm not normally a macho sexist. I was perfectly happy with the sweet and innocent version of Jade. That's a real turn-on, too.*

Oh great, I'm a sexist pig. Lying back on the sofa, Briz fell asleep again.

Hours later, the sounds of people whispering, and cupboards creaking nudged him awake. Slowly stretching, Briz sat up and combed his hair with his fingers.

Across from him, Hubs sat sprawled in the oversized chair, staring at him, a mandolin resting in his lap. Rainbows floated across the man's somber face as the sun touched the prisms hanging in the windows.

Briz reached for his shirt draped on the back of the sofa and slipped it on. Resting his elbows on his knees, he lowered his head and looked at the fresh bandage on his leg. Then he realized that he was clean.

Did they bathe me? He gave Hubs a sideways glance.

The rainbows disappeared. Briz looked out the large window; the afternoon clouds had blocked the sun. Most of the day had passed. His folks would lose it if he didn't show up at home today. Being gone for one night was fine, but two wasn't going to fly.

Briz looked around, ignoring Hubs's penetrating stare. Last night he hadn't noticed the small piano near the front door, the paintings on the walls, nor the family photos showing a young Hubs with his deep brown dad and pale mom and aunties. Not exactly a conventional family. But conventional families were hard to find.

Hunger pangs made his stomach rumble. Right on cue,

one of the mind-reading triplets came from the kitchen carrying a plate of food and glass of water.

"Jaden mentioned ya is a vegetarian. Wasn't sure how strict ya are, so we all just steamed up some vegetables for ya. We can make more if it's not enough."

"Thank you. This is great." Unwilling to make eye contact, worried that she could hear his every thought, Briz took the plate.

"I'm Olympe." The woman walked over to the chair where Hubs was sitting. "Hubs's mama. I know it can be hard telling me and my sisters apart." Settling on the arm of the chair, she ran her fingers through Hubs's hair, arranging his loose curls.

She was right. He'd never be able to tell them apart. Except by her voice. It had that sweet, musical cadence you only hear in the South.

After a few bites of food, Briz gestured to a painting on the wall. "Is that Guyon Manor?"

"It sure is. Back in its day, it was a charming place. My husband, Billy, painted it." She smiled. "Both the house and the painting."

"He's a good artist." Briz smiled back.

"He's gone now. Bless his heart, that man could do anything he set his mind to. Just like Hubs here. Are ya an artist?"

Briz glanced at Hubs's mandolin. "No, but my dad's been teaching me to play the guitar." He took a sip of water. "I'm sorry, I didn't mean to spend the whole day sleeping on your sofa."

"My dear boy, there is nothing to be sorry for. Ya has been through a lot. My sisters and I reckon that after today's rest and the poultice we applied to yer leg all night, ya is gonna be all right. The wounds weren't too deep." A shy grin spread across Olympe's face. "We tried to wake ya. Then decided it was best to let ya sleep while we cared for ya."

They did bathe me.

Briz lowered his eyes back to his plate, feeling his face redden. Without saying another word, he continued to eat until one of the other triplets came out of Jaden's bedroom.

"Tamara, is our patient ready for company now?" Olympe asked.

"I'm certain she'd enjoy seeing *you,* Briz." Tamara gave him the once-over. "She's been asking for you all night. Even when she was burning up with fever."

Briz responded with a tight-lipped smile. Unlike Olympe, nothing about Tamara was sweet and soft. She seemed more worldly, educated. The beat of her words strangled the charm of her Southern roots, as if they embarrassed her. He set his plate down and walked toward the door, wondering what Jaden might have said.

Softly knocking, he peeked into her room. Jaden was curled up in bed wearing one of Hubs's large T-shirts. She motioned for Briz to come in. He sat down, careful not to jar the bed. Black and blue circles framed her eyes.

From the poisons, he thought. Still, he said, "You look like you're feeling better."

"Yeah. I was pretty out of it." She raised herself upright and twisted her hair into a knot. "I don't really remember much about last night."

"You remember being bitten, right?"

"Sort of, yes. It's kind of all hazy. What about you? Are you okay?"

"I'm doing all right." Trying to make light of it, Briz lamely joked, "It was one crazy night."

Jaden didn't laugh. Briz watched her wadding the edge of the sheet up in her hand.

After a few minutes, she asked, "After Datura bit me, was I a horrible person?"

"Horrible? No."

Briz stared at the floor. He could feel Jaden looking at him. He was grateful that she'd lost consciousness at the manor last night before they'd had a chance to give Violet an X-rated performance.

When Briz finally looked up, their eyes locked. Seeing her doubt, he admitted, "Yeah, you were in bad shape. Both of us were. You had a fever and passed out. I found Hubs, and we brought you here."

"Guess you won't want to hang out with me anymore," she said with both frustration and regret.

Briz patted her shoulder, trying to comfort her.

Jaden frowned and pulled away. "Were the triplets with me all night? Or..." She tugged at the top of her T-shirt as if it was cutting into her throat. "I may as well just ask. I'll probably never see you again anyway. Did...did we...have sex last night?"

"What?" Briz choked.

"I mean...I know there would be—"

Nervously laughing, he said, "Face it, Jade, that's what *all* guys want. I'm no different from the rest of them." He immediately felt embarrassed. It was exactly what one of his degenerate friends would have said.

Jaden's face turned bright red.

If your friends are a reflection of who you are, I must be scum.

Briz rubbed his clammy palms on his shorts while looking at Jaden out of the corner of his eye. "No...no, nothing happened."

"It's just that I...it didn't seem like a dream. I thought..."

The more she pulled on her shirt, the more nervous Briz felt. While Ava had made him want to run, right now, sitting on the bed next to Jaden, he wanted to feel her beneath him. Briz took in a couple of steady breaths, doing his best to awaken his one remaining brain cell.

"Jade, did you really think I'd take advantage of you when you were delirious?" He could feel his brows tighten. Last night, at the manor, he'd been more than willing to do it with her. Though in self-defense, he had been poisoned.

He swallowed hard, his gaze shifting around the room, then back at her as he took her hand. "Besides, I know sex isn't all that girls want. They're into every moment leading up to it." Holding Jaden's gaze, he continued, "I mean, girls enjoy the sex part, too. Except they won't if you don't make the journey worthwhile. My three sisters have ingrained that into me. For years they've lectured me on what girls like, how to treat a girlfriend, and how not to. After some...big mistakes, now I try to take their advice when it comes to females."

Briz caressed Jaden's hand. "Just so you know, you will be seeing me again. And, if we do ever have sex, I want both of us fully present, experiencing it together. Not some Mal Rou version of you. And not right now."

"So it was just a dream?" Jaden tilted her head to the side and gave a slight smile.

"You sound relieved." Briz laughed quietly. "Being intimate with me upsets you more than being bitten by a Mal

Rou." He decided not to mention that she'd woken him up last night.

"That's the problem. When I'm around you, I forget all about the miserable cretins." Jaden sat up straighter. "I wasn't worried I'd lost my virginity with you. I was worried that it happened, and I was too sick to remember."

Briz's eyes widened. He ran his fingers back and forth over his chin. This new Jaden was full of surprises. He couldn't stop from glancing down, enjoying the way her T-shirt defined her breasts. *Trustworthy. Mindful. Principled. That's me.*

Briz reached over and released her hair; it flowed down over her shirt, covering her breasts. "You need to have more faith in me, Jade. My priorities are set. Destroy nefarious genetic mutations first—"

"Destroy them? I, I wouldn't know how." Jaden's voice was small. "First our carpenter, Carl, was attacked, then my mom," Jaden glanced at the bandage wrapped around Briz's calf, "and now you've been dragged into this." Looking up at him, she wiped her moist eyes.

"You didn't ask me to come after you." Briz folded his arms around her. Would he have followed her into the field if he'd known what was going to happen? Good question.

There was a tapping on the bedroom door. Jaden leaned back and said, "Come in."

The door opened, but no one appeared. Hubs's voice entered the room. "We h-have to g-go, B-Briz. I w-want to get b-back to town b-before dark."

"I'll be right there, Hubs."

"Miss J-Jaden," Hubs said kindly, "th-this morning, I fi-fixed the lamp next to yer b-bed. In case ya need it."

"Thank you. Hubs?" He was closing the door when

Jaden called his name. Hubs peered around it into the room. "Thank you for everything."

Briz had the impression that the ever-serious Hubs smiled as he nodded and shut the door.

"I have to go, Jade. You'll be safe here."

Briz was finding it hard not to touch her. The back of his hand brushed over her cheek, down her neck. He glided the tips of his fingers along her collarbone, enjoying the way it made her tremble—stopping when the sensation made him want more. He took Jaden's hand in his. "If my folks don't hear from me today, they'll get majorly bent out of shape. I'll be back tomorrow. Then we'll figure out what to do. Maybe Violet can help us."

"You met Violet?"

"She's the reason you're here. You have some interesting friends." Then Briz remembered Violet's description of how the Professor had been changed. "The triplets will take good care of you. You're going to be fine, Jade."

He wanted to believe it was true.

"Oh! My mom." Jaden sat up straighter, her eyes glistening.

"It's okay. Ava was taking her to the hospital. I'll look in on them."

Jaden leaned against him, and he felt her tears dampen his shirt. "Briz, I don't want you to come back." Her words were muffled against his shoulder. "This is my mess. I'll figure it all out."

"Well, I am coming back, so deal with it," he said, stroking her hair.

"You've done enough. I don't want you to get hurt again." Jaden shifted away from him. "Besides, you should be getting ready for your trip to Europe."

"You're joking, right?" He wasn't about to abandon her. And what was he thinking telling Jaden the Mal Rous had to be destroyed? Like she wasn't upset enough. There must be some scientific organization they could call to capture them.

"You told me you've been saving and planning for years."

"Jade, I've plenty of time to help you before I leave on my trip." Briz cupped her face in his palms and placed his lips gently against hers.

There was another tap on the door. It was time for Briz to leave.

The noise of Hubs's boat seemed out of place on the bayou. Briz asked him to identify landmarks in case he'd have to make the trip on his own. Hubs pointed to several inlets and what he considered to be unique-looking trees. Every stretch of water and bald cypress looked the same to Briz.

Ever since he'd moved to Belle Fleur, Briz heard locals say Hubs was mentally impaired. They gave Briz the impression that Hubs couldn't do much more than mop up the cafe.

They were wrong.

Even with their limited conversations as they rode in the skiff, Briz glimpsed the man's intelligence. Hubs just couldn't easily communicate all he knew.

Briz could hear his own grandpa telling him not to judge a book by its cover. Right now, being with Hubs, he truly got what his grandpa meant. People never give Hubs the opportunity to be better than what their petty minds allow him to be.

"Men of few words are the best men," Briz whispered Shakespeare's words. They seemed to be an appropriate description of Hubs. Briz hoped Hubs was a brave man, too.

If Violet was right, and no one believed the Mal Rous were real, what then? They couldn't let the Mal Rous run wild and attack everyone in town. Would Hubs help Jaden and Briz capture the genetic monsters?

We're probably nothing more than human party favors to the Mal Rous. They'd happily string us up like piñatas and whack us apart.

What am I doing?

CHAPTER 24

BRIZ

When Briz passed through the hospital's sliding doors, the cool air wrapped around him like a wet blanket soaked in sickness, healing, and abrasive chemicals. He counted a dozen people in the lobby, some babbling, shivering with fever, others with slashes and abrasions. A man with a deep gash in his arm was mumbling about a rabid *bebette*. Briz recognized the Cajun word for critter or little monster. The Mal Rous had been busy.

Briz asked for Brooke Lisette's room.

The admissions nurse replied, "Through the double doors. Second door on the left. Her *daughter's* with her." If aggravation were a color, it would be the ruddy shade the admissions nurse turned when she said *daughter*.

He nodded. He knew Ava had a knack for sticking her foot—with her perfectly polished toenails—into her mouth.

Briz paused at the open door, imagining a protective shield of light surrounding him. Enhanced with spiked armor. Ava was sitting in a chair by her mom's bed. She raised her head, flopped a fashion magazine onto the small table next to her, and looked right past him.

"Where's Jade?"

"Good to see you, too, Ava." He walked over to the bed.

"Funny, pretty boy," she replied, with heavy sarcasm. "So, where is she?"

"She wanted me to see how the two of you are doing."

"Oh, isn't that just dandy." Ava jabbed her finger at the empty seat next to her. "I want to see her scrawny butt sitting right *here*."

Briz shifted his attention to Brooke. Surprisingly, her pale face exuded serenity. He wasn't sure if she was unconscious or asleep. Memories of Jaden's praise for her mother came to mind—how when devastated by the death of her husband, she'd picked up the pieces of their shattered lives and worked to make them feel like a family again.

No one who had been pulled into this wretched ordeal, from Jaden to Hubs to the victims in the hospital, deserved to be hurt.

Especially not Brooke.

Briz knew that karma, good or bad, doesn't always appear to make sense.

"How's your mom?" he asked Ava, hoping for the best.

"They put eight stitches in the back of her head. They shaved some of her hair off. She's not going to be happy." Ava crossed her legs and jiggled her foot, making her sandal flap against her heel. "Why did Jade think Mom was bitten by a bug or had plant poisoning? They thought I was nuts when I told them that. I had to hound them for hours to test for it."

"Did they find any?"

"Yeah." Ava smiled. Evidently, making the hospital staff appear inept filled her with great joy. "There was oleander poison in her leg, traces of thornapple sap on her gums. They gave her a tetanus shot, put a compress on the bite, but never figured out what bit her. Whatever it was, it caused some kind of temporary paralysis and coma. Early this morning she came to, but she's been sleeping since then."

Despite Ava's superior attitude, she looked tired. Her eyes were puffy and red. Briz noticed a pile of crumpled tissues in the small wastebasket near the bed. "Have you been here all night? Or did you go to your place to get some sleep?"

"Do I *look* like I've had any sleep?"

Briz folded his arms over his chest, remembering that Ava was incapable of having a normal discussion. Verbally clobbering people was her preferred form of communication. If he sent *her* to fight the Mal Rous, they'd probably run away screaming.

"I went to the rental house last night." Ava shivered. "The front window was broken, and the door was ajar. There was no way I was going inside. I got out of there fast as I could." She tugged on the hem of her top, which looked two sizes too small. "I had to buy this at the drugstore."

What are the chances burglars robbed their place? Briz dragged his hand through his hair. *It had to have been the Mal Rous.*

"Did you call the police?" He walked over to Ava and placed a comforting hand on her shoulder. Her tight muscles relaxed at his touch. Maybe she was more vulnerable under her high-and-mighty exterior than she seemed.

"No. The landlady can deal with it when she gets back from New Orleans. I had to sleep in the god-awful lobby. The nurses wouldn't even let me stay in this room. It wasn't like they didn't have space for me." Ava waved dismissively at the occupants of the three other beds. "I mean, I was here before any of *them*."

Briz surveyed the ailing patients, wondering which of the Mal Rous had attacked them. After a moment he realized that Ava's fingers were gliding over his hand. He jerked it away.

For a second, he had actually felt sorry for Ava.

"What's wrong, Briz? Having second thoughts about Jade?"

"No." He was pretty certain he shouted it at her.

"So, where is she?" Ava asked, arching her back like an indignant countess.

"Last night after we left you in the car, she got, uh...hurt. A friend had me take her to some healers that live on the bayou. She's doing better today."

"Are you serious?" Ava raised one eyebrow, intimidating him even more. "You show up at the estate, and my mom gets attacked; you follow Jaden into a frickin' cane field, and she gets injured; then you leave her on the bayou."

Ava stood up, inches from Briz, her hands on her hips. "What is it with you? Are you just all good looks, and no brains? *The bayou.* Even *I* wouldn't have done that to her. You took my sister to some kind of witch doctor instead of the hospital? Why?"

"You're just going to have to trust me. Jade's a lot better off there than she'd be here. They know what they're doing. They've dealt with this stuff before." *A lot better off?* Doubt chipped away at Briz as he looked around the hospital room.

"What do you mean, this stuff?" Ava sat back down, scrutinizing Briz's bandaged leg, his filthy shorts. Her voice rose as she gestured at her mother. "Exactly what happened after you flakes ran off, leaving me to deal with all this?"

Briz shook his head with a huff of frustration. *Why did I mention the bayou? I need to use Hubs's form of communicating when I talk to her—the less said, the better.*

He stared at Ava with narrowed eyes. Being around her was painful on so many levels.

"I don't appreciate that look, *Brisbane*!" Ava enunciated his name like a joke.

He inched back, ready to sprint out the door. Her rollercoaster temperament seemed to subside when she looked at her mother.

"Her vital signs are stronger. They said there's nothing else they can do for her. They need the bed, so they're sending her home tomorrow." Ava's voice soured. "I can't take care of her. What do they expect me to do? Take her to a house that got broken into? And where am I supposed to sleep tonight? In the lobby again?

Briz shrugged his shoulders.

"Real funny, isn't it!"

"Hey, you don't see me smiling." He couldn't care less if Ava had to sleep in the lobby. His main concern was that Jaden and Brooke were getting care.

"Are you going back for Jade? Or are you going to leave that up to me, too?"

"Yes. No." Briz was appreciating Jaden more than ever. "I'm going to get her tomorrow."

Enthroned in her seat, Ava glowered. Briz felt his life force shriveling into a raisin. The combination of the Mal Rous and Ava was too much for him. Ava was too much for him. She seemed more unstable than the Mal Rous.

Briz took a deep breath, trying not to get caught up in her attitude.

"Ava, you have to call your crew. Tell them to take the

week off. There's some kind of feral animal on your property. They can't come back until it's caught."

"Should I have Carl set some traps, like for raccoons?"

"No, no…I'll take care of the traps. Just don't forget to call them, tell them to stay away. Jade mentioned that Carl was attacked. He'll probably be glad to get his workers out of there. Don't go to the estate. Stay away from that place."

"Brisbane, you're kind of weirding me out. What about me? I mean, tonight? I'm not sleeping here again."

"Uh, you can get a motel room for the night."

"Uh…" Ava mimicked him—reminding Briz that he said *uh* way too often. "I'm only seventeen, I can't rent a motel room. Anyway, there isn't one in this town."

"There's one forty minutes north, right off the highway across from the Meadow Seniors' Facility. They'd probably give *you* a room, no questions asked. Do you need some money?"

She angled her body toward him. "No, I have some." Her voice turned velvet-soft. "If I get a room, would you stay with me?"

Briz's eyes widened. He felt like a dim-witted clown.

"I didn't mean in the same bed." Ava's tone changed to scratchy burlap as she stomped her foot on the floor. "I just don't want to be alone. If you won't go to a motel with me, can I stay at your house?"

Briz's brain felt like it was about to hemorrhage from the pressure of holding back a high-pitched scream. He wanted to yell, *No way!* He knew she couldn't go back to her house. The Mal Rous could be there, waiting for Jaden. He had to do the right thing. After all, she was Jaden's sister.

He pressed his thumb between his eyes, trying to bring

up images of Jaden—mellow, easygoing Jaden. He gave a low, agonizing moan.

"Look at these," Ava whined, flinging her hands up. "I've been biting my nails." Glaring at her fingernails, she asked, "Can I stay at your house or not?"

"Okay," Briz squeaked as if he had laryngitis. He'd certainly be safer from her at home with his mom and dad around than alone with her in a motel room. "Only, my parents won't be cool with this."

"Don't they trust you with a woman in your room?"

Was she serious? Briz bit the inside of his lower lip to stop from saying, *You are so not a woman.*

He stood straighter and spoke with authority, "I don't want to have to explain why you're there, or what's going on with Jade. Park your car down the street around the corner from our house. When everyone's in bed, I'll sneak you in through the back door."

His attention shifted to Brooke as she quietly sighed. Looking back at Ava, Briz insisted, "Tomorrow when you pick up your mom, stay at the motel. Call the crew *now.* They've got to keep away from the manor."

"Yeah, I'll tell Carl to come back when my mom's better."

"Don't go over there."

"Yeah, yeah. I get it. I'm not dense."

"Okay. Uh, come over at ten fifteen tonight. By then my parents and sisters should be in bed."

"Excuse me? You expect me to sit here till ten o'clock?"

Briz nodded as he started toward the door. "You remember where my house is?"

Ava's exasperated sigh clearly told him he was a moron. She'd dropped Jaden off there a half dozen times.

He didn't give her a chance to reply. "I'll wait for you by the side of our garage. My folks can't know you're there. Agreed?"

"Give me a break. You're acting all bent out of shape." Ava pointed at herself. "Any one of your friends would be begging for some of this if I spent the night with them. I've seen the way they drool over me."

And when they were done, they'd run for their lives.

"Yeah, well you aren't spending the night with me," Briz clarified. "You're just sleeping in one of our beds. And not the one I'm going to be in." At night, alone in his room, he wanted Jaden lying next to him. Not Ava.

"Wow, I really make you nervous, don't I?" Ava smiled broadly, as if she felt victorious.

Briz couldn't come up with a response. Leaving the room, he didn't look back. "Ten fifteen. Not before!"

CHAPTER 25

BRIZ

What goes around comes around. Eventually a lie will bite you in the butt. Briz knew this. He wondered, *what if you lie to help others?*

Before Briz entered his house, he'd removed the bandage from his leg. The two red punctures were a quarter of an inch in circumference. No one noticed them.

He asked his parents if they'd mind if he went camping with a couple of friends. He knew they wouldn't object. His folks didn't necessarily care for any of the guys he hung out with, but they didn't have much choice. It had been his parents' idea to move the family to Belle Fleur to be closer to his grandparents. They chose to send Briz and his sisters to a public school that was below academic standards, a drastic difference from the private school they'd attended in Seattle.

Anyway, what could they say? He had graduated from high school last month. He wasn't a kid anymore.

Guilt pumped through Briz as his dad helped him load camping gear into his car. Tent, sleeping bag, camping stove

—Briz knew he wouldn't be needing any of it. Except for the flashlight and gut-hook hunting knife his dad had given him "just in case some ferocious critter shows up."

Briz couldn't understand why his vegetarian computer programmer dad would even own a knife like that. At least it might come in handy for fighting the Mal Rous.

How'd I get roped into this? All because I'm jonesing for some girl.

"May I ask if any girls are joining you on this camping trip?" His mom came up behind him. "Do you have protection?"

Briz coughed. Were all women mind readers? Covering his mouth, he stopped himself from telling another lie.

"Carmen, leave the boy alone." His dad patted Briz on the back.

"Don't worry, Mum. I have no intention of making you a grandma. You're way too young."

"I've seen how you look at Jaden. She's way too young to have a child. Just be careful."

"*Mum.*"

"I know. But it's the same way your dad looked at me when we first met. The two of you aren't so different."

"He's going camping, Carmen, not starting a family."

Briz's dad took hold of his mother's hand. "Besides, I'll be ecstatic if he ever meets someone that makes him feel the way I do about you. I remember the first time I saw you."

Briz started rearranging things in his car, thinking his parents would go back into the house. No such luck.

His dad's voice was almost giddy as he leaned against the car watching Briz. "I'd just finished my first year at UCSD— signed up for a couple of summer classes. Your mom was walking in front of me, and I was thinking, *Wow, what a great…anyway,* right then she turned around. She smiled at me like I'd said it out loud. I followed her and sat in on her class."

"Max, you were like a stalker, following me to all my classes."

"Yep. Threw my course schedule right out." He pulled his wife closer and kissed her forehead. "I'd stumbled into my future, and I knew it."

His mom had transferred from the University of Sydney to UC San Diego just for the summer session. When she returned to Australia, his dad wrote her love letters every other day for eight months, then showed up on her parents' doorstep in Brisbane to ask for her hand in marriage.

Who does that anymore?

Briz closed the car door and turned toward his parents. They looked like lovesick teenagers.

Prior to that moment, the danger he was in felt otherworldly. Now the possibility that the Mal Rous could alter his life—as well as his family's—seemed real. With a strained smile, he walked over and hugged his parents, wondering if this would be the last evening he'd ever spend with them and his sisters.

"Just don't do anything stupid when you're with your friends." His mom gave him a squeeze, then repeated one of the principles she worked hard to instill in him. "Be mindful of what you do."

Obviously, he hadn't quite learned that one yet.

At ten o'clock, Briz's mom tapped on his bedroom door and said good night. When he heard the television shut off, he walked quietly down the hall past the pools of light that shone from under the doors of his sisters' bedrooms. He slipped into the kitchen, out the back door. He stood by the garage, the uncertainty of the next few days pressing on him like the hot, muggy air.

"Hey, Torus." Briz looked down as his cat rubbed against his legs. "How you doing, buddy?" Squatting, he scratched Torus behind the ears. "You'd better stay inside. No telling what kind of deadly pests might be wandering around town."

When the cat had gotten enough attention, Briz pulled his phone from his pocket to call his friend Grover. Asking Grover for a favor was on par with licking the sidewalk in the seedy part of town.

"No problem," Grover said, clearing his throat. "I'll cover for you. Where'd you say we were going?"

"Kisatchie State Park. For a week. I told them I'm picking you up early tomorrow morning. So, don't drive down my street...if they *do* see you in town, tell them—"

"Yeah, yeah, I know the rules. I'm the one that made them up. You taking that sweet thing from out of town you've been hanging with lately?"

Briz didn't answer.

"You dog. You just look at some *bebelle* and she'll do whatever you ask."

Bebelle. Jade isn't some plaything. Why did his friends and family think he was such a player?

"Bro, take one sleeping bag, to better your chances of *gogo*."

Gogo. Bedding Jaden was the last thing Briz wanted. Well, almost the last. Mostly, he wanted her to be normal again.

Briz hung up and looked at his phone. Ten fifteen. Right

on time, Ava appeared. Lit by the yellow tinge of streetlights, she slunk down the sidewalk like a panther.

"I'm in big trouble, Torus."

The cat hissed as if it understood Briz's words.

As Briz led Ava along the side of the garage to the back door, he flashed to the morning of his birthday when he'd gone to her house looking for Jaden. Ava had answered the door. Her stare had grazed his body as if she was going to feed on him. Her lips parted slightly as she reached to move the hair away from his eyes. Then her hand stopped, frozen in midair. It smelled of freshly applied nail polish.

"Hi, Briz."

The way she'd said his name had made him feel as if she were going to massage coconut oil all over him. He'd promised himself that if she asked, he'd say no. Tossing her long auburn mane to one side, she'd gestured for him to come in.

When he didn't move fast enough, she grabbed his arm, pulled him into the house, and shut the door behind him.

Briz watched her glide over to the air conditioner, the cool air caressing the perfect figure that her red swimsuit top and shorts pretended to cover. He couldn't help gawking.

She gave a pouty smile. "It's about time."

Time? His eyebrows pinched together.

"Uh, is Jaden here?"

"No." Ava's pout compressed into an angry pucker. "Why? I thought you were here to ask me out."

"I, I wasn't..." he stuttered, trying to figure out why she'd think that. Then she came at him like a feisty dog, her face morphing into a character from Grimm's fairy tales. Torn between cowering and laughing at her, his voice went up an octave. "I just wanted to see if Jaden—"

Ava didn't let him finish.

"What is it with you? Isn't today your eighteenth birthday?" Standing in front of him, she repeatedly poked her finger in his ribs. "Why do you hang out with Jaden? She's a fourteen-year-old kid."

"No, she's not. She'll be sixteen next month." Briz took hold of Ava's finger and stepped back. She was such a reactionary princess. He couldn't help grinning. He'd never been around anyone like her before.

"Whatever! Guess you go for the chaste, immature ones." Ava snapped, pulling her hand from his. "They're so much easier to control, right?"

That was four days ago, before his life spun out of control. Now, alone in his room with Ava, Briz had a rather unsettling realization—being around her didn't make him question his feelings for Jaden, but it did challenge his moral nature.

He'd always thought he had more of a conscience than any of his male friends. With Ava sprawled across one of his twin beds, he realized how much of a guy he really was. He'd spent the last few years denying it. Well, "denying" wasn't exactly the right way to put it. Not being reckless was more like it.

Ava might act like a princess from the dark side, but she was gorgeous. And willing. How often does that combination leap into a teenage boy's bed?

No. If he was going to be hot and heavy with anyone, it was going to be Jaden.

"I don't get it, Briz. Why don't you like me? Guys usually respond really well to me."

"I don't dislike you, Ava," he said flatly.

"Do you ever...think about me...want me?" She said the words as if she was lapping whipped cream from his body.

"Nope," Briz answered too abruptly.

Ava smiled and gave him one of her flirty, come-and-get-it looks. That was all it took. Briz knew perfectly well how one act of indiscretion could change a person's entire life. He went into the living room to sleep on the couch.

CHAPTER 26

BRIZ

Briz groaned as Torus jumped onto his chest. The cat purred contentedly, kneading its sharp claws into the afghan that covered him. It took a moment for Briz to remember why he was sleeping on the couch. Then he groaned again. Now that it was morning, he wanted to get Ava out of the house before his family woke up.

He crept into his room and quietly repeated Ava's name until her eyes opened.

"Mm, I knew you'd change your mind." Ava rolled over, reaching for him.

Briz stepped back. He swore she thrived on rattling him. "No," he whispered. "It's time for you to leave."

"What?" Her arms flopped back onto the bed. "The sun's not even up."

"Yes, it is." Briz pulled open the curtain, prompting Ava to squeeze her eyes shut. "You have to leave before everyone gets up."

"Where am I supposed to go this early?"

"Shh! You'll wake my parents."

Ava opened her eyes and focused on the clock. "It's only six thirty. I can't even see my mom until eight o'clock. The hospital won't get all the paperwork done till noon."

"I don't know. Go wait in the donut shop."

"I. Don't. Eat. Donuts." Ava glared.

"Come on, hurry up. I want to go get Jade."

"Fine."

Ava flipped the covers off so quickly, Briz didn't have time to prepare himself. His hormones hijacked his body as he stared at her magenta panties, the way his ribbed tank undershirt hugged her like Saran wrap.

He had to refrain from yelling, *Help me!*

"You had your chance," she gloated.

When had he become a saint? Grover would be all over her.

Briz sounded as breathless as if he'd just run a fifty-yard dash. "You're a real case."

"I'm a case? And what's *your* problem?" she goaded, as she started to remove the undershirt. "Thanks for the loan. You didn't give me anything to sleep in before you rushed out of here last night. I found this in your drawer."

Briz turned to face the wall, suppressing his impulse to look back around. "Just get dressed."

"Yeah, yeah. Don't have a tizzy fit. I won't be back to tempt you tonight."

"What is it with you? Jade said your boyfriend wears a purity ring as a sign of his chastity. Is it a joke to make his parents think he's not obsessed with sex like other teens?" Briz could feel Ava's grin sliding over him.

When Ava was finally out the door, Briz left for Guyon Manor. He glanced in the back of his car at all the camping gear he wouldn't be using. Guilt and uncertainty undermined his sense of purpose as he tried to grasp all the recent events. *Jaden attacked. Ava in his bed. The triplets. Bayou monsters. A flying human-bug-fairy thing.*

He muttered the words his mom had been telling him since he was a little kid: "There are no accidents in life, no coincidences. Everything happens for a reason." So, why this? What was the reason for it? He should be having a good time. *I could die before I even get to indulge in the sweetness of love.*

Briz laughed shakily, the sound sinking beneath the hum of the tires on the road.

My folks have made me read way too much poetry. Maybe he should have taken up Ava's offer and gone to bed with her to remind himself he was a normal guy.

Once he reached the dirt road, his thoughts shifted to his main goal for the day: not being killed. He looked for the trail where he'd followed Jaden. He couldn't see it. But he knew when he drove past it—the sores on his leg stung, his nerves felt jagged. He felt the urge to speed away.

Why am I risking my life for Jade? He'd only known her a couple of weeks. It wasn't the promise of getting laid. He had plenty of willing girls to choose from. There was something about her.

From the moment Briz happened to follow her into Twyla Mae's Coffee Shop, and quasi-bookstore—the bayou's version of a SoHo hangout—he knew she wasn't from Belle Fleur.

Her backpack had made him smile—a series of small ink drawings decorated the sides, showing the earth being held in masculine hands, the earth having its life squeezed out of it, then the earth tossed into a trash can, its tiny speech balloon pleading, "Help me."

On the flap were a couple of handwritten website URLs. The girl was a walking billboard, encouraging onlookers to save the planet.

Briz had lowered his eyes to take in the way her hips swayed. Turning around, she caught him at it, gave him an indignant look, then marched over to the book aisle.

He waited a minute, then strolled over. She was looking at a volume he'd just read. Gathering his nerve, he said, "It's a good book."

She put it back on the shelf.

He chuckled. "Don't hold it against the author just because I liked it."

This time she smiled.

"I'm Briz."

"Jaden."

Her voice was smooth as the jade ring she was twisting around her finger, her features striking.

A woman who appeared to be her mother walked over carrying a to-go cup of coffee. "Jade, you ready?"

Jaden grabbed the book he'd recommended, gave him another smile, then followed her mom to the line at the register. Briz felt a pang of regret as she walked away. He wanted to know her well enough that she'd let him call her Jade.

What did he have to lose? He asked the cashier for a pen and a piece of scratch paper, wrote down his number, and handed it to Jaden. "If you like the book, give me a call and I'll recommend some others."

He'd known there was a good chance that she would toss his number out. It had taken her a couple of days to call. When she did, he found they had a lot in common. He had no intentions of repeating past mistakes and was going to take things slow.

"What the—" Thoughts of when he'd met Jaden skidded away as Briz swerved the car. It was too late. About forty yards from the entrance to Guyon Manor, something purple shot directly toward his windshield.

Violet bounced off the window, then hit the hood with a thud.

She's definitely real.

"Are you all right?" he asked, jumping out of his car.

"Forgive me." Winded, Violet sat up. "I am having a difficult time flying."

"Yeah, I can see that."

With a tree branch for a crutch, she limped across the hood of his car. Briz leaned over, scooping her up as if she were a bird that had tumbled from a tree.

"The Mal Rous are at the house searching for me and waiting for the workers to arrive." She pointed to a mass of leaves hanging over the stone wall. "I was hiding in that magnolia tree when I saw you coming. I had to stop you."

"Well, you did. Thanks." Briz hoped Ava had remembered to call Carl.

"May I ask why you're here?" Violet inquired as Briz set her on the passenger seat. "Were you able to find the triplets? Where is Jaden?"

The corners of Briz's mouth turned up as Violet posed her questions. Even while stalked by the Mal Rous, she was insistently polite and articulate.

"Jaden's with the triplets. I came to find you so I can take you to their house." Buckling his seat belt, he made a U-turn.

"Oh, no. I can't go with you."

"I'm not leaving you here, Violet." He glanced down at

her, then in his mirror to see if they were being followed. "You'll be okay. The triplets wouldn't hurt you."

"If you have told them about the Mal Rous, they will regard me as one of them. They will be afraid of me. They will hate me."

"No, they won't. The triplets know you helped Jaden and me." Briz paused. Okay, technically he hadn't told them about Violet. "Besides, you're the only one who can help us, the only one who knows the Mal Rous. We have to stop them. They've already started going after people in town."

"I don't know how to stop them."

"Any information you can give us is better than nothing. You could have the answers and not even know it." Briz flinched as he asked, "Since Jade was bitten, aren't all of you sort of related now?"

"We were already related. She has both Dekle and Elvina's DNA." Violet inhaled a deep breath, then released it. "A little more than kin, and less than kind."

"Hamlet." Briz looked in the mirror again.

"Since you have read the play, you are aware that it is a tragedy." Violet sighed.

"Violet, Shakespeare wrote comedies too; *Twelfth Night* and *As You Like It*."

Violet remained silent. Briz took her lead and stopped talking, concentrating instead on finding a way to persuade her to help him. Them. Everyone.

"Okay, Violet..." Briz broke the silence when they reached the edge of town. "I get it. You don't want to upset the triplets. Only it's a little late for that. I'm pretty sure knowing the Mal Rous are back has already upset their world big time. They'll be relieved knowing I found someone who can help." Easing his foot off the gas pedal, Briz looked down at her. "If we don't do anything, the Mal Rous will keep hurting people. How many people would be changed, like you said the Professor was?" With a catch in his throat, he added, "Like Jade."

Violet pressed her hand against her heart. The gesture made Briz hopeful. Tears welled up in her eyes. She quickly wiped them away. Then pursing her lips she stared straight ahead as if determined to shut him out.

Will I have to force her? Briz looked back at the road, wondering just how different Violet was from the Mal Rous. Could she kill him in an instant? Ever so slightly, he turned his head to size her up. She couldn't be that dangerous—she was only twelve inches tall. He swallowed his trepidation like a bitter-tasting medicine.

"Violet, don't you get it? Can't you see how important it is for you to tell us everything you know about them?" Briz's voice rose as he had another thought. "They can't procreate, can they?"

Violet didn't answer.

Oh great. More silence. What's that mean?

A few minutes passed before she asked, "Do the triplets live in town?"

Briz wondered if this was a good sign. *She didn't say yes, but she didn't say no.* "They live on the bayou. I don't think I can find the place on my own. Hubs will take us."

"Hubs. No. I will not be responsible for harming him more."

So she is dangerous. "What do you mean? You're not going to attack him, are you?"

"No. No, Briz. I would never do so. But my presence would be a reminder of what the Mal Rous did to him. Even after all these years, I can hear Datura bragging about every last detail. If Hubs were to see me—"

"How about if I hide you from him? You could talk to the triplets after he goes. Would that work for you?"

They were almost at Hubs's trailer. He had to get Violet to agree.

"Have you read all of Shakespeare's writings?" she asked.

"Shakespeare?" Puzzled, Briz decided that by answering his question with an unrelated question, she had just agreed to go to the triplets. "Not all of them, but more than I wanted to. My mom's an English lit professor. She makes my sisters and me read a lot of stuff most kids don't have to. Poetry. The classics."

"Clearly, you have very good parents. Appreciate them." Violet folded her hands in her lap. "I only had Dekle. He was never a very good role model."

"You turned out pretty good, in spite of him."

"Thank you." Violet gazed down at her hands. "He was the Mal Rous' role model, too."

Briz gave a nod of understanding. Then, scratching his head, he questioned why it felt so normal to interact with this peculiar being, functioning in this utterly surreal reality. Were his sisters right? They'd always told him if he kept reading so many fantasy books, one day he wouldn't be able to tell reality from fiction.

When Briz pulled into the cafe parking lot, Violet climbed in the back seat and tucked herself between some of the camping gear. It was eight in the morning; the heat was already visible as Briz walked over to Hubs's trailer. Moist air circled his feet, rising like smoke signals, as if sending a warning to Hubs, announcing Briz's deceitful intentions.

After one knock, the door swung open to reveal Hubs, his eyes tired and brooding.

With a pasted-on smile, Briz said, "Morning."

"Ya's ea-early. I ha-have to f-finish up at work." The two metal steps sagged under Hubs's weight as he stepped down and shut the door.

"Hey, Hubs..." Beads of moisture sprang out on Briz's forehead, broadcasting his anxiety that Hubs might see Violet, or Violet might see Hubs. "Do you have a paper bag I can use?" he asked, wiping his brow.

It had occurred to Briz that Violet would be less susceptible to heatstroke if she were in a sack instead of stuffed into his nylon backpack. Briz forced another smile. *Oh yes, my feeble plan.*

"Uh, before you go back to the..." Briz gestured awkwardly at the cafe, then stuffed his sweaty hands into the pockets of his shorts.

Hubs scanned Briz from head to toe and side to side. He seemed to be questioning Briz's intentions. Then, opening the pocket-sized door he went back in. Briz peeked in from the doorway.

The place was clean and tidy. A small oil painting of the triplets' house hung on the wall above the kitchen counter; Briz assumed Hubs's father had painted it. Beneath the curved ceiling, a bookshelf held volumes on subjects ranging from auto mechanics to traveling in Italy to how to stop stuttering. On the small dining table sat a laptop computer.

It seemed that Hubs's trailer was his haven. Only those who had proven themselves worthy could enter.

With Violet hiding in his car, Briz was sure he was anything but worthy.

Briz drew his head back and looked down at his feet as Hubs emerged and handed him a bag.

"Thanks, Hubs. I appreciate it."

The more Briz was around this man, the more he believed that Hubs had made peace with the physical and mental wounds he'd received from the Mal Rous. Perhaps even with the residents of this town. What about Hubs's emotional scars, the ones embedded in his psyche? Had they healed, too? Was he ready to face the Mal Rous again?

Hubs walked toward the cafe, as Briz hurried back to his car, unconvinced that his laughable plan to conceal Violet would work.

CHAPTER 27

HUBS

The smells and noises in the cafe were too much for Hubs. He hadn't had any sleep last night, worrying about his mama and aunties, thinking about the Mal Rous. Now the early morning regulars, their chattering coffee buzz, the music pumping through the speakers all made him want to run out the door. Stella, the head waitress who'd worked with Hubs for thirty years, took one look at him and told him to leave. She'd finish up.

He didn't argue.

Hubs tried to steady his head to stop it from swaying side to side as he walked through the parking lot. Briz was standing by his open car door, carefully lowering something into the paper bag. Hubs came up quietly behind him and froze as his eyes locked on the creature Briz was holding.

A scream lodged in Hubs's chest. He felt like he might choke on his own spit. Fear crashed over him. All he could do was brace himself to die. He knew Briz was talking to him, but Briz's words sounded garbled, as if the boy were swimming in a pond of mire and deceit.

Hubs wasn't even aware that his legs had been moving until he was in his car, speeding away. As a child, he'd learned it's better to run than be brutally attacked, whether by bayou *bebettes* or town bullies. The theory of fight or flight was meaningless to him. Fleeing was his only chance of survival. He wished he'd done that when he was six years old, but he'd been too scared.

Memories crept through the fragile layers of his mind as Hubs barreled down the road, memories that he'd spent his life trying to ignore.

Now the scenes played over and over in his head. He was alone in the cottage. His papa had gone up to the estate to help Elvina with some chores. Afterward he was going to take Hubs to Mama's.

Hubs was having fun playing. He'd told his papa he'd be okay, promised him he wouldn't go outside and get bitten by some bayou varmint. Hubs thought of himself as a big kid. After all, he was in the first grade. When the front door burst open, he thought it was his papa returning. Instead, five *rougarous* strutted in. Hubs had heard stories about them, but his parents had always told him they weren't real.

Terrified, he saw how excited the creatures were to find him there. They said they wanted to play. When they came toward him, Hubs realized they were smaller than he was. He looked toward the kitchen, panicking, wanting to run out the back door.

One twirled in front of him, singing, "We got ya...we got ya..."

All of them circled around him, jeering and cackling, saliva splashing from their snouts as they mocked his scared expression.

In one swift motion, they lunged for him.

Their tendrils and tentacles crawled over his skin. Fangs sliced through his clothes into his arms and legs. Claws swiped across his chest and throat. Horns repeatedly punctured his belly. Hubs covered his face as they went for his eyes.

They abruptly stopped when the one with snake-like hair screeched, "Enough!" The creature squeezed a tentacle over Hubs's open mouth and laughed. Then it let Hubs's head roll to the side. "Naw. Second thought, we'll let ya remember what it's like to play with the Mal Rous."

They stood over him, poking his limp body. Then they left him for dead as he lay in a puddle of his own blood and urine.

The memories made Hubs feel as if he were caught in the winter current of the Mississippi River. He drove the car faster, wanting to leave his past behind, knowing there wasn't any road that could take him far enough away.

It wasn't until he saw the Welcome to New Orleans sign that he turned back around.

When he finally stopped, it was at the Meadow Seniors' Facility. This was the only place besides his mama's where he could find a loving heart. Where he'd be safe. Even as the sight of the building helped ease his sorrow, another regret pushed its way in. Removing the key, Hubs rested his forehead on the steering wheel, remembering the day his Uncle Cape had stuck Grand-pere Sep in the home.

His uncle's remarks still angered him. "Stay away, Hubs. You and the triplets are an embarrassment to the family. Don't come around, or you'll never see a dime of your inheritance. If you tell your grand-pere I said that, I'll say you is lying."

The inheritance didn't matter to Hubs. What kept him

away was his uncle's threat to stop his mama and aunties from receiving their monthly stipend.

Hubs put the key back into the ignition. He sat there, trying to talk himself into going someplace where he would be nothing more than a stranger. But he couldn't. Right now, he didn't care what threats Cape had made. He needed to talk with his grand-pere; he'd always been there for Hubs growing up. He'd never cared that Hubs's words didn't come out as quick and smooth as other peoples.

When he entered the Meadow's lobby, a chill pierced Hubs as if icicles were replacing his bones. Outside his grand-pere's room, he paused with his hand on the door, shivering. He wanted to share what had been happening in the last few days with Grand-pere Sep. He longed to hear him say that everything was going to be all right. Opening the door, he found his grand-pere lying in bed with an IV dripping in his arm, keeping him alive, preventing him from moving on to the next world. Hubs had never been any good at hiding his emotions. He couldn't erase the sadness from his face.

"Hubs, my boy, I've missed you." Grand-pere Sep sounded weak, yet his eyes were bright. "Now don't you fret about me. I'm going to be just fine."

Hubs sat in a chair next to the bed. They were silent for a moment, taking in each other's presence.

"It's good to see you, Hubs." Grand-pere Sep took his hand. "I know you don't come around much because of your Uncle Cape. The staff here won't say anything to him. Besides, he hasn't been to visit me since your aunt Laura divorced him and he moved up to Shreveport." He paused, somewhat winded. "I don't know what's the matter with that boy. Don't let him upset you."

"Grand-pere Se-Sep." Hubs was about to tell him how afraid he was, that he didn't know what to do. As usual, the words got jumbled up in Hubs's head. For once in his life, he was grateful for the flaw. The last thing he wanted to do was upset his grand-pere.

"Hubs, you need to come see me more often. It gets lonely here. I enjoy your company. Sure would be nice if you could get your mama and aunties to come visit me. They wouldn't have to see any town folks. Just drive them here on the new highway." With a wink, he added, "Or you could sneak me out of this place for a day."

Hubs smiled, patting his hand.

"Are you still seeing your lady friend?"

Hubs looked down, shaking his head.

"Well," his grand-pere patted Hubs's hand in turn, "maybe you can find someone who lives closer, so you don't have to drive forty miles for a date."

The two men sat together. Their breathing kept rhythm with the drip of the IV. Hubs was grateful that his grand-pere was used to his quietness.

After some time, Grand-pere Sep blinked back a tear. "Did you meet Elvina's granddaughter? Is that why you're here?"

Hubs felt his heart race as he nodded. "Ja-Jaden." He couldn't stop his body from shuddering when he said her name. "Sh-she's at Mama's." Worry knotted itself up in his neck. He rubbed the knots, trying to let go of all the unease he was carrying around.

"My dear boy, do what you can to help her. She's a part of Elvina." With what strength Grand-pere Sep had, he squeezed Hubs's hand. "Elvina was so good to all of you," he wheezed. "Still..." His face creased with fine lines, resembling a piece of old parchment. "No, on second thought, I don't want you to do something that will cause you more pain."

His grand-pere seemed so fragile. Hubs chose not to tell him that Jaden had been bitten. Instead, mustering up a smile, he changed the subject. "I've been th-thinking about t-taking a trip. Always w-wanted to go to Italy."

"We should make that happen for you." Grand-pere Sep wiggled Hubs's hand. Even though Hubs was well beyond middle-aged, he knew that his grand-pere regarded him as his precious grandchild.

Hubs stumbled over his words more than usual, talking about the books he'd been reading, his job, the tablet he'd set up with music for his mama and aunties. As always, Grand-pere Sep enjoyed sharing all the changes he'd seen during his lifetime—how back when he was a mere baby, women had just won the right to vote; televisions and computers didn't exist.

When the time came to say good-bye, Grand-pere Sep leaned forward and gave Hubs a long hug, holding onto him, not wanting to let him go.

"It's okay. I-I'll come b-back soon." Hubs lowered his grand-pere against the pillow, helping him get comfortable.

"Hubs." Grand-pere Sep took hold of his arm. "I know I told you to go away. But this needs to be said, too. I've come to learn that life boils down to confronting our fears. And our regrets."

He paused for a moment, then continued, "I believe there comes a time in everyone's life when they must face them. Sometimes more than one. Some of them bigger than others. 'Cause fear likes to rear up its ugly head. Eventually, your journey is going to lead you right back to it. Hopefully, once it's been denied any power, you'll have an opportunity to go forward on a different path. A better path."

Draped in the Louisiana heat, Hubs walked back to his car. Pushing past the tightness in his chest and the dark omens that were feasting on him, he wondered if he'd ever see his grand-pere again. Not because the elderly man's health was failing him, but because Hubs knew he was about to face his greatest fear—whether he wanted to or not.

CHAPTER 28

BRIZ

Briz watched Violet's pampas grass hair billowing in the breeze. Perched at the front of the boat with her wings outstretched, she seemed to be absorbing the bayou.

"Years ago, I spent time on this stretch of waterway with Dekle." Violet raised her voice over the noise of the motor as she turned back toward Briz. "The Professor's laboratory was in this vicinity."

"His lab? What are you talking about? How could he have a lab way out here in the middle of nowhere? Wasn't it at his house?"

"No, his real laboratory was in a salt cave. They are very sterile environments. At the time it was the ideal location for him to perform his experiments. He did some lab work in his cellar. The majority was done at the cave."

Briz had a lot of questions, yet he remained silent as she continued telling him all that she'd shared with Jaden about the Mal Rous—their sources of DNA, their excellent night vision, their acute sense of smell, the way the Professor had changed after he'd been bitten, as well as information she hadn't had a chance to impart to Jaden. Briz did his best to appear calm as she explained, though worry was taking root in his mind, settling in his heart.

When they approached two channels in the marsh, Violet's wings constricted. She stood, stretching out her neck. Her nose twitched as if discerning a scent.

"What's wrong?"

Violet pointed toward the channel on the right. "I believe *that* waterway would lead you to the Professor's laboratory. If it still exists."

Briz ran a hand through his hair; stimulating his mind, contemplating ways to help Jaden. "The Professor had to have kept records of his experiments. Did you ever see them? Maybe they'd tell us what we can do for Jaden."

"Yes. He kept his journals locked in a metal box, made from silver." Violet's brow furrowed. "Or were there two boxes, made from nickel?" She paused only briefly before adding, "Jaden was of the opinion that they might be at the house. However, in all the years I lived there, I never saw them. And now, as you know, it would not be wise to return." Violet sat. Her shoulders bowed forward. "I never expected to see the Mal Rous again."

"I'm sorry you have to do this, Violet."

Violet shifted her body toward Briz. "And I am sorry you have to do this as well," she stated in her always formal manner. She inhaled a discerning breath. "I know how worried you are about Jaden. I must say, for such a young man, with all the pressure you're under, you do keep your wits about you. Even when Hubs ran off, you had the foresight to go into his dwelling to find the keys to the boathouse and skiff."

Again, she inhaled deeply, as if absorbing Briz's emotions. With her keen sense of smell, could she tell he was also worried about Hubs? About finding the triplets' house? With his lips pressed together, Briz gave her the semblance of a smile, remembering how he had to convince Violet to continue on to the triplets without Hubs. Had she agreed because he'd reeked of desperation?

"Violet, I should probably tell you, the triplets are albinos."

"Yes, the Professor mentioned that numerous times. Oddly enough, he did not mind my appearance, nor that of the Mal Rous. Yet the sight of the triplets disturbed him. Over time, it seems, he lost his ability to be kind and understanding. Perhaps that is the real problem with the Mal Rous. They are not merely cruel, but soulless."

Briz stared ahead as he whispered, "Soulless."

Nothing more was said until the triplets' dock came into view.

"We made it. I can't believe Hubs's landmarks made sense to me." Briz turned off the motor and used a long pole to guide the boat up to the dock.

Violet shivered with apprehension as she climbed inside her paper bag. Concealed in her hiding place, Briz was aware she was placing her life in his hands.

He carried the bag close to his chest as he walked up the steps to the screened porch, his heart beating like a child pounding on a tin drum. Releasing a deep sigh, he rapped on the door. When it opened, he tried to recognize which triplet stood before him.

"Good morning, son. Come on in. Jaden is still asleep." The woman looked past Briz. "Is Hubs down at the dock?"

"He didn't come." Briz quickly shifted his gaze away

from her and guiltily stepped into the house. "Uh, are your sisters here? I mean, yeah, of course they are. I...I have some information that might help Jaden."

"I'll get them, son." Shuffling down the hall, she quietly called out Olympe and Tamara's names.

Briz made a mental note: *Okay, she's Isadora. Like before, she called me "son." She has on a lavender blouse. Her hair's in a single braid.* Isadora and her sister, Tamara, sounded educated. Though unlike Tamara, there was a gentle Southern lilt to Isadora's words. Briz thought the two of them might have spent time away from the bayou. Perhaps at a university, though it seemed unlikely.

Briz sat in the oversized chair. The three women settled next to each other on the sofa directly across from him, with Isadora in the middle.

"And Hubs, where's my boy?" Olympe looked toward the door, expecting her son to enter any minute.

When she spoke, Briz remembered that Olympe's accent was richer than her sisters'. He made another mental note: *Her hair is in two braids, she's wearing a blue blouse.*

"Apparently he stayed behind," Isadora replied. "Briz came here on his own. He has some information to share with us that may help Jaden."

The women sat up taller, their shoulders touching. Their steady gazes rested on Briz, seeming to register the fact that he was being very protective of the bag on his lap.

Briz lowered his hands, letting them rest on his thighs. "Actually, it concerns the entire town."

All three sisters' eyes widened.

He realized from this moment on, everything he said would most likely upset them. *And then I'll top it off by showing them Violet. Great.*

"The entire town? Why?" Olympe asked. "What's happened? Is Hubs all right?"

"Yes." Briz's voice squeaked as if he were going through puberty. He cleared his throat. "Yes, Hubs is okay." He hoped.

The triplets' mouths compressed into thin lines, as if once again they were reading his mind.

"I've, uh, learned more about what attacked Jaden and me...and her mom. And what it might mean—"

"Briz," Isadora said, scooting forward. "Jaden told us her mother was taken to the hospital. She's worried they won't be able to help her."

"I stopped by the hospital to see Brooke yesterday. She's going to be fine." Briz inhaled a deep breath; smelling Violet's fragrance, he curled his fingers over the top of the bag. "When I told you that Jaden got bit—"

Isadora glanced at the bag. "Son, she told us about the Mal Rous. How the Professor changed after he was bitten, and the creature's blood mixed with his. We know she's afraid the same will happen to her."

Briz closed his eyes and quietly said Jaden's name. His attempt at a calm facade started to chip apart. *Jade's going to be dangerous. Treacherous like the Professor, evil as the Mal Rous.* The room felt as if it was closing in around him. All the air was being consumed by his sadness.

When he opened his eyes, tears blurred his vision, melding the three women into one. He willed himself to keep his emotions intact, to focus on finding a solution. After all, that's what he was here for. That's why he had brought Violet.

"We'll do our best to help her." Olympe's words were tinged with doubt. "We had no idea what we was dealing with when they went after my boy. Hubs had called them Mal Rous, but we didn't know what he meant. After a while he called them *rougarous*."

Briz had heard the legends before, but quietly listened as Olympe explained.

"*Rougarous*. The *loup garou*. In the Cajun folklore, creatures with a human body, similar to a werewolf. After four or five years of nightmares, Hubs stopped talking about them."

Hubs. Briz felt guilt sweep through him.

"Briz...son, can I get you something to drink?" Isadora separated herself from Olympe and Tamara, as if they'd been attached by some invisible force.

His lips parted, but no sound came out as he slowly nodded.

Isadora returned, handed him a glass of water, then tucked herself back between her sisters. Briz gulped it down. Looking at each of the triplets, he spoke in a strained voice. "Other people have been attacked. The hospital's filling up with patients. We need to come up with a good plan."

"*We* need a good plan?" Tamara's tone matched her sullen manner.

"I guess I thought you'd have some ideas..." Briz's words trailed off, unnerved by Tamara's stare, "...of how to help us."

"Just what do you think *we* can do?" Tamara's words were crisp. The more annoyed she became, the more she sounded like a Yankee. While her curtness caused her sisters' white complexions to flush with pink blotches, it jolted Briz out of what his grandmother would call a pity party.

I'm such an idiot. They were already doing all they could for Jaden. How could he ask for more? But he needed help. He didn't know where else to turn. Briz gritted his teeth, not wanting to overreact or be disrespectful toward Tamara. It didn't work.

"I don't know what you can do, Tamara!" Briz felt like he was channeling Ava. "For some reason I thought you might be able to suggest ways to capture or get rid of them."

Briz shut his eyes, chastising himself. When he opened them again, Tamara was staring at him, her eyes—like her sisters', the lightest blue he'd ever seen—piercing into him. "Sorry," Briz said directly to her.

Isadora poked her in the arm and Tamara grunted, "Uh-huh," as if being forced to accept his apology.

Be kind. Always choose kindness. Briz could hear his mother's voice in his head. He looked at the wall of bookshelves, then at the triplets. "So, you don't happen to have the Professor's journals, or know if they're still in his laboratory? You know, in the salt cave? I thought maybe you'd been there."

From their dumbfounded countenance, it was obvious the three women had no clue about Dekle's underground laboratory.

"The salt cave?" Isadora's eyes opened wide. "That's where his lab was? That was why he had it declared contaminated."

"The salt cave," Olympe repeated. "Seems being deceitful was second nature to him. That man had no morals." She leaned forward, pressing her hands on her knees, regarding her sisters. "We all took for granted that Dekle wanted to help the town by creating cures for everyone. When Elvina found those demons, we started putting the pieces together...had a better idea of what my boy had been through."

The paper bag crinkled, shifting in Briz's lap. Demons.

He knew the word made Violet nervous. The women focused on the bag as Briz sat up taller, rustling the sack intentionally, as if he'd been doing it all along. "Didn't you help the Professor? Mixing remedies for him?"

"Yes, we did, but we rarely saw Dekle. He thought we were..." Isadora took her sisters' hands, "...unsightly. Most often, he'd give his formulas to our father to pass on to us."

In an almost choreographed move, the triplets stretched out their necks, their matching straight noses rising as they sniffed the air.

Briz stared at their identical images.

Olympe broke from the pose. "Jaden told us all about Violet." She folded her wrinkled hands in her lap. In tandem, Isadora and Tamara folded theirs.

"Violet is not a *rougarou!*" Briz protectively encircled the bag with his arms. "She's intelligent and kind. She wouldn't hurt anyone."

"Yes," Isadora nodded, "that's what Jaden told us. We understand she is nothing like the others."

In unison they said Briz's name.

The implication was clear. The triplets' eyes remained fixed on the object he was shielding. Briz turned his head from side to side. His neck was tight. He was getting a headache.

Hesitantly opening the bag he lifted Violet out, letting the empty sack fall to the floor.

The Bellibone's eyes were as large as cobalt blue saucers. Folding in her wings, she huddled against Briz's chest. Her heart fluttered like a dove caught in an eagle's talons.

Violet had told Briz she had encountered a handful of people many decades ago. Most had viewed her with curiosity and treated her kindly. Two encounters had made her fear for her life. But recently, besides Jaden and Briz, the only other sighting of her had been this morning, when Hubs ran away from her as fast as he could. Neither Briz nor Violet knew how the triplets were going to react.

CHAPTER 29

BRIZ

"Amazing!" The triplets' voices blended together as Briz set Violet on the end table. The three women remained calm. Not one line of fear or disbelief marred their beaming faces. Before they could say another word, Jaden's bedroom door opened. Wearing Hubs's oversized T-shirt, her hair uncombed, she slinked into the room and climbed into Briz's lap like a little girl.

"Hey, babe. I told you I'd be back." Briz moved her hair out of her face. "Are you feeling better?"

Instead of answering, she began sniffing him as if he was a drug she wanted to devour. Her pretense of innocence vanished. Everyone could see what her intentions were— especially Briz.

Not a chance! He grabbed both of Jaden's arms to restrain her from groping his body. Abruptly standing, he dropped her on the floor. He looked down at her, feeling guilty for what he'd done. Jaden didn't seem the least bit upset. She sat there with a seductive pout, looking up at him like an animal ready to mate.

The triplets' eyes darted back and forth from Jaden to Briz.

"Pheromones," Violet said.

Everyone's attention went to the Bellibone.

"Like the Mal Rous, Jaden's sense of smell is now stronger than a humans. She has acquired the abilities, as well as the needs, of an insect, a poisonous plant, an animal determined to survive—to mate. To keep her species alive." Briz stared at Violet, her words slowly sinking in. "There are all kinds of pheromones. All life forms, humans included release chemicals when frightened, angry, nervous, happy."

"And aroused," Tamara chimed in with a smirk.

"Some plants even communicate with pheromones," Violet added.

Briz felt like a lab rat whose breeding habits were being analyzed. He massaged his temples to alleviate his headache and hide his hot, flushed face.

"This is from the bite, right?" Briz looked at Jaden sprawled on the ground, pulling her shirt down over her knees. "I mean, her sister can be pretty aggressive, too."

"I am certain that this is because of Datura's blood." Violet cocked her head, observing Jaden. "It is causing her to function on a base level. Primal. With the Professor, in the beginning, some days were worse than others. It quickly—"

"She wasn't like this when I left yesterday." Briz cut Violet off. He didn't want to hear the rest. He didn't want to be told Jaden would become a soulless Mal Rou. Briz looked at the triplets through slitted eyes. They resembled a row of weathered porcelain figurines on the couch. "Isn't there anything you can give her?"

"You mean besides *you?*" Tamara's acerbic wit didn't sit well with Briz.

Real funny!

Frustration spread through every muscle in Briz's body. Mental, emotional, and physical frustration. From now on, he wouldn't identify Tamara by the way her hair was stuck in a bun, her preference for wearing maroon, or her lack of a Southern accent. He would know this triplet by her so-called humor.

"Huh." Olympe held her thumb against her chin, her bent index finger hovering over her lips as she observed Jaden. "We all thought what we were giving her was helping. She ain't had any since last night. It seems she'll have to be drinking it all the time." She walked over to the bookshelves and pulled down two oversized, tattered volumes which she wielded with ease. "I'll see if I can find a better preparation to balance her system."

Jaden climbed onto the chair and surprised everyone by saying, "You talk about me like I'm not in the room."

They all stared at her. Briz hadn't even considered that she might be following their conversation or grasping what they were talking about. Even two of the lily-white triplets looked stunned.

Not Tamara, though.

She marched over to Jaden. Small as the woman was, Tamara's intimidating presence made her appear large as she loomed over the girl in the chair. "I'll make a balm with licorice root. You can put it in your nose, so you won't breathe in his pheromones."

"I like the way he smells," Jaden replied with childlike innocence.

"Yes, honeychile, so do we—only we can control ourselves." Tamara didn't miss a beat. She spoke with a bit of a twang, chuckling at her own response. Following Olympe into the kitchen, Tamara added, "You being so intent on breeding with your boyfriend is just one of the issues we need to address."

Isadora and Violet gawked at Briz as if expecting him to respond. For a second, he looked toward the front door, wanting to escape. But where would he go? He was in the middle of nowhere.

"We all have a lot to talk about." Isadora shuffled over to the end table and gingerly picked Violet up. "Let's go to the kitchen. We need to see what all we can do for your leg." Isadora nudged Jaden. "Come on, child. You, too."

Violet's wooden demeanor softened. Her lips formed the suggestion of a smile. Briz followed the others, relieved that Violet was feeling comfortable.

He stood on the far side of the kitchen next to the back door, keeping his distance from his sexually hyped-up girlfriend. Jaden lingered near the hallway, fidgeting. She was reminding Briz more and more of Ava, making him increasingly aware of his own repressed desires.

"Spit in this." Tamara stuck a vial in Jaden's hand.

Jaden pressed her lips into a paper-thin line. Taking the vial, she looked over at Briz. He nodded his head like a bobble doll, encouraging her to do it. After she spat into the container, she handed it back. Tamara added water to it, put the lid on tight, and started shaking it vigorously.

"For now, dear, ya can savor this." Olympe offered Jaden a small bottle with drops of licorice oil. "Till Tamara can get the salve made for ya."

Jaden took a whiff. She stared at Briz as if she preferred his pheromones. He was sure she was going to make a mad dash for him at any minute.

"It'll calm your libido." Gesturing toward Briz, Tamara grinned. "And stop him from arousing you."

This time Briz glared at Tamara. She was like a bad comedian that he couldn't avoid.

"Here you go." Tamara walked over to Jaden with the well-shaken vial of saliva. "Every twenty minutes, put a drop under your tongue and rub some on your belly. Let it dry into your skin." Jaden's face pinched with distaste. "Go get dressed. Go on," Tamara insisted. "Isadora washed your clothes. They're sitting on the dresser."

With the bottle of licorice oil under her nose, Jaden disappeared down the hall.

"Now I'm going to make *you* some sage tea." Tamara pointed at Briz. "It's an anhidrotic. It prevents perspiration. It may help the situation by stopping your irresistible scent," Tamara waved her hand through the air, "from wafting through the house so readily."

Briz sat down between Isadora and Olympe. The slight breeze from the ceiling fan ruffled Violet's hair, making her wings flutter as she climbed onto the upside-down mug Olympe had set in the middle of the table for her.

The subtle movement of air wasn't enough for Briz. The house was muggy and warm. Or he was suffering from extreme embarrassment. He couldn't stop rubbing his forehead and tapping his foot. From the corner of his eye, he scrutinized Tamara. Honestly, he wanted to like her and be friends. As she worked at the stove, heating a chunk of wax and the licorice oil in a double boiler, she looked like a glistening snow queen melting in the sun. Removing the pot, she stirred the ingredients that were soon to be Jaden's salve and Briz's protection from Jaden's advances.

"Olympe..." Tamara said, zigzagging her spoon through the herbal mixture as if she were creating a magical potion. "Unlike the time when it happened to Hubs, now we have Violet's help. We'll have more information. We might be able to do more for this girl than we could for your boy."

Might be able. Briz winced.

Olympe appeared to grow smaller, sinking into her chair. *So much for being friends.* Briz thought about getting up and sticking Tamara's beloved spoon down her throat to keep her quiet about Hubs. Oblivious of the impact her words had on her sister, Tamara kept talking.

"If Jaden continues ingesting the bottle of her saliva, it should help to balance her system." Her words were as matter of fact as if she were discussing a new recipe for gumbo stew. "Though it would be a lot better if we could get some of that Mal Rou's blood."

Briz sprang from his seat. "You want her to drink that thing's blood? That's what made her like this!"

"Briz." Isadora took hold of his arm, guiding him back down onto his chair. "Tamara's idea is a good one."

"Whatever you *were* giving her was working? I mean, yesterday she was acting normal. She wasn't sniffing me like a dog." With his elbows on the table, Briz pressed his fist against his mouth as if trying to prevent a sudden onset of Tourette's syndrome.

"Exactly," Isadora said. "Which means it's not working as well as it should. If we could use the Mal Rou's blood, it would be so diluted there wouldn't be a trace. Hopefully, it would trigger her body's ability to heal itself." Isadora's light eyes stayed focused on Briz. "Are you familiar with homeopathic medicine, son? Treating 'like with like'?"

Briz nodded. His grandparents used arnica gel and homeopathic tablets for joint pain.

"Then you understand the benefits of ingesting a substance that is ailing you, in its weakened form, to treat the symptoms. Admittedly, we haven't any proof it would cure Jaden. But it wouldn't harm her, either. We must do whatever we can to slow down the process."

"Please, everyone," Violet unexpectedly joined in. "You must understand. Jaden's desire to mate is merely one of the changes she will experience. She will become more aggressive in all ways."

Briz was grateful Violet left it at that.

"Years ago," Violet paused, visually connecting with each of the triplets, "you brewed a mushroom elixir for the Professor. He referred to it as the herb of immortality."

"I made that there formula." Olympe smiled, clearly pleased with herself for remembering. "The herb of immortality is another name for the Amanita muscaria mushroom. I only made it that one time. He never asked for it again."

Tamara put a cup of sage tea in front of Briz, then went back to preparing Jaden's licorice balm.

Violet continued. "The day the Professor brought that elixir home was when Datura bit into him. A Mal Rou by the name of Talis died from consuming it. So, I—"

Olympe gasped. "Ya mean it was my fault that the Professor was changed?"

"What happened to him was his own fault, Olympe." Isadora patted her sister's hand.

"I was thinking..." Violet lowered her voice as if to make what she was saying less upsetting. "What if Jaden drank a milder form of the drink? Perhaps it would damage Datura's cells and prevent them from consuming Jaden's."

"*What?*" Briz pressed his arms onto the table and leaned forward. "Now you want to give her a deadly fungus. You do realize that killing her isn't the same as curing her?"

Jaden walked in and everyone became quiet.

CHAPTER 30

JADEN

From the way they all watched her when she entered the kitchen, Jaden understood they thought it would be best if she kept her distance from Briz. She stood at the counter, inhaling her bottle of licorice oil, trying not to look at him. Then he said her name.

Jaden almost shoved the small bottle of oil up her nose. When she looked at him, he averted his gaze to the cup of tea sitting in front of him. As if that would stop her from leaping over the table into his lap.

She kept her eyes closed while infusing her nostrils with the licorice oil. Briz's voice eased through her, telling her that her mother was being released from the hospital that day. Instead of feeling overcome with guilt that her mother had been attacked, Jaden was filled with a sense of determination and hope. She would do whatever it took to stop her world— and everyone else's—from spiraling out of control.

Suddenly, as if the triplets had been having a private conversation in their heads, they pushed their chairs away from the table and sprang from their seats. Isadora scooped up Violet, and the three sisters walked over to the kitchen sink. They worked together in perfect synchronicity cleaning Violet's wounds, studying her crushed bones, preparing an herb-soaked gauze, and fastening it to Violet's damaged leg with a stick while discussing her possibilities of recovery.

When they were done, they began scouring Olympe's books for ways to help Jaden—or, as Tamara frequently interjected, something that *might* help Jaden. As the day progressed, the conversation changed from healing Jaden to capturing the Mal Rous.

Jaden's chest tightened. Holding back tears, she imagined Datura's tentacles stabbing into her and sucking out all her blood. "Can't we call a government agency? Get the National Guard?" Jaden's comments were met with pitying smiles. "What if I could get the Mal Rous to drink rat and weed poison?"

"That might work," Isadora replied. "If it didn't, they'd never trust you again. And we might never capture them."

"And the Mal Rous would continue attacking innocent people," Violet added.

"What about hiring hunters to kill them?" Jaden asked, feeling hopeful.

"Jaden," Isadora's tone was compassionate, "I truly believe the fewer people that know about the Mal Rous, the better. I'm certain the creatures would fetch quite a large sum of money if turned over to the authorities. What's more, the authorities just might choose to recreate them—playing with DNA is a big thing these days."

They repeatedly analyzed the list of options and strategies. Nothing the triplets and Violet had come up with had filled Jaden with the confidence she longed for. Jaden surrendered to her pathetic fate of capturing the monsters.

Then she was getting the hell out of this town.

Jaden had finally permitted herself to sit at the opposite side of the kitchen table from Briz when Tamara came up behind her and placed a hand on her shoulder. "However we move forward, it should be Jaden's choice," she announced. "It is her body. Her possible death."

Stone faced, Briz slapped his hands on the table, causing Jaden and Tamara to jump. "Jaden will not die!"

She hoped he was right.

By late afternoon, Jaden found remnants of her old self returning. Apparently, the tonic she'd been drinking had done its job. The wild child within her had been subdued—though she suspected that she'd crave Briz, whether Mal Rou cells were pumping through her or not. Her willpower, the tonic, and the licorice salve seemed the best solution for maintaining her self-control. Still, sharing DNA with both Ava and Datura gave Jaden the feeling that she was genetically doomed. Bracing her head in her hands, she mumbled, "I don't want to be mean and vile."

"Now, we are gonna do our best not to let that there happen." Olympe patted Jaden on her arm. "Izzie, Tam, as I recall, the Amanita mushroom is a hallucinogen. Back when I made the tonic, that mushroom was illegal here in Louisiana."

Really. We're back to that again. Jaden looked over at Briz. His eyes had glazed over. He was either deep in thought or deep in despair.

"In small doses, it shouldn't play with Jaden's mind. Or be fatal," Tamara said, sounding more chipper than she had all day. "Though, we'll need to make quite a bit of the mixture to succeed at killing off the Mal Rous."

"Killing them?" Jaden swallowed hard. "I thought I just had to capture them."

"Yes, well, I'm just stating the obvious." Tamara's sisters silently agreed.

"The mushroom grows in Washington state." Briz held Violet's gaze as if he needed reassurance that procuring toxic mushrooms was the wisest option. "I have friends there. I could get someone to mail it to us. Or I can probably find it online."

Jaden grimaced as the triplets nodded. She would happily give the formula to the Mal Rous. But she had no intention of ingesting the nasty fungus. The one thing they did all agree on was that Dekle's journals might hold the information they'd need to move ahead.

They just had to find them.

After listening to everyone debate the best course of action, Jaden came to the conclusion that she would be spending the rest of her life drinking Olympe's subduing brew, sticking licorice balm in her nose, smearing spit on her stomach, and if possible, ingesting Datura's blood.

Oh, let's not forget. Every boy I date has to glug down large amounts of sage tea so I can restrain myself when I'm around him.

All this represented the upside of her future. There was the little matter of surviving the Mal Rous.

CHAPTER 31

AVA

What part of the word "vacation" doesn't Mom get? Ava blamed her mother and Jaden for her lousy summer. Of course, she was sending a lot of animosity Briz's way, too, for evicting her from his bed early that morning. A bed she never would have been in if her mom hadn't forced her to come to Louisiana to work on that dump of a mansion. Then there was the hospital. It took them hours to prepare a release form.

Brooke, who had no recollection of having been attacked, hounded Ava to know what had happened. Along with her mother's bad attitude and woozy head, she was bound and determined to go to Guyon Manor to get her purse, insisting that it contained her entire world: IDs, credit cards, money.

Ava tried to talk her out of it as she drove her mother toward the estate. No matter what Ava said, Brooke wasn't going to let some wild animal stop her from retrieving her purse.

Using Ava's phone, Brooke called Jaden.

"Why isn't your sister answering? She'd better not have lost my phone, too. Why wasn't she with you when you checked me out of the hospital? You said you'd been sleeping in the lobby."

Ava considered her options. She could tell her mom Jaden was staying who knows where on the bayou, which would only stress her mom even more. Or she could keep it to herself. Use the information against Jaden when Ava could better benefit from it.

"You know we're going to the rental house next," Brooke continued. "I really doubt burglars are sitting around watching our TV."

"Relax, Mom. You're in hyper-mode. What kinds of drugs did the hospital give you?"

Before Brooke could respond, Ava slammed on the brakes. The car skidded across the dirt to a stop. Hearts pounding, they stared across the road. A truck was rammed into the foliage, a man hunched over the steering wheel.

"Isn't that the electrician?" Ava clutched the steering wheel, her knuckles whitening. "I told them not to work. To stay away."

She jumped from the car and ran to the vehicle. Opening the truck door, steam rushed out, along with the stench of broiling flesh. Bile pushed its way up Ava's throat. She gagged out the man's name. "Rick! Rick, can you hear me?"

A pool of blood covered the truck's floor under him. More blood dripped from a hole in his neck, as if from a faucet that hadn't been shut off. It was clear he would never hear anything again.

"*Shiiiit!*" Ava's face turned the color of rotting lettuce as she thought of her mother's wounds, Carl's leg, Briz warning her about a feral animal on the property. She jumped when her mother took hold of her arm, then shrieked, "Mom! Get back in the car. Get in the car before we get attacked."

"What are you—?"

"HURRY!" Ava pushed her toward their car. "JUST GET IN. Mom, call 911. *Call* 911." Ava turned on the ignition and hooked her seatbelt. "Brooke. Hurry. Call 911!"

"Ava, where are you going? We can't just leave him. We have to wait for the police."

Sunlight glinted off the hood of the car, obscuring Ava's vision. Her mother's nails dug into her arm. Some *thing* emerged from the glare, crawling toward the window. Throwing the gears into reverse, Ava put all her weight on the gas pedal, sending the hideous thing tumbling to the ground. She shifted into drive, cranked the steering wheel and went flying toward it, then winced at the sound of a thud.

She stopped, her eyes riveted on the rearview mirror.

Brooke spun around. When the dust settled, they saw a small form sprawled on the road.

"Ava, you killed it."

"I ho-ope..." Ava choked as she looked at her mother.

Brooke's mouth was open as if a scream was trapped in her lungs; her body was slumped in the seat, unconscious.

"*Mama*," Ava whispered. "*Brooke...*"

Ava's eyes widened. Something tickled her neck. She stared into the rearview mirror, watching as tentacles wound their way through her ponytail, then slithered over her throat.

"Aah..." she whimpered, slapping them away.

Claws dug into her shoulders, poking holes in her shirt, cutting into her skin, sending a trail of blood down her arm.

A foul breath hissed in her ear, "Shouldn'ta left the car doors open, ya dummy."

Sharp teeth pierced into Ava's neck. Her head fell back like a slain sparrow in the claws of a cat.

CHAPTER 32

DATURA

The car lurched as Datura turned off the engine. The two women had been a surprise. Good and bad. Datura gave them each a heavy-handed slap for running over Esere. Tig followed suit, then helped Datura push open the car door. Ivan and Anders were already standing next to Esere's smashed carcass. Datura marched over to them, nudging Esere with her foot.

"Maybe he's just been knocked out," Tig said.

A crow circled above; cawing, it dove toward Esere before joining another crow on top of the pickup truck. Their shimmering black heads swayed back and forth, inspecting their next meal.

"Beat it!" Datura yelled at the scavengers. "Just cause we ate some 'a yer relatives, that were a long time ago. Leave us alone. Esere ain't gonna be y'all's lunch." Datura turned Esere's head from side to side, looking for a sign of life. "Anders, get some rope outta the truck and put it in their car."

"What for?" Anders asked, eyeing the close proximity of the crows.

"Just do it!"

Anders didn't budge. "Why?"

"We can use it to tie up 'em women." Datura pointed to the car with a chuckle. "They is Jaden's family—they smell just like her. Now we gonna see if that girl has turned into one of us or not. Heard 'em say their names is Ava and her mama, Brooke. We'll stash 'em in the Professor's cave. Maybe there's somethin' there to help Esere."

Everyone nodded, confirming to Datura that, as usual, she was right.

"Or maybe we'll find the Professor there," Ivan said smugly.

Datura gave Ivan a curt nod. It was an exciting possibility. But worrying. What would be Dekle's reaction when they wandered in with hostages, who might be his unknown relatives? Then learn she'd gone and changed one of 'em. Though Jaden had attacked her first. Datura had done it in self-defense. "Hurry up, Anders," she snapped.

Ivan turned away. Squinting against the sun, he kept his eyes on the crows as Anders clambered into the back of the pickup and dropped two ropes over the side. "And how we gonna get there?" Ivan asked. "You plannin' on sproutin' wings?"

Datura grabbed Ivan's chin horn and yanked his head toward her. "Don't be a bonehead. Same as the Professor would'a. Or we'll walk."

Ivan's eyes were thin slits. "It's too far to walk."

"Just stick Esere and 'em ropes in the car," Datura ordered.

Ivan and Anders dragged Esere over to the car and

stuffed him between Brooke's feet. Slouched over, he looked as if he was merely lounging on the floor.

Datura started the car. She steadied herself on Ava's limp body and steered while Anders crouched between the girl's legs, pushing the gas pedal. The two women were strapped in their seatbelts, their heads waggling as the car sped past the mansion. At the end of the road, Datura plowed through remnants of a cane field, sending clouds of dirt spewing behind them.

The Mal Rous howled and cheered when they spotted the remains of the Professor's boathouse in the distance. Datura turned the steering wheel in its direction, launching a branch into the radiator. The vehicle hobbled forward a few yards, then bellyached, as if mourning its own death. Boiling water shot up in a geyser from the grill, covering the window with steam. The car thudded to a stop.

"Wake up," Datura said, slapping Ava.

The others joined in, excitedly hitting the two women. When their near-comatose bodies were roused awake, Datura climbed from the car. "Get 'em out. We still gotta ways to go."

Tig and Anders unhooked the women's seatbelts and pushed Ava onto the ground. Ivan heaved open the passenger door and shoved Brooke out. Clutching the car's doors, the women pulled themselves up. Ava had barely found her balance when Anders thrust the ropes into her arms. He hollered at Brooke to pick up Esere.

The women staggered through the cane, drugged enough to stay compliant as swarms of mosquitoes fed on their flesh. Fear and confusion dripped from their pores. The Mal Rous breathed in the heavenly aroma.

At the boathouse all they found was a pile of rubble—

another sign that their Professor was gone. The organic sounds of the bayou escalated in Datura's ears. Her tentacles hung softly against her scalp. Tears. She could feel them welling in her eyes. Refusing to grieve, to show any signs of weakness, she broke off pieces of dried sugar cane and handed one to each member of her family—ideal for striking their prisoners—the perfect pick-me-up.

The women pulled away hunks of roof, digging through the debris as the Mal Rous thwacked their calves hard enough to make red welts swell, but not quite hard enough to break the skin.

Datura sniffed the air. Her stomach growled as Brooke froze, eyes focused on a spot two feet in front of her. Datura stepped closer, smiling at the nest of baby snakes. The Mal Rous eagerly consumed the delicious snack.

Once they uncovered the Professor's flat-bottomed pirogue, the women dragged the boat to the water. Its hull was intact, but the motor was worthless.

Tig and Anders jumped in, followed by Ivan. Latching onto one of the paddles, Ivan threatened to bludgeon the prisoners if they didn't do what he said. Brooke got in, placing the ropes at the stern. Anders stuck a paddle in her hands. Datura climbed aboard as Ava laid Esere's body on the ropes. Wading in the water, Ava pushed the boat from the shore, then pulled herself in.

"Ivan!" Datura smacked his shoulder. "Give the girl the paddle or we ain't gonna get nowhere."

Ivan reluctantly relinquished his weapon.

The boat glided over the fetid water. Sunlight filtered through the branches, breaking up the shade with a spattering of light. Datura's tendrils remained extended, sniffing the air, guiding them. The Mal Rous took turns injecting their prisoners with just enough venom to keep them sedated.

As the day progressed in the never-ending maze of channels, the Mal Rous became testier. The appetizing scent of terror that clung to the dirt and sweat covering the women's bodies, soaking their clothes, made the Mal Rous's stomachs churn with hunger.

The sun moved to the west, but the moist heat didn't subside. Datura studied the shore; there was no sign of the Professor's make-shift dock or the tree with the Professor's carving of a double spiral. At last, she saw the gradual rise of the land.

"Row closer to the bank." Datura drew in a breath as they neared the water's edge, tasting the air for a familiar scent. Then she yanked the paddle from Ava and jabbed it into her back. "Climb out and drag the boat onto the shore!" The girl slid into the waist-deep water; struggling, she pulled the boat onto a muddy bank.

Datura turned to Brooke. "Pick up Esere and get out."

"And you..." She pointed a bony finger at Ava. "Carry them ropes."

In a stupor, Brooke lifted Esere's limp body, then gingerly stepped onto the mushy ground.

"Ya two murdered him." Datura gave the women stink-eye. "I ought to do the same to y'all." She paced her words nice and slow, making sure the pain of what she said would be felt. "No, I'm gonna wait so Jaden can watch."

"W-what...what have you done to her?" Brooke spoke as if she were in a trance.

A snide grin stretched across Datura's face as tears fell from Brooke's heavy-lidded eyes. "She's just fine. She may even wanna join in the fun."

Datura stood on the bow of the boat, scanning the foliage. Any remains of the path that led up the small hill to the cave were gone. She jumped down, knocked Brooke aside and shoved Ava into the growth.

"Make us a path."

Slowly licking her lips, Datura watched Ava clear the way. Branches clawed into the girl, adorning her creamy complexion with crimson droplets of blood, tempting Datura to feed. Salivating, Datura told herself to wait until they got to the cave.

A third of the way up the slope, Datura stopped at a small clearing. "We'll bury Esere here."

"Whaddya mean, bury him?" Ivan pushed past the others and stood in front of Datura. "Ya said we was takin' him to the laboratory to find a cure."

"Ya dumb lizard, he's gone. He ain't breathed since they run him over. There ain't nothin' we can do for him. It's best we leave him here."

"Don't ya call me dumb!"

Datura ignored Ivan as she looked out at the bayou. "It's like he'll be watchin' over us."

Ivan stroked his chin horn, then nodded, looking at the view. Picking up a stick, he smacked the welts on the back of Brooke's legs. "Put Esere down and dig a hole for him." Then he hit Ava across her shins. "Help her. Hurry up."

The two women dug into the ground with their bare hands.

Datura's lips pursed as Tig traipsed off, leaving the rest of them to watch their brother being lowered into his grave. By the time Tig returned, Brooke and Ava were already covering Esere's corpse with dirt.

Tig skipped down the knoll singing, "I've found it."

"This ain't no time for celebratin'." Anders tried to trip her as she danced past him.

"Did ya hear me? I found the cave. Come on, it's not far from here."

Datura followed behind as Tig led the way, and Anders and Ivan prodded the two women up the hill.

CHAPTER 33

———————

AVA

Ava could feel the mugginess, hear the mosquitoes swarming her filthy body. Their captors hadn't bitten or stabbed her since they'd left the boat. Her thoughts were scrambled, as if she were coming to after being slammed against a concrete wall. All she knew was that she wanted to escape. Dropping the ropes, Ava lunged forward, grabbed her mom's arm, and mumbled, "Come on, run."

Drugged and disoriented, Ava stumbled over her own feet. Before she even hit the ground, wiry tendrils gouged into her, pumping a thick fluid into her system. Dizzy and weeping, she watched another creature latch his feelers onto her mother's calf.

"Not so much," their leader, Datura shouted. "They has to climb down into the cave."

Immediately the sharp tendrils retracted from Ava's legs.

"We just has to get 'em to the openin'," the taller one said, slobbering on Brooke, "so we can push 'em in."

Ava turned away as inflammations spread across her mother's limbs, grateful that Brooke was too far gone to feel the blisters bursting. As Ava crawled to her feet, her mind plummeted back into a poison-induced hypnotic state.

Near the top of the hill, they stopped at an opening in the earth the size of a compact car. Bleary-eyed, Ava watched as the creatures dragged a decomposing rope ladder out of the bushes and lowered it into the cave.

The ropes that she carried were snatched from her arms, then tossed into the hole. Scampering down the ladder, the tall one called out, "Send 'em down."

Datura led Ava and her mom to the opening, then yelped with glee as she gave Ava a shove. Ava slid over a five-foot incline before falling ten more feet to the ground. She lay there, a heap of bones held in place by her bruised skin.

Bits of sunlight shimmered on the walls. Her mother tumbled down, landing next to her with a loud crack. Brooke's body was twisted onto itself, limp and mangled. Ava heard the rest of the creatures climbing down, excitedly chattering about some professor's laboratory.

Brooke seemed unaware of the blows as Datura kicked her in the lower back. Ava wished they would all just let them die in peace. Then Datura walked over to Ava and slapped her across the face, yelling at both of them to get up.

Ava's eyes narrowed with contempt. If they were going to kill them, they could do it here and now.

"Fine." Datura gave Ava a baleful grin. "I'll just hurt yer mama till ya does what I say."

The beasts howled as Ava labored to stand and worked to drag her mom to her feet. The one with a dragon-like human head and forked tongue cackled and gestured at the ropes.

"I ain't carryin' these for ya."

Tightly holding onto Brooke, Ava struggled not to buckle over as she bent down to pick up the ropes.

In single file, they made their way through a lightless tunnel, descending into the cold, black earth. Though her senses were dulled, Ava could form one clear thought: *This is going to be our grave.*

CHAPTER 34

JADEN

Rays of sunlight pierced the sheer curtain, stirring Jaden from her dreams. The triplets' house was quiet. She had some time to think. To find a spark of courage. There wasn't a clock in the room, but as the morning sun grew brighter, the warmth of the day settled in. She knew everyone would soon be awake.

When she heard movement in the other rooms, Jaden got dressed and went into the kitchen, smiling, pretending that she was okay, ready to find the Professor's cave, locate his journals and triumph over the Mal Rous.

The triplets, Violet, and Briz, were eating breakfast. The five of them looked back at her, mirroring the same forced expression of confidence that Jaden had chiseled on her face. Everyone let her eat in peace. As soon as she finished, preparations for the day began.

While she and Briz loaded supplies into Hubs's skiff, Jaden could feel Violet watching their every move.

"I should come with you." Violet raised her voice, trying to sound convincing. "To help you find the cave."

"No. No way." Shaking her head, Jaden continued loading the boat. "If the Mal Rous are there, they'll kill you on the spot."

Briz glanced at Jaden before looking at Violet. "You've told us how far you think it is from the main channel, and I doubt there are any other small hills around. We'll find it."

Violet conceded.

When they were done, the Bellibone tapped the wood planks of the dock with her crutch. Jaden and Briz gave her their full attention.

"I know that the two of you grasp how serious this situation is. Yet, I cannot stress enough that if the Mal Rous have made their way to the Professor's cave, if they feel threatened, they will have no qualms about eliminating you, Briz—possibly you, too, Jaden. Not to mention the fact that they will find your families. It is most important that you wear the rubber gloves that Olympe has given you. If the Mal Rous are not there, I believe that eventually they will seek out the cave and will recognize your scent on whatever you touch."

The lines in Violet's sweet face deepened as she looked over her shoulder at the triplets, then back at Jaden and Briz.

"Also, I've been thinking. There is a chance the Mal Rous will decide to pursue me. If so, the triplets are now in danger, too. It may take them a few days to hunt us down. Nevertheless, they will succeed in finding us. All of us."

With Violet's sobering words hanging in the warm air, Jaden and Briz climbed into the boat and pushed off to find Dekle's cave.

Quite willingly, Jaden had spent the past few days cooped up in the triplets' home. Now she found being outdoors invigorating, even if it was for such a dire reason.

Unlike her last ride through the swamp, this time she was conscious.

She glanced back at Briz. They looked more like kids out seeking a little adventure than frightened teens on a quest to conquer dangerous predators.

For the moment, Jaden refused to dwell on where she and Briz were going or what they had to do. She allowed herself to be absorbed by the beautiful, primitive bayou that dripped with moisture, plants, and the chatter of insects. With feelings of reverence—and apprehension—she observed the leather-skinned alligators sunning on the banks as their ancestors had done for centuries.

She found herself in awe of the primal landscape. Yet she had no interest in staying any longer than necessary.

Briz cut the motor as they neared the channel of water Violet said would lead to the Professor's cave. From this point on, Violet had felt it would be safer for them to paddle quietly.

"Everything's so alive with color," Jaden whispered, lowering her oar into the water. She looked up at the sky sparkling through the foliage, then back at Briz. "It's like we're sailing through a painting."

Jaden considered that the bayou probably wasn't all that impressive to him. He'd lived in Belle Fleur for a while now. He'd traveled with his family to Australia and Bali—in another month he would be backpacking with his cousin through Italy and France. But Louisiana was the most exotic place she'd ever been.

"You should have more of your drink, Jade. You're delusional." Briz kept his voice low, looking at her with a glint in his eyes. "I feel like we're stuck in a vat of thick green paint."

They smiled at one another, but the purpose of their outing never left Jaden's mind.

The farther they went, the slower time seemed to pass, and she had to agree with Briz; it felt as though they were moving through paint. The air was warm and soupy.

At least a healthy covering of Non-Odeur, the triplets' homemade odor eliminator, on their clothes and bodies prevented the mosquitoes from bothering them as they rowed through the water. Hubs sold it to hunters to prevent animals from detecting them. They hoped that it would work with Mal Rous, too.

When the trees and foliage gradually ascended the banks of a small hill, Jaden and Briz guided the skiff closer to the bog that lined the shore. Ideally, their approach would have gone unnoticed. But their presence was announced by the flapping of egrets' wings as the birds scattered up through the tree canopy.

Jaden and Briz studied the large cypress trees, looking for the Professor's carved symbol of a DNA double helix. Doubtful that it still existed, they weren't surprised when they didn't find it.

"Let's stop here. We must be close," Jaden whispered.

To keep the boat out of sight, Briz maneuvered it next to some overhanging growth, securing its lead to a cypress stump.

The triplets had sent a supply of what Jaden thought of as "don't jump Briz's bones" tonic. Since the acidic-smelling brew had to be left in the boat, she took another big gulp, checking Briz out as she tilted her head back. He removed his knife from his pack and fastened its leather sheath to his cargo shorts. The weapon looked deadly enough to kill a bear.

Jaden's eyes darted over the landscape as she tried to remember where the Louisiana black bears lived.

Briz beckoned her to his side. They crouched in the boat, taking note of his compass to make sure they could find their way back. Neither of them wanted to risk getting lost. Both had heard stories of how crocodiles and alligators shed tears when they ate their prey. They had no interest in finding out if it was true.

Jaden watched Briz sling a bundle of rope over his shoulder, adjust his backpack, check his knife, flashlight, and water canteen. He looked like one hot swamp guide. Well, except for the dorky rubber gloves.

She took another swig of her bitter drink. The smell was so strong she decided to gargle with some of the triplets' odor control. It should be harmless. They'd practically bathed in it that morning. She swished some around in her mouth. After all, it was natural. Then, so was thornapple poison.

They climbed out of the boat, pushed it under the low-hanging plants and made their way through the growth, forging a trail.

Twenty minutes later, Briz pointed to an ancient rope ladder right where Violet had said it should be, hidden in the plants near a weather-beaten sign that read, "DANGER - KEEP OUT - CONTAMINATED: DEADLY - by the authority of Belle Fleur County, Louisiana, U.S.A."

The entrance to the cave was plant-free, the ground too salty for anything to grow. Jaden imagined her grandfather Dekle, Professor Demento, grinning as he hammered the sign into the packed earth, intent on proving himself to the world.

A cave. Jaden squeezed her hands into fists, the way she had when she was a child and her family had gone to

Carlsbad Caverns. She'd cried the entire time. This would be worse. The dormant poison ivy sores beneath her skin simmered at the thought of it.

Briz untangled the ladder and lowered it down, so it hung from its rusting metal stakes into the uncertainty below. He glanced at Jaden as he fastened the triplets' rope to one of the stakes. "For back up. I don't want to get stuck down there." As the rope slide over the edge of the opening, he pointed at pieces of cracked, brittle cable that poked from the foliage disappearing into the cave.

It had already been decided that Jaden would climb down first. Briz had been berating himself all morning for that decision. They both understood it made the most sense. Jaden should be relatively safe if the Mal Rous thought she was loyal to them. Briz was a different story. Jaden believed they would tear him apart and demand that she join in.

She wondered if she was strong enough to overpower Briz, drag him back to the boat, and the two of them could get out of there.

Then what? Suppose she managed to talk her mom into leaving town? Could she just abandon the triplets and Violet, knowing the Mal Rous would eventually track them down?

Not trusting the Professor's old ladder, Jaden kept one rubber-gloved hand on the rope they'd brought. She inched her way over the sloped entrance, down into the void, where she was engulfed by semidarkness. Her body tightened as her foot searched for another rung that didn't exist. Taking hold of the triplets' rope with both hands, she slid down the remaining distance to the cavern's floor.

Her feet met the ground sooner than expected. She lost her footing—gripping the rope, her fingers slipped, clammy in the gloves. She swayed back and forth on the balls of her feet like a bell ringing, sending out a warning of possible danger.

Shivers went up her spine as she found her balance.

The dark, the dankness, being underground—it had just never seemed right to her. She was fine flying in an airplane thirty-thousand feet above the planet. But graves were in the earth. For Jaden, this felt as alien as landing on Mars. Yet during the last few days, what hadn't seemed alien? Freakishly unreal?

Above, specks of sunlight snuck past the outcropping of dirt and salt that blocked her view of the opening. Jaden stood listening, waiting to hear the Mal Rous prowling behind her.

The goal was to find Dekle's lab and his journals. Not Datura and her pack of genetic mutations. Jaden pulled a small flashlight from her pocket and quickly scanned the cave. The size of a three-car garage, its walls resembled dirty milky glass, woven through with blue threads.

When nothing came charging at her, she signaled with a tug for Briz to begin his descent.

He was halfway down when a rung of the ladder broke. Before he could grasp the rope, he fell the remaining five feet. Jaden rushed to him. She helped him up, relieved he wasn't hurt, glad it hadn't happened to her, and nervous that the thud of his body colliding with the ground would alert their enemies if they were near.

Briz placed his hand on the small of her back—even that subtle action caused her to jump—and pointed to where the beam of his flashlight created a halo around two black holes.

Tunnels, exactly as Violet had described. Jaden's shoulders

edged up toward her ears at the knowledge that she had to venture deeper into the earth. Briz leaned closer. His lips brushed across her cheek, his mouth hovered next to her ear. She couldn't help thinking, *If the monsters are here, they are so going to smell me. Fear, plus lust pheromones—how potent is that?*

"I'll go first," he whispered. "When we come to the next chamber, you'll have to enter it before me, in case the Mal Rous are there."

Jaden's eyebrows knitted together in one tight line as Briz's gloved hand gently steered her to the tunnel on the right. Once their flashlights clicked off and the darkness concealed them, they glided their hands along the wall for guidance. The path sloped steadily downward, leading to more underground chambers. Briz's loud breathing in the cramped space made it easy for Jaden to follow him. Her own breath kept tempo with his in what seemed like a rhythm of potential defeat.

When the tunnel ended, smooth walls expanded around them. Jaden stepped past Briz into more blackness.

Violet said the Mal Rous could see well in the dark. Jaden wished she'd already acquired their trait of great night vision along with their arrogant, homicidal temperament. Both would help a lot right now.

Cool air chilled her skin as she emerged from the tunnel. Turning on her flashlight, she shone it around. The chamber was the length of a large swimming pool. At the far end, the ceiling was only a couple feet from the floor of the cave, gradually ascending to a height of about twelve feet directly above them.

No Mal Rous were in sight. Still, Jaden wasn't convinced that they weren't here somewhere, hiding in another tunnel, biding their time, waiting. Walking farther into the cavern, she longed for the security of Briz's touch.

Before she could speak, he stepped close beside her. The beams of light from their flashlights rested on a mound of dirty clothes in the middle of the room.

They moved nearer. In the same instant, both of their minds registered what they were seeing.

Bodies.

Briz held his light over two blank faces. Jaden gasped. Her sister and mother! She'd never expected this. She thought they were both safe back in town. Were they dead?

Jaden's heart banged like a clock ticking. Clicking away the minutes of her life.

Briz crouched down and felt Brooke's wrist for a pulse while Jaden pulled her father's knife from her pocket and frantically spun in circles. Her jiggling flashlight created demonic shapes across the walls. She listened to the sound of footsteps coming closer.

Jaden was determined to keep her family and Briz safe. She'd kill whatever was there. She'd shred it to death with her puny knife before she'd let anything near them. Turning every which way, she heard the sound grow louder. Cold clammy fingers latched onto her leg. Jaden lept back, angled her flashlight down, ready to strike.

"Jade...Jaden, calm down. It's just me," Briz said quietly, squeezing her ankle.

Hyperventilating, she accepted that what she'd heard was her own rapid heartbeat thumping in her ears. She knelt next to Briz. He tried to reassure her.

"They're both alive." Gently raising Brooke's eyelids, he shined his flashlight into her eyes. "Her pupils are reacting to the light. That's a good sign." He did the same to Ava, then studied both of their faces. "I doubt they even know we're here."

The two women were bound at the ankles and wrists. Filthy rags were stuffed in their mouths. Jaden couldn't imagine why. Who on earth would hear their screams out here in the bayou? The ticking clock in her chest grew louder, like a bomb ready to detonate, imploding her world.

Briz rested Ava's head against his arm as he removed the rag.

Jaden pulled the dirty cloth from her mother's mouth, took hold of her shoulders and started to shake her. "Wake up," Jaden pleaded, choking her back tears. "Goddammit, wake up."

Briz clutched Jaden's arm, holding it firm until she stopped. He pulled the canteen from his pack and handed it to her.

Jaden braced her mother's head, letting the water trickle over her cracked lips into her mouth. "We're going to get you out of here. We'll take you to the triplets. You'll be safe there." Jaden lowered her to the ground.

Both women were listless, too far gone to know Jaden was there, let alone what she was saying.

Briz moved aside as Jaden slid next to Ava. Supporting her head, Jaden allowed the water to drip into her sister's mouth. She wasn't aware that Briz had left until a clanging echoed through the hollow cavern.

She heard muffled footsteps, their volume increasing as they came closer and closer.

A dim light crept toward the opening, then blinded her as Briz entered the chamber. Jaden leaped up, her stance rigid, as she strained to see if the Mal Rous were prodding him forward.

"Come on. I'm sure I've found the lab." The tone of Briz's voice alleviated Jaden's fear that the Mal Rous were close behind. "I thought we should go in together." Reluctantly, she slipped her gloved hand into his and walked away from her mother and sister.

At the end of the tunnel was an oak door framed with large rustic beams crusted over with a layer of salt.

"Look. The cable we saw coming out of the bushes runs all the way back here." Briz pointed his flashlight at the ground where a cable peeked through the salt that had accumulated over the years.

He had already pried open the lock on a door that had kept intruders out for the past fifty years.

"That's it?" Jaden asked. "One measly lock to keep all his secrets safe?"

"Would you be wandering around an allegedly contaminated cave on the bayou if you didn't have to?" Briz removed the lock and rubbed his gloved thumb over its surface. "It looks like the Mal Rous tried to open it. These scratches aren't from my knife, it's their claw marks." He aimed his flashlight down. "They also tried to dig under the door."

"Why would they even want to get in there?"

"Well, they've lost the Professor. And their home. This is probably the safest place they could think of."

Jaden pushed open the door. Shining their flashlights around the cavern, they stepped inside.

The space was larger than the other two caves. It had a domed ceiling. A layer of salt coated everything. Test tubes lay askew on lab tables that were in the process of corroding to the ground. Salt-encrusted light fixtures hung from above like glistening chandeliers. Oak shelves held oversized jugs like the ones Jaden had found at the shack.

She shuddered to think what might lie dormant within them. Next to the jugs were small bottles, blanketed in a white sheen.

"Have you ever seen the movie *Doctor Zhivago?*" Briz asked. "You know the scene when Yuri takes Lara to the shimmering ice palace...?"

"Yeah, but this place feels like a tomb."

The cable reappeared in the room, connecting to an old generator with plugs to power the lights and a small, rusted refrigerator.

"Wow, check it out." Briz pointed his light at the cable. "It must have provided the chamber with solar energy created from salt. Your grandfather really was brilliant. Crazy, but brilliant. Ahead of his time."

Jaden cringed, hearing Briz refer to the Professor as her grandfather. In her mind, he was some wacko man set on ruining her life from beyond the grave. "How did he get all this stuff down here?"

"It would have been a lot of work for one person. But if he was young, strong, and determined, it probably didn't take him too long. Who knows, maybe someone helped him."

Briz guided Jaden along behind him as they looked around in awe at what Dekle had created. They stopped in front of a desk coated with salt, where a metal box sat buried under a dusting of white. Jaden tightened her hold on Briz's hand. Right now, he was her safety net from insanity and despair.

"Just like Violet described," Briz said, glancing around. "I only see one box. The other one must be in here somewhere. Do you have Amelia's key?"

"Yeah, in my pocket."

Jaden brought out the key. This was it. She'd find the mushroom formula and learn how to eliminate the Mal Rous. The white beam of Briz's flashlight struck the tarnished box as if challenging it to try to keep its secrets from them. Jaden slipped the key into the lock; it almost disappeared in the keyway.

"It doesn't fit!" Frustrated, she slid the key back into her pocket.

Briz removed his knife from its sheath, jammed it into the lock and popped it open.

For days, Jaden had been walking around wearing a layer of guilt like a heavy suit of armor. She exhaled loudly, but her tense muscles didn't relax. She raised the lid. The discolored interior glared back at them as their flashlights lit up the stack of five journals within.

Briz began placing the journals in his pack while Jaden hurried back to her mom and sister in the other cave. She was untying the rope from her mother's ankles when Briz reappeared at her side.

"I covered the box with salt again," he whispered. "I didn't see any other boxes. I tried to make the lock on the door look like it hadn't been opened. If the Mal Rous try to get in again, maybe they'll just think they were able to break it this time."

Jaden nodded. Right now, all that mattered to her was her family. "Come on, we have to wake them. Get them out of here." Sniffling, she removed the rope from her mother's ankles. "I can't stand seeing my mom like this. Her last memory of me is of us arguing."

"Jade." Briz touched her shoulder. His voice was

strained. "We have to leave them here. If we take them away now, the Mal Rous will come after all of us. All of us."

"What are you talking about?" Jaden recoiled. "I'm not leaving them. I'm not going to let them die!"

"Jade—"

"NO!" Jaden picked up the canteen lying next to Ava, ready to hit Briz with it.

He grabbed it from her. She reached out to swat him, but he stepped back.

"NO! NO WAY!" Her words bounced off the cavern walls, magnifying her outrage. She didn't care if the Mal Rous were nearby. She didn't care if she'd just announced their presence. "We have to get them out of here!"

"Your mom and Ava won't be able to travel for days." Briz spoke quietly but firmly, his composure upsetting her even more. "By then it could be too late. The Mal Rous would have tracked us down. What about my family? You know they'll be targets, too. And Hubs? The triplets? Violet said the Mal Rous would come after all of them."

"I DON'T CARE! *I DON'T CARE!*" Jaden's head felt as though it was exploding.

Briz knelt next to her, still annoyingly calm. "We can't carry them out of here. And they're not going to walk out on their own. They should be safe for now."

"Should be safe?" Even without Briz's flashlight shining on her face, Jaden knew he could feel her rage, sharp as a dagger. "We don't have to carry them. We can drag them. They're dehydrated, starving, poisoned, beaten. I'm not leaving without them."

"I just saw Ava yesterday. At this point, neither of them is starving." Briz took Jaden's hand. "Jade, please. Listen to me. To get them out of Belle Fleur alive, we need to find something the Mal Rous will trade them for."

She pulled her hand away. "The only thing Datura would be willing to trade them for would be the Professor. Do you honestly believe he's alive?"

"No." Briz's breathing was shallow as he forced out his next words. "If you consider everything Violet has told us, the Mal Rous may be willing to trade them for...*for you.*"

A spastic huff came out of Jaden. She wanted to spit on him. "Are you trying to make me feel better? Because you *so* aren't."

"Yeah, I know it's a crappy answer. But I'm betting they won't kill them if it means losing you. The Mal Rous have probably figured out that they aren't going to get the Professor back. In their warped minds, you're his replacement."

"You're willing to gamble my family's lives? My life? What's wrong with you? I thought you cared about me. I thought you—"

"I do care. That's why I'm here."

Briz lowered his head as he drew in a steady breath. He exhaled slowly before looking at her again. "Let's go back to the triplets and read your grandfather's notes. We'll find a solution that will work for everyone. For everyone, Jade— you, me, Violet, our families." Awkwardly stroking her hair with his rubber-gloved hand, he softly repeated, "For everyone."

"Don't touch me!" Briz's hand dropped to his knee as Jaden raised her voice. "Are you going to tell me you'd leave your parents and sisters in here to be tortured—"

"No. Probably not. But I'd hope you'd find the right words to convince me that I had to. That I wasn't abandoning them. That I was finding a way to save them. To save all of us."

He reached out to her again, then stopped. "Jade, I feel the same way about my parents and sisters. And if we don't put an end to the Mal Rous, they'll go after my family, too. They'll go after everyone we care about. Everyone they possibly can."

Briz was right. Jaden knew it, and she hated it.

What was worse, it was all her fault that her grandfather's vile mutations were free. It was her ill-fated destiny to try to finish them off. For reasons she couldn't even begin to fathom, Briz was willing to make it his destiny, too.

She placed the rags back in Ava and Brooke's mouths. Not as far in as before. Just enough so that the Mal Rous wouldn't notice any difference.

Briz walked toward the tunnel as Jaden tied the rope around her mother's ankles. Slowly rising, she turned toward him.

"I don't want to leave them."

"I know you don't." He looked years older in the light reflecting from their flashlights off the dirty white walls. "Believe me, neither do I."

Angry as she was, Jaden could sense his pain.

"Jade, I just don't want to ruin the chances of all of us surviving this."

Without looking back at her mother and sister, Jaden walked over to him. She felt as if the blue threads embedded in the salt were pulling free from the cavern walls and wrapping around her neck, strangling her.

"Okay," she choked on the word. "But we're coming back for them tomorrow."

Briz bent down to kiss her, but she stepped back.

"Or I'll come back by myself if I have to!"

"We'll get them."

Chapter 35

Jaden

On the boat ride back to the triplets', Jaden should have felt relief at finding the journals. She should have felt encouraged at being a step closer to getting out of their mess. Instead, she felt as if the ability to ever be happy again had been ripped out of her. She couldn't stop thinking about her family. Her rib cage constricted as if a manacle was tightly cinched around it, squeezing all her grief and anguish to the surface.

When they got to the triplets' house, Briz took Jaden's hand to help her out of the boat. Even his touch left her feeling numb—no electric shock, no pangs of desire. The wooden walkway felt like a ship's plank to her. She saw herself standing at the end of it, leaping off into an ocean seething with demons. Unable to tread water. Unable to save the people she loved.

Jaden stopped. Briz turned back toward her. His eyes met hers and she lost it. Her inevitable breakdown had arrived. The past few days of stress caught up with her. Her mind sank into a deep pit of emotional sludge. Her tears flowed like water cascading over a falls.

Briz dropped his pack and gathered her in his arms. It didn't help. Jaden clutched the back of his shirt and hung on as if to stop herself from falling into a black hole of desperation.

Her hysteria mounted. Her chest heaved. Briz held her tighter. She knew he was trying to be strong for her. Still, she could feel him weeping, too. They were both just kids. And kids shouldn't have to do battle. But that's what the next few days had in store for them. They both knew it.

Jaden knew they weren't the only ones in the world going through a horrific ordeal. Every time there was a war or natural disaster, children much younger than they were had to grow up in a heartbeat. Becoming orphans in a matter of seconds. Thrust into instant adulthood to fend for themselves. Jaden understood that they were on the verge of joining those kids and becoming part of a piteous global tribe, a club of child survivors.

Now it was time for Jaden and Briz to grow up fast. To keep their families and friends alive.

Maybe once they won this weird, eldritch battle, if they won, they could go back to being innocent, unaffected.

Or maybe there was no way to go back to being a kid once you've had to fight for your life.

Briz didn't shush her, didn't try to calm her as she held him tightly. He let her break down. It was unavoidable. Necessary. His arms relaxed their embrace when she stopped crying and trembling and grieving over what she had caused.

When Jaden and Briz entered the house, silence hung in the air, thick as the humidity.

Jaden knew the triplets and Violet had witnessed her entire breakdown through the window. Olympe, always the caregiver, led them to the kitchen and gave them cups of calming tea. Then everyone left them alone.

Once their emotions settled, Violet and the triplets joined them. Jaden let Briz do the talking. The triplets were beside themselves with excitement when they heard about the journals. Jaden realized they'd done a good job of hiding their doubts about her and Briz's chance of success earlier that morning. When Briz started to tell them about her mom and sister being abducted and battered, Jaden left the kitchen. She felt strangled by guilt and shame. Worn out, she nestled in the chair overlooking the bayou.

Soon they were all in the living room with her. They gathered around a table where the Professor's journals were put on display.

Violet fluttered clumsily over to them, weighed down by her injured leg. Jaden realized that the triplets had stopped burning their homemade incense that kept the mosquitoes at bay. Violet was all they needed.

Jaden was relieved that no one tried to dissuade her when she opted out of reading Dekle's writings. Diligently sipping her "anti-Briz tonic," she found that when there wasn't a harrowing event occupying her thoughts, her attention went back to Briz.

Isadora picked up one of Dekle's journals. Thumbing through the book, she read aloud.

23rd of June, 1953 ~ Dr. Whiting has asked if I could help him come up with a remedy for an epidemic of poison ivy that is spreading through the town. The fool. He hasn't a clue. The town residents' health will continue to be 'compromised' by my Mal Rous, until, lo and behold, I create the perfect formulas for the cures, making me appear a compassionate, caring person. I'll ask those inane triplets to prepare the mixtures. It will give the three of them something productive to do with their lives.

As Isadora continued reading, Jaden's ability to focus faded. She wanted to pay attention, to help the others find an answer, but hearing what Dekle had written made him even more of a monster to her.

There was no inner sense they were somehow connected, that he was her grandfather, or that they were related in any way other than sharing traces of Datura's DNA.

Jaden couldn't help evaluating her situation. Even if they captured the Mal Rous and pulverized their bodies into mush, what about her? What was going to save her from becoming like Dekle? Or the Mal Rous? Tuning back into Isadora's voice, Jaden was grateful she hadn't heard most of what had been read.

19th of November, 1954 ~ I brought more of the Amanita muscaria mushroom tincture home for the Mal Rous. I'd developed the formula several months ago. The mixtures I brewed originally must have been milder. That mousy triplet made this batch. It was too potent. Datura could smell it in my satchel. As soon as I removed it, she snatched it from me and refused to let go, determined to open the bottle. She wouldn't let me come near her to help. My impulsive pet broke open the bottle by biting it. Her gums were bleeding. When I tried to retrieve it from her, she clawed at my arm and plunged her fangs into me.

She didn't understand what she was doing, mixing her blood cells with mine. I experienced convulsions. A fever swept through me. Soon after, a bitter cold took hold of my flesh. When I woke the next day, my arms were covered in dried blood surrounding open sores.

Violet told me that while I lay unconscious on my cellar floor, Talis died from drinking the entire bottle of brew. I must tell that good-for-nothing triplet not to make it again. I was wrong about the tincture. It will not make the Mal Rous stronger. Quite the opposite.

As I posted in my earlier reports, until now they'd healed from any injuries within a few days. Even when that hunter shot Esere, he'd stayed alert, cheering on the rest of the pack as they killed the man. My studies showed that Esere's rapid healing and recovery, his ability to regenerate, could be attributed to the properties of his tardigrade, newt, and plant DNA. The Amanita mushroom formula is the only thing I have found that can end their lives.

Elvina questioned me this morning. She saw the truck in the garage and knocked on the cellar door. When there was no answer, she became worried. I have threatened her sufficiently to prevent her from trying to find a way into my lab. She says she loves me. I don't believe her.

Tamara interrupted Isadora and began reading from a different volume. Jaden figured the words wouldn't bother Tamara, however upsetting they might be to everyone else.

10th of December, 1958 ~ When I go to town with the Mal Rous to observe them, I enjoy breathing in the scent of blood. Like a coppery, metallic liqueur, it causes me to salivate. Now I take along hunks of raw meat to chew on as I watch in awe.

Jaden sighed shakily. At least I'm not like that, she thought. Not yet. She shivered as Tamara kept reading.

30th of December, 1958 ~ I forced myself on Elvina again last night. I had to have her. I wouldn't stand for her refusing me—not that she had any choice in the matter. As before, she cried, begging me to stop. Afterward, I left her sobbing while I went down to the kitchen and devoured a large serving of raw meat. When my darling Mal Rous returned, I sat in the cellar with them listening to music on the phonograph, quite satisfied.

All the content in the journals was disturbing, but these words haunted Jaden. Dekle's declarations of excitement at assaulting Elvina made her wonder—was her father conceived on such a night?

Jaden didn't want to become like the Professor, but she felt everyone in the room knew that the transformation was already happening. Violet had described a lot of this before. It hadn't meant as much to Jaden when it was about some dead madman she'd never known. Now it felt like it was about her.

The triplets, Briz, and Violet decided that all further reading would be done in silence. As the five of them scoured the Professor's books for the mushroom formula, the quiet pressed against Jaden's eyelids and she drifted off. She had no idea how long she'd been asleep when Olympe's voice woke her.

"Dad burn it! Why didn't I save that there recipe?"

"Olympe dear, that was over fifty years ago. You only made it once, and you didn't know what it was for," Isadora said reassuringly. "Besides, Dekle said it didn't work, so it wasn't important at the time."

Jaden watched Olympe's reflection in the window as the woman stood up and walked toward the kitchen. Jaden was still gazing into the glass pane when a faint image stared back at her. Olympe had returned. She set a container of licorice balm on the table next to Jaden, along with another large glass of her tonic.

Apparently, what they were reading in the journals made them decide it would be best to keep her tanked up. Jaden knew they were right. Briz's pheromones sang out to her whenever she took a deep breath.

So from this point on, my life will consist of eating raw hamburger, being sexually aggressive, and finding enjoyment from acts of violence. Jaden shuddered.

"Listen to this..." Hearing Briz's voice, Jaden wanted to walk over and climb into his lap. Discreetly applying the balm to her nose and taking a gulp of her drink, she listened as he read aloud the last entry Professor Dekle Thatcher ever wrote.

24th of April, 1959 ~ I had only gone out for a short time. When I returned to the cellar, I tasted Elvina's perfume in the air. HOW COULD SHE DO THIS? She knows she is never to come into my workplace. The lock was not damaged, which means she has found my other key. She saw the Mal Rous and Violet. That is where her perfume lingered most strongly. Without question, she will confide in her trusted Dr. Whiting. I have hastened back here to my lab. I am mixing up liquid placenta in which to store the Mal Rous. I shall hide them where no one will ever find them and return for them as soon as I can.

"Liquid placenta?" Briz looked up from the journal. "I bet you it was similar to perflubron."

Jaden and the others stared at Briz, waiting for an explanation.

"You know, liquid air. My science teacher talked about it. It's an oily, clear liquid that's rich in oxygen. Pretty wild, having your lungs filled with a liquid that's twice the density of water and not drowning from it. Humans can only breathe it for a short time, but I guess since the Mal Rous only have a small percentage of human DNA, their insect and plant DNA allowed them to stay in it...well, for decades. That means Dekle discovered how to make it before anyone else. Or he befriended someone who had and stole the formula." Pressing open the pages, Briz continued to read aloud.

I must clean out my cellar, make everyone believe Elvina imagined it all. I am thankful I acquired a vial of the rabies virus. I will inject Elvina with it. Everyone will think that she has gone mad. No one will listen to her. They will pity me and agree that I must send her away. It will be easier to bury the Mal Rous on the plantation until I have Elvina taken away and committed to an institution. Once the rabies virus has spread to her central nervous system, her death is inevitable.

It is important that I go through my lab reports, eradicate any reference to the mushroom formula in case tonight does not go as I have planned. If it fell into the wrong hands, my life's work could be destroyed.

Datura...if only our blood had never mixed. England...I miss the damp, cool air of England.

"These are his journals!" Briz gripped the edges of the book. "Not his lab reports with his actual experiments. We have to go back and find them."

"He said he was getting rid of the formula." Jaden spoke louder, more sharply than she'd intended.

"Well, we won't know unless we look." Turning away from Jaden, Briz studied the triplets' faces for confirmation that he was right. "I mean, why would he even write this, telling everyone the one thing he doesn't want them to know?"

"Because he was a raving mad egomaniac!" Jaden's

words were biting. Was having a mini hissy fit a good sign? Did it mean she was recovering—or that she was becoming more like her grandfather?

"Does anyone have any other suggestions?" Briz asked, scowling at Jaden.

"All right, fine." Jaden sat up straight and scowled right back at him. "First thing tomorrow we go back to get my mom and sister out of there, and we'll look for his records. Then I'm going to the shack to see the Mal Rous to convince them I'm their new best friend, so they won't hurt anyone else."

Briz set the book down, then snatched up the remaining unread journal as if it was his enemy.

The other four nodded at Jaden. What choice did they have? They all knew she would have to be the bait.

CHAPTER 36

BRIZ

Briz looked up from Dekle's writings as Olympe closed the journal she'd been reading and placed it on the table. Her sisters continued thumbing through the pages of Dekle's notes. Even though they knew they wouldn't find the formula, they still sought the answers.

Olympe gave Jaden a sidelong glance, then went to the kitchen. Shortly after, she handed Jaden yet another glass of the special brew. Then without a word, Olympe shuffled down the hall, the late afternoon light casting a flaxen sheen on her pale skin. Briz heard her bedroom door close.

He understood the woman needed time to herself. Caring for Jaden, hunting through the journals, worrying about Hubs—they were all in need of rest.

Briz went back to scanning the journal. A mere moment later, Jaden began to cry. He immediately went over, slid next to her in her chair and placed his arm around her, doing his best to comfort her without stirring up her urge to mate with him.

"Olympe," Tamara called out as she hurried down the hall. "Olympe, what do you put in that calming tea?"

Jaden's crying erupted into wails. Briz sympathized. Jaden felt like her life was being shredded into tiny pieces—he felt the same.

They had all been trapped in a state of physical, mental, and emotional turmoil for days, with no way out until the Mal Rous were eliminated. And if they weren't? If Jaden didn't survive and win, it could mean everyone's downfall. Hubs, the triplets, Violet, his own—they were all a part of this now. Young as she was, Jaden was their only hope. Their lives were in her hands. It was a heavy burden for her to carry. For anyone.

Olympe entered the room carrying a tray with a teapot of her special blend and cups for everyone, followed by Tamara on her heels.

Tamara's pale eyes focused on Jaden.

"Does that girl grasp how much Briz cares for her? What he's sacrificing for her?" Tamara directed her questions to Olympe, but her intent was obvious. She wanted everyone to hear. "It reminds me of when Billy left his family behind to be with you and Hubs."

Olympe didn't reply. Instead, she silently passed around cups of tea.

"It will cool ya down," Olympe said as Briz shifted away from Jaden and lifted the cup to his lips.

He knew it was true. The hot drink would make him sweat and lower his temperature. But he still longed for an ice-cold drink.

Before he could take a sip, Jaden's howling abruptly stopped, her eyes fixed on Violet. The Bellibone was sniffing the air.

A hush filled the room. Briz heard the sound of footsteps, quiet-like, sneaking across the porch. He could tell the others heard it, too.

They all held their breath and froze, like cursed prey. Briz knew everyone felt the same gnawing terror that the Mal Rous had found them.

Olympe's saucer and cup rattled in her hand. Her tea spilled as she set her cup down. Ever so quietly, she whispered, "We was being naive, thinking the Mal Rous wouldn't track Jaden here so quickly."

Briz watched Tamara grab the lamp from the table as if she were going to pound one of the brutes to death with it. Briz stood up, no better prepared, with only his teacup in hand, ready to charge them.

The screen door creaked. The air felt thick with dread. He swore he could hear everyone's hearts hammering.

The doorknob slowly turned.

Briz dropped his cup and rushed forward.

Violet shouted, "No!"

But it was too late. Briz slammed against the door, trying to shut it, but something was shoving it against him, pushing steadily inward. Briz's feet slid out from under him, and he fell to the floor.

The door opened against Briz's back as Violet said, "It's not—"

Hubs peered in, and Violet's words trailed off, "the Mal Rous...."

The sight of Hubs sent an eruption of sighs through the room as everyone expelled their fears and inhaled relief. Armed with a boat oar, Hubs stepped inside.

"S-sorry, I di-did-n't come s-sooner." Hubs leaned the oar against the wall. He stood taller than normal as he pulled

Briz up off the floor. They stared into each other's eyes as he said pointedly, "I di-didn't have a b-boat."

Olympe hurried over and wrapped her arms around Hubs. "Oh, my boy, ya must have been in a panic hearing Jaden's yowling. Most likely ya'd been expecting to find all of us being tortured by the Mal Rous."

Hubs gasped as he caught sight of Violet.

"It's okay, Hubs." Olympe took hold of his hand. "Now, this here is Violet; she's a...a Bellibone."

Hubs's gaze remained locked on Violet. Olympe stood in front of him. Placing her hands on his face, she gently tilted his head down and stared into his eyes until there was a silent exchange between the two of them.

Olympe lowered her hands, and Hubs rigidly tipped his head toward Violet, acknowledging her. It would take time for him to learn to trust the Bellibone, but this was a start.

Violet nodded back understandingly.

Olympe led Hubs over to the sofa.

"I'm s-sorry, Mama." Childlike embarrassment clothed Hubs's words. "I was s-scared." He glanced at Briz, then stared at the floor. "I drove away. G-got all the way to N-new Orleans b-before turning b-back. Went and s-saw Grand-pere Sep. Then locked m-myself in the trailer. When I wasn't s-scared anymore I f-found a b-boat I could b-borrow."

Olympe took her son's hand in hers. "I've been so worried about ya. I'm so glad yer all right."

"Everyone out," Tamara ordered, lifting Violet into her arms. "Let's give them some time alone. Briz, clean up that broken teacup, then come help us get dinner started."

Isadora and Jaden obediently followed Tamara into the kitchen.

"Ya know how much I love ya, Hubs." Briz heard

Olympe say as he picked up the pieces of the porcelain cup. "That's why I want ya to go back to town tomorrow and stay there till this here deed is done."

"No, Mama," Hubs said firmly. "Not less y'all c-come w-with me."

"I can't do that, Hubs. This here is my home. Yer Papa built it."

"M-maybe it's time to f-find a new home. M-move closer to Grand-pere Sep."

Briz sopped up the tea he'd spilled on the floor with a pile of cloth napkins. Then, stacking everything back onto the tray, he left Olympe and Hubs in the living room, where they sat huddled together talking, disagreeing, negotiating until daylight faded and it was time for dinner.

While eating, Briz and Jaden sat at opposite ends of the table, stealing glances and conversing in playful banter. Jaden seemed more like her old self, which Briz attributed to the calming tea and tonic. The energy from their bodies floated across the room like luminous fibers spiraling around each other.

"Has ya two ever had a chance to go on a real date together?" Olympe asked.

"Not yet," Briz replied.

He knew Olympe missed her husband, Billy. She'd told Briz how his passing had left a void in her life. Briz considered that back when they were young, the two of them never dared to go out to dinner and a movie. With her lily-white skin and Billy's ebony-black, it's likely they would both have been lynched. They couldn't even marry legally until the law prohibiting interracial marriage was changed in 1967.

"Well then, if you survive the next couple of days," Tamara said dryly, "you should take Jaden out."

Olympe discreetly raised her finger to her lips, silencing her blunt sister—though they all knew Tamara was right. After hours of discussing a dismal array of "battle strategies," it was clear that their chances were slim. "Don't be silly, Tamara. Of course they are gonna survive."

Briz and Jaden were washing the dishes when Briz overheard Olympe say quietly, "Meantime, they can enjoy tonight. Hubs, why don't ya go and put some nice music on?"

CHAPTER 37

JADEN

"That's it." Jaden handed Briz the last dish to dry. Turning around, she realized that they were alone in the kitchen. She wasn't surprised that she hadn't heard the others leave. Whenever she was with Briz, she had an uncanny ability to tune everything else out.

She expected to find everyone in the living room. Instead, Jaden found music playing and candles flickering on the end table. The curtains were closed. She couldn't see the porch, but assumed Hubs was sleeping in the hammock. His jumpiness at being near Violet was obvious, though he'd relaxed slightly as the evening went on.

Given the spine-chilling drama that she was currently living, Jaden thought she should feel more like Hubs, nervously awaiting a fight for survival.

Hubs should drink some of my tonic, along with that calming tea. Jaden had consumed buckets of it today, and it seemed to have done its job. Her more aggressive nature, and her obsession with Briz, felt relatively contained, though she wouldn't have thought the triplets would trust her to be alone with him.

On cue, Briz walked in. Sliding his arm around Jaden's waist, he twirled her through the room, making her head feel like it was filled with Fourth of July sparklers. When the music slowed, he pulled her closer. Their bodies swayed to the beat.

"What are you doing?" Jade asked giddily as her contained feelings frolicked back to life. "I didn't know you could dance."

"My sisters always made me practice with them when we were kids. Guess some of it stuck."

Jaden inhaled his scent as if drinking an elixir of ambrosia. She knew it wasn't just her own desires that were reawakened. His touch was causing Datura's cells to reignite, overriding the triplets' brew. The song ended, and Briz waltzed her over to the bedroom door. Jaden smiled in anticipation of his invitation to lie down with him.

"Hey, I'm spent," he said. "I'm going to crash. It's been a long day."

She frowned. Clearly, he didn't find her pheromones nearly as tantalizing. Maybe they were a little too heavy on the heartless monster side.

Jaden knew he was right. She should be exhausted, too. Instead, energy surged through her. "Why don't you sleep in the bed, Briz? I'm not tired yet. I'll stay out here on the couch. Anyway, I'm going to get something to drink."

A smile toyed at the corners of his mouth. Briz knew what she'd be guzzling down. It didn't stop him from briefly kissing her on the lips before he retreated to the safety of the bedroom—alone.

A few days ago, all she'd wanted was to be kissed by Briz.

Now she wanted to bypass second and third base. How quickly her world had changed. *She* had changed.

Jaden plopped down on the sofa, all too aware of her hyped-up feral senses. She was feeling brave, cocky, and determined, not just about Briz, but also about saving her family, and putting an end to the Professor's mutations. Jumping up, Jaden went to the open bedroom door.

Briz had taken off his shirt and lay stretched out on the bed, the candlelight from the living room bathing him in a golden glow. The mosquito net was pulled aside, as if inviting her to join him. Without warning, a fabulous glitch clicked in Jaden's brain; she had the delightful sensation of losing control.

All her innocence, hesitation, and insecurity flew out the window. Out of the house. Out of the state. She didn't know, or care, if Datura's cells had anything to do with it.

Jaden marched into the room, climbed on top of Briz, and straddled his hips. She leaned down, letting her tongue touch his lips as her mouth embraced his. His fingers entwined in her hair, guiding her closer, deepening the kiss. She lowered her hand to his shorts and was fumbling with the zipper when he pulled his lips away from hers.

"Jade, we can make out, but that's all."

His comment stung her ears, but not her willingness or her ego. "Why?" she heard herself whine like a child who wasn't being allowed to play with a new toy. "You started this," she said, her face hovering over his.

"I was dancing with you, Jaden. Not coming on to you. I thought you were going to drink some of your brew."

Jaden pushed herself up so Briz could better see her glaring down at him. "For being so appealing and cool, you can sure spoil the mood."

"It was my mistake. I wasn't thinking. Dancing can—"

"What's wrong with you?" Jaden interrupted. "Are you creeped out that I might be contagious?" She kept talking while he moved her body off his and sat up, making certain his zipper was up. "Afraid you'll catch the incurable Datura disease?"

Jaden laced her fingers around his neck, drawing him toward her. He systematically pried himself free and held her arms to her sides.

"Jade, seventy-two hours ago we had our first kiss. Maybe we can slow down."

"Slow down? I don't get you."

"*Me...?*" His eyes quickly scanned her face. "This isn't even you." He released her arms, adding, "And this time, I'm not letting things get out of hand."

"This time? When was there a last time?"

"The other night..." Embarrassed, Briz lowered his head. "At the manor."

"You told me nothing happened."

"And it didn't."

"So why not now? Come on, we're in a life-or-death situation. If we don't do it tonight, we may never get another chance." Jaden knew if a guy used this line on her, she'd be angry and out the door. But she needed Briz to touch her, tenderly, lovingly. To distract her from her worries about tomorrow. "Do you even like me?"

"Uh...yeah, I like you a lot. The real you. If I didn't, I wouldn't be here." He rubbed his forehead. "This new altered version can be a lot to handle."

She couldn't argue with him about that. Datura's blood flowing through her was making this whole teenage coming-of-age thing way too intense.

"You're the only person in this town I can relate to, that I want to hang out with. You're different from everyone else." Stifling a chuckle, he added, "Now you're a little too different. Normally, you're a lot of fun to be with—when you're not acting like your sister. Or a Mal Rou."

"What's that supposed to mean? You think I'm like Ava?"

"No, not normally."

"You just don't *want* me the way I want you."

"Of course I do. You're a total babe, smart...a good person." Standing, Briz stepped back, putting some space between the two of them.

'Total babe' was all that Jaden heard. It was as if he had recited a love sonnet to her. "So...?"

"It's not you. It's..." Briz's hands went to his hair, tugging it as if he wanted to pull it out by the roots. "You have no idea of how much self-control I'm using."

"Self-control," Jaden scoffed, ogling his bare chest. "I'm offering myself to you. What's stopping you?"

"I know you think I'm some kind of puritanical prude. I'm not. It's a lot of stuff." Giving his scalp a reprieve, Briz stuffed his hands into his pockets.

"Like Datura changing me?"

"Datura's definitely changed you."

"Yeah, well, my wanting you isn't just because of her bite," Jaden barked. Briz was right. She was acting like her sister.

"I know."

"You know, but you aren't interested." Jaden twisted the bottom of her top and considered pulling it off before he could stop her.

"Jade, I feel the same way about you." Exhaling, he

sounded like a trapped bull. "You're making too big a deal out of this."

"Haven't you noticed how everyone in the house has vanished? Even Violet isn't here to protect you from my lewd advances. The candles, the music. Maybe nobody has much faith in our ability to survive the next few days. They're giving us some privacy, the opportunity to, you know..."

There was a brief silence as Briz stared at Jaden, his jaw tight. Then he snapped, "Do you really think I carry condoms around in case I get lucky?"

"Briz, are you gay?" she asked, hoping he'd prove her wrong. "I mean, it doesn't matter if you are...But I'd stop bugging you."

He pulled his hands out of his pockets and waved his arms in the air. "How can you ask that after the other day? No, I, I just..." He started sputtering. "You know, ever since you got bit...You're not even legal. I could go to jail."

Jaden's forehead creased with lines of doubt. Was he that much of a law-abiding citizen? He did seem pretty conscientious. But she wasn't buying this. "I could die tomorrow. The Mal Rous might decide to knock me off. You can have 'a departed virgin lies here' written on my gravestone."

Jaden knew she should be freaking out about tomorrow, not forcing herself on Briz. Her grandfather's face plopped into her mind. *Talk about a mood killer.* Jaden didn't want to be like him. She truly believed this was completely different. She would never treat Briz the way Dekle treated Elvina. Right now, what she needed was to be loved. To experience tenderness. To feel less like a monster. Less afraid.

Briz sat down on the edge of the bed and put his head in his hands. After a few minutes, he straightened up and faced her. "Jade, without protection, you could get pregnant. Have you thought about that? How that would change your life, our lives? Do you really think you're ready to have a baby when you're still in high school?"

Jaden hadn't thought about it at all. When she was around Briz, thinking wasn't her priority. Apparently, he made all her brain cells disintegrate. Stifling her impulse to climb in his lap and kiss his luscious lips, she moaned, "Nooo."

He shifted away from her, lowered his head back into his hands and released a guilt-ridden sigh. "When I was your age, I got a girl pregnant."

Briz's confession crashed through Jaden's desirous intentions. She hadn't seen that coming.

"You may think because you're almost sixteen you're a grown up, but when you're slapped in the face with reality, it suddenly feels real young."

Jaden almost opened her mouth to argue—the Mal Rous wanted to turn her into their homegirl. It didn't get more real than that. Well, an altered version of reality...but still.

Briz lifted his head to speak. Jaden could see his pain and humiliation.

"We'd been dating for eight months. My family was getting ready to move here from Seattle. When I told them she was pregnant, they put the move on hold, said I had to take responsibility for my actions. Three weeks later, Abigail had a miscarriage. I know this sounds bad, but we were so relieved. Abigail and I were given a second chance. My folks insisted we stay in town for a couple more months. They said it wasn't right to just leave her, after all she went through."

"Both of you," Jaden said, touching the side of Briz's

knee with the tips of her fingers. "What both of you went through."

He took her hand in his. "Trust me, it's a lot harder on the girl. I'm not putting someone through that again. And I don't want to be a dad when I'm just a kid myself."

"Did you love her?"

"I was a fifteen-year-old guy. Love had nothing to do with it."

"So are you any different now?"

"Hmph. Funny. Yeah, I've been eighteen for a week. Now I'm real mature." Briz grinned wryly. "My dad always says, 'Don't be a walking hormone.' I'm trying to take his advice. But you're not making it easy."

"And you've decided to be a monk?"

"No. I'm just..." Briz paused and exhaled a loud breath. "I'm more mindful, conscious. More creative when I'm intimate." Jaden scooted closer as his words registered. "I want to care about the person I'm with, Jade. Not that I didn't care about Abigail, but I don't know..." He looked at Jaden. "I'm not making the same mistake twice. Besides, there are other ways. Other things we can do."

"What? When?"

"We have time, Jade."

"Actually, tonight might be the only time we have."

"I don't believe that." Briz kissed her hand.

Jaden knew he was right. She didn't want to get pregnant. But what about those other, *more creative* ways to be intimate? She was hungry for him. For any crumb he was willing to throw her way.

Briz stood up and crossed his arms over his bare chest as if guarding his body, the promised prize. And the conversation was over.

Jaden sighed. It was time to direct all her pent-up energy toward tomorrow. Trying to stay alive while undermining the Mal Rous would take some doing. She slid off the bed, grabbed her nightshirt from the dresser and headed to the bathroom. Then straight to the kitchen for a long, steady swig of her drink. When she returned, Briz was lying on the couch. The candles were out, the music had stopped.

He probably feels safer from me out here.

This night wasn't ending the way she'd imagined. Jaden got into bed and faced the wall, hoping she'd fall asleep quickly and dream about what she was missing.

Then Briz's warm, lean body slid next to hers. His fingers moved her hair aside. Her skin heated up as his lips swept over the nape of her neck.

"It's lonely out there. I thought we could sleep together."

From the way he said "sleep" and the fact that he was fully clothed, she knew it was all he intended to do.

She slipped around to face him, and his lips met hers as if he were enjoying a lush Georgia peach. She savored the moment. *Who cares about the Mal Rous?*

CHAPTER 38

JADEN

Tig floated off the triplets' kitchen counter to the ground, singing a lyrical tune about swallowing a coral snake whole. Her screech wasn't as shrill as before, Jaden thought as she regarded the Mal Rou. With her sharp fangs sticking out, the small creature appeared a bit manic, yet funny. Even cute. Climbing back onto the counter, Tig carefully separated Jaden's matted hair into dreadlocks similar to Datura's wormy strands.

Jaden's dream came to an end as Briz slid out of bed and drew the sheet up over her shoulders. Her eyes blinked open. She lay admiring him as he walked to the door and quietly shut it behind him. Snapping fully awake, Jaden felt her hair and was relieved to find there weren't any dreadlocks forming. Still, something was wrong.

A chill spread across her skin. She hadn't had any elixir since last night when she gulped half of a bottle to make sure she wouldn't harass Briz. This felt different. It was as if she'd woken up in the wrong body—a Mal Rou's body. Her stomach churned with hunger as she saw visions of succulent toads.

Jaden had barely stepped into the kitchen when Isadora stuck a small bottle in her hand. "This is for you, dear. Put a dropper-full under your tongue every half-hour."

Jaden remembered the other day when the triplets pricked her finger. They'd been planning to mix drops of her blood with ground mosquito larvae and pulverized thornapple seeds in an attempt to make it similar to Datura's caustic system. According to what Violet had said about Datura, this was as close to a homeopathic formula as they could create without actually using Datura's blood.

Jaden did as she was told, then sat at the kitchen table, where Olympe immediately set a glass and a bottle of brew in front of her.

"This here mixture is more potent than the first one. Plus, we added some of the homeopathic remedy. In case you forget to take it." Olympe's mouth crumpled into a thin line as she walked over to the stove.

"Aren't you going to tell her?" Tamara looked at her sister. Olympe gestured to Tamara to go ahead. "We have no idea if, or how, this new formula will work. You'll just have to give it a try. If it seems too strong, stop drinking it. We won't be with you, so you're going to have to be the judge. We researched all the ingredients and don't believe the combination will be harmful to you. But we can't be certain."

Wonderful. If the Mal Rous don't kill me, the cure will.

Jaden opened the bottle. The smell hit her and her face went limp as a wrung-out washcloth.

"You're kidding me. You want me to drink this?"

"Yes," Isadora said with both regret and pride. "Do your best, dear."

Tamara set a bowl of grits in front of her. "You should have some food in your stomach when you drink it."

Jaden caught a glimpse of Tamara as she poured herself a glass of the slimy mixture—the woman looked concerned—feeling like a disgruntled guinea pig, Jaden took a sip. The flavor was hard to pinpoint. Perhaps swamp water with a hint of liquefied toad. She wiped her mouth as if to erase the taste. "Violet, do the Mal Rous eat toads?"

"No. They lick the fluids from their skin."

With a loud thud, the back door swung open. Hubs and Briz came in lugging a five-gallon cauldron. Whatever was in it stank worse than Jaden's brew.

"That better not be for me. This is harsh enough." Jaden forced down the rest of her drink.

"It's for the Mal Rous." Violet, sitting on a throne of Olympe's herbal books, pointed at the three sisters, who started filling containers with the thick, stringy solution. "The triplets have been brewing it out back for the past two days. I am surprised you didn't smell it."

Jaden had forgotten all about the broken-down house next to the screened garden, the one Dr. Whiting and his wife had originally helped the triplets build. Even when it was new, it couldn't have been more than a hovel.

The foul odor of the mixture permeated the room.

"I can't breathe," Jaden whined as if she'd inhaled a bad attitude. Tamara switched the fan on high, but it didn't help get rid of the stink. "Why don't you have more fans in this house, or air conditioning?" Slurping up a second glass of tonic, Jaden considered the possibility that it was making her feel as bitter as it tasted.

Violet aimed her twig crutch at the cauldron. "Of course, this formula for the Mal Rous is not nearly as potent as the one made with Amanita mushrooms. But it is the best the triplets can do for now. It should sedate most animals." Her weary eyes focused on Jaden.

"We do not know for certain how the mixture will affect them. I drank a small glass of it earlier. It made my extremities tingle. I became inebriated and remained unconscious for approximately thirty minutes. Hubs was able to get prescription sleeping pills, which the triplets are adding to the mixture."

Only half-listening, Jaden stared into space. Violet tapped on the table with her crutch to get Jaden's attention.

"Jaden, as long as the Mal Rous think you have changed as the Professor did, they will trust you. And trusting you is our only hope of stopping them. If you can persuade them to drink this, and they have the same reaction I did, you should be able to capture them."

It was all Jaden could do not to laugh in Violet's face. *Oh yeah, that'll happen. Just capture them, no problem. Or maybe we could get some Agent Orange and spray them with it.*

She was on her third glass now. Her fingers were twitching, her heartbeat felt erratic. It dawned on her that the piddly bug was still talking to her.

"Are you all right with that plan?" Violet asked again.

Jaden had no idea what Violet had just said, but she nodded in agreement.

"Good. Then that's settled." Violet sounded like a tired schoolmarm. "You will locate the Mal Rous first. After they are sedated and tied up, you will go to the cave to retrieve your mother and sister and Dekle's records."

"Remember," Tamara directed her words at Jaden, "the mushroom formula needs to ferment for seven days, before we can put an end to the Mal Rous."

Jaden responded to Tamara's well-intentioned words with a rude gagging sound. She had to refrain from throwing her glass at the triplet. "Let's just get some explosives and blow them to bits!" she practically yelled.

Everyone's heads snapped in Jaden's direction.

"Well, we could do that," Isadora said, observing her. "Excepting, Dekle seemed to be convinced that the Mal Rous are capable of regenerating. There is the possibility all of those bits might go into a state of hibernation or take to seed and eventually grow into more Mal Rous. That's not a chance we want to take, child."

"Don't call me child!" Jaden muttered as she slammed her glass onto the table.

"Hey," Briz leaned over and whispered in her ear. "Chill out."

Jaden ignored him and held up her empty bottle. "All gone. Can I have another?"

Olympe pulled a bottle from the refrigerator and placed it next to Jaden's bowl of grits. "You haven't touched your breakfast. You need to get some food in your stomach."

Bypassing her glass, Jaden pressed the fresh bottle of brew to her lips, enjoying the comforting sensation of the liquid crawling back up her throat, winding its way behind her eye sockets, snuggling around her brain.

"W-we could s-sedate them, then bu-burn them." Jaden had forgotten Hubs had ensconced himself in the antique recliner. "Lots of p-plants die when ya bu-burn them."

"That's a good idea, Hubs," Briz agreed. Tipping his chair back, he drew his fingers through his hair.

He does that all the time.

Jaden wanted to whack his hands. Maybe she would shave his head when he was asleep.

Clearly this new concoction was working. Jaden wondered what else the new formula would give her an aversion to, besides Briz. Hearing these people's ideas about how to eradicate the Professor's creations was making her feel protective. Why would she want to harm the Mal Rous? They were a part of her now.

Jaden ate her grits and sucked her drink as she studied the haggard faces around her. Compassion for the Mal Rous continued to steal its way into her heart. The little vermin weren't all bad. Her empty bottle hit the table harder than she'd intended. She didn't think anyone was paying attention. Then she realized they were all looking at her.

The triplets had said they weren't sure how this mixture would work, or if it even would work at all. Jaden was pleased with how she was feeling—a little angry, a bit wicked. Briz interrupted her thoughts by placing his clammy hand on hers.

"Come on Jade, it's time to get ready to go."

She pulled away from him, picked up the bottle, and sucked out the last drop.

CHAPTER 39

JADEN

Until this morning, Jaden had wanted to capture and exterminate the Mal Rous. Now doubt was growing in her like an invasive weed. Her stomach growled during the drive toward the shack. Despite her breakfast grits, she was hungry again—this time for a hunk of meat.

"Will you do it? Please?" Briz asked, talking on his phone.

Jaden hadn't heard the beginning of his conversation. She'd been too preoccupied with thoughts of food. Her body went rigid as she listened to his voice now, all sugary sweet.

"Come on. It's just a toadstool. For a science project I'm working on."

Someone was squawking on the other end of the line. "You graduated. You don't have any school projects."

He was talking to a girl. *Probably Abigail.*

"It's a friend's project, for summer school. Don't worry, I'm not ingesting it."

Jaden detected delight in Briz's tone. Was he thinking, *Better Jaden than me?*

"Send it to the P. O. box I gave you? Address it to me, care of Hubs. H-U-B-S. Let me know how much I owe you." Briz glanced at Jaden. "Yeah, me too. We'll talk soon. Bye-ee."

Bye-ee. Jaden wanted to puke. Out of the corner of her eye she could see Briz giving her a crooked grin. From guilt?

She stared out the front window, aware of the tiny hairs on the back of her neck curling like pinworms and wriggling around. Another Mal Rou trait? Her legs were jittering. She was ready to jump out of her skin.

Jaden savored a mouthful of her tonic, letting it barrel through her like a fat snake intent on strangling her heart. The stuff was working. She didn't feel like a wuss anymore.

"You okay?" Briz placed his grimy paw on her knee as if that would calm her down. She refrained from slapping his hand away. Nodding, she held in a cackle that was trying to burst free.

"After I drop you off, I'll park a half mile down the road." Jaden flinched as the sound of Briz's voice scraped over her skin. "Once the Mal Rous finish their drink and pass out, call me. I'll be at the shack fast as I can to tie them up. I'll bring more bottles in case we need them."

Yeah, yeah, you have a carload of brews for them, plus more for me. Shut up about the plan already.

Jaden bit her lip, trying not to taunt him. They'd been over it a hundred times. Jaden couldn't believe the jackasses really thought it would work. She opened the passenger door before the car came to a complete stop.

"Are you sure you're okay?" Briz removed his hand from her knee and hesitantly touched her forearm. "I know you're stressed and scared, Jade. But I'm here for you. I'll do my best to not let them hurt you."

Jaden nodded. She wanted to be rid of the smelly jerk. She climbed from the car, barely able to hide her contempt. The weight of the overstuffed backpack, heavy with drinks for her and the Mal Rous, challenged her slender arms as she lifted it.

Briz was still talking as she slammed the door shut. He lowered the window and handed her a half-empty bottle.

"Here." He paused. "Maybe you should finish this."

What is it with him? Can't he just zip it? Jaden grabbed the bottle from Briz, swung around and charged into the foliage, grumbling to herself, "Everyone's always telling me what to do. Drink this! Do that! Set the Mal Rous on fire. You're all disgusting!"

When Jaden reached the shack and stepped into its moldy interior, she took a deep breath, relishing the mustiness. The place was comforting, even homey. Much nicer than the triplets' rank-smelling house.

"About time ya came back. Where has ya been?" Datura sauntered from the kitchen, picking cockroach legs from between her teeth. "Did ya go off with yer little boyfriend? Did ya have yer way with him? Did he promise to make everythin' better? 'Cause there's no way to do that. Didn't that pathetic Bellibone tell ya? It's too late now."

"I haven't even seen that lame bug. Besides, why would she help me when I'm one of you now?"

"One of us?" Datura smiled.

"Don't act like you didn't know," Jaden sneered. "I can feel your scummy cells moving through me." She dropped her backpack between them, and it landed with a thud, denting the weak floorboards. "You think I'm your godly Professor now? Well, I'm not. I'll help you however I can, but I'm not your nanny—or your slave."

Jaden was supposed to convince the Mal Rous that she was as obnoxious as they were. She just hadn't expected the words to flow out of her so effortlessly.

This must be how Ava feels all the time, empowered to the ninth degree of odious. Jaden laughed out loud. *Odious. Now I'm repulsive, too.*

"Don't ya disrespect me!" Scowling, Datura took a step forward. "Ya'll never be like the Professor. He was a great man. Ya is just a simple-minded kid."

"Ha! Look who's talking."

"Ya is the simple-minded one! Only ya is all we got." Datura's tentacles twitched. "Ya'll learn real fast, I'm the one in charge. From now on, yer gonna do what I tell ya to do."

"I bet Ivan wouldn't appreciate you calling yourself the leader of your hideous little pack."

"Ivan's opinion don't matter. I'm the smartest. I'm in charge."

Jaden cocked her head back and looked down her nose at Dataura. "Well, if that's the prerequisite, I should be the one in charge."

A growl came from the other side of the room. Jaden turned and saw Anders leaning against the wall. "Ya is nothin'," he snarled. "Ya couldn't hurt no one. Ya ain't never gonna be powerful as us." Dropping down on all fours, he charged at Jaden.

She didn't cower or move out of the way. Undaunted by Anders, Jaden pulled her flask of water from her pack, and chugged half of it down. Was this new calm because of the tonic, or was she mutating into a Mal Rou sooner than expected?

Anders's pace slowed as he realized his game of intimidation wasn't working. Tendrils stretched out from the back and sides of his head, pecking at her bare legs, making him drool. "Yer sister is smarter than ya is. She done smashed Esere. He's dead."

"Anders, shut up!" Datura's tentacles crimped, twisting into tight ringlets.

"My sister killed Esere?" Jaden chuckled. "That's funny. It must be a lot easier to get rid of you than I thought."

"It wouldn't 'a happened if our Professor was here." Datura stroked her wormy strands of hair to calm them down.

"Face it, you little rodent." Jaden felt good calling Datura that. "The old man is dead and gone."

Datura's lips curled back. Pushing Anders aside, she leaped at Jaden and slashed her leg with a claw, releasing a plume of fresh blood. She sniffed Jaden's skin. "Ya reek 'a that boy."

"Get away from me!" Jaden stepped back. "You're dumber than you look if you think I'm with him. My sorry-ass sister wants him, and she can have him. They both make me sick."

"Well then, I has a real treat for ya."

"What are we going to do, lick some toads?" Jaden raised her eyebrows. Suddenly toad-licking sounded genuinely appetizing. Glancing around, she asked, "So where's the rest of your gang of morons?"

"They ain't morons! And they is makin' the rounds."

"What, patrolling for wayward rats?" Jaden knew what Datura meant. But she didn't care if they went after some chump who strayed onto the property or parked his car nearby.

"Rats. They come in all shapes and sizes." Datura sniffed Jaden again. "Come on, girl. Let's get."

Jaden reached for her pack.

"Leave it!" Datura snapped. "We'll be back soon enough."

Jaden was going to argue, then again, she had no desire to lug the bag around. Besides, she was feeling a bit of camaraderie toward the Mal Rous. When they returned, she'd decide if the Mal Rous were worthy of befriending or killing.

Sweat trickled over the remains of the dead mosquitoes on Jaden's skin as she walked behind Datura and Anders through the cane field. Observing their ridiculous bodies scurrying along, bonding with them seemed absurd. She didn't need the Mal Roos. She didn't need anyone.

"Are you going to tell me where we're going? Or do you just enjoy strolling in the heat?"

There was only one place they could be heading—the cave. Jaden had guessed it when Datura asked if she had a flashlight. She had taken it out of her pack and waved it in front of Datura's face. Plus, Anders was babbling about how lucky it was that they'd brought their boat farther down the bayou, closer to the shack.

"Stop gripin'! I told ya I got a present for ya."

Jaden knew she'd better act surprised when she saw it. Her nostrils pulsed as she took a deep breath. Datura's cunning scent reminded her of a savory cologne.

When they reached the pirogue, Jaden eyed the murky water, longing to quench her thirst. Anders climbed in ahead of Jaden. As soon as she sat down, he shoved an oar into her side; snatching it from him, she rowed up the marsh, pretending to be clueless about their destination.

Other than giving Jaden directions, none of them spoke. This was her second jaunt on the bayou today, and she found the sights even less intriguing. She didn't care about its beauty or its ugliness. She just wanted to get on with her life, whatever that meant. She wasn't interested in being her mother's daughter or Datura's servant. Just no more games. Or maybe that was what being a Mal Rou was all about, and she'd have to get used to it.

Her arms were worn out from rowing when Datura broke the silence. "We is here!"

Jaden tied the pirogue to a tree stump, then the three of them walked along a path, stopping for a moment at Esere's grave. This trail was easier to hike than the one she and Briz had forged. When they arrived at the Professor's KEEP OUT sign, Datura gestured toward the bushes.

"Jaden, get that there ladder and lower it into the cave."

Relieved that Boy Scout Briz had remembered to put the ladder back after they climbed out yesterday, Jaden did as she was told, hopeful that if any of their odors lingered inside the cavern, Datura would think it was the smell of Briz on Jaden's skin.

This time, Jaden found it easy to climb down the ladder. *Best thing about my new drink: I don't give a damn about being in a friggin' hole in the ground. I don't give a damn about anything.*

With her flashlight guiding her way, Jaden followed Datura and Anders into the tunnel. In the second cavern, Datura took the flashlight from Jaden and aimed it into the middle of the room. Jaden pretended she didn't know what she was looking at.

"You had me row all the way out here to show me a pile of dirty laundry?"

"It's yer sister, dummy." Datura strutted over and kicked Ava in the gut.

Jaden laughed. "She looks dead."

"Ya thinks this is funny?" Datura kicked Ava again.

"Well, I didn't expect to see *her* in here," Jaden lied. "That's what I'd call bad karma." Judging from Datura's expression, she'd never heard of karma. "You know, 'what goes around comes around,' 'the golden rule,' 'do unto others.'"

Jaden stomped over to Datura, took back her flashlight and aimed it at her sister. "The princess deserves whatever she gets. You'd be blown away by how mean she is." She paused. "Well, no, *you* wouldn't be. The two of you have a lot in common."

"What do ya mean? I ain't no princess."

Anders sniggered and took a step back before Datura could hit him.

"Yeah, you are," Jaden insisted. "You both have a hateful streak. You'd shrivel up and die if you couldn't be mean and nasty." As Jaden looked at the crumpled figure on the ground, it was strangely easy for her to act detached. "She's not as bad as you, but she can hold her own. Once, when we were kids, my dad was going to punish me for some lame-ass thing I'd done. Ava jumped around all excited shouting, 'Kill her, Dad, kill her! Come on, kill her!' He told me to go outside and play. I guess he decided that my having to live with Ava was punishment enough."

Her jaw tightened as she stared down at her sister. "It all sounds so sappy now. I was a wimp, and she thrived on pushing me around."

Jaden questioned why she'd told Datura anything. She should have let go of it a long time ago. But how do you love someone who has spent years tearing you down? When their dad died, she'd thought their grief would bring her and Ava closer together. But it put even more of a wedge between them. While Jaden's heart had felt battered, vulnerable to the world, Ava's became an empty shell.

The idea of forgiveness darted through her mind, but she instantly dismissed it. "If you're going to murder her, I want her fully awake. I want to see the terror on her face. Payback for all the years she mistreated me—and for lying to me about Briz."

Despite the coolness in the cave, perspiration suddenly seeped from Jaden's pores, smelling of her brew—followed by the sensation of hundreds of centipedes biting the inside of her head, trying to escape.

"Ya is not so dumb and mousy after all," Datura crooned as if she was about to start singing a Broadway song.

"Well, *you* are." Jaden's testy response caused Datura to chirr with pleasure. "This is what you dragged me out here for? Did you think you'd have to intimidate me into submission? Have you forgotten? My emotions are dried up now, like yours. What do you want me to do with her?"

Jaden winced as the question left her mouth, realizing her emotions weren't dead.

"I got yer mom here, too." Datura giggled like a schoolgirl. "I been thinkin' 'a feedin' 'em to the gators. I thought ya should be here for the auspicious occasion."

Auspicious occasion? Violet was right. Datura was smarter than she let on.

Datura's words were meant to be uplifting. Instead, at seeing her mom, the hallucinatory horde of centipedes finished gnawing through her skull and began vacating her head, causing Jaden's grisly attitude to collapse as her conscience shut down her vengeful ideas. Compassion reared up, squelching the urge to be cruel.

Compassion for who, though?

Jaden craved her tonic. It brought out the best in her, accelerating her transformation. Vacillating between her loyalties to the Mal Rous and to her mom and sister, drops of sweat crept down her forehead. Jaden wiped the moisture away, wishing the act would remove her confusion. She felt like an addict going through drug withdrawal. If she could just slug down an entire bottle of her drink, she knew it would help her think more clearly.

Jaden reached in her pocket and grasped her father's knife, squeezing it as if to invoke his spirit and ease her confusion. Should she save her family or not?

Earlier, Jaden had been so certain about her choice.

Feed them to the gators. A burst of energy raced up her spine, and her body shivered as if desperate to reconnect with her old self. That comforting feeling she'd had earlier, of her drink snuggling around her brain, was fighting a losing battle against the sweet girl she had been so happy to abandon. Pointing the flashlight down at Datura's face, Jaden felt like a marionette that the Mal Rou had been manipulating with invisible strings, not only moving her arms and legs, but also controlling her thoughts.

"Yer not as tough as ya act," Datura smirked. "But ya will be...ya will be. Ya is doin' better than I thought ya was gonna with only a little 'a my blood."

"What are you wasting my time for?" Jaden's words carried a hard edge, masking her erratic emotions. "They're already half dead. If you want to get some kind of a reaction out of me, stop drugging them with your venom."

Jaden flicked the beam of light over their bodies. Kneeling, she looked at her mother and sister, as the unbearable thought of losing them settled in.

She worried Datura would smell the change in her pheromones, breathe in the aroma of Jaden's distress on her skin. Jaden aimed the flashlight directly into Datura's eyes, blinding her, as she pulled the knife from her pocket. Concealed in her hand, Jaden flipped the lever, releasing the blade.

"Rip into them when they're conscious!" As Jaden spoke, she tucked the knife into her sister's palm. "Let's have some real fun."

With all her strength, Jaden slapped Ava's face. "You've always been a raging bitch." Then she slapped her mother as hard as she could. Inside, Jaden was screaming, *wake up. Wake up and get out of here!*

Some part of her knew she loved her mom and sister and that they loved her.

Chapter 40

Briz

Briz was having serious second thoughts about their plan as he sat in the car. Why did he agree to let Jaden meet the Mal Rous at the shack on her own? Shouldn't he have gone with her regardless of the risk?

Part of him thought he should call the authorities. But he knew they wouldn't listen to his crazy story. They'd think he was just some smartass kid feeding them a line of bull. Until he and Jaden could get their hands on the Mal Rous, no one was going to believe the monsters were real. Even then, the triplets were worried the authorities might hand the Mal Rous over to another mad scientist.

For now, he'd stick with the plan.

He had to remind himself that of all their idiotic ideas for capturing the Mal Rous, this one was the best the triplets and Violet had come up with. And it was the only one he and Jaden had been willing to try. Briz locked the car doors, then silently laughed at himself as he rolled the windows down so he wouldn't suffocate.

For the millionth time, Briz questioned his decision to

follow Jaden into the field that night and to race into the shack despite what he saw through the door. He could have just turned and run.

He looked into his eyes in the rear-view mirror.

"Love." His lips barely moved as he mouthed the word. He stared at his reflection as he questioned the way his heart swelled with acceptance.

"I love her," he whispered. "I love her open heart. Her kindness. Her sense of compassion for animals, people, the planet...I love her. That's why I'm doing this."

At that moment, passion, desire, lust...love, it was starting to feel like a form of mental illness. Why else would he be sitting here waiting for Jaden's call? A call that could possibly end his life. Or turn him into a Mal Rou. The thought didn't help the nervousness that was taking root in his stomach. Jaden had been acting strange all morning. Then again, lately, what exactly was normal for her? His new girlfriend was currently possessed by wild beasties. Wild beasties with attitude.

Surrounded by a heavy silence, he imagined the spirits of slaves and sharecrop workers roaming through the abandoned fields. He wanted to start the car, turn the air on high, listen to music, and distract himself from the heebie-jeebies that were taking over his thoughts. He surrendered to the fact that he had to be quiet. Who knew how well the Mal Rous could hear?

Every word he'd read about the Mal Rous, all the stories Violet had told him, were fresh in his mind, including their names, appearance, how they preferred to hunt in pairs, and each of their "specialties."

It was vital for him to stay alert, but as he rested his head against the back of the seat, the stillness and heat weighed his eyelids down.

Briz woke to the sound of his own voice crying out like a wounded soldier on his deathbed. His head snapped up as wiry feelers gouged his neck. He gasped, and his breath became caught in his lungs. He couldn't exhale, and he couldn't take in more air as he glimpsed Tig's head inches from his, her body draped over the back of his seat.

"That's enough, Tig. We gotta stash him," Ivan said, standing on the seat beside him.

Tig's tendrils pulled free. Her high-pitched voice shrilled in Briz's ear. "What 'bout that girl? Datura said she'd be with him."

"Yeah, well she ain't." Ivan slid his claws up Briz's arm as if searching for a tender spot to bite. "Start the car and drive to the house."

A distant voice in Briz's head was telling him to throw Tig and Ivan out of the car and speed away. The voice faded as Tig's poison turned his brain into a sponge that felt like it was squeezing mind-numbing fluids through his entire body.

"Start the car!" Ivan commanded again, slapping him, then wrapping his claws around Briz's wrist.

Briz's limbs felt detached from his torso as he pressed the ignition button, pushed his foot down on the brake, then the accelerator. Tig remained on the back of the seat, her feelers caressing Briz's face. Arriving at the estate, he had just enough reasoning ability left to know it was his last chance to make a run for it, but he didn't have the physical capability to try.

Ivan shut off the engine while Tig climbed onto Briz's lap, stretching up as if to kiss him, jolting him out of his fog, until her feelers sank back into his neck.

The next thing Briz knew, the afternoon sun had replaced morning light, and the humidity was even more oppressive. He was sprawled on the ground next to his car, his face smashed into the gravel. His wrists were bound tightly behind his back, his feet were loosely tied together, and Tig was looping a coarse rope around his neck.

"Put this here over his eyes." Wielding a ten-inch boning knife, Ivan cut off a strip of Briz's shirt. "He don't need to see where we's takin' him."

Tig wrapped the cloth around Briz's head, ripping out hunks of his hair as she tied a knot.

"Stand up." Tig kicked him in his ribs, laughing when he curled up in a protective ball. "Oh, he wants his mommy. We should go get her for him."

The thought of his mother being hurt pained Briz more than Tig's physical abuse. Abruptly, his hunting knife was ripped from his belt loop.

"Well." Ivan slobbered on Briz excitedly. "Ain't this a pretty thin'."

Ivan's saliva singed Briz's arms. Blisters popped out of his skin and bored deep into his muscles.

Tig kicked him again. Raising himself to a standing position, Briz tried to twist his hands free from the ropes. He stopped when Ivan pressed the tip of the knife into his tailbone, driving him forward. Briz shuffled along, until Tig yanked hard on the rope, intentionally making him fall. With shrieks of joy, his captors yelled at him to get up.

Briz hauled himself onto his knees. Tig tugged on the rope as if it was a leash, forcing him to follow her. His shins scraped the gravel as he shimmied along like a blindfolded animal being led to slaughter.

If they're doing this to me, what have they done to Jade?

A door opened; damp, stale air filled his lungs. A harder yank on the rope caused Briz to topple forward, his chin grinding into the dirt floor. He rolled onto his side and raised himself back up.

The Professor had kept the Mal Rous hidden in the garage cellar. Briz assumed that was where they were taking him now. Tig pulled on the rope. Wobbling forward, Briz heard another set of door hinges groaning, a guttural sound that raised the hairs on the back of his neck.

"Watch yer step," Ivan said cheerfully. With a shove, he sent Briz tumbling down a flight of wooden stairs.

Lying crumpled on the ground, Briz wanted to groan from the pain, but he wouldn't give them the satisfaction. They yelled at him to stand up again. Ivan's claw struck his face, gouging it beneath his eye; he could feel blood bubbling up.

"No! Not his face." Briz heard the impact as Tig smacked Ivan. "He's pretty. In fact—"

Tig crawled onto Briz's chest. Her tongue slinked across his face like a leech dipped in warm olive oil, lapping up drops of blood as they slid down his cheek.

"Yum." She licked Briz's lips and tried to poke her tongue into his tightly sealed mouth. Giving up, she moved her tongue along his jaw, gyrating it into his ear. Briz thought he would vomit.

"Enough, Tig!" Ivan knocked her off of Briz. "Ya can play with him later."

They didn't have to yell or smack Briz any more. He willed himself to stand.

"Move it." Ivan pushed the knife into Briz's tailbone. "Tig, open the lid. Hurry up!" Ivan's slobber spread across

Briz's legs, raising fresh welts to match the ones on his inflamed arms.

Briz stopped moving forward when his knees hit the edge of a wooden crate. His muscles tensed as Ivan's knife dug in deeper.

"Do it now, Ivan...*do it now*," Tig chirped.

Ivan's fangs touched Briz's leg. They lingered on the arteries behind his knees, signaling what was coming. His skin popped as Ivan's fangs dug in. The venom flowed into Briz's body as if Ivan were pumping gasoline into an oil tanker. Tig chomped into his other leg as if it were a piece of fried chicken. Briz went weak from the pain. Ivan's teeth disengaged from Briz's flesh, his tongue hovering over the wounds as if he wanted to strike again. Briz tumbled into the darkness as Tig's fangs pulled free from his calf.

When Briz regained consciousness, he thought he was dreaming. Then the sensation of a noose cinched around his neck made him weep. *A dream would be nice. Night terrors would be nice. This is real.*

He had no idea how long he'd been there. Minutes, hours, days? Filled with poison. Slowly dying. Convulsions rocked his contorted body as he struggled to rise, pushing his head against the lid of the crate. It didn't budge. He tried to extend his legs, to get free of the ropes that bound his wrists and feet, but the wooden box constricted his movements.

The poison ivy sores itched to the point of making him want to scream. Sweat seeped from his pores; he felt like an egg being poached. Concern for Jaden, pain, and intense thirst kept him conscious. He had to will himself to pass out again.

Chapter 41

Jaden

The trip back through the bayou had been excruciatingly long. Jaden was thirsty; she craved her drink. After tying up the boat, she ran all the way to the shack, finished off her container of water, then grabbed a bottle of her tonic. A voice in her head warned, *don't drink it.*

Her body won.

It didn't take long to get used to it again, to find enjoyment in the way it slithered down, filling her lungs, before settling in her belly. By the time she drank two more bottles, Jaden's confusion was gone. She knew where her loyalties lay. She was pleased with herself for telling Datura that her mother and sister should be coherent when the Mal Rous tortured them.

What was wrong with me, leaving my knife with Ava? Why would I want to give her and mom a chance to escape from Anders?

She looked down at Datura, ready to confess, but didn't.

Anders will be fine. He'd keep guard at the cave until the games began in two days. By then, the women would be fully awake. And the fun could start.

"Let's go," Datura said, interrupting Jaden's thoughts.

Jaden grabbed her backpack and followed Datura. The two of them walked silently along the road toward Guyon Manor. A purr rumbled from Datura's chest. Jaden sighed contentedly, knowing that Datura was delighted with her progress.

So was she. Jaden found the changes in her personality liberating. She was grateful her new improved tonic helped her feel more like a Mal Rou.

A powerful sense of pride welled up in Jaden as she stood in front of the estate's massive gate. It was a pride Datura had always felt. This was the home of Jaden's grandfather, the brilliant man who excelled in genetic engineering. In the 1940s, while other scientists were arguing about DNA structure, he'd already begun experimenting with cloning. He achieved far more than his so-called colleagues were even beginning to understand at the time.

"Stinky magnolia blossoms," Jaden grumbled as they strode the length of the driveway.

The sight of Briz's car made her recoil. "What's he doing here?"

"It's all right." Datura's words were like a cool, calming liquid flowing over Jaden. "If Ivan and Tig did what I told 'em, he won't be botherin' ya no more."

Jaden glugged down the dregs of her tonic, opened Briz's car door, tossed the empty bottle inside, and grabbed three full ones. Then she strutted into the house after Datura.

CHAPTER 42

AVA

There was a painful rumble in Ava's head, as if a semi-truck was parking in it. Her eyes were sealed together. When she cracked them open, all she saw was blackness. A droning hum filled her ears. She tried to lift her arms, but they were a numb, heavy weight wrenched behind her. Gagging on something that was stuffed in her mouth, she felt sores on her lips. She spat out a rag and relished the sensation of her saliva glands kicking in, filling her mouth with moisture.

Where the hell am I? Ava stared into the dark emptiness. As her pupils dilated, the room expanded into layers of gray. She couldn't understand where she was, or what had happened.

Then it hit her as if someone had sucker punched her in the gut. She remembered finding Rick dead in his truck, being kidnapped by strange mutant aliens, and being dropped into a cave. It didn't seem possible. But lying there, helpless, she surrendered to the fact that this was real. For the first time ever, Ava prayed.

She prayed that her mother was alive. Prayed that

someone would save them. Her prayers were followed by an all-consuming feeling of panic. Her life had never been threatened before. She wanted to cry the way she had when she'd hidden in her bedroom on the day she learned her father had died. Another part of her wanted to fight.

Her aching, bruised muscles convulsed, sending a prickling sensation swarming over her numb hands and feet. Her body lurched backward, bumping a lifeless form.

"Mom...Mom?" Her words were quieter than a whisper. Pressing her lips together to stifle the sound of her sobs, Ava rocked against her mother, trying to wake her. She kept telling herself that her mom was unconscious, not dead.

She squeezed her cold fingers together, stopping as a sharp edge pressed into her palm. A few days ago, Ava would have griped about the discomfort. Now, a wave of relief swept through her. She recognized her dad's pocketknife. She'd know it anywhere. Hadn't she spent years hiding it from Jaden, threatening to toss it out, just to upset her sister and see her cry?

How had it gotten into her hands, in this place?

"Mom." Ava leaned her head toward her mother and spoke softly. "If you can hear me, I'm going to get us out of here."

There was no response.

With the blade at an awkward angle, Ava repeatedly slid it across the rope that bound her wrists. The process was tedious, but each slice filled her with determination to survive. Her tired fingers cramped, and the knife fell to the ground. Her need to throw a mini tantrum came and went. She was determined to remain silent.

Alive.

Ava arched her back, twisting her body until her

fingertips touched the precious blade. Wiggling her fingers, she shimmied the knife back into her hands, then continued the arduous task of sawing her way to freedom. Her fingers ached as she sliced through the last bit of rope—freeing her wrists she untied her feet.

She removed the rag from her mother's mouth, loosened the bonds from her hands and ankles, then felt her wrist for a pulse. Ava couldn't detect anything. Trying not to panic, she pressed her fingers against the artery on Brooke's neck. The faint beat gave Ava a heightened appreciation of how irreplaceable her mother was. Lovingly holding Brooke in her arms, Ava began rocking her back into consciousness.

When Brooke took a deep breath, Ava leaned close to her ear. "It's me, Mama, Ava. Don't say anything. You aren't dreaming. We were kidnapped—"

Her mother nodded slightly.

"We're in a cave. I don't know if anyone else is here. We're going to find a way out."

Ava rubbed her mother's arms and legs, chasing the numbness out of her limbs until Brooke reached for her hand. Slowly standing, leaning on one another, they steadied themselves. It was all they could do to keep their dehydrated, weak bodies from tumbling back to the ground.

Not knowing where their captors might be, they held each other's hands and used the subtle movement of flowing air to guide them to what they hoped was an exit. Stumbling forward, Ava gripped her mother's arm, struggling to keep the two of them erect as they reached a tunnel.

Ava led the way, knowing they might be walking right into the monsters' den. With each step, she pushed past the pain that gripped her bruised and battered body. Her determination escalated as she mentally prepared to fight for her life.

The two women tried to quiet their breathing as their fingers skimmed over the slick, chiseled walls of the tunnel. Finally, a dim light flickered, beckoning them forward with a promise of safety. At the end of the passage, they paused.

Ava reached back and squeezed her mother's hand, gesturing toward thin shafts of sunshine that filtered down from an opening at the far end of the chamber. Remnants of a rope ladder hung from the ten-foot drop. They could see no signs of their captors.

Ava drew Brooke closer. "When I let go of your hand, run for that ladder. No matter what, just get out of here."

Their hands slipped apart as they hurried toward the opening.

Ava made a choking sound and squeezed the hilt of the knife as tiny claws grabbed her calf. Brooke looked back at her.

"Mom, go! Get up the ladder," Ava shouted, the words rising painfully in her dry throat. "I'm right behind you. GO!"

Streaks of sunlight showed the human-like creature as his long tongue wrapped around her ankle and his tendrils stabbed into her leg. Turning, Ava thrust the knife downward into one of his bulging eyes. His tendrils pulled from her flesh. She twisted the knife free as he stumbled backwards, snarling.

Ava ran to the ladder.

With the creature right behind her, she jumped up and grabbed the remains of a wooden rung. Her legs dangled like bait. Before she could pull herself up, sharp claws dug into her ankles. Ava glanced down, and saw the monster's massive jaw opening. She screamed as it locked around her foot.

Her mother's hands clasped onto her wrists, pulling Ava higher. With her free foot anchored on a rung, Ava gripped the rope and heaved her body from side to side, swinging the ladder, knocking the creature repeatedly against the cavern walls. She cried out as a hunk of flesh was torn from her heel and the beast fell to the ground. Ava stared at him lapping her blood off the floor as if it were raspberry jam.

"Ava, hurry!"

They crawled out over the lip of the cave into heat and blinding sunlight. Shielding her eyes from the brightness, Brooke looked past Ava, her face contorted. Ava turned to see the creature's head emerging.

"You little bastard!" Brooke dropped to her knees and wildly shook the ladder.

Ava ran the blade of the knife back and forth across the ropes as fast as she could. As she cut through the last strands, the ladder slid from her mother's hands like a pair of decapitated snakes, dropping with the creature down to the cave floor. They both stared at the opening, expecting the barbarian to reappear.

Then Brooke focused on the knife in Ava's hand. "How did you get—?"

Ava shrugged and slipped the knife into her pocket. She didn't have an answer.

"Let's go," Brooke said in a hoarse voice.

Ava led the way, limping downhill on a trail she had hazy memories of climbing, until they passed a mound of dirt. "Guess we're going in the right direction."

"What is that?" Brooke asked.

"One of those *things*. You don't remember burying it?"

Brooke shook her head.

"We should make our own path. In case the others show up." Ava pushed her way into the thicket without waiting for her mother's reply. Ignoring cuts and scrapes from the branches, she found she had a whole new level of tolerance for pain.

Brooke squinted up at the sky. "From the position of the sun, it must be midmorning."

Ava had forgotten what an outdoorswoman her mom used to be—all those camping trips the family had taken when her dad was alive.

"Ava, we need to clean your foot."

They made their way to the brackish water. Ava stared at it, wishing it were drinkable. Brooke stopped at a massive bald cypress tree and motioned for Ava to sit.

Ava had no interest in the bloody, muddy mess sticking to her sandal. She closed her eyes as her mother scooped handfuls of murky water to rinse it. Peeling a strip of bark from the tree, Brooke wrapped it around the wound, and secured it in place with the tie from Ava's straggly ponytail. Then she helped her daughter stand up.

"Which way?" Ava asked.

Brooke looked at the dense growth, the flow of the water, then up at the treetops. "I'm guessing that direction is south and would lead us toward the marshes. It would be our best chance of finding someone to help us."

"Let's go." Ava swatted away the bugs that hovered in front of her face. "Those alien *things* might come by in their boat." Looking at her arms, she swore all thirty-nine species of mosquito that lived in Louisiana were lunching on her. At least the bloodsuckers were distracting her from her throbbing foot, the damp clothes sticking to her like a second skin, and the water moccasin she spotted undulating through the green water.

As they headed away from the bayou, Brooke said, "Your sister was telling me the truth, but I didn't believe her."

"What are you talking about?"

Brooke shared the story Jaden had told her about discovering the Mal Rous. She spoke quietly, yet the meaning of what she said was loud and clear to Ava.

"This is all *Jaden's* fault. You're telling me *she* freed them?" Ava's raspy voice cracked as it cut through the air like a whip. "It figures. That worthless little...If she's not already dead, I'm gonna kill her!"

"Oh, no. She can't be." Brooke stopped in her tracks and stared at Ava.

"Well, if she is, it'll save me the hassle—"

"Ava, please—"

"After what she—"

"Please, Ava, stop it. Now." The lines in Brooke's face showed sadness, regret, anger.

Ava didn't care.

"Mom, look what she's put us through."

"Enough! No more cruelty!" Ava hadn't expected her mother to have the energy to snap at her. To be so angry. "I love you, Ava. You're my daughter." Her mother swallowed as if to ease her dry throat. "You just saved my life. But Jade's my daughter, too. And your hostility toward her hurts me as well." Brooke's tears mixed with grime, weaving moist patterns on her cheeks. "Ava, I realize having a sister has been a great inconvenience to you. From the day Jade was born, you've acted like a princess, angry because you'd been dethroned. You're not a kid anymore. It's time you stopped."

"Why are you amping on me? She hates me, too."

"If she does, whose fault is it? Jade adored you until you beat any love she had for you out of her. For her own self-preservation, she learned to cater to you, or to avoid you. I'm to blame for that, along with your dad. We always told her to let you have your way because it was easier. We were wrong. It wasn't fair to her. It certainly wasn't fair to you. It was lazy parenting!"

Oh, bite me!

Every muscle in Brooke's face tightened, as if she heard her daughter's thoughts. Ava couldn't care less.

"Ava, you're stunning and smart." Brooke's tone was sharp, her expression pained. "But that doesn't entitle you to be a bitch and a bully."

"I don't get it. What'd *I* do? Why are you pissed off at *me*? I didn't release alien assassins. *Jaden* did."

Her mom was physically and mentally fried and taking it out on her. Well, she was maxed out, too! From the open wound in her foot. From being told she was a bad person when she'd just saved her mom. From being a pincushion for a pack of mutants spawned in the crud floating in the bayou. From thinking she was going to die. She was stuck in this hellish inferno with bugs swarming over her, all because of Jaden. Every horrible experience they'd been through was because of Jaden. No matter what her mom blamed on her, she couldn't say any of this was Ava's fault! It was *all* because of *Jaden baby*.

Brooke eyed her daughter.

Ava stared back. All she'd said was that she wanted Jaden dead. She said it all the time. It's not like she really meant it.

Without another word, Brooke turned and worked her

way through the growth. Ava limped after her. They continued in silence.

Ava had never been so quiet before. She'd always avoided being alone with her thoughts. But she wasn't about to speak now. She let her resentment grow steadily in her like a tumor. She found it comforting.

Miles later, they entered a grove of ancient bald cypress trees that stood like giant death totems in the black clay gumbo soil. The ideal place for those little Mal Rou monsters to lurk, to jump out from behind the tree trunks and force them back to the cave or leave them lying there as food for the vultures.

Ava's foot was swollen and became more and more painful with each step. Without speaking, her mom gestured for her to sit down. Brooke packed mud on the gaping hole in Ava's heel and attached a fresh hunk of bark to it.

When the late afternoon rains began, Brooke showed Ava how to catch raindrops in oversized leaves. The small amounts of the water they dribbled into their mouths only left them thirsty for more.

At last, they came to an overgrown sugar cane field. It was the most wonderful sight Ava had ever seen.

"It's ours, isn't it?" Ava asked.

Her mom sighed and took hold of her hand. "I think so."

Misshapen smiles appeared on their tired faces. Leaving their angry words behind them, Ava and Brooke climbed through the thick foliage together, moving in the direction of town, determined to avoid the dirt road, the mansion, and their captors.

CHAPTER 43

JADEN

Jaden awoke alone in the mansion. She wandered aimlessly from room to room as if trapped in a glass snow globe, small flakes of awareness drifting around her. Her brain might as well have been a fried computer chip. Sparks of memory surged through, stimulating random nerve fibers. Hugging herself, she studied her reflection in the bathroom mirror. Her eyes were sunken and vacant. She looked as if she had died and was coming back to life.

That wasn't possible. Was it?

She got into the shower and let the cool water flow over her, cleaning off the grunge and some of her confusion. Slowly Briz, the triplets, Hubs, and their plan emerged from her fractured thoughts, reminding her what she was *supposed* to have done—only hadn't.

There was a vague memory of Datura happily declaring that they were allies now. Was it true? Had an unexpected alliance been formed between the two of them? Had Jaden willingly ceded to Datura and become her minion? Because of Datura's blood mixing with hers, or did the triplets' brew have anything to do with it?

Jaden dried off with a moth-eaten towel, pulled her grimy clothes back on, and made her way down the grand staircase, the emptiness inside her echoing off the walls. Without Datura around, Jaden hoped to be herself again. Whoever that was.

In the kitchen, Jaden found her backpack on the floor surrounded by empty bottles. The sight of it brought back a memory of the Mal Rous' reactions when they'd discovered the special beverages.

She recalled the way Datura's bulbous nose had throbbed with excitement, her tentacles rippling over her head like serpents, as she encouraged Jaden to drink the runny slime. Unwilling to admit that it had been made to drug them, Jaden had sipped it slowly, unwisely using her own mixture as a chaser. The combination had made her feel loopy and punch-drunk.

When the yellow glutinous drink hadn't made her keel over, the Mal Rous excitedly guzzled down the rest of the bottles, including the ones they'd found in Briz's car. She couldn't remember if the drink had any effect on them, or how much they had made her swallow.

Jaden opened her pack. A smile spread across her face when she found her mom's cell phone. She could escape. Sneak off, hide in the cane field, and call Briz to pick her up. Turning on the phone, she was relieved that the battery was still charged and noted the time, 4:57 P.M. Then she saw the date and sank down onto a chair.

Was I passed out for two days? That's impossible. What did the triplets put in—?

Jaden's eyes widened as she noticed an object on the

table. Briz's hunting knife. Sticking straight up, the tip of the blade wedged into the tabletop. A glimmering bad omen. She smashed her palm against her chest, trying to stop the sensation of razor blades slicing off pieces of her heart. Briz... *He won't be botherin' ya no more.* Datura's words thrummed painfully through Jaden's bones.

With shaking hands, she checked the phone for messages. There were none. She called Briz's number. She heard his voice on the phone telling her to leave a message.

Jaden reached over and grasped the knife's handle. Even in her not-quite-transformed state, if he were hidden in the house, wouldn't she have smelled his pheromones? She'd been in every room.

She had to find him.

She crept out the back door onto the porch. Her heart stilled, then sped up as her attention settled on the weather-beaten garage. Scanning the grounds, she couldn't see any sign of the Mal Rous. There was a chance they were far away, scavenging for food. At least if they were feeding, they couldn't be torturing the townspeople. That would come later, after sunset. For fun.

Jaden stepped into the light falling rain and let the damp grass swaddle her bare feet. Then she ran to the garage and opened the door.

Narrow rays of light leaked in through the decaying siding and broken window. A rusted machete hung on a wall above a termite-eaten workbench. Glancing behind her, Jaden shut the door, fearing that the Mal Rous were spying, ready to strike and punish her.

She understood that their allegiance to her was as unpredictable as hers was toward them.

As her eyes adjusted to the dimness, she saw the door at

the far end of the room. Fleshy chicken skin erupted on her arms, and Jaden knew.

Briz was on the other side.

She walked over and opened the door to the Professor's cellar. The quiet rushed up at her. Every pore in her absorbed his scent. She stood motionless, staring into the bleak space.

Her fingers trembled as she flipped on the light switch. Nothing happened. Taking the phone from her pocket, she punched in Briz's number. A muffled ringing sounded from below. She inched down the stairs, the phone in one hand lighting her way, Briz's knife in the other.

Softly she called his name.

When the phone disconnected, Jaden was surrounded by shadows that hovered in the room like ghosts. She pressed redial. Again, a muffled ringing guided her forward. She wanted to cry out for help. But there was no one. This was it.

She was the rescuer, not the one to be rescued.

Jaden pushed redial. She followed the sound to the corner of the room, where a wooden crate looked like a small coffin. Tiny air holes had been drilled into the lid. What had her grandfather kept in there? Sliding the latch, she lifted the top. Her stomach leaped into her throat, then quickly dropped. She choked on the sickly odor.

The phone's light bathed Briz in a cold silver glow, as if he were drowned in the depths of a gray sea. His face was sunken and hollow. A blindfold partly covered one eye. The other was swollen shut. Scabbed blisters covered his arms and legs.

She could see the rise and fall of his chest. He was *alive*.

Shuddering at the sight of the noose around his neck, Jaden carefully removed it and shook his half-dead body.

When he didn't respond, her hands curled into tight fists. She struck his arms, his chest, the tops of his thighs—he didn't stir. She sliced the rope that bound his feet. With all her strength, Jaden tried to raise him out of the crate.

The more her slight frame tugged, the more his weight resisted. Her tears tumbled onto him. She had run out of adrenalin. Pure terror was keeping her going.

Jaden knelt down, cupped his face in her hands, and pressed her lips against his until his mouth opened.

He tasted like poison.

Like her.

Moments later Briz's lips responded. His breathing grew louder as he kissed her back. Gasping as if he'd been underwater for too long, he managed to cough out two words.

"You're real."

Jaden helped him stand, then cut his wrists free. He lifted a shaky leg over the edge of the crate, then fell against her. Bracing him, Jaden helped him move the other leg. She closed the lid and lowered him on top of it. They sat leaning into each other, dripping with sweat and tears.

"I have to go back," Jaden said quietly. "If I'm not there when the Mal Rous return, they'll know something's up. Stay here."

She helped Briz prop himself up against the wall. Edging away, Jaden started to stand. He took her hand and pulled her back to him until their lips touched.

This kiss wasn't passionate. It was desperate.

At the top of the stairs Jaden closed the cellar door. She tasted the salt from Briz's lips on hers.

This nightmare has to end!

CHAPTER 44

JADEN

Jaden was aware that the Mal Rous would sense her intention to obliterate them. Even she could smell the predatory pheromones escaping from her skin. She opened the door at the side of the garage and paused.

In the distance, beyond the layer of cloud and mist, soft shades of blue filled the sky. Her gaze drifted down, across the yard, and rested on Ivan, his coppery skin glistening with moisture.

And her mother, kowtowing to him.

Ivan's talons squeezed Brooke's wrists, his tongue spiraled over her arm, leaving a red trail of poison ivy sores.

A few yards behind them, Ava crouched before Tig, rendered helpless by the feelers pawing her face and the fangs grazing her neck.

Ivan lifted his head. Like a satisfied snake, he hissed, "Look what we found wanderin' out in the field."

Jaden's mother and sister looked scared to death. Or perhaps by now they thought death would be a welcome form of escape. Jaden was surprised that seeing them this way didn't make her want to cry.

It made her mad as hell.

She glanced around the yard. Where was Datura?

Hiding. Waiting for the perfect moment to appear—fangs exposed, claws extended.

With Briz's knife behind her back, Jaden took a step forward, then stopped, laboring to inhale a deep breath. It felt as if her chest had collapsed and, like a dying star, her heart was sucked into a black hole. Right now, everyone she cared about was in danger.

Including the Mal Rous.

Ivan cocked his head, looking at her.

Jaden's sweaty hands held the knife tighter. As she took another step, her foot slipped on the moist ground, sending her to her knees. She stood back up. Her mind sputtered like an old jalopy, slipping in and out of gear. She failed to mask her vulnerability.

"Hah! I thought ya'd be a worthy opponent. Worthless is more like it." Ivan nodded toward the garage. "What was ya doin' down there?"

Jaden didn't answer. It was obvious that he already knew.

"Ya has double-crossed us."

She wanted to say she hadn't meant to be a traitor. But no words came out. No snide comments. No lies. Jaden stood there; her emotions locked in uncertainty. She was filled with hatred of the Mal Rous. At the same time, she felt compassion for these lonely, malformed beings that her grandfather never should have created. No matter how much she'd bonded with them, she never wanted to become like them, nor like her grandfather. She wanted to be human. All human. With normal emotions of passion, love, even anger.

She thought with the triplets help, she would be able to suppress their traits, but she couldn't change the fact that she carried Datura's DNA.

"Cat got yer tongue?" Ivan laughed.

Jaden looked over at the large trunks of the oak and magnolia trees, then at the house, sensing that Datura was nearby, watching her, shrewdly calculating what would cause Jaden the most pain. The obvious choice would be ending the lives of Jaden's family and Briz.

Except, this was Datura, and cruelty was her strong suit. No, ending their lives would be the compassionate thing to do. Datura would be thinking about mutilating them, and of course, making Jaden participate in the process. It would be an agonizing, lifelong reminder that Jaden had made the wrong choice. That her loved ones' miseries were all her fault.

Her attention shifted back to Ivan and Tig, who were excitedly waiting for a sign from their leader to determine her fate.

With a nod from Ivan, Tig coiled her feelers around Ava's wrist like bracelets, ready to send her into shock. Ivan shoved Brooke flat against the ground, his fangs near her throat, threatening to inject her with venom and paralyze her breathing muscles.

A high-pitched whistle came from the upstairs window. Jaden turned toward the sound, then spun back around as her mother screamed. Ivan's teeth were sinking into Brooke's throat.

"Leave my mom alone, you—" Ava yelled at Ivan before Tig's feelers broke through Ava's skin, silencing her.

Jaden started sprinting across the yard, determined to save their mom.

She glanced at her sister as Ava twisted onto her side and kicked Tig. Kicking out again, Ava caught the side of her head, knocking Tig onto her back.

"Run, Ava!" Jaden called out.

Ava scrambled to her feet. She slid on the wet grass, regained her balance, took another step, then sank back to the ground as Tig latched onto her ankle, and her tendrils gouged into Ava's legs.

"Let me go!"

Ava's eyes met Jaden's as Tig pulled the bark from Ava's foot and dug her claws into the raw flesh on her heel. In that moment the two sisters released agonizing screams, Ava's full, guttural, filled with pain: Jaden's heavy with remorse. Jaden looked away first as she ran faster toward their mother.

She stopped inches from Ivan, her bare feet pressed firmly on the ground, her legs steady, her choices clear. She sucked in a sharp breath as he moaned with pleasure, releasing a steady flow of snake venom into Brooke.

"Let me help you, Ivan," Jaden said affectionately. "You and I are family."

He looked up at her with annoyance, his eyes narrowing as if not trusting that she'd changed her mind so quickly and sided with the Mal Rous after all.

Jaden smiled.

Then she drove the gut hook knife into his ear, twisting and scraping into his ear canal. Ivan swung his arms, scratching her legs, trying to stick his claws into her.

"I can do this all day, Ivan." Firmly holding his shoulder, Jaden wedged the knife deeper into his ear until his jaw released Brooke's limp body.

She tightened her grip on the knife as Ivan turned his head and spit on her. The familiar sensation of poison ivy bubbled up on her skin. Jaden braced Ivan's head, pushing the blade in as far as it would go—at the same time, she watched her sister.

Even as Tig's feelers pumped poisons into Ava, causing her to convulse, Ava kept fighting. Jaden admired her tenacity. Ava was a survivor. And her cruelty had forced Jaden to be a survivor, too.

Ivan tried to jerk his head free. Jaden wrenched his head back. Tugging the knife out of his ear, she held the blade against his throat.

"Go ahead. DO IT. Ya can't kill me."

"I wouldn't be so sure about that. Esere died. You can, too."

When Jaden had awakened in the mansion that morning, she'd felt as if she were on the verge of becoming her sweet, kind self again. That girl was gone. With one swift movement, she sliced Ivan's throat. She let his twitching carcass fall, blood poured from the gash, draining from his soulless body.

Tig looked at Ivan's form sprawled on the ground. Screaming profanities at Jaden, she pushed her feelers deeper into Ava.

Ava reached her hand into her pocket. "Eat this, you little mother!" She raised her arm, and crammed Jaden's pocketknife into Tig's wide-open mouth. Tig's tendrils recoiled, but her claws dug deeper into Ava's heel, stopping Ava from crawling to safety.

"I thought ya was one 'a us."

Jaden winced at the sound of Datura's voice. She turned

toward the house as the Mal Rou stepped off the back porch. "But ya ain't."

Jaden walked toward her, putting as much distance as she could between Datura and her family, stopping when she reached the oak tree near the house.

Datura's nose bulged as she inhaled the fragrance of Jaden's betrayal and savored her fear, anticipating what Jaden would do even before Jaden herself knew. Datura looked over at the garage.

Jaden followed her gaze and saw Briz staggering out like a drunken lunatic, waving the rusty machete, his skin and clothes were drenched with sweat. His heavy-lidded eyes passed over the yard, not seeing Jaden where she stood by the tree, settling on Brooke and Ava.

Datura watched calmly as he approached Tig and swung the machete at her face, forcing the pocketknife further into Tig's mouth, striking the knife repeatedly, ramming it until Tig fell back, her claws releasing their grip on Ava's heel.

His body swayed, and he dropped to his knees.

Jaden was trembling, but Datura appeared unaffected. She seemed to be confident that Tig and Ivan would survive. Or was she so cold-blooded that she didn't care? Looking into Datura's eyes, Jaden saw contempt, along with scorn, and... hurt. *She's hurt that I've chosen Briz and my family over them. Angry that I'm not loyal. That I'm not the Professor.*

Jaden tried to hide her emotions behind a smug expression and come up with a plan, hoping her agony wasn't spreading across her face, exposing her heartstrings. She had no doubts that Datura had already made a plan of her own. Datura wasn't going to let Jaden win. Ever.

"Ya gonna be all mine now. Like yer grand-pere was."

With a sadistic grin, Datura began dancing around Jaden. She howled with delight, mumbling and jumping as if she were performing some ancient Voodoo ritual—puncturing her own gums with her sharp claws until blood poured down her chin.

The heat of summer pressed against Jaden's skin, but the realization of Datura's intentions turned her insides bitter cold. Datura wanted a new, improved, more potent Jaden—a Jaden with so much of Datura's DNA in her that she could never change back. Then she would be like the Professor, and she wouldn't have the desire to betray them.

Jaden clutched the hilt of the knife, swiveling on the balls of her feet, mirroring Datura's movements as the Mal Rou circled her, ready to strike.

What was she waiting for? Jaden lunged. Datura sprang effortlessly out of the way.

Jaden rushed toward her again, swinging the knife.

Datura twirled into the air, propelling her body into Jaden, digging her claws into Jaden's chest. Her tentacles latched onto Jaden's forearms, squeezing them like tourniquets, stabbing spiked tips into Jaden's skin.

A loud bellow filled the air as Jaden cried out in pain— for herself, for her family, for Briz. For their forgiveness. For their sakes, she couldn't give up. Jaden wrenched her arm upward and swept the knife across Datura's tentacles, cutting off as many as she could while they engorged her limbs with poison.

Datura guffawed, as if delighted by the challenge. Clinging to Jaden, she thrust out her foot and knocked the knife from Jaden's hand.

Jaden had never punched anyone. Now seemed the perfect time. She made a fist and struck Datura in the face.

Unfazed, Datura kicked Jaden in her belly. *Whump.* The sound and impact came again and again. Jaden doubled over. Staggering backwards, she seized Datura's leg. *Whump.* Datura kicked Jaden with her other foot.

Jaden lost her balance and fell back onto the ground with Datura still clinging to her chest.

Datura released a savage belly laugh as she scraped her claws over Jaden's neck. Jaden's blood bubbled up as Datura's fangs pressed against her skin.

Suddenly Datura squealed. She yanked her claws out and ripped her remaining tentacles free.

Jaden's eyes widened.

Briz was coming toward them, roaring like an animal, the machete over his head. Jaden braced herself as Briz slammed the machete down onto Datura's back. The impact flattened Jaden hard against the ground. He hacked the machete into Datura until there was a cracking sound and her spine wrenched open. Her body hung on Jaden like a malignant growth, with the machete sticking out.

Before Jaden could move, she heard a high-pitched shriek. Briz grabbed his hunting knife from the grass, headed for the middle of the yard, and stopped.

Tig, moving like a black widow, blood brimming from her eyes, was scuttling across the ground on all fours, screaming at Briz. Holding the knife at his side, he waited for her. Her tendrils whipped out, reaching toward his scent. As she blindly flung herself at him through the air, Briz raised his knife. Tig slammed into the blade. Falling, she slithered around on the ground, unable to strike her enemy.

When Tig's body became still, Briz knelt on the grass and pulled the knife from her chest. His body sagged as he stared at his hands.

Jaden breathed in the metallic smell of blood mixed with the gentle rain and fragrant magnolia blossoms. She began pushing Datura's corpse off her body when, with an ugly laugh, Datura jabbed her blood-covered fangs into Jaden's neck.

As the DNA coursed through her, Jaden's eyes closed, sealing in her defeat and grief.

Satisfied, Datura pulled out her fangs, stood up, and shook the machete free from her back.

Jaden's limbs jerked uncontrollably, her mind caving in on itself. Forcing her eyes open, she fought to stay alert and saw Datura—the gouge in her back fleshy and red, her gait unsteady—lurch up behind Briz.

Jaden slid her hands over the grass until her fingers found the machete and closed around its hilt. Her feelings for Briz burned in her stronger than Datura's blood, building a fire of hatred for the Mal Rous.

Datura's stride had become stealthy and confident. Her tentacles slithered through the air like Medusa's hair. The stumps of pieces Jaden had cut off appeared to be shaking back and forth at her like stubby fingers, saying *no, no, no.*

Jaden meant to spring to her feet like a cat, but her legs were like rubber. Weaving toward them, Jaden swung the machete to one side, preparing to decapitate Datura.

"Briz!" Jaden called out as Datura launched herself through the air, digging her claws into Briz's back. Her teeth were poised at his neck. Her tentacles twitched, preparing to stab his flesh.

Briz didn't move.

"Don't do it, Datura." Jaden lowered the machete. "You win. I'll do whatever you want. Just leave him alone."

Datura shifted her head to the side. Eyes, snout, and hair

stretching back, she peered at Jaden. "Why should I trust ya?"

"Look at me." Jaden's voice cracked, her body shivered. "You just sent more of your blood into my veins. I am you."

Datura's eyes stayed fixed on Jaden's, determining Jaden's sincerity.

Jaden held Datura's gaze as Briz slowly raised his arm.

Briz plunged his knife into the top of Datura's head. Stunned, Datura retracted her claws. Her tendrils went limp as blood bubbled up around them. Growling, she yanked the knife from her skull and lashed out at Briz, missing him as he rolled to one side. He labored to get to his feet.

Eyes gleaming, Datura spun back toward Jaden.

"Traitor," Datura sneered as she sprang up and thrust the knife deep into Jaden's stomach. Then she stood back and smiled.

A callus grin spread on Jaden's face as she looked down at Datura. Stepping forward, she jammed the machete into Datura's heart.

Datura's eyes continued to sparkle with life as she fell. Reaching her hand up, she whispered, "Jaden..."

Jaden pressed down on the machete unrelentingly, forcing it all the way through Datura's back into the earth, making certain she was dead this time.

The sparkle left Datura's eyes. A whistling sound escaped from the hole in her chest, as if announcing that the fight had ended.

Jaden's eyes glazed over, her mind drifted through a labyrinth of distorted images. She pulled the knife from her belly and pressed her hand against the wound. Blood, slimy and thick, coated her fingers.

She looked at Briz.

All the color had drained from his face. He took off his shirt and was stumbling toward her when she dropped to the ground. Jaden released a shallow breath, her body slumped and her eyes closed.

CHAPTER 45

JADEN

Am I hallucinating? Is it the thornapple poison? Datura's DNA? Jaden tried to hear the beat of her own heart as Briz sat on the ground, cradling her in his lap.

"I'm okay, Briz. I'm okay."

He didn't hear her.

Jaden gazed in awe at the luminescent silver cord tethering her to her body. *I'm dying*, she thought as she floated above Briz, watching him rock her crumpled remains in his arms. Blood seeped from her neck wound, smearing across his chest. Tears streamed down his cheeks as he pressed his wadded shirt against her stomach, trying to stop the bleeding.

Jaden moved closer, placed her palm on his shoulder, but her hand was like air.

His head lowered to the side as if he wanted to rub his cheek against her hand. Only nothing was there.

Jaden glided over to her mother and watched the rising and falling of her chest. Next to her, Ivan lay motionless, his head barely connected to his lizard-skinned body.

Ava lay curled in a ball, eyes open in a blank stare. Tig's poisons had done their job. Jaden trusted that Ava would be all right. Her sister would never let a deranged rodent get the best of her.

A crow cawed. It was calling Jaden's name as it circled her ghostly form. It gestured with its head, encouraging her to follow it above the treetops.

From that height Jaden could see a car racing down the dirt road in the distance.

Hubs.

Hubs has come to help. He's not afraid.

Jaden watched as his car pulled up to the gate, then drove slowly down the long driveway. He got out, shut the door ever so quietly, and carrying a pistol, he walked toward the front door.

"Hubs, back here. We're back here," Jaden called.

She wasn't surprised when her words weren't heard, knowing that her voice, like her body, was invisible in the mist.

Moments later Hubs came out the back door onto the porch. A pain-filled expression froze on his face. His legs moved as if they were stuttering, like his words, as he spoke Jaden and Briz's names.

When only Briz turned in response, Hubs's features caved in with grief.

Jaden, hovering above the yard, looked at Datura. The crow swooped down, hopping around the creature. Jaden wondered if Datura would miraculously regenerate. If all the Mal Rous would. As the Professor had believed.

She watched as Hubs pulled his car around to the back of the house and unloaded supplies. Briz continued to hold his shirt against Jaden's stomach, watching dully as Hubs tied the Mal Rous up as planned, with duct tape, rope, and bundles of wire.

"Does the re-refri-figerator work?" Hubs asked Briz, while he stuffed the small bodies into gunnysacks.

"I think so," Briz answered softly.

"I'm gonna st-store them in it. My mama says w-when the mu-mushroom comes, w-we should boil them all in the mixture."

Jaden understood why the triplets wanted to boil them. They couldn't risk the smoke from the Mal Rous' burning bodies impregnating everyone's lungs, poisoning the entire town, altering people's cells, transforming them all into Mal Rous.

Like me.

One at a time, Hubs hauled the burlap sacks into the house. Jaden wanted to tell him where Esere was buried, but she knew Ava would let Hubs know when she was conscious. She assumed Anders was still in the cave and would be easy to drug with the triplets' concoction.

Briz stroked Jaden's cheek. Her ethereal body lowered next to him, wishing she could feel his touch.

When the Mal Rous were sealed away, Hubs locked the doors of the house. Then he came outside and stood near Brooke and Ava. Rubbing his fingers against the faded scars on his throat, he stared at their bodies.

With great care, Hubs carried each of them to his car and placed them in the back seat. He opened the front passenger door and walked back to Briz. He put his hand on Briz's shoulder to let him know it was time to move Jaden.

Hubs bent down, lifted her into his arms, then patiently waited for Briz to stand.

Briz got up and held out his arms to carry Jaden himself.

Like a butterfly, Jaden flitted above him. She wondered what would happen when the car drove off. *Will my silver cord break, setting me free from this world, this reality?*

Briz rested her body on the front seat of the car.

The crow flew up behind Jaden's ethereal form and hung in mid-air, stretching its shimmering black wings. They curved around her head, ruffling her hair and covering her eyes.

All she could see was blackness.

Then Briz's lips were pressing against hers.

Breathing him in, Jaden's body shivered and spasmed as it reunited with itself. Waves of unconsciousness swept over her as Datura's venom completed its journey.

CHAPTER 46

HUBS

Hubs drove in silence, wishing he could turn back time. If only he'd arrived at the house sooner. If he'd come looking for Jaden and Briz yesterday, no one would have been hurt. He glanced at the glove box where he'd stashed the gun he'd borrowed from his friend Stella. Shooting the Mal Rous may not have ended their lives. But it might have incapacitated them. Stopped them from harming everyone.

His passengers, including Briz, remained sprawled in his car, unconscious. Hubs knew his mama and aunties could help the boy and Jaden's mama and sister. Jaden needed a real doctor. The knife wound was deep. He prayed Jaden would survive.

As he neared town, Hubs slowed to the speed limit. Now was not the time to be pulled over by the sheriff.

"Where are we?" Briz asked, stirring awake as they pulled to a stop in front of a well-kept house.

"My Aunt L-Laura's." It was obvious from Briz's expression that he didn't know whom Hubs was talking about. "She's a d-doctor...Dr. Sc-Schilling."

Hubs knew his grand-pere had told Aunt Laura that wild animals had attacked Hubs at Guyon Manor when Hubs was a little boy. It was probably for the best if she didn't know the animals were mutant experiments.

He worried that she wouldn't help him, that she'd turn them away. Then he reminded himself that his aunt was nothing like his Uncle Cape. Maybe she'd sew Jaden up, no questions asked. It was Hubs's only hope.

Five hours later, Hubs pulled his boat up to the triplets' dock. Briz carried an unconscious Jaden, while Hubs carried Brooke, then Ava, into the house.

CHAPTER 47

JADEN

The cool air pressed against Jaden's skin as she looked down at the swampy wetlands and marshes weaving through the bayou. She smiled, stretching her arms, letting the tips of her fingers touch the tips of a crow's wing as it soared next to her. Then the sound of a snarling twang sent her plummeting toward the water.

"Wake up! Come on Jaden, wake up!"

Over the past few weeks, that voice had become implanted in Jaden's brain. Jaden sat upright in bed and stared into Datura's face. Certain that she was dreaming, Jaden pushed Datura aside. "But you're dead."

"Ha! Ya knows we can't be destroyed. A rusty machete and a knife wouldn't put no end to me. Knock me out for a bit, give me a world a hurt, but not kill me. Get up! The others are waitin' by the dock. Come on." Datura started pulling the covers off Jaden.

They all survived. Esere, too? Had his body healed in his grave?

"I'm not going with you." Jaden yanked her covers back

from Datura. "I missed being a nice person. It was exhausting being afraid and angry all the time. Go away."

"Ya is nuts. It's in yer blood. Yer a natural. Look at yer sister. It runs in yer family. Ya didn't need my blood to change. I just set yer inner demon free."

"You changed the wrong sister. This was never supposed to be my path. I wasn't meant to be hateful and mean."

"Sure, ya was. Ya is just like us. Come on. Ivan said he forgives ya for slicin' his throat. Fact is, he admires ya for bein' so bloodthirsty. Me, too. But we're all in agreement 'bout that boy Briz. *His time is up.* Tig can't wait to bite into him, watch him die. Unless 'a course, we change him, too. The two 'a ya could spread our bloodline to yer offspring."

"No! You're not changing Briz. And I'm not spreading your bad blood anywhere."

"Hey, ya weren't the only one changed. I never had a conscience till I bit into ya."

"Well, it didn't help you much. I never saw any improvements in your personality."

"Some things take time. Now get dressed. We gotta go."

"Leave me alone. You can't manipulate me anymore. Anyway, I'm tired. I can't help you. I need to sleep. Even then, I'm not making any promises."

Datura raised her hand, her claws extended. Her tone was menacing as she said, "Fine. Only, we has to leave before the sun comes up."

For some reason she didn't strike. Maybe she was changing after all.

As Datura climbed from the bed and walked out of the room, Jaden recalled the triplets had wanted her to get some of Datura's blood for one of their homeopathic cures.

Later. If this isn't a dream and Datura's really alive, I'll get it later.

Jaden rolled over and went back to sleep.

When she awoke, Datura was nowhere around. Jaden felt gauze taped over the holes in her neck, saw well-healed punctures in her arms. Pain shot through her stomach when she sat up. Pulling up her shirt, Jaden stared at the stitches, and vague memories appeared in her mind, like one of her unfinished pencil drawings, missing the details. She thought she recalled Hubs by her side as someone cleaned and stitched her wound.

I remember!

Datura pumped thornapple into me. Did her blood prevent it from working?

She looked around the room. The morning light had not quite reached Violet, who was asleep in a chair near the window. On the table next to her sat a dirty glass and half a bottle of Jaden's brew. She had the uncomfortable feeling that she might have fought with the Bellibone and triplets when they'd been trying to get her to drink it.

Jaden lowered her feet to the floor, wincing at the pulling sensation she felt in her stomach with each step. She tiptoed into the living room. She was relieved to find her mom and sister there, alive, sleeping on cots near the large window. Marks from Ivan's fangs resembled fading birthmarks on her mother's neck. Ava's wrist was bandaged. The set of her mouth was tight even when she was asleep.

Ava already hated me. There's no way she's ever going to let me forget any of this. And why should she?

Forgiveness. Jaden didn't believe there was any likelihood of that. Not after everything she'd put everyone through. How would she ever be able to show her gratitude to the triplets? She owed them her life. She owed them the lives of everyone she loved. A lifetime of servitude wouldn't be enough to repay them.

And Briz. He could have died.

As if her thoughts drifted through the air and captured a scent, her attention and body moved toward the couch. Even asleep, Briz drew her to him.

She saw that his poison ivy had cleared up. The triplets had undoubtedly kept him covered in their pink ointment. There was a small red scar under his eye. She remembered how it had been swollen shut and trusted it would eventually fade.

Jaden flinched, recalling the expression on Briz's face when he had hacked Datura with the machete and stabbed Tig. As their blood soaked into the ground, had it taken a part of Briz's sweetness with it? Growing up wasn't meant to be a dangerous experience. As soon as he woke, Jaden was going to send him home before he lost the rest of himself.

Hesitantly stepping onto the screened porch, she tensed. Would Datura be waiting there for her? When the Mal Rou was nowhere to be seen, Jaden let out a slow breath. Their little chat really had been a dream.

Or would the ghost of Datura haunt her for all of eternity?

Jaden thought of the one Shakespearean quote that she knew. It was from *The Merchant of Venice*. She'd told it to Briz once, trying to impress him since he'd read so many of the plays. "If you prick us, do we not bleed? If you tickle us, do we not laugh? If you poison us, do we not die? And if you wrong us, shall we not revenge?"

It was time for revenge, to get even. To finish off the Mal Rous.

Get even? Revenge?

Where had Jaden gone? Who was she now?

"Enough," Jaden whispered. "*Enough.*"

She was ready to stop thinking about genetic crossbreeds and deadly bloodlines. She wanted to forget, at least for a while. To just watch the sunrise. To appreciate the beauty of the bayou when its dense air hadn't yet settled close to the earth.

Behind her, the floorboards creaked. She turned and saw Briz watching her through the screen door. Bare-chested, in rumpled shorts, with gauze wrapped around his leg. He was gorgeous. Biting her lip, Jaden was aware that she still had Datura's DNA flowing through her and would probably be drinking the triplets' concoctions for the rest of her life.

Briz's eyes leisurely swept over her. All she had on was one of Hubs's shirts. She was relieved when she didn't have the urge to lunge through the screen door and throw herself at him. For the moment, her lustful impulses seemed contained.

Briz slipped out of the house. "You're awake. How are you feeling?"

"Achy and wobbly, but alive." Her voice was barely a whisper. She cleared her throat. "I am alive, right?"

"Yes..." He chuckled softly as she turned back toward the water. "You're alive!"

Briz came up behind her, and Jaden felt a familiar tingle at his proximity. She wondered if her subdued desires would be fleeting, how long it would be until she felt compelled to wrestle him to the ground.

"How many days have we been here?" she asked instead.

"Four."

"My mom and Ava? They're going to be all right? And you?"

"We're all fine." Jaden turned her head and, with a raised eyebrow, looked up at Briz. "Honest. Everyone, including Hubs and the triplets, is tired, worn out. But we're okay, Jade."

Jaden didn't press him for the truth. Instead, she leaned against Briz as he wrapped his arms around her. She could feel his heartbeat, his chest expanding with each inhalation, contracting when he exhaled. Her body moved in kind. She relaxed, the rhythm of her own breathing keeping time with his.

As they listened to the birds announcing the day, Jaden considered how, from this point on, her image of life would be like one of the triplets' patchwork quilts—remnants of events held together by a thin thread. Briz would be a piece of smooth satin fabric stitched into the quilt. His presence, the memory of him, would forever validate her experiences. They'd gone through so much together. There was no going back to being the kids they were five weeks ago.

In the distance came the sound of a motor laboring through the water. Hubs would be arriving soon, the household would awaken, and from the depths of her heart, she would beg her family for forgiveness, as well as the triplets, Hubs...Briz.

A feeling of gratefulness spread through her, knowing they'd all survived the chaos and terror they'd experienced these past weeks. As if he knew what was on her mind, Briz leaned down and kissed the top of her head.

In a few weeks, he would be traveling through Europe. By the time he returned, she'd be back in Colorado and would most likely never see him again.

Jaden turned to Briz—reaching up, she guided his head toward hers. Their lips met, and passion replace her feelings of guilt and anxiety. She savored the moment, feeling like nothing and no one else existed.

The sound of Hubs's boat grew louder, coaxing their lips apart. Jaden looked toward the dock as the rumbling motor went silent. Dread crept over her. It was time to implement the final demise of the Mal Rous.

IMAGINE JADE GONE

Enjoy reading the first several chapters
of the exciting sequel to
Sweet Desire, Wicked Fate

The bayou holds terror that can devour her alive.

After barely escaping a horrifying pack of hybrid mutants, all sixteen-year-old Jaden Lisette wants to do is put the episode behind her, especially now that her future includes the sweet and sexy Briz Nolan. But falling in love may not be their fate. As Jaden battles her new living nightmares, an old adversary returns, intent on revenge. This time, every last ounce of her strength and courage may not be enough to save the ones she loves...or herself.

IMAGINE JADE GONE

Book 2 of Sweet Desire, Wicked Fate

PROLOGUE

Jaden sniffed the air. A pungent odor filled her nostrils. Once again, she felt a glass pressed against her lips and a stringy liquid slide into her mouth. She smiled drowsily. At first, she'd found the taste and texture revolting. Large hands had to physically restrain her to get the foul solution into her mouth. She'd gagged repeatedly as it was forced down her throat. But now, she didn't mind as the drink pulled her from her dreams of Professor Dekle Thatcher, the brilliant grandfather she'd never known, and of his genetically engineered creations, the Mal Rous.

Ahh, yes, more, she thought, swallowing the savory, delicious interruption.

People swore the Mal Rous were monsters, that the Professor had been deranged to create them. But Jaden understood his devotion to the Mal Rous. Especially the one called Datura. After all, Datura's blood now ran through Jaden's veins; they were partly kin.

A vision of Datura dying flitted through Jaden's mind.

Was that because of me? She thought of the other Mal Rous: Anders, Tig, Esere, and Ivan. *Did I kill them all?*

She swallowed more of the thick liquid.

The glass emptied too soon. Jaden struggled to open her eyes as the coolness of the glass slid from her lips. She tried to speak, to demand more, but her mind dulled as unconsciousness stole her away.

This time, she dreamed her sister, Ava, was chasing her down a dim corridor lined with windows that framed the dark night beyond. Jaden looked back, then stumbled as Ava morphed into a creature with horns and fangs. Jaden moved to run again, then stopped. Glancing at her reflection in the window, she realized she had become a monster, too, deadlier than her sister. She turned and stared into Ava's fiery eyes. Jaden's eyes blazed hotter.

Confront the beasts that torment you. Then allow forgiveness to find its way. Unleashed from her mind, the words thundered down the hall, pushing against the walls and shattering the windows, the broken glass sparkling as it fused into rivulets of water. Jaden spread her arms and flew into the night. She looked down and saw Ava, no longer a monster, watching her.

Jaden's eyes popped open; the dream withered away.

Perspiration seeped from Jaden's skin. Blearily, she stood. Multiple hands pushed and pulled at her, forcing her back into bed. Voices tumbled around her, some badgering her to respond, others declaring she wasn't in her right state of mind, vowing they'd find a way to help her.

Jaden snarled and lunged as nylon straps were tied to her wrists and ankles, then fastened to the frame of the bed. She thrashed, struggling to get free.

The badgering voices returned. This time, they cooed

that Jaden would be all right, implored her to calm down. But Datura's blood and the feral Mal Rou instincts within told her to trust no one. Soon she found another glass pressed to her mouth, followed by two more. The concoctions within tasted familiar, not as pungent as what she'd been given before, less stringy.

Her body felt heavy. Had she been drugged?

When Jaden dreamed again, she found herself soaring above the bayou, smiling, the tips of her fingers touching the tips of a crow's wing. The cool air whispered of changes to come, promised that eventually the nightmare she'd been living would end.

"When?" she asked. Then a shrill voice called her name, and Jaden plummeted downward, knowing the nightmare lived on.

CHAPTER 1

JADEN

Surrounded by the early morning bayou, Jaden stood on the triplets' porch. The large T-shirt that served as her nightshirt hung loosely over her slim body as she leaned back against her boyfriend Briz's chest. Jaden felt she'd been transported to another world. A peaceful world. A sane world.

Briz's arms wrapped around her, comforting her. Jaden placed a hand on his and squeezed gently, confirming that he wasn't an illusion—that she was alive. When Jaden woke up this morning, after four days of drifting in and out of consciousness, she was unsure of what was real and what was not.

The sound of Hubs's boat rumbled in the distance. Jaden wasn't ready for this moment of tranquility to end. She felt calm and wanted the feeling to last.

She needed time. Time to be with her family. Time to be with Briz. Time for all of them to heal.

Physically. Mentally. Emotionally.

Somehow, they had all eluded death. The horrifying

version of her life that she had been living for the last few weeks was so close to being over that she could taste it.

Taste it...the words brought images of Datura and the other four Mal Rous to Jaden's mind. No doubt, with Datura's blood pumping through her veins, it was a trait of the mutant creatures that Jaden would have for the rest of her life: smelling and craving fear, tasting elation.

She touched the gauze taped over the wounds on her neck. Then lowering her hand, she let it hover over the stitches in her stomach, wondering who had sewn her up. Jaden drew her slender fingers together, then flicked them open, wanting to magically erase the memory of her shock when Datura had stabbed her, of when she had jabbed the machete into Datura, killing the small Mal Rou to save Briz.

Jaden faced Briz, guiding his head toward hers until their lips met. For a moment, passion replaced her feelings of anxiety.

Hubs's boat went silent.

Jaden turned toward the dock. A soft sigh passed from her lips as Briz kissed the top of her head. Resting his chin where his lips had just touched, the two of them watched Hubs come up the wood walkway to the house, nodding at them when he reached the porch.

Jaden was grateful for all the help Hubs had given her, her family, and Briz. If he hadn't brought her here to the triplets' house when Datura had first bitten her or brought her mom and sister after they'd been attacked, there was no telling where or what any of them would be now—fledging Mal Rous, mere shells of who they were when they'd first arrived at Belle Fleur. *Or dead.*

Hubs handed Briz a small package. His stutter was more pronounced than normal. "The f-fresh m-mushrooms f-from yer f-friend in W-Washington." His eyes filled with compassion as he regarded Jaden. Then he looked back at Briz, the lines on his face holding back a question. Not uttering a word, Hubs opened the screen door, and like a phantom, he glided into the house.

Jaden looked over her shoulder at Briz. With a shrug, Briz guided her back against him. Her head resumed its place against his chest as he wrapped his arms around her.

She had forgotten all about the mushrooms. Which seemed impossible. As far as they knew, a formula made from them was the only thing that would kill the Mal Rous. How could she not remember they were going to boil the little mutants in it until their bodies dissolved—it was going to be an added precaution in case they could seed and sprout back to life.

Mal Rous. Jaden thought of the nickname her crazed grandfather, Professor Dekle Thatcher, had given his creations. Mal, Latin for bad, evil; Rous, a play on the word rougarou—a beast from Cajun folklore, part human, part animal. Their scientific name, *Cerophagous Cautelosus.* Cerophagous was Latin for flesh-eating; Cautelosus, for treacherous, cunning. She cringed, knowing their blood now ran through her veins.

With the soft squeak of the screen door, she felt Briz turn his head.

The scent of Olympe preceded the woman as she padded her way toward them. During the time Jaden had spent with the triplets, she had learned the obvious and not-so-obvious differences between the identical albino sisters.

Olympe's scent was soft like a fading flower, motherly like fresh-baked cookies; the cadence of her speech was infused with the essence of the South. Her sister Isadora's accent was lyrical, not as strong as Olympe's; she smelled musky, rich as her vast book collection. While Tamara lacked warmth, she ran hot with a spicy scent and a biting tongue.

Jaden moved away from Briz to greet Olympe. The petite woman was wearing a blue bathrobe that was slightly darker than her pale blue eyes.

Olympe handed Jaden a large glass of her herbal brew. The mixture kept Jaden's system balanced, more human—less Mal Rou, less aggressive, less angry.

"It's yer original blend," Olympe said with optimism, stressing the word *original*. "We added some spearmint, trying to improve the taste."

"Thank you, Olympe. Thank you for everything." Jaden's voice was meek as she reached for the glass. She'd hoped to sound filled with lifelong gratitude; only her words came out like Olympe had just served her a cup of hot cocoa, not saved her and her family's lives. Jaden raised the glass to her lips. "I really need to give this stuff a name."

"How about *Envie* Tea?" Briz offered with a smile toward Jaden. Answering the question in her eyes, he spelled the word. "E-n-v-i-e. It's pronounced 'ahn-vee.' In English it means envy. But envie is Cajun...or is it French?" He looked at Olympe for confirmation. "Anyway, the old timers in town say it when they have a craving for something." This time Briz's smile reached his eyes. "I was thinking it was a good name because you drink it to stop your cravings for me."

Embarrassed, Jaden sipped the mixture, thinking, *Envie Tea it is.*

Briz and Olympe stood at her sides, reminding her of guardian angels—*or perhaps*, she mused, *they were guards, not guardians*. She wasn't ready to face her family, and they knew it.

Olympe turned and went back into the house. As Jaden and Briz walked over to the screen door, Jaden heard Olympe's sweet voice greet Brooke and Ava.

"Oh, good morning. I hope I didn't wake ya."

The triplets' living room was large and open. Normally, the sofa was placed in the middle of the room; it had been pushed closer to the entrance to make space for Brooke and Ava's cots.

"So is Jade...*finally*." Ava sat looking at Jaden through the screen door, with an expression that Jaden couldn't read.

Concern? Confusion? Contempt?

No.

Loathing!

Jaden could see that Ava's foot was wrapped with gauze—more bad news. How was she going to ask for forgiveness? She had ruined everyone's lives.

"Jaden, are you all right?" her mother asked.

Briz opened the door wide enough for Jaden to enter the house. It was clear he thought her moment of reckoning had arrived. It was time for her to face her jury.

Yep, guard, not guardian angel, Jaden thought. Briz's eyes were no longer smiling at her; he motioned with his head, signaling Jaden to go inside.

Jaden wished she'd just pass out and fall onto the floor. She wondered if she could fake it. Delay the inevitable for a bit longer. Probably no one would think it was odd—just another reaction to Datura's poisons in her blood.

She looked at her mother and Ava sitting on their cots. They didn't appear to be as bruised and battered as the day they were attacked by Ivan and Tig.

"Sweetie, please." Her mother's weak, concerned voice beckoned her in.

Jaden sucked in a breath of air like a boat sputtering out of gas as she tried to suppress her tears. "I'm, I'm so sorry," she mumbled. "Please forgive me for everything." Shoving her empty glass into Briz's hand, Jaden dashed off the porch into the yard.

CHAPTER 2

JADEN

Jaden expected someone to follow her, to escort her back to the house so they could have a nice long chat about genetic monsters over morning coffee. But no one came.

The ground was moist, soft under her feet. Keeping an eye out for snakes, Jaden went around the corner to the triplets' first home on the property—now it was where they created their brews, though the place was nothing more than a shack. The weathered gray structure leaned to one side, ready to collapse. Pieces of screen were nailed haphazardly over the termite-eaten walls; crooked door hinges were attached with wire.

Jaden looked through a grimy window. The rotting floorboards had been replaced with bricks. Two cauldrons sat on a stone fire pit. Above them, the ceiling had a vent for smoke to escape.

The sisters weren't into Voodoo as far as Jaden knew, but maybe her grandfather Dekle had been right when he'd written in his journals that the triplets seemed to be a little Wiccan. Jaden could imagine them at night, dancing outdoors, whistling to stir the wind, drawing down the moonlight, conjuring up spells.

A whisper of stuttering words drew her away from the window. Jaden peeked around the corner of the shack.

She could see Hubs on the porch talking with Olympe, a blue housedress having replaced her blue bathrobe. The two of them went back into the house. The sound of chatter swelled, then subsided, and swelled again. Everyone's words were muffled, though Jaden recognized the irritated cadence of her sister's voice.

With her jaw set, Jaden shook her arms like a prizefighter preparing for a match. She took a step toward the porch, but immediately changed her direction and went around to the back of the house.

Jaden looked out across the yard. It had no ending or beginning. She understood why the triplets had purchased this land; it was one of the highest patches of ground for miles and wouldn't flood every spring.

Jaden jumped as Briz's hands embraced the sides of her waist. She hadn't smelled his pheromones or sensed him walking up behind her. She smiled. Maybe she was less Mal Rou than she'd thought.

She could feel Briz's breath on her hair as he murmured, "Come on babe, everyone's waiting."

The clouds released a drizzle of rain on them as Briz placed a hand on her shoulder, encouraging her to return with him. Jaden wanted to go anywhere except back to the house. She pulled free of his touch.

"Jade...you have to do this." Jaden's muscles tightened at the sound of Briz's now firm voice. "Look, I've been here every step of the way for you. I'm...I'm not bailing on you now, but your family wants to talk with you. They've had a tough time, Jade. We all have."

He was right. With all they'd been through, he'd always been there for her...*always*. Her shoulders dropped as she exhaled.

Briz continued with his unsympathetic tone, "The other day, when your family came to, we told them everything. Well, almost everything."

Jaden wondered what Briz and the triplets *hadn't* explained to her mom and sister. Did they tell them how, if she didn't drink her Envie Tea, that she'd be aggressive, violent, lustful? She remembered the way Hubs had looked at her. Briz was leaving something out.

"And me?" Jaden turned to face him. "What aren't you telling me?"

Briz looked past her, the sounds of the bayou ticking off the seconds.

"Yeah, well..." Briz's gentle voice was back—but it wasn't comforting. "I guess now's as good a time as any." Jaden lowered her eyes and stared at Briz's T-shirt. "When Hubs brought all of us here, the triplets plied you with bottles of that *improved drink* they'd made for you, to balance your system," Briz said with light sarcasm. "At first, they had to force you to drink it. Then you started crying out for more, like you were addicted to it. Isadora went into the kitchen to get you another glass. She was only gone for a moment."

Briz's words were guarded, as if he was unsure of how much to share. "When she returned...you," he exhaled, taking Jaden's hand in his, "you had a pillow over your sister's face. You were trying to suffocate her."

Jaden's heart stalled, then spasmed as it labored to beat again.

"Ava wasn't aware of what was going on," Briz added in a pathetically reassuring voice. "She was still full of Tig's poisons."

Jaden could barely speak. "I, I'd never do that."

"No, you wouldn't." Briz's words swelled with sympathy. "But...Datura would."

"You mean Datura was here? She's alive? I thought I'd dreamt it."

"No, Datura wasn't here." Briz squeezed Jaden's hand. "Jade, you have her blood. She's..." Briz didn't finish his sentence.

Jaden felt nauseated; she knew exactly what he was going to say. After all, Datura had pumped more of her blood into Jaden. She pulled away from Briz. "What are you even doing here? I'm more like Datura now...like the Mal Rous, with the heightened need to harm others. Get away from me while you can! Before I try to murder you, too!"

"It wasn't you, Jade." Briz drew her into his arms as he whispered in her ear, "It was the drink."

"You're wrong!" Jaden stepped back. "You should leave. Go back to town," Jaden demanded, clenching her fists. "I don't want to see you anymore."

"Jade, you saved my life." Briz's tone wavered between annoyance and sympathy. "If it weren't for you, I'd be dead in that crate in your grandfather's cellar."

"Get real!" Jaden glared at Briz. "If it weren't for me, you never would have been in that crate. You never would have been captured by the Mal Rous."

"I'm not leaving you!" Briz reached for her. "You're still my Jade."

CHAPTER 3
ESERE

A dense pressure pushed against Esere's eyelids, forcing them to stay closed. Engulfed in darkness, gasping for air, he swallowed hunks of dirt. More filled his mouth as he attempted to spit it out.

The small Mal Rou's heart pounded as he realized he'd been buried alive.

He forced his fingers to move through the weight surrounding him and started to dig until his hands broke free from the earth. The damp air soaked into his leathery skin as he clawed his way out. Crawling from his shallow grave, he sat upon the fresh mound of dirt. His skin rippled over his bones as he shivered and stared into space.

"Where am I?" His throat was thick with particles of dirt. "How'd I get here?"

Had he upset Datura? Was this her way of punishing him?

"No. No..." He paused, spitting out pieces of mud. "I 'member bein' with the others and torturin' some man in a truck."

He looked at the dirt on his hands, the remnants of roots sprouting from under his claws. He reached up and felt sprouts on the tips of his ears, the horn on top of his head.

A smile filled his ashen-colored face as he considered what a truly unusual creature he was—that all the Mal Rous were. How clever the Professor had been, creating him with DNA from scorpion, Calabar bean, and vulture.

He and each of his four siblings had a unique blend of rodent, insect, newt, and poisonous plant DNA—most importantly tardigrade, and a tad of the Professor's own DNA.

The Professor had always believed the combination made the Mal Rous virtually indestructible.

Esere lay back in the hole and looked up at the sky, watching the clouds. As the rain washed the dirt from his skin, he could feel seed pods germinating in the core of his cells, pushing runners through his veins the entire length of his twelve-inch body—filling him with life.

When the movement in his veins diminished, he sat back up.

A secretion oozed from the tip of his chin horn. Slowly sliding his long tongue over his dry lips, he extended it down toward his chin to lap up the bitter drops of his scorpion venom. When the precious nourishment dwindled, Esere's tongue slithered back into his mouth like an eel into its den.

Esere looked out over the bayou as he removed hunks of dirt from his ears.

"I has been here before." Esere coughed, clearing his throat. He swiveled his head from side to side, taking in his surroundings. "Am I near the Professor's cave?"

Esere called out with his weak voice, "Datura, Tig...Ivan, Anders..."

He waited for an answer.
All he heard were insects chirring and buzzing.
His eyes moistened.
"I gotta find my family."

CHAPTER 4

AVA

Ava sat next to her mother on the sofa and watched as her sister entered the house; Jaden's movements were hesitant as she came toward them. Without a word, Jaden knelt in front of Ava and Brooke—despite of all their physical wounds, the three of them embraced. Surprising herself, Ava leaned her head onto Jaden's shoulder. Jaden's nightshirt felt damp and smelled of rain.

Regardless of their differences, they were family, and as her grandmother Jin would say, their lives were tightly knotted together like an Asian ikat weaving. Tears welled in Ava's eyes, but she refused to let the moist traitors escape. They nearly found their freedom as memories of her father's death when she was twelve years old came into her mind. How she and her mom and sister had embraced, and for one brief moment, the three of them had experienced a heartfelt connection.

A bond. Ava thought the word had an uncomfortable ring to it, like the words *helpless* and *powerless*. But right now, she needed to feel a sense of closeness. She hated feeling weak—being kidnapped, abused and traumatized would do that to a person.

Not to mention waking up in a strange house in the middle of the bayou, with identical-looking albino women, forcing you to drink some strange herbal concoction.

Ava felt Jaden turn her head, saw her give Briz a smile, as if Jaden wanted to include him in their personal, loving, supportive interlude of *we are family, we are a friggin' ikat weaving*.

Ava looked at Briz, then back at Jaden. An ache spread through Ava's chest as she pulled away from Jaden and their mother. She tried to cover the hurt in her expression, knowing Jaden would never care about her. Why should she? From the moment Jaden was born, she had been the enemy, forcing Ava to share the attention of her parents. Why would anyone form an alliance with the enemy?

Her entire life, Ava had done all that she could to distance herself from her younger sister. Now she swallowed back the bitter taste of regret.

"You only came in here because he made you."

Jaden shook her head. "No...no that's not true."

Her sister's timid voice was all it took to alter Ava's moment of remorse. Sneering at Jaden, Ava reclaimed her normal combative self. "You should be begging for our forgiveness you little fu—"

"Ava," her mother cut her off.

"What, Mom? She doesn't care about us." Ava let her anger roll off her tongue. "I really think it's okay to cuss in this situation. *Especially* in this situation!"

Ava stood abruptly and wobbled for a second on her bandaged foot. With her hands on her hips, she watched as Jaden cowered back.

"Because of you, this happened to me." Ava pointed to every wound on her body. "Do you even care that one of your monsters ripped a hunk of my heel off. I watched him lap up my blood from the cave floor. But why would you even notice?" She flipped her hand, gesturing toward Briz. "You care about him more than us!"

Jaden raised herself up; sitting on the edge of the sofa, she looked down at Ava's foot. "They...they aren't *my* monsters," Jaden said in a mousey voice. "I'm sorry, Ava. I screwed up."

"You should be sorry." Ava mentally ran through her list of reasons that Jaden would never be good enough for her. "I can't believe you're so dumb that you set them free."

Brooke reached over and rubbed her hand over Jaden's back.

"What are you comforting her for?" Ava glared at the two of them. "I'm the one that stabbed that hideous beast in the eye to save your ass. Every horrible thing that's happened to us is because of her."

"I am so sorry." Jaden gulped in a tear-filled breath. "But it...it's not *all* my fault."

"Not all your fault?" Ava laughed. She could see the little wimp's tears threatening to undermine her determination to defend herself.

"You...you p-pushed me out of the car," Jaden stammered. "You told me to, to go off and die. None of this would have happened if you hadn't made me so damn angry and then dumped me in the middle of nowhere!"

To die—the words hung over Ava's head. She waved her hand through the air, as if to push them aside. "What? You're blaming me for your stupidity?"

"I knew you'd never forgive me," Jaden muttered as she slumped against the sofa.

"Forgive you? Forgive you—"

"Ava, calm down." Brooke rose and placed a hand on Ava's arm. "Sit back down—you need to stay off of your foot."

"I don't want to sit." Ava pulled away from her mom. "Why would any of us forgive her? She messed up big time, and you're coddling her."

"I didn't mean to set them free." Jaden straightened up; pursing her lips, her eyes crinkled. Ava realized Jaden was mirroring her own annoyed expression. "You told me you had sex with Briz, then kicked me out of the car when a storm was coming."

As her mother sat down, Ava saw a flash of awareness in her eyes. For a second, the sound of rain pulled Brooke's attention to the ceiling before she looked at Jaden, then at Ava.

"Ava, you had *sex* with Briz?" Brooke questioned with an exasperated sigh. "You told me Jade was upset because Briz had asked you on a *date*."

"Really, Mom! Aren't we a wee bit past that now? Because of Jaden, we were almost killed by depraved monsters." With her hands back on her hips, Ava glared at her mom before looking at her sister.

Bond with Jaden...what was I thinking?

"Ah, ma'am." Ava looked over at Briz, standing at the front door, taking everything in. "Since Ava wants this to be all about her, how she's the victim, you should know—I've *never* had sex with her. And I *never* asked her on a date."

"Butt out, Briz!" Ava raised her voice as the beating of

the rain grew louder. "This doesn't involve you. This is my dysfunctional family's problem, not yours!"

"Doesn't involve me!" Briz jerked his arms through the air like they were exclamation points. "You've got to be joking! Being locked in a wooden crate for two days—saving *you* from that monster, Tig. I'm as much a part of this as anyone else here!"

He stopped gesturing and dragged both of his hands through his hair as he walked over to her. "We're all on the same side, Ava, but you don't see it. We have to figure out how to move ahead, and you're acting like a dethroned princess."

Princess. Ava flinched.

"You diss your sister all the time." Briz stood in front of her as if thinking his six-foot stature would be intimidating to her. "Are you even aware that Jade saved your mom's life? Our lives?"

Ava didn't look at Jaden, but she could feel her sister's delighted expression. Briz was defending her, so once again Jaden wouldn't have to fight her own battle.

"And are you aware none of us would have been in danger if wasn't for her, the immature twit! What's more, I'm not a princess!"

"Oh yeah, you are a princess!" Briz snapped.

"You didn't seem to mind when I was in your bed, did you!" Pleased with her response, Ava smirked and folded her arms under her breasts, propping them up, drawing Briz's attention to them.

From the corner of her eye, Ava could see the way Jaden was clutching the sofa cushion to brace herself as if the floor was moving. Knowing how much Jaden was into the guy,

Ava figured that right now her little sister felt like seismic shock waves were moving through her.

While Briz wore a stunned, embarrassed expression, his eyes lingered on Ava's breasts. She smirked again.

He looked at Jaden, shaking his head.

"I slept on the couch, Jade. I let her sleep in my room when your mom was in the hospital—she didn't have anywhere to stay. The Mal Rous had broken into your apartment."

Briz looked back at Ava. "Christ, Ava. What is wrong with you? I would think that almost dying—twice in one week—would have changed you for the better. But you're still a manipulative, bitter, egocentric princess!"

"Stop calling me a princess!" Ava raised her hand, ready to slap him across his face.

Briz grabbed her wrist. His eyes creased, challenging her as he squeezed tighter. Ava let her hand go limp, and he released his grip.

Her shoulders sagged as she heard her father's words—the last friggin' thing he'd ever said to her—before he was shipped out to fight in some war and was killed.

For your mom's sake, take it easy on Jaden. Be nice to your kid sister. Don't act like an evil princess or the ultimate ice queen. No words of comfort, like, "I'm going to miss you." Or, "You're my little darling, my favorite daughter." He must have told her he loved her...? Why couldn't she remember hearing it?

Her eyes met Briz's scowl as his words admonished her. "Implying that we've slept together...telling Jade we'd had *sex.*"

Ava took a step back as Briz threw the word "sex" in her

face, like she was the last person in the world he'd want to be close to.

He was looking right at her. How could he not see her pain?

She glanced around the room. Violet, the diminutive, fairy-like Bellibone Ava's grandfather Dekle had created, was sitting on the piano, her broken leg in a makeshift cast. Supposedly, Ava's grandfather had created her by combining damselfly DNA with violet and pampas grass, along with her grandmother Elvina's DNA. Like Ava, Violet had Elvina's nose. Disgusted by the thought, Ava quickly shifted her attention to Hubs in his oversized chair, taking everything in.

Everyone was so charmed by sweet little Jaden that no one could see her. Ava. *If I scream loud enough, if I continue to withhold my love, will they bother trying to understand me?* Ava met Briz's gaze—there was a hint of compassion in his eyes—maybe he did see her pain. Or perhaps it was pity. That was worse. It made her feel vulnerable, uncomfortable. Ava raised her chin in defiance.

"You find power in hurting others, especially Jade." Briz took in a breath, the understanding in his eyes gone. "If you're going to dish it out, you'd better learn how to take it."

Ava stood taller, deciding to give everyone what she knew they expected from her.

"It was her stupidity that almost got us killed. I suppose you think it's funny...a big joke that she set the Mal Rous free."

"She didn't do it on purpose!" Briz shouted.

"Yeah, well, she did let them out, and from what you've told us, now Jaden's a she-devil just like them!"

* * *

CHAPTER 4

TO READ MORE

IMAGINE JADE GONE
can be purchased through

<u>Amazon</u> - <u>Barnes&Noble</u>
<u>Kobo</u> - <u>Apple Books</u>

Author's Note

Thank you for reading *Sweet Desire, Wicked Fate*. If you enjoyed the book, please spread the word. Your reviews are invaluable, and I would be very grateful if you would take a moment now to write a review. It can be as short, or as long as you like.

Just go to wrayardan.com/post-review.

Thank you,

Wray

Acknowledgments

The late Joseph Campbell, author of *The Power of Myth*, was an advocate of following one's bliss. Apparently, my bliss is about the art of rewrites.

Writing *Sweet Desire, Wicked Fate* has taken me on a journey of learning to face my fears and insecurities. I have learned when writing a book, one is dependent on good friends who are willing to be honest and straightforward with you.

I'd like to thank Steven L. Smeltzer for not only creating the sculptures that inspired the story, but for telling me when I could do better.

Special thanks to my first readers, starting with my sister Robin for cheering me on and for spotting my typos. Viki Alonzi, for reading many drafts of the story, as well as designing my website. Ed Monroe, for pointing out annoying repetitions. Kathy Kasprzycki, for letting me bend her ear and her unfailing enthusiasm in the project. Cheryl Mayville, for her honesty and encouragement. Victory Wallace, for her detailed notes.

Thank you to Dr. Eve Berman for answering my strange and sometimes gruesome questions. Authors Anne D. LeClaire and Linda Himelstein for their encouragement. Debra Bassett and James O. Murdock III at Bassett

Productions. Thank you to my editors, Lisa Levine, Paul Wood, Aharona Shackman, and Meredith Narrowe.

I would also like to thank all the developers of the World Wide Web. The gift of the Internet has simplified the research that goes into writing a book and has enabled writers to become authors through eBooks.

ABOUT THE AUTHOR

WRAY ARDAN lives on an island in the middle of the Pacific Ocean with an artist, four cats, and a parrot. Her award-winning romance horror trilogy, *Sweet Desire, Wicked Fate*, was inspired by sculptures created by her partner, artist Steven Lee Smeltzer. In Steven's mind, the ceramic characters appeared mischievous; in Wray's novels they became the deadly Mal Rous. As well as being a writer, Wray, along with Steven Smeltzer, has set up a creature shop for a computer animation company, worked as associate producer and set designer on a television pilot, and had a series of their characters featured in a young children's animated movie.

To post reviews and learn more about Wray Ardan, visit her website at wrayardan.com.

www.ingramcontent.com/pod-product-compliance
Lightning Source LLC
Chambersburg PA
CBHW031929110726
47902CB00001B/102